ANOTHER KIND

ANOTHER KIND

ANTHONY WEST

HOUGHTON MIFFLIN COMPANY BOSTON
The Riverside Press Cambridge
1952

TO FRANK MORLEY

The Riverside Press
CAMBRIDGE • MASSACHUSETTS
PRINTED IN THE U.S.A.

Part One

I

WALTER JACKSON climbed up onto the bus top and found a seat on the left-hand side of the upper deck, so that he could look down onto the pavements and watch the people as he rode along. He didn't bother much with the people sitting in the seat in front of him, gave them a half look as he sat down, then just knew they were there. The woman was wearing a little round hat with a red and blue ribbon on it, the man was a naval officer with a white summer top to his cap; his voice burred on indistinctly, and she kept saying, 'how extraordinary,' 'how extraordinary,' in a thin, high-pitched voice. They got off at a stop in Wigmore Street while Walter was staring, fascinated, into the windows of a medical hardware store in which the display was as strange and romantic as the stands of arms in a medieval armoury – arranged in very much the same way too, with a feeling for pattern and rhythm spiritually remote from the use of the scalpels, scissors, saws, forceps, and so on, involved. Contrasted with the hard brilliance of the metal tools there were the softened, rounded shapes of a number of curious earthenware vessels which spoke of strange needs of helpless or crippled bodies.

Walter tried hard to imagine a body in that state of helplessness and failed; he was in his early thirties and his whole experience of life was of an upward movement to maturity, it still seemed to him that his body was strengthening and hardening, and that his mind was broadening and deepening with increasing knowledge of the world.

'I am not one of the herd,' he thought, 'I am not one of the helpless ones. I make my own life and my own conditions of living. I shall never be one of the people who need those things. When I go I shall go quickly, and I shall die on my feet. The death of Emily Brontë, that was something like it.' He pictured his own death. He would be a magnificent old man, not so much aged as weathered by time – like a ship's figurehead stripped of

6

paint and gilding by the scalding sea and the bleaching sun – the sun, that would be it, he would ask them to take him out into the sun. He would stand in the blaze of the sunlight magnificently upright, there would be a woman attendant – two perhaps – his daughter and some other woman – they would be immensely moved by his uprightness in the sunlight. 'Father you'll tire yourself, you must sit down.' 'I am beyond tiring now,' he would say, and then in a few seconds it would be all over.

The bus jolted forward in the traffic stream and although he was not aware of it, consciously, the movement altered the stream of his thought. Who would want, after all, to write the biography of an architect of independent means, who consumed most of his time in visionary projects, and only a third of it on buildings that achieved substance, concrete, steel, and wood?

He passed at that moment one of his 'jobs', a moderne front attached to an old late eighteenth century house, and looked at it in the vain hope of catching some fleeting reflection of his own mind or character. But all he could recognise was the standard units of which it was made. The base of the design was the show window on the ground floor, and the size of that was dictated by the dimensions of a device – a standard device – for preventing the plate glass of the window from acting as a reflector to the busy life of the street, all its other proportions had been imposed by the relationship between the size of that device and the size of the original building. And even then, when the proportions had been worked out it was a matter of arriving at the nearest possible approximations to them. Messrs. Wilmer's steel windows were chosen because they were only .756 of an inch away from the ideal measurement, and with Grandisons' standard panel blocks, enabled him to get closer to his idea than anything else. The building was really, when he left it, nothing more or less than an exhibit of manufacturers' standard products – it was like the work of ninety and nine out of a hundred modern architects.

Grandisons' had reproduced it in colour once in a full page advertisement, Wilmers had used it for two or three months in one of their appalling series – *Light and Airy in the Modern Manner, Windows by Wilmers, of course!* Later on Wilmers had run a double page spread illustrating the fourteen buildings they had, the

7

right word was pilloried, publicised in the series. No one would have known that the work of fourteen individual architects was in question – his own was *Light and Airy in the Modern Manner* like all the others. It was not surprising that although his work often appeared in advertising sections of the architectural papers it never made the editorial pages . . . he jerked himself away from the sight of the façade and its jaunty demonstration of his mediocrity.

He leant forward to try to pick up the thread of the officer's story, to try to find what it was that the woman had kept saying was so extraordinary. He wanted to listen to anything but the voice saying, you're middle aged, you're no good. He was ready to grasp at anything, no matter what, that would stand between him and the terrible futility and emptiness of that facade; which, he realised, was all the reality that his dreams would ever have.

He was shocked to find the pair had gone without his knowing it, that he was leaning towards the shoulder of a fair girl with upswept hair who had apparently magically replaced them. She was a real blonde; the strong hair sweeping upwards was a whity gold right down to its roots; in the exquisite furrow down the back of her neck there was a fine golden down. Her skin was not pink or white, it was several colours, white, violet, pale blue, and pink. Her shoulders were wide and strong under a grey flannel suit, and she carried her head with pride; Walter could just make out the line of her cheekbone, her forehead, and her jaw, and he could see that she had a big, well drawn face without the cramped, caricaturish meanness which disfigured so many of the faces that he saw in English streets.

He suddenly found himself in the grip of an insane hunger for her, he wanted to lean a little farther forward to plant a kiss in the soft curve of her neck below her ear.

The violence of his daydream was such that for a second he believed that if he did she would sit silently accepting him, until after a moment or two she would swing her head slowly, like a statue coming to life, and give him her mouth. He looked uneasily round him, concerned because he wanted the woman so much that his desire seemed like a real presence that must be obvious to everyone else near him. He expected to meet disapproving

8

looks, but all he saw were blank grey faces swaying to the movement of the bus, faces from which life had for the time being retreated. Even the girl was unaware of him.

When the bus stopped the girl stood up and turned to go back to the stairs; turning she faced Walter for a moment, almost motionless. Without thinking he started at her toes and travelled staring up her body, at her wide hips, at her well set breasts, at her wide red mouth, at her violet eyes. She as unthinkingly looked back, for another moment right into his eyes, and then with a faint smile, blushed, and stepped away past him, down the stairs, and out of sight. He was paralysed, somehow terribly disturbed by the abrupt realisation that she was not merely a physical presence that he could want or not want, but a person, who could return his look, and weigh him.

He looked down the side of the bus, hoping to see her again as she stepped off onto the sidewalk, and then found her, already some distance away, walking slowly, slowly, down a side street. She looked splendid, a proud, strong young woman; there could be nothing more in life than to be walking there in the street with her, in her world, in her brain, part of her pride and youth, her lover.

The bus lurched on again, and bore her off down the stream of time, into memory, transforming her from a thing of flesh and blood and infinite possibility into an image, as sterile, and as doomed to fade as a cut flower.

But about four hundred yards up the street the bus stopped at traffic lights: they were green when Walter first saw them, and he said to himself, if they turn red and stop the bus I'll go back to try to find that girl.

When he found himself standing on the pavement he felt oddly out of breath and excited, as if the natural order had for the moment suspended its laws to allow him to go back in time to his youth. He thought the girl would have had time to go about another four hundred yards at her slow, idling pace, he would be about eight hundred yards from her. He almost ran back to the ground where he'd last seen her, expecting to catch sight of her down the long eighteenth century street. But she wasn't there.

He went down the street over two crossings, looking to right

9

and left up the side streets, seeing nothing. He walked slower and slower feeling the deadness of the places in front of him! A hunter's instinct told him that where she had passed the air would be alive for him, warmed and kindled by her being, that he was going out of the zone in which she made a tension for him.

That was the first time he saw her. He walked the rest of the way home hoping to beat his desolation and his longing for the stranger out of his blood before he faced his wife and his two children. He walked away north towards St. John's Wood, up the interminable straight streets, trying to drive the idiocy of this sudden passion down into the hot pavements. He thought of all the pleasure he had had out of the children, and of the long stretch of living he had shared with Margery. There was something real there, something solid, that outweighed this mere appearance. He reasoned it that way, but the emotional fact remained, that what he had seen had somehow devalued everything he had. The town, which he usually liked in an on the whole, more or less, way suddenly seemed intolerable to him. He smelt the bitter reek of poverty and ill-health in the sweat of the people hurrying past, the sour whiffs from uncleaned trashbins in the areas, the polluted soil around bomb-cracked drains wakened by the unexpected spring heat, the pungent odour of the dry rot fungus breeding in the old houses. Towards St. John's Wood there were more trees, and flower-festooned shrubs hung over the garden walls. But the heavy town air stole their freshness and the blooms looked too exhausted to set fruit or seed. He found himself beating up against a tide of nice looking, nicely dressed people setting away from Lord's Cricket Ground after the day's play. They looked like the flowers, he thought. They were still the same British middle class that had skimmed the fat off the world's trade for their own benefit for so long, superficially, but they looked tired now, years of war underfeeding, and years of socialist planned underfeeding, had taken the freshness out of them and the animal vigour. They dragged their feet a little through the scatter of hawthorn blossoms that had fallen on to the hot paving stones of the sidewalks, worn out after a day watching cricket. He found himself at the traffic roundabout by St. John's Wood church where the cars circled endlessly amid bluish exhaust fumes round the bronze image of St. George, frozen in the moment of victory over the dragon of evil. Jackson eyed it bitterly. 'That damned dragon,' he thought. 'That time it was the Kaiser's Germany. We've just killed it as Hitler's Germany. Next we'll have to kill it as Stalin's Russia. And every time we kill it we get weaker and it gets stronger.' He looked at the lance spearing it, with the horseman's weight and the horse's weight pushing the lance home, and felt the rending tissue and the sense of accomplishment. 'The next time we kill it we will have nothing left.' There was so little time left to get what you wanted out of life, so little chance of getting it. He walked on towards his home.

'You look tired, darling,' said Margery.

'I've had a disappointing day.'

'My poor dear, I hope nothing special went wrong on any of the jobs.'

'No. Just the usual things with permits. They still won't let us have the licences for the Waldegreen job, and the Phillipsons' house is still held up by the timber permit. It's maddening.'

'They must let you have the permits soon.'

But there was no must about it, as they both very well knew. She brushed his cheek with a kiss.

'Try not to be unhappy darling, it's the same for everybody.'

'I mustn't be unreasonable, I suppose.' He smiled. He thought that the image which was excluding almost everything from his mind, so that he looked round the edge of it at his wife, at his children, and the familiar, pretty house, would fade in a day, two days, or a week. Then he could be reasonable again.

Later he read aloud to the children as he always did when he wasn't out of town on a job. They had their bath and then ate their supper silently, listening to a favourite story about some children who conjured up a real mermaid with an invocation.

'Sabrina fair
Listen where thou art sitting,
Under the glassie, cool, translucent wave
In twisted braids of lilies knitting
The loose train of thy amber-dropping hair . . .'

They finished two chapters and then it was bed time. It was

the rule that every night when their lights were out they should each have a couple of minutes of secret talk alone with him, before Margery came in and said a last goodnight. He said goodnight to his son Francis first and then went and sat on the edge of Jeanette's bed thinking of the woman divided from him by circumstances as if she were in another element like Sabrina under the glassie, cool, translucent wave.

'There is a sort of magic, isn't there?' Jeanette said.

'No. But you have feelings that are like magic.' He didn't want to take it from her altogether.

'There ought to be magic.' She took his hand. 'If you want something very, very, much you can make it happen can't you?'

I ought to say no, he thought. But he remembered being young suddenly, and the world before the war, before everyone was tired and dull. 'If you're young,' he said, 'and if you want the right things perhaps there is a sort of magic. Now I've got to say goodnight.'

Going down stairs he whispered the Sabrina fair invocation and dreamt for a moment of the woman coming slowly towards him from some remote greenish depth, but his wife passed him on the stairs, going up to the children, and the dream shattered. He would never see her again.

It was three weeks before he did. He was walking with a little time in hand to a lunch with the Waldegreens at a West End restaurant where they were to discuss whether it was worth going on with their project for building a house. He saw her walking towards him and smiled easily, because he had seen her so often in his waking thoughts and reveries that she seemed an old friend. She smiled back, and slackened her pace as if she expected him to stop and speak to her.

'You look even prettier in that green linen dress than you did the other day, when you were in grey.' He wondered if she had remembered him at all.

'I remember now, you stared at me on the top of a bus.' She smiled at him with amusement. 'But you didn't speak to me.'

'I suppose it was very rude of me.'

'It's a sort of compliment. But it was silly of you not to speak to me – if you wanted to.'

12

'I did. But I was bowled over. I got off at the next stop and came back to find you, but you'd vanished into thin air.'

'I'd gone into a dressmakers . . .' they were drifting down the street in her direction '. . . for the last fitting on this dress. You haven't got long this time either, I'm going to vanish into thin air again – into a restaurant this time. I've got to meet somebody for lunch.'

'So have I. Damn it, I wish . . .'

'It's no use wishing. You'll have to be direct and purposeful. If you aren't I may vanish for good this time.' She was laughing at him.

'Haven't you got time to have a drink with me?'

'I'll be late, but I will.'

They went into a bar, and as they sat down at a little table he suddenly felt an acute embarrassment. He wanted her so much and there was nothing else to say.

'You're behaving as if you were fifteen or sixteen,' she said. 'Haven't you ever picked up a girl before?'

'Yes, but this is different. I don't know why . . . look, I still don't know your name or your address, or anything about you, and it's very important to me that you shouldn't just vanish again.'

'You're doing this all wrong. Women don't like men to get all grim and serious at them. This ought to be nice for you. It ought to be quite a cheerful adventure.'

'You're teasing me.'

'You're very teasable. Intense people are. Now your face has gone dark like a child's face. But you're sweet in a funny way. I promise you I won't vanish. I'll make things easy for you. 'Look' – she dipped in her handbag – 'here's my card. There's my name, and my address, and my telephone number. Now you know all about me and I can't vanish. Now you can be happier.' She looked at the clock. 'I've got to go now, or I'll be hideously late.'

He looked at the card as she got up. Anne Horne.

'Miss Horne – Anne – you don't know my name . . .'

'You can tell it to me next time. Call me, and tell me. I've got to go.'

He was left to pay the check, and she was gone. But she had said 'next time.' The Waldegreens were surprised by his buoyant mood, and were happy to be convinced that it was worth going ahead with the long drawn out battle to get their building permits. They had been rather disappointed by his willingness to give up, and had had the impression that he had asked them to lunch to tell them that everything was quite hopeless. They were delighted to hear him saying: 'After all, if you want a thing to happen enough you can make it happen. You've got to take what you want from life, nowadays more than ever. Nobody's going to give it to you. We'll see if we can't get hold of somebody in the Ministry. . . .'

He called Anne Horne in the morning three days later. She was still asleep, although it was ten o'clock.

'I'm sorry I woke you. But it's such a beautiful day that I thought it would be a good idea to go on the river. . . .'

'Oh no – not that. But it is a wonderful day. I'd like to do something, but nicer than that. We could go and look at the sea.'

'The sea . . .?' He saw miles of railroad track unwinding ahead of them, a laborious journey, and flinched from it.

'Don't say it like that. Come round and fetch me. I'll be ready by the time you get here. We'll go somewhere – I don't know where.'

She hung up abruptly, and he slowly put down the telephone, wondering about her, suddenly doubtful what he was getting into.

She made him take her to Newhaven, and after a quick look at the meagre port they started walking out along the stretch of beach leading towards the white cliffs over beyond Seaford. They passed a few boats hauled up for the winter, some still sheeted and dead, some coming alive again as they were scraped and repainted for the new season. There was the fresh smell off the living sea, and the clean, tart, smell of tar from the boats. The waves flounced gently up against the coarse grained beach with a shusshing sound. They walked on the wet margin bared by the falling tide and she collected a handful of sea bright, sea worn glass, smooth edged flakes of violet, green, and amber.

They grew dull as they dried in her hand and she threw them away. He watched her, and she watched the clouds sailing in the brilliant sky, and the jumble of short steep channel seas, chalky green, cold grey in the cloud shadows, occasionally breaking into white horses.

'I love this.' She put her hand on his arm. 'You ought to know why I hated your idea of the river. It seemed so hopeless, somehow, taking a girl you'd picked up for a day on the river. You ought to have known better than that. It was a shopkeeper's idea.'

'I didn't think it was possible to do anything as nice as this, without planning and arranging it beforehand. I still can't quite believe we've done it.' He looked at her, suddenly aware that it was not just desire, that he was in love with her. 'With you I believe I could do anything; anything I wanted would happen.'

She brushed her hair off her forehead, tilting her head back for a moment and shutting her eyes. She didn't answer.

They sat on a sea-bleached log washed up to the limit of the sea's ground, where the plants began, wiry grasses and a few wild cabbages, a plant or two of stiff leaved sea holly, and ate the fruit and drank the bottle of wine they'd bought on the way to the train. The wine was chianti, and as he tasted Italy in it, he started telling her about the villa that his parents had taken, several Easter seasons running, on the hills of Fiesole, above Florence, and the way that he had first seen life there – people living at the top of their bent, letting themselves go, absolutely, in joy, grief, anger and panic as the mood was on them. Then memories of the campaign overwhelmed him, when Italy was the soft underbelly of Festung Europa and the guts were ripped out of it, and that whole pagan life was overrun and trampled on by the glum ones from the north, from the Protestant, power-crazy countries. When he started being serious and defeated, she stopped listening to him. He felt that she had left him, and fell into a glum reverie about his professional frustrations. She looked at him with an expression of pity for a second, and then got to her feet. There were snail shells among the marram grasses, striped in colours that ranged from deep dark red to pale gold on a white background. She began gathering them with an idea that, shellacked, and strung on a cord, they would make a pretty summer necklace. But when she had gathered a number of them she saw that although they would be pretty for a child, they would be wrong for her. She brought them back to show to him, and knelt beside him holding them for him to see in her open hand. He took her hand, spilling them, and tried to pull her down to kiss him. She tore herself brusquely away from him, and stood up, stepping back.

'You're so very beautiful. And I'm so much in love with you.'

'Don't say that. It's absurd. And besides . . .' She looked down at him and her expression of anger gave way to a smile. '. . . it's drinking that wine with nothing but fruit to go with it. You can say nice things to me – there's quite a lot you can say, about wanting me, and about my looks. But don't say anything about love.'

'But I . . .'

'Don't. I told you not to.' Her voice was suddenly hard. She walked down to the edge of the water and stood with her back to him. He buried the wrappings of the fruit and the empty bottle in the sand before he went down to her.

'We've got to go back,' she said, turning to him, 'the sun's going. It'll be cold in an hour. We've got to go back.'

'I suppose so.' He felt like Adam, tormented elaborately by being allowed back into the garden for half a day years after the expulsion. He'd felt young and happy with her, for a few hours he'd believed that you really could force events into a pattern of your own choosing. They'd done it. And now they were going back.

It was dark when they got back to London and leaving the station a lighted flower shop, glowing in the darkness, caught his eye. He hadn't bought flowers since before the war, and he wanted to, partly as a demonstration against the narrow, economical, budgetted life he was leading, partly because he wanted to leave their loveliness with her opal loveliness when he had to leave her. She said she didn't want them, that they were forced flowers, not real flowers, stiff things out of hot houses. But they had a dark red rose, with a green vein on the petal, that seemed a black red, in the shop, and she accepted

16

some of them. And he persuaded her to accept some carnations when he discovered that they breathed out the sweet scent of cloves. They cost more than five pounds, and while he was paying for them he looked up into a looking glass, hung high among the upper vases of flowers, and saw her watching him with an odd, puzzled look, as if she had suddenly become mistrustful of him.

When they got to her flat she still had the same expression, and she seemed uneasy while she went to and from the kitchen, putting the flowers in water, and arranging them. When she had finished he took her in his arms, meaning to kiss her. But she pushed him away, her body wooden. He heard her voice speaking, as if it was a great distance from his ear to the part of the brain where the words were received and understood.

'No, you can't have me like that – for a few nice words and a few flowers. I don't have lovers. You'll have to give me money, like anyone else.'

'But . . .' he held her, refusing to let her go, refusing to understand what she had said. 'It's some kind of horrible joke. . . . You didn't mean that. . . .'

'How can anyone be such a fool? You must have realised what I am. . . .'

She gave him a steady, utterly cold, look that he couldn't bear to meet. He turned from her, nauseated, suddenly mad with anger. She stepped away from him appalled by the violence of his revulsion. He looked about him and the flowers mocked his idiocy, intolerable symbols of what was so valuable to him, so worthless to her. He stepped over to the carnations and plucked them up out of the big glass jug in which she had arranged them in a dense mass. The jug teetered and spilt as he stepped away, looking round the room for the roses. As he went towards them, seeing them only as a blur of colour, she tried to stop him, grabbing at his shoulder. He hit her arm a backhand blow to make her let go. She flung up her arm so that his hand slid up her forearm and struck her on the side of the mouth. He gathered up the roses from their bowl and straightened with his arms full of flowers, feeling the water from the flower stems soaking cold, through his shirt to his skin. She stood by the empty fireplace, watching him, stony-eyed, dabbing at the blood that had begun to ooze from her split lip.

'You're mad. . . . I ought to send for the police.'

'I loved you. Now I hate you. You could tell them why.'

He walked out with the flowers in his arms, their colours and scent appealing for mercy, through the hall and out into the street, to the salvage bins decorated with an appeal for pig food a couple of hundred yards away at the next crossing. He felt that the girl was behind him staring after him as he went, but he didn't turn around. He knew that she was there in the doorway, watching, until he had stuffed the last thorny ends of the rose stems into the bin, among the spoiled and rotting leftovers of food. Then he heard the door slam, and he knew that he was alone.

He walked a little way with a staggering gait, like a punched out fighter, and then stopped to steady himself, holding on to the cold iron standard of a street lamp. 'I am in love, I have been in love, with a whore. Nothing in my life has meant so much to me as this. Nothing will ever be the same for me.' He pressed his cheek to the iron, and felt its chill seep through to his bone. He heard the door slam behind him, again, echoing in his memory. It had slammed for good on the whole dream world of magic and enchantment. 'I am in love with the most worthless thing in the world, with glamour, with nothing.' He walked home in a dream and found himself facing the blank face of the house behind which slept the people who loved him. He stared up at the dark windows and felt the fever of longing still burning in his blood. He had come home, but sooner or later he would go back to Anne – whatever she was.

2

ANNE HORNE slammed the front door and went back into her flat, furious, loathing the man. She loathed him most for being incomprehensible. It had been all right at first; she had known then exactly what he wanted, and it had been just what she was prepared to give, – and then suddenly he'd wanted her to be something she wasn't, and couldn't be, something soft and yielding that she didn't want to be.

She went and stood in front of the looking glass to examine her lip, finding the cut a small thing and resenting that less than the water spilt on the chimneypiece when the carnations had been jerked up out of the water jug. She could still smell, or imagine it, the last faint breath of their spiced clove scent.

She didn't, couldn't, understand what he had been so angry about. She thought with fury of the far too expensive flowers in the dustbin – she'd despised him when he bought them because they weren't the sort of thing which made her give what she had, or was willing, to give to men – and she thought he was a fool to pay for them. He should have known that they wouldn't be enough.

She thought, it was like a splinter under her fingernail, of the roses and the carnations among the tea leaves, and the butts of old loaves, and bacon rinds. She thought of herself in the dark squalor of London and of the ugly trap that her life might make it. She turned down her lip with a finger and looked at the split; tiny, it must just have touched the top of a tooth, it had already stopped bleeding and certainly wouldn't swell. She rubbed a little blood from the tooth with a fingertip, then closed her lips firmly – not a trace.

Honestly, it was a pretty good face; honestly, you couldn't blame a man . . . but then if he'd wanted her why get so wrought up about finding he could have her on her own terms? If he had hoped or thought she was a good girl why did he try to pick her up on the street? Was it just that he hadn't got the money? She

19

thought of his white-faced, crazy look again . . . it must have been something about goodness loose in his head. If it was he must have been mental – she stood back in the room, where she could see all of herself from the knees up in the glass – 'no one in their right mind could meet me that way and think I was good . . . although I do take a lot of trouble not to look obvious . . .'

Being an outsider was one of the few things that worried her, and she was at pains, always, to make herself look as much like an insider – one of the people who belonged – as possible, choosing her clothes carefully from the fashion magazines, watching the jewels the nice girls wore; the bags they carried, their shoes, and the way they did their hair, fitting herself out so far as possible with the things they used at the stores they went to.

But still she belonged on the outside and was determined to stay there. She looked into the glass over the fireplace beyond her reflection to her childhood, to the misery and squalor that was her lot on the inside: nobody would trick her back to that with sweet talk about love and loving.

She turned away, refusing to be upset by a fool. She went over to the wireless and clicked it on, and then went into her bedroom, not listening to it, to wash some stockings and underthings in the washbasin. The clock showed seven as she finished hanging them out to dry on the towel rail, and she wondered for a minute or two about going down to the Ironsides Club for the evening before deciding that what she wanted was a quiet night.

She went to catch the last house at The Classic in Baker Street instead, walking through the twilight alone, taking a single one and sixpenny, and sitting alone in the dark.

She didn't think much of the film, it was a revival of a musical and she'd known and forgotten all the tunes. When it was over they had all come back, and she hummed them quietly to herself as she went up the almost empty street to the brasserie under the block of flats at the top.

The sky was copper green shading to dark blue from west to east, and the houses now seemed to be made of black velvet, pierced here and there by lighted windows, like little peep-shows. A man read a newspaper in that one while a woman walked up and down, talking and gesticulating with one arm; in another two completely motionless people read, one on each side of a huge, fringed lampshade; in one of the flats over the brasserie a party was warming up, you could see people in evening dress dancing and drinking in little groups, all through the rooms of a big flat, and a confused burr of talk spread out through the wide open windows into the street. A few airforcemen and soldiers with their trotties stood round the coffee stall on the corner looking up enviously, pathetic children with unformed faces, the girls with their tight skirts well above their knees so that their smart ankle strap shoes seemed madly indecent, dirt in the street.

She went down into the cellar and ate under dark plastic linenfold panelling enriched by the arms of the leading public schools, while the head waiter stood by her and talked to her.

'. . . it's all I can do to catch the last train – and it's late by the time we get there right out at the end of the extension – and then there's the walk out from the station. It's not very often I'm in bed by half-past one – and then we start serving here, lunches, again at twelve-thirty. Mr. Carmody is pressing for me to open at twelve – we're always turning people away he says – but it's all I can do I tell him – it means getting here at ten as it is – well I don't have to tell you what it means, and then my missus, if you please, has me on the carpet. Charles you don't take any interest in the children, Charles you're getting so bad tempered . . . all that – and Charles when you are here on Sunday you don't take any interest. I told her straight, we've moved out too soon I said. This would have been all right if I'd retired, but as things are we'd have better stayed in the old place opposite the Pineapple, dingy it may have been, but, I said . . .'

'Poor Charles,' she said now and again, and then went home again through the darker, quieter streets.

On her way she began thinking about the man again, and he stayed with her while she undressed and went to bed, on into the time when she should have gone off easily into the dark and quiet of sleep. She lay watching the lights on passing cars making patterns on the ceiling, looking through the night vision back into the day, and seeing him going past her again and again with the flowers in his arms.

Damn you and your fury. What about me? What about what I think of you? You black ugly brute, you scowling ill-tempered lout – hitting a woman. What gave you the right to hit me? Because I didn't fit into some dream you had about me? I never asked to be in your dream. I'll make you sorry for doing that to me, you'll wish you had never been born.

She twisted and turned; flung off the bedclothes because it was too hot, then pulled them up again because it was too cold. She began to run through scenes in which she wounded him beyond his bearing, so that he covered his face with his hands and sobbed as if he was retching while she stood a little way off, not caring. She – but that would mean having him about, and she certainly wasn't ever going to put up with that; she'd never see him again, not if she could help it.

About three in the morning she gave in, turning on the light to lie smoking and reading a detective story. She ran out of cigarettes after the fourth, and couldn't find another packet anywhere in the flat. She came back to bed ice cold and went on with the book, shivering. It was a thriller more than a detective story, written in imitation American – she'd been recommended it by someone who said it was dirty as well as exciting. Presently she fell asleep, with the book spread out on the rumpled sheet and the electric light blearing through the room.

The sun called her back from the dark void, sending a bar of light in through the crack between the heavy curtains that made the lamplight seem dim. Anne lay awake watching the motes dancing in its beam but doing nothing about being awake for twenty minutes when a church clock some streets off told her through the hum and stir of the traffic noises that it was eleven, and fetched her out of her lair.

She padded into the hallway in a house coat to fetch in the milk and any letters, and back in the flat again sat on the rim of the bath tub while the water ran in, reading the only letter there was.

Dear Miss Horne,

 I must apologise for my absolutely unforgivable behaviour yesterday. I don't know how I can ask you to forgive me, but

22

all the same I do. The minute I saw you I knew you were the most important person for me in the world. I don't know how, or why, but I just did, and I still know – more certainly than before – that you've something to give me more precious than anything I'll ever get from anybody in the world. I don't think many people know what love is – I know I didn't before this. I feel there's something between us that's going to develop into one of the great things – the loves that enrich the world and life after the lovers have gone.

I hope you'll forgive my special beastliness about the flowers. I've come to realise since that I've no right to criticise or even question anything you do or have done. If I may I'll call on you at seven this evening with some flowers to give to you – to the real you, not to some idea of my own about what you ought to be – I don't want you to be anything but what you are – I hope you will be no one but yourself for me tonight because I want nothing other than that.

Yours with all the love in the world,
Walter Jackson.

She tore the letter, damp with the bath steam, across and across into little squares, and then let it dribble square by square into the little platted straw basket under the handbasin, along with the balls of cotton wool greasy with the cold cream she'd used to clean her face. How could anyone be such a fool as that, or expect anyone to fall for such slush.

The man who had frightened her was diminished, shrunken away from a dark perplexing menace that might be amusing to torment and break, shrunken down to the ordinary thing – a wet young man who wanted it for nothing. She marched him out of her mind and wondered at herself for having spoilt a night's sleep on his account.

She had a bath, dressed, and went round the corner to the Basque Snack Bar for lunch. She ate her meal in nine minutes and forty-seven seconds sitting perched up on top of a high leather-covered stool at the quick service counter between a man reading an early edition of the *Evening Standard* and a woman reading a Daphne Du Maurier novel in a brown paper wrapper.

In the afternoon she shopped down through the West End looking for nylons and ended up staring at a film, one of the twelve or fourteen people in the eleven and sixes in the middle afternoon. Someone was beaten up in an alley, someone else trod on somebody's hand, a woman in black satin tried to seduce a plain-clothes detective from the path of duty, there was a gun battle in a warehouse full of barrels that was won by the right people, the really bad man got away in a car, but presently it went through a queer looking white fence and after turning over and over several times it burst into flames, then it turned out the girl in black satin was good after all and a nice old man with platinum blond hair parolled her in the detective's custody. Then there was a comedy about a woman-hating author who had taken a job as lecturer at a woman's college under the impression that it was a men's university. His daughter and his estranged wife were somehow or other enrolled in the student body, he didn't recognise them for a long time because they wore dark glasses. When the news reel came on Anne recognised it as the same edition she'd already seen twice with other feature programmes and she went home.

It was one of her pleasures to come out of a show after an idle morning and afternoon, cool and fresh, into the mob of people going home after a day's work. They were all used up, grey faced and finished, she was just coming fully alive – the excitement of wondering if she'd get off with anyone, and who it would be, what sort of man, already stirred in her, making her feel that the world had been slowed down a little while her perceptions had been speeded up.

It was still broad daylight, but the night was coming. The sun stood over the buildings in the western sky but it already had the metallic glitter of its death round it: a fissure in the protective tissue that had grown over her past, her youth and her childhood gaped momentarily and her father looked at the sun under a brown farmer's hand foretelling from that glitter that it would be another haymaker tomorrow. She could almost hear through the traffic the rattle of mower knives in the fields of her home place, and the ticking of the mower wheels as they were turned short at the corners of the uncut grass; everyone round about would be working late to catch the weather, on into that cool dewy twilight in which the fallen grass would breathe the sweetest of all scents. She closed her mind to it, and shutting her eyes for a second or so opened them wide and dreamless to Oxford Street.

She had another bath when she reached home, and lay in it soaking, remembering how she used to wash her body standing in a big tub set on the floor beside the copper in the farm kitchen. Her mother used to be angry with her for not being ashamed to stand there naked, cleaning herself, ruddy in the light from the fire under the steaming copper. 'Like an animal,' she said, with her deep country shame of her own body. 'If your father ever catches you he'll tan your hide.' She wondered if her mother had ever realised why she had been, after all, right to tell her to hide herself from her father's eyes, and just what it was she had to fear. A spasm of disgust shook her – it had been the same thing that that man had tried to trick her into with his talk about love, and his flowers.

She saw him again, with that awful stricken look, taking his flowers away. And now he was coming back with more flowers. She climbed out of the bath quickly and began to dry herself, hurrying now to make sure that she would not be there when he arrived. She went down to the Ironsides Club and took up her station in the bar, sitting at one of the little tables against the wall looking like a girl who was early for a date. The barman sent over her usual drink, an imitation Tom Collins that had no gin in it and she sipped it quietly as an hour melted away. Towards eight o clock a girl she knew who modelled for a dress designer she occasionally worked for, came and sat beside her sipping from the same innocuous child's drink. They talked desultorily, with long pauses, they didn't really like each other.

'I heard from Leila the other day.'

'Leila? Oh, I remember, what's she doing?'

'A Greek shipping man took her to Alexandria, she's having fun.'

'I'd be scared. It would be so awful if you got dumped in a place like that.'

'I suppose it would.'

Anne thought idly for a moment about Leila, a girl who

25

drank too much and was always borrowing money. There was not much hope for her in Alexandria – anywhere.

The girl beside her lit a cigarette and stirred restlessly.

'This place is dead tonight.' She looked about. 'You can't blame Leila, only foreigners seem to have money nowadays.'

She lapsed into silence, looking sulky, until another thought strayed into her mind.

'Your friend Charles Ross was here last night.'

'Oh, I'm sorry I missed him.'

'He was in a horrid mood, sad and miserable. He said he was looking for you.'

'It doesn't sound like Charles to be sad.'

'Well he was. He got drunk all by himself, then he quietly vanished away.'

'I wish I'd been here.'

She thought about Charles Ross sad, and couldn't imagine it. She had first met him during the war when she was in the ATS. He had picked her up on a train when they were both coming into London on leave. That time and every other they had been delighted with each other because he had never been interested in anything but her physical attributes and her response to his natural and uninhibited love making. And he had never wanted more than she had been ready to give. She remembered his absolute lack of interest in her private thoughts with something like affection. So many people came to her in muddles, despairs and miseries, and he always had come as a happy animal.

The girl slipped away and left her alone and she sat on while the clock crawled on towards nine, hoping Ross would come. He came at last and stood in the doorway looking at her as if he wasn't sure that it was her, even though she smiled. When he came over to her it was with an uncertainty that was unlike everything she remembered of him. It came back to her after they'd been talking for a little while, she knew what was wrong.

'I saw about your engagement in the papers. I thought you'ld be giving me up. You ought to be being happy with her. You shouldn't be here with me.'

'Let's not talk about it. I was expecting you to cheer me up.'

26

'I don't know that I'm in a very good mood to cheer you up. Not tonight – I'm upset myself. I don't know why.'

'Well, let's try a change of atmosphere. There's death in this gloomy hole tonight. We'll go somewhere more cheerful, and get stinking and tell each other how miserable we are.'

They went to The Jongleur and danced twice, the only people on the floor; there were six other people in the room and the food was frightful.

They went to several other places and found them pretty much the same: at the last one they were all alone with the waiters and the band. The band leader chanted a song through a megaphone which got at them and insulted them in a way that it was difficult to do anything about, except by going.

'No tip, sir?' said the waiter. 'You can get your tip from that wizened little jerk leading the band.' The bandsmen all snickered, leaning forward to listen; Anne couldn't quite hear what the leader called over to the waiter as they went out, but she could hear the burst of laughter that rattled among the empty tables and chairs.

'What a joint, and what an evening!'

'You see what comes of trying to have a good time with a girl like me when you're engaged to a nice girl,' said Anne.

'You don't know what you're talking about.'

'Yes I do, there's a black dog on your shoulder and we'll have a dreary time whatever we do.'

'We'll find out about that.' He leant forward and slid open the glass panel dividing them from the cab driver, and muttered a change of directions to him that Anne couldn't catch. 'I just don't know what you mean by "a girl like me." You're no worse than anyone else. You're better than most.'

' It's sweet of you to say that, but you wouldn't say it if you weren't a bit drunk.'

The cab stopped and she got out looking curiously to see where he'd taken her. It was the wrong sort of place, and she shivered when she recognised it. That man Jepson, Jipson, Jackson, or whatever he was had brought bad luck, smuggled it into her flat with the flowers, this was the sort of night that would end in some sort of trouble. She fished in her bag for the

27

lucky gold fish an American had given her, desperate for a moment in fear that she should have left it behind at the flat. While she felt for it she looked down to Piccadilly at the bottom of the street, saw it sluicing by like a river in flood, with tree trunks and wreckage in it.

'Come on.'

'Look,' she felt the plump gold body of the fish slide between her fingers and felt reassured, up to a point. 'This isn't my sort of place you know. We'll meet the sort of people you go about with. Ought you to . . . ?' She snapped her bag shut. 'Suppose we just went back to the flat.'

'When I get inside, and compare the dreary lot I know with you, I shall probably ask you to marry me. You're being tiresome, Anne – it isn't like you. Come on like a good girl.'

The waiter at their table smiled and said, 'Good evening, Mr. Ross,' politely. He had clean hands and there were no thumb prints on the card he gave them, the linen was clean, and the silver had been washed with some care.

Anne looked round the well-lit room and was surprised to see so few ugly people, so many people who had the air of always having lived in clean, well-lit places, so many people amusing themselves without violent grimaces, jerky gestures, or shouting and bawling, idiot laughter. There wasn't a single party with a funny man, and yet there was a buzz, and a great deal of pleasant laughter rising out of it all, that said quite certainly that people were having a good time.

'It's fun having you here with me. Your eyes have been enormous ever since we've been here – it's like taking a girl out who's never been out before. You're not sorry you came now, are you?'

'I'm scared stiff. Any minute I'll do something that'll give you away. Do the wrong thing with my hands; dance in the wrong way; smile the wrong sort of smile; use a word that'll grate on anyone who happens to hear it like a sour note from the band. I'm on a tight rope.'

'You're doing all right.'

'Oh no I'm not. Every so often I catch someone having a good look at me and then they lean over and say something quietly and

28

then two or three people have a good look at me and smile at each other. It's spreading slowly round the room. Nobody's been actually unpleasant but I can hear them thinking that I don't really belong. I've only got to put a foot wrong and they'll all click together. "That girl over there is a tart." One woman's on to it already – I can tell it every time she looks at me. She's . . .'

He turned round and had a look at her. 'Oh that girl . . .' he said, 'she's the girl you read about in the papers.'

'The one you're engaged to.'

'Yes.'

'Did you know she was going to be here?'

'I had a pretty fair idea, to tell the truth.'

'You just wanted to bring me here to hurt her.'

'No. That crossed my mind I'll admit. I brought you here to give you a trial run in this sort of place. You'll learn, even if you aren't the thing yet. I was going to ask you to marry me.'

'You're absolutely mad.'

'That's my look out. Will you?'

'No.' She looked round the alien crowd. 'They'd all laugh at you and be horrible to me. You'd hate it, too, pretty soon. It's all very well coming to me when you just want what I've got, and then you clear out when you like and it's finished – but tying yourself up with me just to sock that poor girl in the teeth is a mug's game. There'd have to be a messy divorce before you could get straight again – you don't want to marry me.'

'I'd give you a pretty decent settlement – it would be just the same really. Wholesale instead of retail.' He grinned at her and she suddenly felt her flesh crawl with repulsion, it was as if she had suddenly found a louse on her body.

'That isn't my idea of marriage,' she said.

'Oh,' he laughed again, 'don't tell me you believe in orange blossoms and living happily ever after with your professional background. Perhaps I ought to have said "I love you" a couple of times before I asked you – I didn't realise you had a romantic side that needed looking after.'

'I don't know what's the matter with you. In the old days we used to have fun. You were just a man who wanted a woman.

29

Now you're all twisted up and beastly. I don't like you any more. What's it all about?'

'Love.' He gave a quick look round at the girl at the other table who was looking elsewhere with her chin held high and turned back again. 'You haven't told me your idea of marriage.'

'I don't know what it is quite. In a year or two I'll have enough saved to buy a boarding house or a café in some seaside town down in the west. When I've got it I'll get some nice steady chap – a navy man or something like that – who'll be handy round the place to help me run it. I'll be done with all this – you know – I'll be a good wife and we'll live out our time like decent people.'

'Nothing about love.'

'I see what it does to people.' She looked at him, the drink had softened his face and it was sagging off the bones. A good man's face, rotting. The dancers circled in discreet abandon, the controlled laughter slid between the talk and the music, nobody looked straight at anything, and all the important words were reliably unspoken. The bright lights and the cleanness hid more than the dirt and the darkness in the other places.

Ross was just crossing the borderline into maudlin drunkenness, one or two other people were well away, but it would all come to nothing – at the most a wry smile on the face of the friend or waiter who steadied the drunk out to the gentlemen's cloakroom and then to a waiting taxi.

Ross wanted her to put on white satin and orange blossom, and to go in front of a priest to make promises before God that wouldn't mean anything, just to break through it all – just because he couldn't cross the room and say a couple of sentences to the girl with the hard line to her jaw and the eyes brimming – Anne looked under her hand to make sure of it – with tears.

He really wanted to take her out onto the dance floor and make love to her to involve them all in some monstrous humiliation.

She imagined it. The dancers circling on looking over them, the people all round the floor looking away at an angle of forty-five degrees, the good waiters paying no attention, the *maître d'hôtel* and an *aide* moving quietly forward with a large black cloth into which they would be silently folded and removed –

with no more fuss or bother than a dropped plateful of food.

'What on earth's keeping you from that girl – what's all the agony about? Why can't you just do it and get it out of your systems? You're crazy for her and she looks crazy for you – I just don't see it.'

'You wouldn't understand. That's just what I like about you. That girl over there is a woman of principle and colossal moral rectitude. She can see through me like glass. You see I'm good looking, and you know I've got plenty of money, and that's enough for you. Well she looks at me with the eye of love and she can see weak lines round my mouth and a shifty look in my eyes. When I get tight she doesn't think it's fun, she thinks I'm dodging something – she thinks it wrong of me to take my money without doing anything for it. She says it's no sort of life for a man, living by selling capital. She wants me to do some damn thing or other – work – I tell her it just means socking out more in taxes – and then she starts crying and saying she loves me and she can't bear me and we break it off. And then when it's broken off she wants to try again – she just wants to work me over like sculpture – when she's got me she sees she can't do it – when she's away from me she thinks she can – she's a born reformer – she thinks she can make something grand out of me, disclose a better self. Tommy rot.'

He turned again and gave the girl a belligerent glare, by an unhappy chance catching her eye.

She smiled bleakly, cracking his face into an answering mockery, and they lifted their hands to each other in the smallest of friendly salutations, perhaps more like the movement some savage peoples make when the dead are mentioned – to keep the spirits underground.

'She's not wearing a ring,' Anne said.

'No. She gave it back to me a couple of days ago.' He fished in a waistcoat pocket. 'Here, you have it. It's worth a lot of money. It's not worth anything else.'

'You're being stupid. I'll take it if you go on holding it under my nose. You know me . . .'

He drew his hand away from it, leaving it lying on the white table cloth, and after it had been there for a few seconds, glittering and glinting from its cold blue heart she picked it up and slipped it onto her finger.

He opened his mouth as if he was going to say something and then shut it again with a slight change of expression, a barely detectable loss of colour, that set her heart beating and filled her with an excitement that was better than the excitement of drink or lovemaking.

She felt she was gigantic, a huge marble statue, still and remote, on whose altars the hearts were torn out of living men. It was the end of Ross's effort to be large enough for the love he had called up in the other woman's body, from now on he would rot alive, drunkenly casting himself away in the sterile bodies of women like herself who cared for nothing. She had pushed him over the edge of the cliff.

She looked across at the woman who loved him, turning the ring on her finger, it was the end of a lot for her, too – the huge structure of her marriage was in ruins, its bare shell would never be roofed, never be fitted out with floors, or windows; the children that Ross might have fathered would never come out of its doors to grow into men and women. A long chain reaching forward in time had been snapped at its first link, to fall away into the dark.

At four-thirty in the morning his misery was talked out; he had lain with her, wept while she stroked his hair in the stillness and emptiness, and presently fallen asleep. She got up, dressed quietly, and telephoned an all night car hire garage for a cab to take her home, speaking softly into the instrument in the dark drawing-room lit by a single table lamp.

When she had done with the telephone she snapped that out too and stood for a few seconds looking about her by the ghostly reflected light of the street lamps outside, which glistened faintly on a variety of polished surfaces that gave back in return little winking recognition signals that meant nothing to her.

When she walked up to them she could see that they flashed and winked from porcelain figurines, from silver boxes, carved boxwood statuettes, a tortoiseshell cabinet with silver filigree inlay and handles, a multitude of familiar little things and pieces which had been accumulated slowly in generations of family life. The signallers were not so much the things themselves as the ghosts in the room, of Ross's great-grandparents who had jointly chosen this cabinet in Venice, of his great-great-grandparents who had contributed the "good" but stiff armchairs and the cabinet, of remoter connections in the seventeenth and even the sixteenth centuries.

In the bedroom where Ross now lay with his mouth open and with his drowsy blood slowed by alcohol moving thickly like a dying man's, there was a picture of a house somewhere in the country from which all these things had come.

It had been for sale for twenty years, an impossible place to live in, to maintain; a wrecked ship breaking up in the surf of an alien time. This room in the block of modern flats, duplicating with its things something of the old house was a ship's boat, a life raft, flung out to carry a survivor's last hopes.

Tonight the signals seemed to ask desperately for pity; a great green sea had swept over the boat, leaving its gunwales flush with the water and a spreading ruin of oars, floorboards, water kegs and sodden biscuit about it, and among the other debris the last man of the crew, stunned and helpless, for one final moment alive and recoverable.

When Ross woke in the morning and found the whore gone and the ring gone his heart would split and he would go down without a sound; the things in the room, the tokens of four hundred years of continuity and order would be worthless junk, mere scum of the face of the sea.

She turned from them and went over to the window and leant out, watching for her car's arrival at the entrance to the block of flats six stories below. The streets under the exhausted lamplight looked like the bare beds of streams, they had their stripped, worn look as if the daylight's traffic were an abrasive force like a mountain torrent.

A bicyclist, head down, slid by in absolute silence; two policemen standing talking parted and walked off, becoming immensely solitary when they were a few paces from each other; the traffic lights by Oxford Street changed from red to green and green to red over the empty tarmac.

33

She looked idly along the house fronts for a peepshow, but there were none now, the windows were all black. There was a man or a woman, perhaps a man and woman asleep in the room above Ross's twelve feet above him; there was another sleeper or set of sleepers the same distance below, and below them, and below them. She imagined the house transparent, and its columns of sleepers exposed, eight high – there were six flats on each floor, there would be six such columns. In the larger block opposite there would be stacks of servants in the servants' quarters as well as stacks of masters in the master bedrooms, each one within speaking distance of the next, unaware and unconscious of the other's existence.

She tiptoed from the window back to the bedroom and looked at Ross, lying on his side, his eyes shut, his quiet breath barely audible, as utterly shut off from her as if he lay in a grave.

She went back to the window and looked at the reddish grey of the clouds reflecting the London glare, four and a half million people lay blind and dead under that dome of half light waiting for the morning's resurrection. Their feet pointed to all the quarters of the compass card as they lay, some curled up in tight balls, some relaxed as if they lay praying on their sides, some rigid and straight, others back upwards with their heads twisted round sideways as if in repulsion, on their pillows, others spread face upwards like St. Andrew on his cross, all breathing in and out, waiting for their spirits to return.

They stretched away for miles in every direction, lining each side of the roads and streets, a few paces apart, mile after mile: before they lay down and shut their minds they spoke of love, friendship, and kinship, now they were parted so that they might be at the farther ends of the universe. If she passed among them looking into face after face until she found Walter Jackson he would not know that she was beside his bed; she could even lie beside him, hour after hour, without his knowing. In ten days, a month, a year, he would have forgotten her face, she would have forgotten his.

That was the truth of all these relationships so agonisingly built up and maintained, the truth each night confirmed – they were all alone, just as she was alone, whatever they might pretend.

A car slid up the street and came to a stop at the entrance to the flats: Anne threw a coin down to attract the driver's attention and waved when he looked up, to let him know that he needn't ring, then silently left the flat, leaving nothing behind her that could have told anyone that she had ever been there.

3

MARGERY JACKSON looked across the breakfast table at her husband with distaste. He looked green, greenish white. If it had been another man she would have supposed that he had been drinking, but he didn't ever, in that sense, drink. He had just been 'out' the night before, he was now 'in' but she wasn't much better off – he was still 'out' so far as she was concerned.

About half his time when he was theoretically with her, 'in', sitting in the room with her, it was like this – he'd only answer a remark the second time it was made. What was more maddening about it still was that sometimes when she challenged him – 'didn't you hear what I said?' – it appeared that he had heard, and even recorded, whatever it was but that he just hadn't bothered to come back from his private world, and wasn't prepared to come back unless dragged by insistence and repetition.

At first she thought of it as the onset of deafness. 'My poor old Walter is getting middle aged,' and she'd talk to him about his deafness and the importance of doing something about it – she was anxious about it because she loved him.

It was a wounding discovery when she began to recognise it as indifference; now she could see that it was really more than that, he withdrew from her deliberately, it was no longer merely that he did not bother to listen.

The children had finished breakfast and were upstairs dressing for school. As long as they had been in the room Walter had been at least partially present.

It had puzzled her, the way he had behaved with them, treating them with a curious solemnity, a heavy, almost tragic affection. After the elder, the girl, had risen from the table she had run round to stand by his chair with her head against his shoulder, and he had bent his head down to hers and there they had stayed, cheekbone to cheekbone in an unbearably senti-mental pose for nearly a full minute.

Margery could have slapped them both – she hated the mawkishness of it.

She liked her little boy, much more than the girl, because he, reliably, didn't do things like that. If he wished to tell you that he loved you he would jump up onto your knee, and bounce there, bruisingly and exhaustingly, saying, 'I love you, I love you, I love you,' as if it were a jolly song.

She did not trust this quiet flowing stream with surface eddies only to give one misleading information about the main run of the current.

The children rushed into the room to say good-bye before getting off to school, looking pink and fresh in their grey uniforms, filled, radiant with life and happiness. They momentarily dispelled the heaviness and the tension. They were both wonderfully themselves, and yet, marvellously, also Walter and Margery.

It was one of the days when they were both looking like Walter, unblighted, one of the days that made Margery feel that the long wearisome business of being married was worth while. There had been love, very great love, and it had left these children. The children carried it with them in their rush into the room and made the air in it sparkle with morning freshness and delight.

But when they ran out of the room, off to school, they took it all with them and left Walter and Margery facing the emptiness. Sitting in silence Walter felt his wife brewing up an outburst, but he couldn't say anything to forestall it, couldn't bear to involve himself further with more unnecessary words – he didn't want to add a straw or a feather to the existing burden of commitment. He switched his mind away, almost off, and concentrated everything in him on the china on the dresser. Margery knew exactly what he was doing as he stared with a fixed, stubborn look at the lustre ware, at the patterned eighteenth century china, and the country-looking coloured mugs.

'Speak to me, speak to me, speak to me,' she suddenly shouted at him, 'it's not fair, just sitting and sulking – at me . . .'

'I'm sorry . . .' he muttered it, almost inaudibly, staring at her hands which trembled crazily as if they belonged to a machine that was, although still running, seriously out of order.

37

'Sorry? Sorry?' she stood up with a plate in her hand and he wondered if she were going to throw it at him until it smashed in the corner of the room. 'Damn you.' They stood facing each other, she still trembling and desperate, he white faced and mute, across the loaded table. 'Isn't there any way I can break through to you? Haven't you anything to say?'

'There isn't anything,' he looked from her to the smashed plate and back again, 'to say.'

She sat slowly down again, her violence broken on the immense solid front of his sullenness, burying her face in her hands. He looked in sudden unbearable distress at the shards and brilliant white chips of china scattered on the floor, and then filled with a desire to make some gesture towards the restoration of order, he carefully refolded the newspaper until it looked as if it had never been opened and read.

'If you've found another woman,' she said abruptly, drawing her hands sharply away from her face, 'you'd better say so at once and have done with it.'

'I . . .' His feeling for Anne returned to him so strongly as he tried to speak that he felt as if she were there in the room, pressed against him, between him and his wife, and that they had been caught together locked in each other's arms – so that there was nothing whatever to be said, no need at all for words.

'You have found another woman!' she cried. 'You've found another woman and you want to leave me and the children. I can see it all over your great sulky face. Well . . .?'

'Yes . . .' he was surprised by the thin sound of his voice coming, reduced, through his contracted throat, 'that is . . . not the children. I don't want to . . .'

'Oh, oh,' she started up with her hand to her cheek in a fantastic, theatrical gesture of horror, 'you want to walk out, to walk out, and take the children, to take my children away. . . .'
She ran suddenly from the room, leaving the door swinging wide and fled away upstairs.

He went into his study and smoked a pipe, walking up and down, occasionally pausing to look at the work on his drawing board.

He had roughed out ideas for three big jobs that were up for open competition, but hadn't been able to decide which to concentrate upon. Now he saw the rough sketches spread out before him with complete detachment – as if he had left them and come back to them after a year – and he could see that they were no good. For the first time, too, he could see why, they were bad just where he was forcing himself away from his inclinations and gifts in the direction of fashionable idioms into falsities.

In any case none of the three projects – for a technical school, for housing in one of the new towns, for a sanitarium–were in the least attractive to him as work. He had slipped away from the conception of architecture as architecture, he had just been pursuing the fat job; the problems set, the possibilities, did not interest him in the least. Because I've let myself die in my living my work has died too, he thought; it's time for a clean break.

He set to, methodically destroying everything that might record the dead patch, old projects realised and unrealised, old letters, even photographs of his work, shredding it all and burning it, piece by piece, in the grate. The sun shone in through the tall plate glass windows, mocking the dingy flames with its morning brightness, showing up the squalor of the mass of black and grey flaked paper ash, and asking if he meant to burn the children and the woman. All he was destroying was duplicated either by papers at his office, or by buildings squatting their tons of steel and concrete on the ground. All that he was destroying was paper, nothing that mattered.

He stood in doubt over the pile of ash, there hadn't even been anything decisive in the way of a break with Margery, everything was still to be said.

She lay upstairs on their bed, no longer sobbing, with a dry dispassionate agony in place of her first wild rush of grief. Her thoughts came by slowly while she thought very fast about them, it was like watching balloons drifting past in a high wind.

She thought, well it's been coming for years, and looked bleakly over the string of years; we've been drying up on each other, and saw all at once all those moments of not looking up when one or the other came into the room, of actions continued across talk, of neglect, of gathering unawareness. It's over now, over now, over now – this one was out of control, dragging car, ropes, and a grappling iron along behind it, bringing down a shower of tiles, uprooting small trees and plants, gapping hedges, leaving behind it a great scar.

The tears welled up in her again, she wept for failure, and for having loved so much. The tears burned away three, four years, like acid, and she recovered with the solidity of a crystal ball the whole of the love and the abundance of happiness of the first seven years of the marriage.

Aaahhh, she cried through her clenched teeth, like a woman in ecstasy; her children were born out of her body again with great pain and the greatest satisfaction she had ever known, and passing away left her body to body with him in the best of everything they had known together.

It is over now – she lifted her hand to her mouth and bit hard on the thin strip of flesh she could raise from its back with her teeth, to make that pain drive away the other, and to prevent herself from groaning aloud.

She heard the door click, and rolled her head to see Walter standing in the doorway white faced, with a look of shock and concern.

She wanted him desperately to remain silent, to come to her as a physical presence; she could accept anything that his body did, or was, or needed, but wordlessly, without questions, and without answers. She opened her hands, half uncurling their fingers, so that they lay in flowerlike generosity at each side of her mass of auburn hair: he could come from any woman to her, he could go to any woman from her – her passionate love for him had returned with its full force.

He stood in the doorway blinded by another love and saw only her grief. Thin, ill fed, words crowded into the room to divide them.

'I'm sorry . . .'

'You mustn't say that – you mustn't be sorry – it's my fault – I know – I've been worn out with the housework and the children . . . I've failed you . . .'

'Oh, no . . .'

'You've failed me, too.'

'I know . . .'

There was a moment of silence between them; outside in the back garden the wind stirred the leaves of the pear tree and the big bay with a sound like whispered talk. His throat relaxed and he suddenly felt free to speak, while the pain deep in her body that had been closest to the surface in her breasts died slowly away into a dull ache, generalised and unassuageable.

'Is it bad – are you very much in love with this woman?'

'Yes.'

'Does it mean the end of us? Must it mean the end of us?'

'I'm afraid it does.'

'We had something so good . . . won't it come back if we try . . . couldn't we get right again?'

'I don't know . . . I don't want to hurt you . . . I don't want to be cruel . . . but I don't think so . . .'

'Oh . . . darling . . .' It was a mere whisper, an exhalation of pain, the air escaping from a lung wound.

'There's nothing between us any more,' he raised his voice challengingly, 'is there?'

'There has been . . . there could be . . . you know it.'

He came and sat at her feet at the end of the bed, his face downcast, his hands awkwardly in his lap. She had liked his hands, there was something about their being at once smooth and hard, they were firm, square palmed strong fingered hands. She moved a little and stretched one of her hands towards him, he took it, and of old habit their fingers interlocked. They were hand in hand.

'Couldn't we try to get back what we had?'

He gently disengaged his fingers.

'I told you . . . I love this girl.'

'Who is she?'

'Nobody you know.'

'Is she nice enough for you?'

'I don't know.'

He rang her door bell again, a few minutes after seven, and heard the bell pealing out in the empty flat. He went back again at eleven, at midnight, at one, at half-past one, at two, and at three, listening through the empty hours of night to the bell ringing in the silent rooms.

'Is she pretty – prettier than I am?'

'She's very lovely. She's the most beautiful woman I have ever seen.'

She, too, suddenly heard the faint pealing of the bell behind the unopened door, and realised with terror that this was all that he knew about this other woman, that she was beautiful.

'How long have you known her?'

'Not long.'

She gently took his hand again, watching a faint flush spread along his cheekbone, pitying him for his inability to tell the truth and wondering for what brief contact their marriage was to be thrown away.

'Look at me.' She shook his hand gently until he lifted his head and faced her with a dog's eyes. His look of shame and fear took her back to the beginning of their relationship, when he, unformed, changing, and developing had clung to her maturity. She had known then that behind what she loved there was something weak and poor that always might simply go bad.

Ever since they had been married Margery had been troubled by this sense of being a guardian of something that, however precious to her, might prove in the end to be worthless. Now she felt the burden of guardianship weighing on her more heavily than ever, because she felt that Walter was on the edge of finding out for himself that he was no good. He was filled with a sense of failure in his work, and in their marriage, now he was desperately plunging on a new relationship – like a gambler changing over to a new system towards the end of a bad season. If this new thing failed there might be nothing left but failure to live with.

She felt that she had caught him throwing a knotted rope over a beam, or holding a shot gun with one foot bared. He dropped his eyes, he was unable to face his own fears in her. She began to prepare a line of retreat for him, that might blunt the teeth of failure, and preserve something to her.

'Walter . . .'

'Yes.'

'Let's be sensible. We won't part, or divorce, or anything . . . for six months . . . not until you've found out what this thing really means.'

She was appalled at the thin sound of her voice, hollowed out by her lack of faith and conviction like the voice of a little boy talking tough.

'You go off and have your affair . . . if it grows into something bigger than me and the children . . . then so be it.'

The bay tree and the pear tree whispered for a few moments that life could not be ordered as easily as that and to drown their voices she spoke again in a firmer voice.

'I think you'll find me and the children beyond it. I think you'll come back, knowing more about yourself – better for us.'

He sat dejectedly looking into his lap, until she crawled to him and began kissing his hands. He slipped one away and stroked her hair, feeling her kisses and her warm tears on the other, the tears rolling heavily over his knuckles until they were blurred into wetness by her lips down near his wrist. Presently he pushed her gently away from him, and left her lying crying on the bed while he moved about the room, and in and out of the bathroom, packing a bag.

When he was gone she lay there listening. He went downstairs and down in the hallway silence closed over him. She wondered for a moment if he were going to come back up the stairs suddenly awakened to the reality of their relationship, and then the front door was shut, carefully, discreetly, and without wounding violence. His footsteps went off purposefully down the empty street and died away.

The outer world, crowded with other people, stole back into her mind, slowly building itself fragment by fragment.

A dog barked a few gardens away, a gust of wind set the trees whispering, a piano student began to play a familiar piece, one or two cars passed and the street became filled with other footsteps, and the tiny bedside clock began to sound triumphantly through the room. You grow old, you wither, men seek young flesh, it said, talking its metallic truth, your children have taken the firmness from your breasts, knowledge has put lines at the corners of your eyes, you grow tired as the light begins to go.

It is in the nature of things that he should go, men wither later than women, and you married young.

She lay, drained of tears, listening to the clock, to the voice of the reasonable little wheel swinging on its hair spring; saying, he'll never come back.

And then a change in her position made her feel the slow movement of her blood within her body, the pulse marking another time, the blood speaking another language. She had heard his heart beat, they had been together, she was part of his knowledge of life, and he of hers. They might leave each other, and go as far from each other as it was possible to travel, but the distance would be no barrier to that knowledge – it would crowd in wherever they were, or whoever they were with. The implanted tissue might be cancerous and deadly, but however much one might wish to be rid of it there was no easy way to slough it off or cut it out. However brutal and direct one might be in handling the knife, however deep one trenched, there would be no coming to an end of those delicate fibres and filaments which extended into the farthest corners of the body and the mind. There was no escape as easy as this – walking out and shutting a door carefully behind you was only the beginning.

Pray god, she thought, that I can take what is coming. Let me take it without bitterness; let me go on wanting him to be happy; let this be a birth and not a death. The clock talked on, everything dies, everything dies, but she lay quietly listening to the beating of her heart.

4

ANNE HORNE was still fast asleep when Walter rang her doorbell, lying on her back with her clenched hands drawn up each side of her head and the light from her bedside lamp glaring down on her face.

She had not slept right away when she got to bed, as soon as the light went out the girl Ross had been engaged to came weeping to beg her to give him back to her, railing at her for being cruel and cold.

She snapped on the light again and told herself she wasn't like that while she took some pills to make her sleep.

But as soon as the light was off her fears came back, the more frighteningly through the drug. So the light stayed on to keep the ghost away and burned on while Walter stood on the doorstep pressing the bell.

The bell brought her back a long way: from an estuary whose black waters were flattened by catspaws of a violent seaward wind. The boat she was in slid away from the land heeling madly when the gusts struck, then standing up again with the sails flap flap flapping like pistol shots as the wind eased. She would be blown out to sea if she didn't cut away the masts and sails, and the sea would be terrible.

She hunted about the empty decks for an axe, for a knife, for anything, but couldn't find what she wanted for a long time. While she searched she heard hootings, and looking up saw across the leaden water the river bank crowded with jeering, hostile people – hating her.

She went to hide from them in the shadow of a deckhouse, and, cowering down, found herself under a stand of fire buckets and fire axes. Now she had an axe she didn't know where to begin, and masts stood like huge forest trees and the sun bleached spider's web of rigging reared up secure in its incomprehensibility. Doubtfully she laid the axe to one of the shrouds – it's steel wire, she thought, it'll kill the edge of the tool, it's no good.

45

It parted like silk, and flailed upwards, streaming out in the wind.

The whole rigging began to run like a piece of knitting, the slatting sails flogged into ribbons and blew away in ragged strips; then the towering masts, mizzen, main, and fore, went silently over the side like divers, the last of the rigging sliding after them with the smooth purposefulness of snakes.

For a moment she thought, I'm all right now – but the wind pressed solidly against the black hull, moaning through the spokes of the big double wheel aft, and round the deck houses, driving the ship on down the river.

They were in close to the bank now, too, and the brutefaced crowd were stooping, picking up stones, and throwing them. Most fell short, some rattled briskly on the decks, one struck her on the lip. She tasted blood, and a great delighted shout went up from the bank as she turned and ran below decks in terror.

It was dark at the foot of the steep companion ladder, and she made her way for comfort to a small oil lamp which burned dimly at the far end of the corridor, swaying slightly with the movement of the boat. When she reached the pool of light she found herself by a teak door with a glinting brass plate on it, saying, Captain's Cabin.

The captain was in there, lying on his bunk in the half dark, bound and gagged. His eyes followed her as she came in with the lamp and tried to untie him, but she could find no ends to the rope, and could do nothing.

She managed to force the gag out of his mouth and asked him what she ought to do, but he turned his head away and whispered, faintly, to the wall. 'It's a secret, a secret I am not allowed to divulge.'

She heard the stir of the water outside the skin of the boat and felt that it was swinging round and round as the current carried it away towards the sea. 'Tell me what to do. Tell me where I can find a knife to cut you free.' He shook his head slowly from side to side and whispered again, 'I can't tell you anything. It's forbidden.'

The ship lurched and water ran in from the corridor to settle into a deep pool on the far side of the cabin; she was suddenly

46

terrified of being caught below decks in these shadowy rat runs, these little gravelike boxes of cabins, by an inrush of water.

It was a long way up the narrow stairs onto the deck, longer than it had been coming down, and she fell on her knees, exhausted, when she at last came out onto the sunlit glare of the deck.

She looked up and saw that the boat was being swept down towards a bridge, like old London Bridge in the picture books, with a row of houses built over dozens of little arches. The boat swung stern first into the bridge and struck one of the stone piers.

She fought to get up off her knees, but she couldn't, though she could feel the ship shuddering and breaking up beneath her.

She knelt there while the hull disintegrated into strips of raw planking which swirled off under the arch of the bridge. The tied and bound captain appeared among the wreckage bobbing on the surface for a moment before he was swept off under the arch into the rearing darkness.

The water ran up the deck and put a heavy arm round her waist, she could feel the weight of it pressing her down into disaster, but just as she felt herself going she reached out and found a heavy iron ring leaded into the pier of the bridge.

She took it, and immediately an alarm bell began ringing, high up overhead and out of sight. A man came down the face of the bridge, swinging down on a rope ladder from the window of one of the houses. When he got to her he began forcing her hands off the ring. 'You've got to let go, I can't help you if you won't let go.' She felt the water's heavy weight about her and couldn't let go. 'I can't, I can't.'

Tears ran down the man's face. 'I've got to have it,' he said and he took her wrist muscles in his hands and broke her grip on the ring. 'You've got to trust me, not that,' he said.

She felt her wrists slipping out of his grasp as she looked up into his face knowing him for the man who'd given her the flowers, pitying his tears. The water took her from him into the dark while the bell shrilled out, louder and louder until she remembered what it was.

She rolled over into the pillows fighting to get back, beyond the electric clarity of the dream into the black indifference of sleep.

47

But the bell went on.

She went out to the door, gathering her dressing-gown about her, angry at having to face anyone without her make-up, and sinkingly sick still with the anxiety and terror of the dream. When she opened the door the anxiety and terror crossed the boundary between dream and daylight and moved into her waking heart.

He stood there, with the scared unhappy face he had had in the dream, but real, with the life of the street going on sanely behind him; an electric milk float tinkling with empties moving one way, a gravel lorry dripping water the other, someone scrubbing a step and whistling something from Brigadoon.

Just before she opened the door the full realisation had come to him that he had jumped over the bridge of his marriage, out of the life he had made for himself, into a void in which he might fall, alone, for ever; he was as ill-equipped for living what remained of life as for the death that lay beyond it. For the moment he was without faith in his dream of the woman behind the closed door, the shuffling in the passage would be something, someone else arriving, and when the door opened it would assert another identity, shiver his illusion, and pitch him headlong into the gulf.

The door opened, and she stood there, all gold, as he treasured her in his mind.

He heard the clinking milk bottles, the whistled song, the rumble of the lorry, and saw her mouth moving. 'Go away,' she pulled the lapels of her dressing-gown together in a defensive movement, 'I don't want to have anything to do with you.'

She had meant it to come out clear and strong and final, but the words were whispered out over the weakly modest gesture.

He took a step towards her, to hear her better. 'Go away.' She said it again, but it was too late; she no longer had any authority of will or intention to enforce the remark. It died and passed her lips as a ghost. She could no longer pretend that she had nothing to do with him; the violence of his emotion had established a relationship.

Though everything on which she had based her life fought against the idea she knew she was going on with it, that she couldn't, to save her life, do anything else.

For the first time she felt that she was unalterably fixed in some pattern or sequence of events, she belonged in a particular place in the pattern, she had a function there. She fought it because she knew the man, not she herself, was the centre of the pattern; and her brain, reasoning against her heart, told her it was her right to exist at the centre of her pattern, to weave her own web, and that to be woven into any other web was an infringement of her rights.

But somehow she couldn't prevent the infringement; there was a deeper need, that was also new to her, to do something to remove that look of sick anxiety from the man's face, to give something. And she felt suddenly that she might, by giving that something, discover a way out – that here was the thing that truly would save her life, the need for which had become so strong.

'No, don't go.' She reached out towards him with a reassuring hand and then suddenly wanted to repudiate the loving gesture. 'We'd better,' she injected a metallic hardness into her voice, 'find out what all this is about. You'd better come in and explain your filthy way of going on – if you can.'

'Thank you.'

She went into the sitting-room with a new tremulous embarrassment.

She was abruptly ashamed of being caught so late in the morning in her dressing-gown, and with last night's dress, underclothes, and shoes, flung into a chair. She gathered them up hurriedly, and vanished away through the half open double door that separated the room from her bedroom.

'I'm so sorry, the room's in a state . . .' she murmured out of sight.

'It's very nice,' he said, his eyes roaming over the room, dodging the unemptied ashtrays.

The furniture was expensive and ugly, there were no pictures on the walls – nothing in the room spoke of a personal choice. Even the small things, the clock, the cigarette box, the ashtrays, a bronze statuette, were impersonal – expensive gifts from givers concerned only with their expensiveness and not at all with what they were.

49

'I love you,' he said, but it didn't mean anything in that room surrounded by those things, they were just words without any particular value.

'What did you say?' she said from the back room.

'Nothing.'

'I thought you spoke. . . . Would you like some tea? I'm making myself some tea.'

'Thank you.'

She appeared after a few minutes with a tray; brown china tea pot, milk bottle with the cardboard cap still on it, Tate and Lyle sugar packet and two white utility cups.

'I've forgotten spoons,' and she came back with two Georgian silver spoons.

'These are beautiful,' he was startled.

'Oh, are they? A man gave them to me . . .' she bit it off and blushed.

For a half second they looked at each other, then she bent her head and poured tea. She was wearing the same grey flannel suit with the white pin stripe she'd been wearing when he had first met her. She was even more beautiful than he'd thought. She had strength, and with it the richness and fullness of youth. More important than that a dignity of proportion made her beautiful, and not just pretty; she had a dignity and fullness that outweighed the deadness and lack of character in the room. When he again said 'I love you,' the words did not just die among things, they were received, and they meant that life went on.

She pretended not to hear, but she had, and she waited silently, without moving, bent over her cup, pretending not to accept it or submit to it, but waiting all the same.

'It's difficult to explain . . .' he said.

'It must be . . .' she flung her hair off her face with a swing of her head and stared at him, 'it's impossible to explain – if I were you I wouldn't try – but you've chosen to act this way – so I suppose you must.'

'You see, I love you.' He groped and found the wrong words. 'I want you more than anything in the world.'

'Oh that . . .' her face hardened and darkened. 'Men generally do want me. You're no exception – and they generally want me more than anything in the world while they want it – that doesn't mean very much. What I don't understand is why you should come and make a disgusting scene when you found you could have me?'

'Can't you?'

She looked at him and blushed again. She could feel the blood rising to her skin, and it made her feel angry.

'I can't understand love mixed up with contempt.'

'Nor can I – when I went away I saw I was angry with something rotten in me and I loved you all the more. That's why I came back.'

'All this about love!'

She drank down her tea and, getting up, walked over to the window. There she rounded on him, black against the net curtain that held the glare of the street in a white mist.

'Doesn't it,' she finished, 'only mean you want me for nothing?'

'No,' he wiped his hand across his face as if he were scraping something off it. 'No.'

'Well then – what does all this nattering mean, about love, about wanting me, about being important?'

'It means I want to give you all of me, everything I have, and know, and feel. And I want all that from you.'

'You want to make me part of some dream you've dreamed – you want to tie me to you – to wrap me up emotionally,' she grimaced as if there was something bitter in her mouth, 'you don't know me. You don't even know anything about me. How can you? I was with a man last night – I've known him for a couple of years – he could be important to me. You couldn't. . . . How can that fit with your dream?'

'I'm more important to you than he was. I know.'

'You're talking like a fool. You're not important to me. You're nothing to me, nothing at all. I wouldn't care if you walked out of the room now and never came back.'

'Shall I go?' he asked. He looked into her eyes for an answer, but she gazed back with a curious repelled, but fascinated, stare that he couldn't meet.

He shut his eyes and waited for the appalling word. The horrid, expensive, little clock struck, a new hour began.

She stood clasping and unclasping her hands, fighting to say the words, 'yes, go,' and she couldn't do it. Go, and leave me alone, and free, she wanted to say, and yet there was someone else with a say in her voice who wanted to be involved and unfree. This new person wouldn't let her speak, and hadn't yet found a voice. This new person was badly afraid, but didn't want to avoid what it was afraid of: the feeling was new to a mind familiar with the calculated risk, and habituated to the wise choice of risks. Pain was a bad thing, and the risk of pain was bad, and all that had been safely ruled out. Now she could see clearly pain coming, and uncertainty, and round the mouth and eyes unreliability. And yet she wanted to undertake those things for the sake of what would be interwoven with them. She looked at him standing in front of her, illuminated impartially by the filtered reflected sunlight without shadow, a rather ordinary man in rather ordinary clothes, without any of the signs of power or success about him, and she wondered what it was she craved in him.

He took a step closer to her and moved his hands slowly from her shoulders down her back, while he kissed her neck, the bone of her chin, her cheekbones, and the ʻcorners of her eyes. His hands came to heavy rest on her hip bones, solidly and possessively holding her, and she shook her head away from his kisses. She wanted to say, no, it's not that way that you're taking me; it's not as easy as that – that's a game I can play any time with anyone and win – this is something else. He felt this grain of opposition gritting between them and shook her gently.

'Look at me, look me in the eyes,' he asked, 'do you want me to go?'

She tried hard to turn her face to him and look him straight in the eyes, but it was almost impossible to do. She found herself looking at his neck and the line of his jaw. When she lifted her head to bring her eyes up to meet his her eyelids dropped half shut so that she couldn't see anything above his mouth.

Her sense of her own weakness disgusted her; being held like a baby in these great hands, being so gutless and abject, and wanting to be like that – which was so much worse.

She opened her eyes, suddenly furious; it was just a matter of having a good look at him and seeing that he was just a man like any other man – then all this glandular magic would loose its power. She looked deep into his eyes and he looked steadily back without flinching.

The will to be alone and apart broke in her. Her tears rolled down her cheeks as she wept for the loss of all the certainty and sureness that she knew. Now she was part of a pair, and about the other half she knew nothing except her need for it. She knew nothing except that it had come wantonly and extravagantly into her life, and might as wantonly vanish. And yet under it there was a mysterious joy: lost and afraid though she might be she wouldn't have it any other way. This could be love – the word might mean something after all – she turned her face up to his, eagerly, the woman asking for the fruit of the tree.

Walter fed at her lips; drinking up her youth, her need for him, and her absorption, forgetting what he wanted to be and was not, forgetting his age, his responsibilities, his part of his marriage.

His marriage had begun like this, with lovers forging out of the call of one body for another something that was to outlast the body's frailty and to challenge time itself. He renewed all those promises now without any doubts, they had been made before by another man, in another life.

5

ANNE and Walter left Beaumaris Street as soon as they could; Anne, like Walter, in flight now from what she was, and the surroundings where she had become used to being that.

They caught a two-fifteen train to the country after a desperate scramble, they seemed to have a bigger chance of leaving things behind if they moved quickly. They looked about curiously as they went to the station in a cab, and stared at everything – even the most trivial and familiar things – under the acres of dingy glass roof in the station – it would all be changed beyond recognition when they got back, it would never be the same again.

There was the usual ' go-slow ' half strike on the railway.

The packages in the parcels section stood in immense swollen piles, bulging out of the parts of the station designed to hold them, and great men with strong muscular hands moved the little packets one by one onto trolleys which moved off very slowly to the trains.

The slow moving railwaymen were watched by angry people waiting for late trains, people who were too well behaved, too half alive, to say anything. They stood round hating the railwaymen, and the railwaymen smugly and slowly hated them back, but there was no jeering and no real feeling, just a corrupting, half dead sullenness.

The senior officials and the managers walked about looking contemptuous but not trying to get anything done – they knew it wasn't any good – looking cool and detached in their braided uniforms or their dark suits and not speaking to the men who pretended in revenge not to see them – men who had worked together all their lives.

Occasionally some more frantic member of the public would rush up to a man in a peaked cap or a morning coat and with a white face, not far from tears, beg them to do something: the train for Cornwall, or North Wales, was just going to go, and there was all their luggage standing on the platform; couldn't somebody help, couldn't somebody do something. And the nobles of the railway with restrained grief and still not looking at their men would do it; or perhaps a few of the other passengers, soldiers or sailors on passage would do it, and handle the trucks into the guard's van. Then there would be the anti-climax while the passenger was effusively grateful with an end of her worry, embarrassing the volunteer helpers by overdoing it, and the train just sat there, not leaving, for ten, twenty, or even thirty minutes.

Anne and Walter moved about among it all feeling like foreigners, amused and apart. They had taken a tremendous step in their lives, everything was changed for them, they were excitingly alive.

They felt like birds flying low over a stream bed in a droughty season; the water had stopped running and the sluggish fish were dying in the stagnant pools beneath them, but they were sweeping on, other kinds of creature in a happier element.

The railwaymen thought much the same thing in a rather different way, when they thought about them at all: they would give Anne an indifferent look as a nice bit of stuff if you liked that sort of thing, and then flare into interest – how do people like that have money and time to travel in mid-afternoon in the middle of the week? How does it come so easy for them and not for us?

And they looked at Anne and Walter and decided to not-work all the more stubbornly so that they would get more money and be able to put on flash clothes and travel in the middle of the week too.

Anne laughed when the two-fifteen pulled out at five-past three, remembering Walter's anxiety because it had taken him a whole four minutes of the seventeen minutes they had left themselves to catch the train, to get a taxi: and feeling that she was really, now, being taken away out of her world into his world.

She seemed to be shedding things with every turn of the train wheels, as they went round things that were bound round her were loosening and uncoiling.

She lent against him and felt happy – when they arrived they were friends as well as lovers. They were able to walk in silence down the quiet mile of road from Lemlade Station to the Carp Inn.

There had been bad moments in the five hours' train journey, moments of unease when they had both felt a desperate need to rattle with talk to cover up strangeness and unawareness, but these had somehow gone at Oxford Station.

There they had strolled up and down the platform, waiting for their branch line train to start, among milk cans warm in the sun's glare, wicker packets of pigeons astray en route for Swindon, and drying chip baskets of watercress.

There was a wailing cat in a basket somewhere in the stack of passenger goods, and it had taken some finding. It had taken a good deal of argument, too, once it was found, to get a saucer of milk out of the refreshment room for the poor thing: finally the cat had been brought into the refreshment room and given aid and comfort on the bar counter.

It was sick with thirst and its sticky coat stood up in patches with heat, misery, and fear.

The Irish girls behind the bar talked of it in their singing, drawling voices with cold loathing as a filthy beast, an insult to them to bring it in, an insult to them to give it milk from china they would have to wash, an insult to the clientele.

The clientele drank tea dumbly, bewildered by the intensity of the row about whether a cat should have milk or not. On the whole they were for Walter as a merciful man, on the whole for the Irish girls on the propriety of the thing – refreshment rooms are not, after all, for cats.

Both sides being right there was, clearly, no side to be on; so they just watched with clear blue eyes under sandy lids, surprised that anyone could bother.

That Walter had bothered, and had not asked about whether he should bother or not, but had just solidly gone through with it, had established an understanding between him and Anne.

There would be time enough to say everything, they would do what they wanted and there was no need to hurry time with conversation.

There had been a shower just before they got to Lemlade

and as they walked down the station approach out onto the lane the ground stank of greedy, hot, wet earth.

Great drops of water hung on the rank growth at the hedge bottoms, and the domed white panicles of the cow parsley were bowed over with the weight.

The clouds had cleared away and the first stars were winking out in the clean, fresh, evening-green sky.

They stopped on the way to change hands with the suitcases once, and then to watch a youth chasing five lean fit hunters out of a hay field.

The boy was red faced and angry, and the horses laughed at him, moving easily, springy, away round behind him on their thin, delicate legs, scattering spray off the long, sodden grass. Presently the horses tired of their game and the wet field, and ran out tossing their pretty heads. The boy ran after them to shut the gate for fear they might come trotting as gaily and as lightly back.

The shining field was criss-crossed with their dark tracks and the running boy made one last dark bar across the pattern as he ran to the gate. His trousers legs were sodden wet, and they swung heavily from side to side as he forced his way through the tangled hay, stumbling and weary.

'The horses, weren't they lovely, the horses?' She said, 'I love riding, will you ride with me?'

'I can't bear horses – they're such stupid animals – with no brains in their long empty skulls.'

'You only say that because you don't ride well – I know.'

'How the devil do you know me as well as that already,' he said it laughing with her, but it disturbed him a little. It was quite true.

'Oh, I know about you, all about you,' she said. 'But you'll ride with me.'

He looked over his shoulder, back into the field. To him the important thing in the scene, the thing that had come most keenly into his mind, was the franticness of the boy when the horses wouldn't do what he wanted.

He knew that maniac feeling, when he wanted to take time, events, things, and people together into his hands to force them

57

into conformity with his will – and the time ran on and things and people ran off tossing their heads. He felt with the boy, through the despair at the wilfulness of the horses, the cheap trousers getting heavier and heavier and wetter from the jewelled grass. The boy might have a mile or more to walk or cycle home with the clinging wetness about his legs chilling and chafing. The damp would be through to his bones by the time he got home. . . .

He began to say something about that to Anne, but when he turned towards her there was nothing but light in her face. It was no good calling her back to the awkward, angry figure now fastening the gate; she was with the proud quickly moving horses in the far meadow, not with the underdog.

And when he looked at her he stopped thinking underdog thoughts; he could see that if he thought them he would be left behind with Willie Wet Legs in the wrong field, he belonged in the sunlight with the proud animals.

They were happy at the Carp Inn from the minute they arrived.

It wasn't merely lovers' self-absorption either. Walter to his great surprise began to work there. At the end of three days his head began to spin with ideas. The section of the new town that was open for competition stopped being a vague indeterminate fog of specifications and site problems and took shape as a set of dignified and handsome buildings well planted on the fine Northumberland hillside.

He forgot, too, all about the photographs that the smart architectural photographers would take through their red filters, the pictures that would catch the eyes of the coterie readers of the architectural papers, and gave his designs an unphotogenic solidity and comfort that would mean home to people living there in Northumberland in another hundred years or more.

He gave the designs the quality he liked best: in that hundred years, perhaps sooner, people wouldn't be saying, as they came up to the houses with their collars turned up against the weather, what a clever chap that Walter Jackson was, they'd just be thinking that the houses had always been there and probably always would be.

He was bothered at first because he hadn't got his adjustable sloping drawing board, with its tricky balance weights and gadgets, and all his little bottles and pens and drawing implements; but he soon found it easy enough to get down to work on the huge solid mahogany table in the unused dining-room at the back of the public house.

After all Yvele, and the builders of such places as Cunault or Albi, hadn't had gadgets to do half their work for them – and when you came to think of it the gadgets didn't do any of the work – whatever you might think when you bought them.

Walter found himself in direct contact with his work and able to concentrate in a way that he'd almost forgotten.

While he was thinking or drawing he withdrew into his brain pan and was alone in there with his stored up knowledge and experience, to the absolute exclusion of what was going on about him.

At the beginning this had been a worry to him, he was afraid of what would happen to Anne and him when he left her and went into work like this, because he felt their relation depended on his absorption with her. If he withdrew into his inner world and gave himself up to the egotism of the artist she might be gone when he came back – or worse she might anxiously, like Margery, try to follow him into those shadowy caverns to drag him out.

Walter had an earthy, ordinary egotism as well as his artist's egotism – it told him that Anne might vanish if he stopped thinking about her.

But when he retired into his work, turning from her, and dropping her mentally, to become absorbed in wringing ideas out of his brain and getting them onto paper, she retired into herself quite happily too.

He was forgetting, or disregarding, her nature, not recognising her passionate striving and longing not to be thought about. His working, and leaving her to work, was just what she wanted.

She could tolerate and enjoy him while their senses locked them together in a physical obsession that banished thinking, but his efforts to weave himself into her thoughts were different.

When she felt his mind working at her, when she became

conscious of his mental gropings for an understanding with her, she could feel the term to their love. His efforts would finish them, they depended as lovers on the unquestioning surrender of what they were to each other.

When he withdrew into his professional mind, and sat over his board like a hen hypnotised by a chalk line, conjuring ideas onto paper, she felt a great relief. It meant the end of these efforts to get at her for a time, the past was safe, the disparities were undefined, they were still together.

When he came back he was mentally worn out, he was in search of rest and recreation, to play with the world and her.

When he began to turn his rested and restored mind, curious again, towards her she could drown it in her beauty, annihilating him physically.

It was her great happiness – feeling herself overwhelming him, engulfing him, taking him down into a great abyss of smoothly flowing sensation in which he was powerless to create tension and unease, where he could rest untroubled by doubt and uncertainty.

It was an addition to her happiness to find that his work, too, took him to this great good place, and that it was an ally not a rival. When he was back there working, away and impersonal, she could gather up more calm and silence round herself; sitting curled in a chair in the shadowy front parlour, or lying on the white bed cover in their room upstairs, stretched out watching the reflected sun dapple on the ceiling, or down by the river sitting among the twisted roots of a big tree watching the changing light filter down through the green tent of leaves into the brown river water.

But though Walter had this happiness, and treasured it, there was this rottenness in his mind that made him want to dredge up something that would spoil it all.

He was thankful, instinctively, for this stillness in her, and her ability to wait; but secretly, deep down, he was disturbed. It was all very well to get on with his work – but he was afraid of this motionless waiting.

The sea might wait for you like that if it knew that you were going to die by drowning.

He could see that it was a big part of her life, and he wondered, with that itching intellectual, analysing side of his mind, how she had learned to do it. He could see her stretched out like that, waiting, in numberless anonymous rooms like her own flat.

There she was, stretched out on something white, characterless, and unchosen, consuming time without thought. He could see her there in lodgings and hotels, gone tomorrow or the day after, forgetting the name of the place, being nothing, wishing to be nothing, growing and becoming beautiful like a plant.

And when he had these cold intellectual moments he began to nourish a suspicion that the perfect physical content they achieved together was just another unfurnished room for her, another dark silent place without character or interest, that the magic of enjoyment they shared was a secret dangerous magic of hers, charming him into nothing.

Her stillness might be more dangerous in the long run that the bustling, pursuing triviality that a silly woman might corrode him with – but she had only to look at him with a special slow, spreading smile and that suspicion was gone. Then he only wanted to be deep with her in her still pool of darkness, whether he were to be betrayed there or created.

Every afternoon they walked out into the upper Thames plattes, walking through the lush, intemperate, late June wealth of green things and flowers.

The trees were towers of blue-black shadow under the brassy sun, and the willows with their grey strips of leaf like drifts of smoke along the water course and the ditches. The hot air quivered over the drought cracked fields where the hay crop had been lifted; even the insects seemed to swim slowly in something a little thicker than normal air. A few round white clouds hung about the sky, like a small herd of cattle in a large field, and beyond Faringdon, to the south, on the far side of the snaking Thames the downs lay, blue behind the shimmering glare.

They walked slowly to Buscot Lock and bathed, most days, and sometimes went on down to the Eaton Inn to tea.

The Eaton Inn was on an island in the Thames; they served an abundant tea with sweet strawberry jam there, on the pointed lawn heading into the stream as if it were a moored boat.

Or they would take a boat at Ford's in Lechlade and slide down the stream to take tea, at the Swan at Radcot, staying till late evening, coming up stream and home again in the gathering dark, with all the river scents coming out strongly as the air cooled.

Walter had a love of marshes and wet places, and this flat Thames head country was the dearest place in the world for him. Its plants even were precious; the coarse leaved, gross growers, on their thick hairy hollow stems, the delicate amphibians with their white water roots and their darker mud roots and green-veined white flowers, and the dusty flowered and dull leaved, seeming mediocrities, which from obscure glands scented the whole riverside with mint.

He had brought her here because it was the happiest place he knew and the most ordinary, and if she was possible or right here she would be possible and right anywhere.

And swimming up against the air silvered water pouring and foaming through Buscot weir, or diving off its soft coloured stone walls into the dark earth tasting river pool below, she was right – the plants were right, or as the pike in the river, or the swallows skimming low over it, were right, as beauty is right anywhere.

He was right with her and she was right with him as long as it was the natural order they chose to relate themselves to; while they did that they could walk together with linked fingers just being happy.

But there was a part of him, always present, that was afraid of the silence, the darkness, and the cold impersonal actuality of the natural order.

He found a new plant, new to him, with small oval dark green leaves, and little bronze gold flowers like small, delicate, snapdragon flowers, growing on a shelf under the bank downstream from Buscot weir and it worried him that he couldn't put a name to it or identify it as belonging to some family or other.

He couldn't just take its beauty and admire it, and leave it, as she could; he had to pick it over in his mind, tear the little flowers to pieces until he understood the structure, and puzzle over it.

He had to go into Cirencester and search through books in the public library until he found it and all the dead information there was to be had about it, columns of small close print, which he handed to her the next day, well learned, as they leant over the bank and looked down onto it from above.

She felt that it was all dust settling on the moment of discovery, when they had both suddenly noticed it gleaming by the edge of the water as they swam past. He was substituting something valueless for something valuable in a blindly murderous way.

Even his voice changed – took on an improving night school deadness as he discharged the rehashed botany – and she felt that he had become some quite other person than the swimmer who had found the plant, someone who had forgotten being there in the river beside her looking at the blaze of gold across the level glitter of the water, a stranger.

This stranger had a trap set for her among the river meadows she presently discovered.

When she sat on the lawn in front of the Eaton Inn on the island in the river she could see to the north, across a water meadow white with big ox eye daisies, a bank of trees, sheltering a rick yard, barns and some grey stone houses.

There was something nice about the way the place sat there, it looked snug, and welcoming, and presently she thought it would be nice to walk over and look at it – to see if it really were as nice as it looked from a distance.

He didn't say anything to her when she said she wanted to go, he just got up to go with her, with an evasive and secretive expression on his face.

She led the way over the wooded footbridge across the river, and he followed her without saying anything, watching her.

And he followed her, watching her, along the footpath across the meadow which was trodden short and smooth like a mown lawn by Kelmscott people coming and going from the river crossing and the Inn.

When they came to the barns and yards about the house no one was there.

Wet nosed bullocks, with their nostrils beaded with crystal, looked over the half doors of the fatting sheds and grumbled in their deep throats, cattle fashion.

Walter smelt the country smells, which were exotic to him, without realising that they were home and childhood for her; he was half intoxicated by the hot over-rich smell of the ripe dung heap, the different scents of the hay and straw ricks, the close, stuffy, smell of wheat piled in sacks in the barn.

She just thought, they have better animals than we had, and they must have about three times the land we had, and aren't they fine beasts.

'What's that feathery fluffy green stuff, growing there under the wall?' she asked.

He bent down at the foot of the silvery grey manor house wall and pulled a branch of fennel, then rubbed its aniseed reek onto the palm of his hand for her to smell. She held his palm like a cup under her nose, and when she had captured the odd pleasant-beastliness of the scent, touched the centre of his hand lightly with the tip of her tongue.

'We didn't have anything like it at home,' she said. 'What do you call it?'

'I don't suppose you did – its fennel. . . .'

He looked at her with that smugness again, he was teaching her things. He was imagining her, not knowing fennel, poor creature, a gangling lovely adolescent with thick plaits, sitting in some slum close in Stepney or Southwark under a sooty leaved fig tree waiting for meagre flowers from a few potted carnations or geraniums.

She was thinking of sea holly and tamarisk and other things that, like the fennel, didn't seem to altogether belong in England, that grew at the seaward end of her father's farm.

He led her out of the farm gate, into the beginning of the lane leading into Kelmscott village, past a little narrow gate leading into Morris's garden. This was to be the beginning of a new life for her.

Walter stopped in front of the door, putting his hand on the draw string of the bell.

'Shall I ring, shall we ask to go in?'

She looked up at the grey stone cliff of the house rising beyond its wall, her gold hair falling back on her grey-blue man's shirt. She assessed it as dead, hostile, at least irrelevant.

If it were some sight to be seen he should have told her about it, and asked her if she wanted to see it – he hadn't asked her, he had brought her there for some purpose he wasn't prepared to admit to – with some complication in mind – she wouldn't be entangled.

'No, it's not our place, it's nothing to do with us. Let's go on, up that way.' She pointed them on up the lane into the village.

He walked beside her with a rather pale face, seriously considering if she had failed him or not.

They walked by the church and he peered over the churchyard wall at the green damp stained gravestones over in the corner where the Morris's clan lay dead and done with, opening his mouth to begin to say something about them, and then not saying it.

She watched him wondering what of his lay in the dank shade over the lichened wall, and why he should want to speak about it and not be able to – increasingly annoyed by his craven dumbness and disappointment with her refusal to go into that dark alien looking house.

He spoke at last when they were clear of the village and its big stone farms.

'Do you know anything about Morris?' he asked.

'He's very rich and makes cars – nothing really,' she said.

'I meant a poet, William Morris,' he said.

'That's your teaching voice, again,' she said. 'I hate it. You turn into something dry and dead when you try and teach me things.'

'I'm sorry.'

He said it with a slightly amused, patronising intonation, and she turned on him, gleaming and golden, so that he cowered for a moment thinking in terror that she might really have some witch's power to blast and wither him with.

They were apart and at war as they had been in the street in London, she was despising him and leaving him, and he was sick with desperation to get her back.

'Sorry! You set a trap for me back there,' she said, 'I won't be trapped by your dead poets. I won't. We're alive together and we've got to live together. It'll be all right if we live together. But you'll make it impossible if you drag in all that dead book stuff.'

She saw that gold plant by the river wilting and fading under the load of library smuts that he had tipped out over it, and she glared at him angrily as if he were trying to murder her too.

For a moment he wanted to argue with her about the life of poetry and the immortality of poets – they are alive, they speak to us. That was the proud part of him, another part wanted to cringe and apologise; and there was the real man in him who saw that words or begging or weakness would all be equally fatal to them.

He saw that it had been a trap, a shabby, low, sneaking trap, too, that he had set for her. He'd brought her to a place he knew about just to expose her ignorance, it had just been a trick to put her there below him, where she would have to take from below what he, godlike, handed her from above.

It was contemptible.

'I love you,' he said, 'whatever you know or don't know, whatever you are or become or don't become. I love you and the hell with all that back there, behind us.'

For a moment she hung back stiffly looking into his face with a lingering doubt, and then she let him take her into his arms. It was a workable base for their living together: she had killed the stranger, or had left him broken backed in the trap he had set for her.

They walked back along the lanes leading towards the Carp dreaming a common dream, utterly content.

The sun was going down in the usual glare that said the weather wasn't going to break, and the trees cast long shadows clear across the boxlike riverside paddocks as it became a yet more beautiful evening than any they had so far shared.

They strolled on hand in hand, wanting to stay there in that lane, in that moment of time, in that complete unity, for ever.

When they were nearly home they turned up a small lane branching off their road to the right just to spin out their walk. But as they went up it they both knew that it wasn't a by-road,

66

it led somewhere, and it was the only possible road for them, although it couldn't take them home. It was the right way to go, and the feeling of its rightness grew every second. They had found out how they were going to live together, and now they were going to find out where they belonged – they knew it – the road was taking them there.

Half a mile up the road they came to a stone-built mill standing in a deserted garden. A green, weatherbeaten agent's board told them that it was Paradise Mill, and that it was for sale.

They walked over the weed masked gravel to the open doors of the mill, and hesitated under a vine, looking into a great shadowy room with stone floors encumbered by mill machinery.

They called into the cobwebby darkness, but no caretaker or guardian came, and at last they ventured in, moving quietly and whispering.

There were two upper rooms in the mill, thirty feet long and the width of the building, beautifully lit with long bars of windows in the south wall, and square casements in the curved north wall. These northern openings looked up along four hundred yards of still water pent up behind the mill dam, a long avenue lined with rushes and paved with water lilies.

Water spilt over the dam in a flurry of white foam that ran round the curved back wall of the mill with a steady rushing and a faint vibration.

All three great rooms were full of the murmur of the moving water and the whitewashed ceilings were luminous with its soft reflected light.

On the second floor they found a small round headed door under a low arch that went through to the mill house by way of a corridor bridge that hung over the motionless, moss-covered, wooden mill wheel.

The little house beyond breathed friendliness from its two sitting-rooms and four bedrooms, its proportions and solidity combining to give them assurances of cosy uneventful happiness if they would only come to live in it.

Best of all was the mill's generous heart, the biggest room in the house, the kitchen out at the back surrounded by its nest of dependencies, slate shelved dairy, cool north facing larder with narrow shelves all the way up the walls, and scullery with gigantic copper and brick vaulted bread oven built into a corner.

It was quiet and empty, but it was impossible to see it that way; as they looked at it the room filled up with its own life.

It was the sort of kitchen in which the bread lives in a huge earthenware tub, on the floor near the two big glazed jars full of eggs preserved in waterglass. Hams and a side of bacon hung from the ceiling, along with ropes of onions and bunches of sage and dried herbs – they weren't there at the moment but they belonged there and both Anne and Walter could see them perfectly clearly.

And they could see how life was lived there – if you came in an hour late for a meal you would find a pot with a pigeon and rabbit stew – the potatoes and carrots and turnip in with the meat – waiting for you on the top of the stove and an apple tart in the bottom oven.

You would put the hot things on the table in the middle of the kitchen – a table scrubbed and scrubbed till its grain stood up in ridges – and go through to the larder to draw off a pint of home brew and fetch the cream jug. While you ate an old fashioned Pennsylvania clock would tick heavily and you would hear the geese out in the orchard hissing, at a child, or a dog, or a woman pegging clothes out on a line.

They turned away from it reluctantly and went out at the back door onto a stone-flagged terrace, noisy with the rush of water. A low parapet edged the terrace, broad enough to sit on, still warm from the day's sunshine when they touched it.

They sat on it for a time, close to each other, dangling their bare legs over on the water side, just tipping their toes into the glassy curve of the water where it swept over the dam.

Presently they put their shoes on again and wandered off to explore the little track that led along the mill bank behind the house.

It took them into a quarter-mile long orchard which stretched out by the water, the grass under its gnarled apple trees almost shoulder high. Just by the entry to the orchard a little coach house, really only big enough for a pony and trap, had been engulfed by an enormous rambling York and Lancaster rose

68

vine. It was dappled with its streaked flowers, white broken by a soft purplish red.

As they walked up beside the water, like a looking glass in the evening calm, a fish leapt and fell back with a heavy plop; that decided a pair of wild duck that it was time to go, and they broke from the reeds and took off, leaving behind them a line of ripple rings and a wild scatter of diamonds flung out over the lily pads.

'I want to live here, Anne,' he said, 'could you live here?'

'Oh, yes, I'd love it. I do love it.'

'You wouldn't be lonely, and bored?'

'It would be the loveliest place in the world to live.'

'All right, it's our place; we'll live here.'

She lived there while they stood watching the evening shadows bank up behind the mill and under the trees. She lived there a long time, filling the house with life but not changing the place – she saw that the gnarled orchard would slowly decay, that foxes would creep through the long grass to take young fowls in spring time, and that they would spy on the wildness of the mill pool from inside their life, leaving its life alone.

He stood by her with his hand on her shoulder making other plans – plans in which realities had no part. He would have his drafting office on the top floor of the mill, he would get the mill wheel working to make power for electrical machinery that would run a printing press on the other two floors. He had always wanted his own press, he would have it here – The Paradise Press – they would publish fine editions – on architecture and art, mostly, but also poetry – the place would become as famous as Kelmscott already was.

The house could be done up, and the kitchen electrified by the power plant.

He even pruned the trees in the orchard, cut them right back, and brought in a machine to mow the grass. He saw trees, healthy again, loaded with fruit, and the windfalls rolling to rest across a smooth lawn.

But as he only felt her happiness, and she just felt the content through that heavy hand on her shoulder, it didn't all get into words, and they stayed together in their drugged, physical unity.

But they were oil and water, really. However hard she fought to make him oil he remained water, and however much he tried to change her to water she stayed, not even stubbornly, just irredeemably, oil. And whenever they came out of their physical trance and stopped dreaming they flew apart, like oil and water.

There was nothing for it but some sort of disaster if they stayed together, and as she wanted that, and he wanted that, it was going to be disaster.

The mill waited, immensely solid, for them.

Meanwhile they were very happy and they walked back to the Carp radiant, so that the men they passed in the lane, going home from work, saw it and envied them.

That night in bed Anne told Walter that she hoped she would bear him a child, she would never be untrue to him, never, she said, and she would die if he left her, die. I'll never leave you he told her, never, because I love you. They took the murderous knife by the blade and loved the wounds it made.

6

JEANETTE and Francis came back from school with their round felt school hats over their arms like baskets, slung on the elastic chin straps they wouldn't ever use for keeping the hats on. It was one of their days of secret nonsense; they were having private giggles about Tibbytabac and Tabbytabic who lived at the bottom of the Highgate ponds and ate children who got lost on Hampstead Heath.

'. . . But they can claim sanctuary if they get to the Spaniards,' said Francis.

'Yes – they have to blow a silver slug horn . . .'

'What's that?'

'. . . like in Browning, "dauntless the slug horn to his lips he set" . . . you know a silver trumpet . . . it's in Childe Roland . . . they have to blow this slug horn hung on the fir trees, and then they have to call on the Spaniards, "Gardez mon foy, a mon aide monseigneur".' She called it out three times and Francis joined in, loud and clear.

'Gardez mon foy, ammonade monseigneur,' he looked puzzled, and beginning to hop on one foot said, 'what does it mean?'

'I don't know – I got it out of a book on Old Guernsey customs – it's feudal – or something . . .'

'Guernseys are a sort of cow.'

'. . . anyway – when they've cried it – the call – the Spaniards come rushing out in their broad brimmed black hats, and long coats . . .'

'. . . with scarlet linings . . .'

'. . . their long swords flashing . . .'

'. . . smoke curling up from their primed matchlocks . . .'

' "Yield, yield, cravens, these children are under ban and arriere ban! We the Spaniards have spoken!" '

'And Tibbytabac and Tabbytabic turn and bunk like anything for the ponds and safety.'

'Foaming and snarling . . .'

71

They both, by a common impulse, flung their hats and school-books onto the chest in the hall and went hopping madly through the open drawing-room door. Margery was lying down on the drawing-room sofa, she had taken an aspirin for a headache.

'You're making far too much noise, children, please be quieter or go out and play in the garden.'

'Sorry, mummy.' They were both still standing on one leg.

'Why must you come hopping in like that, can't you come into a room in a civilised manner?'

They looked at each other. 'Tibbytabac and Tabbytabic are monopodes,' said Jeanette.

'Monopodes?'

'Like quadrupeds, but with only one leg,' they burst into giggles.

'Oh, please, please, be sensible . . .'

'Sorry, mummy.'

'But seriously, mummy, why is it called the Spaniards, and Jack Straws Castle?'

'I really don't know.'

'Was there ever a real castle there?'

'I don't think so, they're just the names of public houses.'

'What's a public house, mummy?'

'You know,' said Jeanette, 'they're on corners.'

'Oh, yes, I know that – but what are they?'

'They're places where people can go to buy drinks.'

'Could I go and buy drinks there?'

'No, you're too young.'

They went on through tea, grinding away at her nerves with their excess of energy and their bouncing innocent appetite for the world and everything it contained.

Margery loved them, really, but they were so boring – so utterly limited to taking and not giving – that she found it an enormous strain to be with them, talking to them, for hours at a stretch.

Her cheekbones began to ache with boredom after she'd been with them any length of time – she felt she just had to get away and lie down. That was her usual reaction and in the afternoons she could just hold on through tea until Walter came back from his office. He always had enough energy left to deal with their simple physical bounce, perhaps because in the office he was primarily engaged on contemplative mental work. It was the consoling thought towards the end of their long tea time, daddy will be back in a few minutes, never later than half-past five.

Every day she looked forward to that relief, and she still did, quite automatically. It was always an effort to remember that there was no relief to look forward to.

She finished putting the tea things away and stopped looking fixedly at the hands of the clock with the gilt face which sat under a little glass dome on the chimney piece, at the tiny pendulum swinging so firmly, at the drum on which the finicking little platinum chain was half unwound. She stared and stared at the clock, until, quite suddenly it seemed it was a quarter to six. It was another day when he hadn't come back. When would he come back? He might never come back at all.

'It's too late for daddy to come back today, isn't it?'

Jeanette was standing beside her, and she put her hand to her head and stroked the child's hair with an uneasy fondness. She wanted to be honest with the child always, because she did truly love her, but she also wanted to protect her from uncertainty and pain. She didn't want to face this particular truth herself, and she very much didn't want to hurt the child with it. She wanted to stave it off for as long as possible – after all, it might never be necessary to scar her small heart with it – the passions of middle-aged men, or of men slipping consciously into middle age, flared up, and flared away.

'Oh, I didn't really expect him. This job in the North is a big affair – they're making a whole new town – he'll be away some time – I don't know how long.'

'He'll write to us soon, won't he?'

'I expect so. But I expect he's terribly busy. He may not have time for letter writing.'

'Oh, I see.'

He didn't write. There were no letters, there was no word; just a threatening, enduring, silence that ate away Margery's reasonableness.

The children were allies of the silence, steadily fraying at her

73

nerves with their energy, and their frank, open questioning. Why doesn't daddy write? Why doesn't daddy come back? Where is he? Don't you know where he is? Is that why we can't write to him? Is daddy angry with us?

Poison came into her, a sour bitterness at what she saw in the children's eyes when they saw that she was fencing – that she couldn't bear to answer their questions. They were hurt, and by her; they thought she was doing something to them that deprived them of their father.

It all bred an anger in her that hunted for an outlet.

She could see the easy confidence of her daughter breaking slowly, a reserve came into her that hadn't been there; and the boy began to develop a certainty of unchallenged possession of her, that was a bad, unbalanced thing the rivalry for her was gone out of his life.

He began to develop a funny little cockiness and matter-of-factness that was superficially attractive – but superficially only – strangers said he was such a manly little boy, but she knew it was all wrong. She knew it was rank growth, not the healthy thing that would have, should have, come out of trust in his father's manliness. It was knowingness, mistrust; he was making a hard outer crust inside which he could shrink away from the world.

She began to hate and despise Walter for the weak failure that had allowed her children to go wrong like this – and yet she still loved him, and the hating and despising were a small part of what she felt.

The main feeling was longing for him back, and a sickening fear of what might be happening to him.

And she felt terribly ashamed and humiliated because Walter had vanished and she knew so little about what he was doing that she couldn't even fabricate a convincing lie to account for his absence.

He was just missing, out of touch, in thin air.

One day about a month after Walter had walked off into emptiness Margery's mother asked her to come to tea.

They sat in the long expensive drawing-room of Mrs. Courtenay Bannerman's Georgian house by the river at Chiswick and wondered about each other. They were at the back of the house because in hot weather the mud banks under the Eyot smelt at low tide, and the hot muddy smell was more than usually bad that day.

They sat by French windows opening onto the little orchard at the back, because it was so nice for the children to run in and out. Mrs. Bannerman had good reasons for everything she did and felt better when she had told people what they were.

Her husband's small sailing boat was laid up under the trees and the children were romping over it happily.

'Does daddy ever sail, nowadays?' said Margery.

'Oh, men,' said Mrs. Bannerman. 'Courtenay always says he's going to sail when the fine weather comes if I tell him he ought to sell it to a younger man.'

'Poor daddy, it would be like selling his youngness.'

'Well – it's just rotting there – nobody's getting any fun out of it.'

'The children love it.'

'Francis gets more like Walter every time I see him . . .' Mrs. Bannerman seemed to catch at the words as if she would rather have left them unsaid, and then realising that her pause might be more unkind and tactless than words went on in an altered voice: 'How is Walter?'

'Oh, he's all right,' said Margery, dry mouthed now the crisis was in the offing.

'He's away, isn't he?'

'Yes, he had to go north – on that Carterdale job – the new town, you know. I don't know when he'll be back.'

'My dear?'

'Oh, he has to go off – sometimes.'

They pretended to be watching the children, but they were only conscious of each other.

Margery was trying to will her mother's mind away to something else, trivial for preference: she had a strong belief that telepathy worked on occasions like this, or would work if one concentrated hard enough.

Mrs. Bannerman was knitting unhappily with confused thoughts running through her mind.

75

Walter was up to something that might mean unhappiness for her daughter. It might mean making more unhappiness than was necessary if she did or said anything to impart her knowledge. But then that knowledge might be a comfort to her daughter – she was certainly very tense and upset – and the hard facts might ease her mind – perhaps her trouble was that she didn't know.

Speaking rather fast, looking down to the far end of the orchard, right over the children's heads, a long way away from her daughter, she let it out.

'Your father and I went up to spend the week-end with the Costersen's at Windrush. We took the car and stopped for lunch at that pretty little pub with the fish's name – Chubb or something – just near Fremlade – Walter was there – having lunch. We came back the same way and he was there again. He seems to be staying there.'

Cloud shadows ran over the lawn: Margery knew that wasn't all and couldn't bring herself to ask what the more was.

'Didn't you speak to him?' she asked in a flat voice.

'Well – he didn't seem anxious to be spoken to.'

'Oh, mother . . .' she just couldn't contain herself, 'what was she like?'

'She was very fair, and young, and good looking – a very pretty woman really – but I don't know, she looked hard . . .'

There was an intimate moment of trust in which tney looked into each other's eyes, but it didn't last.

Margery didn't want to be intimate with her mother about this thing, and wondered awkwardly how to conceal her shrinking. She didn't want to expose wounds or share her grief, and yet she wanted to know more. How could she ask without letting her mother know what was being done to her, and the children?

Mrs. Bannerman wondered how she could comfort without being intrusive, or, more especially, without seeming greedy for her daughter's emotion. She felt guilty at knowing what the poor girl should have come to know first, it was an insult to her that she should have the information at all – it belonged to her daughter. She decided that the only thing she could bring herself to do was to pretend that her daughter knew everything.

76

'I'll be very angry with Walter if he's making you unhappy.'

'I suppose all men have these – episodes – it's only natural, really.'

'I suppose so – they want mothers and they want fun women – all the same they've no right to hurt the mothers. Walter's no right to hurt you.'

'Oh, mother, Walter's not hurting me. He was all fussed up over this girl – he said he had to go away with her for a bit – so I told him to go off and have a good time. He'll get her out of his system soon. He won't be away long. I know Walter.'

She smiled at her mother, hating Walter a little for the rancid taste of the lies in her mouth. But pitiful to her mother she wouldn't be.

Mrs. Bannerman knew when her daughter was fibbing – she itched to offer sympathy, to stroke the hair of a weeping girl child again, to snuggle her into her kind bosom to have her cry out.

But Margery had grown up and grown away; she was like granite, sitting there behind her bright smile, shutting the doors of her life firmly in her mother's face.

'Well, you're a grown woman now, darling, you know what you're doing . . .' but the tone of her voice doubted it.

'I think so.'

They left it, at that.

'We've more or less arranged to have the Wincklemann's house in Cornwall for the rest of the summer,' said Mrs. Bannerman. 'Phil's got a marvellous new job in Washington, so they won't be using it.'

'Phil Wincklemann always gets the most marvellous jobs.'

The conversation went on safely and boringly to relatives and friends, and to the ailments of the girls who had been girls in the houses where Mrs. Bannerman grew up. Margery always found that talk with her mother ran into those easy subjects in the end. If they tried to talk about anything else they always ended up with hot spots on their cheeks and tight mouths, agreeing with each other effusively, and thinking inwardly how unreasonable, narrow and prejudiced they were. But there was ease and room for love so long as they gossiped about all those women of an older generation that Margery scarcely knew.

77

Perhaps it's just as well, she thought to herself, that Walter and I have bitterness mixed up with our love – that'll keep us from turning into podge-puddings like mummy and daddy. 'Where is daddy, today?' she asked.

'Oh, he's fishing on the Wye – so he says – I know he's really sitting in the Snarrett Arms drinking whiskey and pretending he's waiting for the rain to stop, or the light to change, or something. Men are such humbugs. He's gone for a fortnight.'

'You see, he has to break out now and again, too.'

'Oh – him – he's finished with all that – long ago.'

As it happened Mr. Bannerman hadn't gone fishing, that was only his cover story. He'd really gone to have things out with his son-in-law.

He'd taken a quick look at the register of the Carp Inn while he was waiting for Mrs. Bannerman to come out of the Ladies.

Every inch the old soldier and man of action, he'd made an appreciation of the situation and decided that if Walter was staying with the girl under an assumed name, Smith, or Withers, or something like that, he'd take it that it was an episode and the least said soonest etc.; but if Walter was staying under his own name and describing the girl as his wife, he meant business and his daughter was in for trouble.

And there it was, plain as a pikestaff, Mr. and Mrs. Walter Jackson.

He wasn't going to have his daughter's life messed up, so he was going up to the Carp for some plain talk.

But he felt a little lost when he pulled the car up on the gravel outside the inn, because the plain talk that had seemed so possible in London had become, somehow, impossible on the way. Back there it had seemed quite reasonable to say – Walter, you must go back to Margery and make her happy. Since then he had remembered a good deal that he had forgotten about Walter, about his daughter, about his wife, and about people generally.

Driving out of the dingy suburbs, and leaving the rubbish bordered by-passes behind, had been like driving out of the land of death, and coming into the farming countryside, whitish yellow with ripening wheat, tufted with blue black elms, had been like coming back into the land of youth where his blood moved and recollected its unreason.

Walter was a rather nasty fellow in many ways, and Margery might be well advised to say good riddance to bad rubbish while she still had the looks and youth that would get her a decent hard working husband.

When she'd married Walter he had warned her – pretty plainly – that these bohemian artists and writers and architects were not very sound people. When you leant on them they slipped away.

He'd told her to look out for squalls, he knew, for a fact, that the man had been involved with other women before Margery. She would have only herself to blame if she saddled herself with a man who wanted a fresh woman every so often.

Margery hadn't argued, she'd just looked a little strangely at him. From that curiously direct look he'd known that she'd been the mistress of one or two men, and that she knew enough about them to know rather more than he did about what he was talking about, and perhaps about him.

He, as a matter of fact, knew pretty well what Walter was like in that respect because he was pretty well the same – he liked a fresh woman now and again himself.

All through his career in the army there had been periods of separation from his family – when tours of duty took him to places unsuitable for young children, or special duties took him briefly to places where it was unsafe, or not worthwhile to go the expense of taking out the family and setting up house. And of course there had been women at these places, jolly companions even if they hadn't counted – that was the point, of course, and the saving grace – they hadn't counted. He'd never been disloyal to the family, and he'd always come back to his duty.

It was pretty clear in his mind what not counting meant, and he had a strong feeling that going back to do your duty to your wife and children was right, but he couldn't quite put it into words. It was difficult to explain, and he felt reluctant to tell his son-in-law to sit down to that cold and rather tasteless dish.

His duty was all, in the end, he had ever done in his whole life – and it didn't amount to very much.

He had not, as he very well knew, made Mrs. Bannerman very

much in the way of happiness, and he had always been quite remote from Margery. Paying the bills and so on, that didn't amount to very much however the psychologist-Johnnies might prattle away about the craving for security.

And being tolerated, and rubbed along with, and being mildly loved, and mildly pitied, and mildly teased, didn't amount to very much either.

He didn't know that he could be very sincere about saying to Walter go back and make my daughter happy, when he meant – go back to be tolerated, to be rubbed along with, to nullify yourself, to get under the yoke, so that you can wear out, clean, ineffective, and harmless, if a little boring, like yours obediently Courtenay Bannerman.

Still it had to be done, it was his duty, it just had to be done.

When he arrived at the Carp the bars were still shut and the front door was locked, in the way of English inns outside permitted hours, so he went round to the back to see if he could find anyone.

There was nobody there to do with the hotel, but down at the far end of the lawn, by the pool under the bridge he saw a glint of fair hair. She was there, curled up in a big wicker chair.

He walked straight up to her, regretting as he went that she was so much more lovely than Margery. But then, in his experience, and he supposed in everyone else's, that sort of woman always was.

He looked down at her and coughed to attract her attention. She looked up, gave him a cold look, and turned away – a dirty old man at work she thought.

'You're staying here with Walter Jackson, I think,' he said.

'Well, yes, I am. Do you know him?' She prepared to be friendly.

'Yes – I do – as a matter of fact –' She was very lovely indeed, he wanted to be friendly, very much, but there it was – there was duty to be done, come what may. 'I am his father-in-law. My name is Bannerman, Courtenay Bannerman.' She quietly turned to stone, enemy stone, under his eye.

'I don't think we've anything to talk about,' she said. 'My

name is Anne Horne, if you want to give it to a lawyer or anybody.'

'I want to avoid that if I can, Miss Horne.'

'Well then there isn't anything we can possibly talk about.'

She turned herself away, and became absorbed in watching two swans idling against the current in the river, just holding themselves in place against it with an occasional powerful stroke of their grey rubbery legs, watching for the scraps that the stream carried down under their noses.

'I'm sorry. I'm rather gravely concerned about the happiness of my daughter, and the future of the two children. I thought I'd like to have a friendly talk with you and Walter about the situation.'

'There isn't any situation to talk about. Walter's everything in the world to me – and I'm everything in the world for him. Your daughter should have seen that her marriage didn't die on her – if she really wanted to keep him I don't suppose it would have – anyway I've got him now – he's mine until I fail him. I don't mean to fail him. I know he won't fail me.'

'I wonder how you can know that, Miss Horne. After all he's just walked out on one woman and a couple of children – perhaps he's the walking out sort. Perhaps he'll walk out on you.'

'Anyway, if he should I won't send my father round after him, like a dun. I'd be ashamed.'

'Margery didn't . . . damn . . . I'm sorry, the last thing I meant to start was a slanging match. I just meant to have a straight talk . . .'

'You just felt like interfering. You must have known it wouldn't do any good.'

'Please listen to me – just for one moment – I don't know you, or anything about you. I know my daughter and I'm fond of her and her children. I know things aren't right for them with Walter away from them – here with you. If you don't love Walter – if you're only having some fun, having a good time, or whatever you like to call it, for god's sake give it up. Let the man get back where he belongs. And even if you do love him, remember he's got his responsibilities to three other people. And there's one thing I have learned in life, there's no real happiness to be got from other people's unhappiness.'

81

'You're a poor dried up, withered old man and you've forgotten all you ever knew about love and happiness. You don't calculate like that about love – it's just that I can make Walter happy – your daughter can't any more. Happiness is the only important thing in the world. We'd be doing wrong if we turned our backs on each other. It would be a terrible thing to do.'

'You won't give him up?'

'No.'

She sat up, straight backed and proud, burning at him with love magic. He was warmed by her, and he envied Walter the strong passionate animal that was so eager and aggressive for him. Her loveliness was unanswerable, it was as futile to argue with her as it would be to stand on the bank and try to persuade the swans that they would be more useful and practical as geese or egglaying ducks.

It would be useless to argue with Walter, too, with that intoxication upon him.

He went away across the lawn and drove off without making any further effort to see him, or to part them. As he went on through Gloucestershire he rather envied them. His mind was full of her golden being: he felt his life had been very sterile, very empty of that kind of quickening experience, and that kind of woman.

He should have left Katie Bannerman for someone like that when she had begun to turn stale and discontented on him – perhaps he never should have tied himself down – if only he'd had the courage to be reckless, to let the blood course through the veins as it should, perhaps he would have known what that girl was talking about when she spoke of happiness.

He looked down at his hands on the wheel, well kept, thin now, with many blue veins clearly visible through the transparent flesh: if they had never grasped flesh and blood in forgetful passion, they were at least guiltless, they had done no wanton hurt. He had, with his limited liability affairs, done all he could to avoid grief and pain, he could hold his head up on that score. He argued to himself that his dull way had, after all, its merits: Walter would in the end explore with that woman a world of regret that he would never know.

82

As he bowled along the country roads Mrs. Bannerman walked up and down her drawing-room looking rather bleakly at all its good pieces of furniture and porcelain.

Her daughter had seemed so terribly unhappy behind her defences, and it made her sad not to be able to do anything about it.

She was tempted to write to her, or to telephone to her, to tell her it might be for the best.

She remembered how unbearable the slow death of her love had been; how she had slowly become used to a tepid answer to the fullness of her love, what unbearable pain there had been in finding no answer to her generous natural flow of emotion, and how desolate she had felt as its source ran dry. When Courtenay's at home it's rather like having an unburied corpse about, she thought, you could keep a man and it might be much worse than being left, much, much, worse.

7

THAT evening Anne told Walter about Mr. Bannerman's visit to the Carp, and gave him an amusing parody of what had happened. It made Walter laugh a good deal at the time, but in the morning he was furiously angry – so angry that he couldn't settle to work. He sat down and wrote to Margery instead.

Dear Margery,

When I said good-bye to you I tried to make it plain that I wanted time to think and get myself straightened out. I told you I was too tired and strained to be reasonable and that I had to get off and put my ideas and feelings about us and our situation in order. I thought it might take six months – I didn't know how long it would take. You agreed to that – we weren't to do anything definite or to commit ourselves in any way for six months. Now, in complete disregard of that agreement, you've chosen to set your father on me – inside a month. I don't know what good he was meant to do, or what you'd told him to say to me, or how dragging him in could possibly help us to straighten out our difficulties. In any case he seemed to be well aware of it, and being ashamed or afraid of facing me, contented himself with making a disgusting scene on the lawn of the hotel here which poor Anne had to deal with. That hasn't improved matters at all – in fact it's convinced me that I can't wait six months. I know my own mind now. I want to be free of our failure altogether. This business of sending up your father has finally convinced me that there's no hope – if you could hope to make me love you again by bringing a sort of blackmailing pressure on me through your family – with whom I've never had any sort of sympathy – it means we're so utterly out of touch that we might as well abandon the pretence that any real relationship exists. We'd better break, and break clean. I'm staying here with Anne Horne and we are quite open about being man and wife. Tell your lawyers to send someone down here with the necessary papers, and some snooper to look at us – whatever has to be done. There's no alternative to a divorce – it's the only thing, it's not possible for us to go back – we've got to go on, and I'm sure that the only way we can go on is to follow separate paths.

Yours,

Walter.

Margery read the letter and as soon as she had reached the last word rolled it into a small ball between her hands and threw it away from her.

The cat patted it about for a time until she decided that it was too nasty even to have about, she picked it up and dropped it into the dustbin. Eugh, and she washed her hands as if she had been touching something very unpleasant and defiling.

But really, how could her father have been such a fool? And how could Walter be so utterly ignorant of her ways of thinking, how could he really think that she had sent her father after him?

And how could he write to her at such length without saying a word about the children? And how, that was the unbearable thing, could she still love him?

Dearest Walter,

I'm very angry, but I can be angry with you and still love you. I'm afraid it is so. There has been love between us, and it still is the real thing for me. That's not the only thing that makes it impossible for me to slide off as easily and conveniently as you would like. We have had two children and they are not yet grown up enough to understand this sort of thing. I believe in an old-fashioned family as the place for children to grow up in – the sort of family with a mother and father in it. I want you to come back and do your proper job as father to our children. I know very well that men want lots of women in their lives to make them feel bold and strong and successful – I don't in the least mind your having affairs with other women. I know there is so much between us that I'm the important woman for you, in ways that are only partly tied up with sex. I'm not so young as I was, and I know I can't be everything you want now – but that doesn't worry me enormously though it makes me a little sad. I don't mind what is happening. You can have a liaison with this girl Anne of yours

85

– I hope it's nice for you – but I want you here to be a father to the children most of the time. They're feeling rather horribly hurt and unwanted now, and I don't want them to grow up to be difficult problem burdened adolescents. I want you to come back and make them sure of you. If Anne's really nice I wouldn't mind having her to stay when you wanted her – if she got on with me I'm sure it would work all right. If you couldn't bear that you could go off when you wanted to. But you can't rip my insides out, and hurt your children like this, just for an affair. I'm not going to do anything about divorce until the six months are up.

I don't know how you can be such a fool as to suppose that I sent father to you. You must be in an absurd mental state even to think of it – it was his own bad idea and I had no part in it. He was probably just trying to be kind – it was unfortunate but it wasn't my fault – it's your fault that a situation in which his interference was possible existed.

Come back soon, and be sensible – I do love you – even if I get angry when you are not sensible, I love you all the same.

Margery.

'Ach,' said Walter, and flung the letter by the corner, like a boy flicking a cigarette card, across the breakfast table to Anne.

She read it slowly, and gravely, propping it against the brown china teapot while she went on eating toast and marmalade.

It was the first time she had heard of Walter from outside – lying at his side in the dark of night she had learnt a great deal from inside – about what he had done and what he was. She had been told among other things about a marriage that had died slowly until it existed as no more than habit and custom, that was not a real thing.

The letter brought less comfortable knowledge, from the other side the marriage was, apparently, real enough, and worth fighting for – if it had been in a dead patch the crisis had restored something lost to it.

She went to the end of the letter and then read it immediately all over again. On the whole this Margery was fighting very well – she could see that she was a complicated thought-weaver, like Walter, and she could see that a lot of the ideas in the letter were like burrs, subtly hooked to cling, and to work into the flesh.

86

All that permission and tolerance was very nicely calculated to bring his new love down to a little thing . . . and then this about the children made her feel a little uneasy.

Walter had said enough about the children to make it plain that there was a very powerful tie there, and that was another thing from the love of a woman.

It was nothing Anne could magic away with her body. Instinctively she hated the idea of bearing children, she didn't want to be fat and gross, she had a horror of finding a being, a little, helpless, pink worm, utterly dependent on her – and she couldn't bear the thought of it greedily nuzzling at her for milk – the idea made her bowels crawl with a sort of nausea.

She remembered her mother's last five children too well, when the ninth came she was just over eleven, quite big enough to wash napkins, and she'd done more and more for the four that came along after that one.

And it hadn't escaped her that her father had loathed the whole messy, smelly business, and drank more, and was out more, and was worse tempered, while it was going on. He had hated her mother for being caught, and the baby for taking her away from him, and the wormish helplessness of them – he couldn't bear to have anything to do with them until they were two or three years old – when they stopped smelling and began to talk.

She had an idea that all men felt like that, and that a woman who had a child said good-bye to her man for about a year and a half, if not longer.

This was no time to try to checkmate this Margery woman with that sort of thing – besides she couldn't do it as part of a battle with another woman, as a considered plan – it would be too loathsome.

She stared out of the window, forgetting the letter for a moment – she felt that, and yet she did want a child with Walter. She could sometimes feel his love wrapping her about, and then she felt that it would be very easy and pleasant to make a Walter-Anne person, that making that composite being was what she was for.

But she couldn't do it abstractedly, for a purpose.

She shuddered and handed the letter back.

87

'I shouldn't answer it. I wouldn't have written in the first place. You don't have to answer it.'

'No, it was stupid of me to write to her. . . .' He kissed her and went off to his work room, pretending that he was just going to work in the ordinary way – pretending to himself as much as to Anne. He'd told her in his letter that it was finished, and he told her what he wanted her to do, so there was nothing more to be said. But Anne knew from the way he held himself as he went out of the room that thoughts were tumbling angrily about in his head, and that he was surely going to write to Margery.

She saw them weaving themselves together with their busy minds, tying themselves together with a web of letters, their obsessed anger slowly excluding her from the charmed circle. Well, she could write letters too, and she'd catch the post if she got down to it.

She wrote a bad, dead hand that showed that she didn't write often, and hadn't written much since she'd left school, it was a child's characterless handwriting.

Margery despised it, and the cheap blue paper that she wrote on. It was a small sheet, four by six, and very bright blue. When Anne decided to write she had to go into Lemlade to buy a pad, and that was the only one she had been able to get at the combined grocer, stationer, and post office. She never had writing paper because she never had any occasion to write letters, and had, indeed, been at pains to order her life so as to have nobody to write to.

Dear Mrs. Jackson,
    Walter showed me your letter and it made me very sad because I love Walter so much and it is clear to me that you love him too. I know I ought to give him up because he made promises to you and because there are children and they're as much his as yours. But I can't give him up because there's a rightness in love that's more than that sort of rightness. All I know is that I found Walter terribly unhappy and that he grasped at me as if he was drowning and I know that if I gave him up he'd start drowning again. I can't let him drown in unhappiness because I love him and I couldn't bear him to get desperate with misery and all wound up inside himself the

88

way he was. You must see from the way Walter has gone off that you weren't enough for him and that he's gone off to find what he really wants. If you're really thinking of Walter's happiness you'll let him go. If you love him I'm sure you will. I know you love him because you said in your letter you would share him, and that I could have part of him. Because his love for me is so real I know that would mean me having the most important part of him, and I think that would be rather embittering and horrid for you and would make an atmosphere which would be an unhappy one for his children. I think it would be better for us both if you let Walter have his way now and much better for the children. He'll be angry if you don't and I think you'll lose him altogether. If you give him up now there will be a bad six months or a year, while the divorce goes through, but then he will be your friend again soon, and you will be able to come and stay with us at our mill here as a friend without tension or unpleasantness. The mill is a lovely place and I am sure his children would like it. But I think if you try and thwart him there will be a fight, and there will be all sorts of beastliness and bitterness that will make friendship impossible in future. I hope you will see what is best for us all. I'd give Walter up tomorrow, I promise you, if I thought it was best for him or even good for him.

Yours sincerely,

Anne Horne.

Really, Miss Horne, really, said Margery to herself, as she folded the letter neatly and put it away in her letter case.

She felt it would be almost her duty to save Walter from such a creature, even if she didn't love him. She imagined her writing the letter carefully, forming each letter of each word deliberately with the tip of her tongue between her lips.

Some vulgar hard little blonde person – she dared to imagine herself queening it alongside the educated man she'd dazzled – playing hostess to his wife and his children – well, thank goodness, that couldn't last. He'd see through her soon enough.

His letter came by the next post.

Dear Margery,

Your letter was a nice exhibition of everything that's detestable in you. When you turn on the feminine wisdom,

89

oh so much older than the ages, I feel nauseated. That letter with its cruelty and grasping greediness disguised as kindly benevolent thought for the children gave me all the choked throttled feeling that living with you has given me in these last ghastly years. I don't know if it's that, or if it's your pretence that the first real disinterested love that's come into my life is only an affair – to be dirtied with your obscene suggestions about concubinage – that sickens me most. I want you to try to understand that what has happened to me has turned me into a new person. I've never known what love was before. I just knew what it was supposed to be. With you I managed to fake up something that was good enough to pass for the real thing – while I was young enough and green enough to be taken in. I've got the real thing now, at last, and I'm not going to give it up for any pretences or shams you want to poison the children with. Think of trying to make a life for them by starting them off with the biggest and most complete lies we could think of. I'd like to be your friend and their friend when our systems have been cleaned of lying and deceit. The children could come and stay with us then, when we've set up our home here. I won't fail in my duty to them, never fear, not unless you contrive a gulf between us that makes it impossible. Believe me, I am being sensible and reasonable. You're being cruel to yourself, and to the children, by refusing to face the fact that what was between us wasn't good enough at best and is now dead and done with. We've tried and failed and the only sensible thing to do is cut our losses. Break clean and start again. Be honest with yourself, go to your lawyer, and start the thing going that will set us free to make a new relationship as friends.

Walter.

'If that is what you have made of my dear Walter, Miss Horne, you deserve to have him,' Margery said aloud, when she'd finished the letter.

The words resounded startlingly in the empty room.

When she had come in from the shops she had seen the letter in the letter basket, and had put her things down at once. She didn't want to lose a second in getting in touch with Walter again. She hadn't even shut the drawing-room door, or sat herself down in a chair. She had just dropped, half sitting, on to the arm of the sofa and ripped the letter open.

Now the words, which she had spoken aloud quite unwittingly, fled out through the open door, echoed in the empty hall, in the empty stairwell, and against the doors of the empty rooms.

They came back, from every surface, with the same report. Something is dead in the house, there is no hope, there is no use pretending any longer.

She walked to the window, and stood staring out with one cheek set against the chill glass.

The cat came straight tailed and rubbed its fat neuter's head against her legs, purring. She knelt absently to caress it and grief overcame her. Crouched, she bowed her head and began to weep, the cat from time to time darting a green intent look into her tear-blurred eyes. It wanted something to eat and couldn't understand why she didn't feed it.

She felt broken and humiliated, as if her long tolerance of the side of Walter which was now crudely uppermost was disgraceful to her. 'It was my own fault, pussy,' she said, stroking the animal, 'I should never have had anything to do with him.'

If Walter and Anne had appeared before her insect size she would have been too repelled to tread on them – to be concerned, to dirty one's foot, would be intolerable.

And how was the stain already there to be scalded off? Letting it wear off with the effluxion of time would be too slow. She would shut him out, she would never think of him, or mention him, or regret him, or long for him ever again.

That letter, oh, god, that letter, had turned over a page and on the next one there wouldn't be even a clue that would enable anyone to guess that Walter had ever been part of the story.

She went up to the bathroom to bathe her eyes with cold water so that the children wouldn't see she'd been crying, she would never show anyone the trace of Walter again. She did not answer either letter.

Anne watched the post for answers, but she was not at all surprised when no answer came – she had not intended Margery to answer her, she just wanted to shoulder her way into the argument so that there would be no doubt about the third party to it. Margery and Walter could say things that mattered to each other on the intimate basis of their marriage, but it was quite another thing to let a stranger into the middle of the heart. She didn't think Margery could write to her, and she felt she'd shown in her letter that writing to Walter would be writing to her. Every day those two were physically and mentally apart the higher and stronger grew the Anne-Walter wall of common experience: Given time it would shut out Margery altogether – but it had to be given time.

The summer towered on, hotter and hotter, through July.

The white wheats turned from ashy white to brilliant yellow, and the fields of red wheat looked as if they were grown on red hot soil. With the other country sounds they began to hear the binders cutting the early fields of oats, the clattering of their knife blades, and the regular clumping as the bound sheaves were tossed off at the side of the machine.

Here and there combine harvesters were at work, eating into the big fields of grain, like insects eating great yellow leaves; they were curiously bug like, and, with their whining drone, less attractive than the bustling, rattling, reaper-binders.

It was pleasant to be in the middle of this hard-working countryside without being devoured by it, as spectators, free of anxiety about the thunder heads lying southwards over the downs and rumbling in the early morning, free of the daily strain of four or five hours' extra work until the last sheaves were carted, free of the fear that the gold in the fields would be turned by a break in the weather into mould-scented rubbish.

Anne remembered, walking through the lanes and watching, how her father used to get sick with the nervous tension every harvest time, and how it always meant rows and scenes before it was safely in.

Walking and watching, too, she could understand how it was that for the rest of the year her father had looked forward again to the harvest, saying farming wouldn't be farming without harvest, and that it was what one farmed for.

Even the year wheat was eighteen shillings for two sacks of two hundred and fifty pounds weight he had to have his wheat field, although he had been sour mouthed and bitter, snapping everyone's head off, whatever they did, from the time it was cut to the time it was put up into the stack.

They carted that lot in a wet time, with the water running out at the cart-tail, and made a narrow stack to let the wind blow through.

Mark Stephens had built the stack and had let the roof run into a ridge too quickly so there was a half waggonload left when the rick was built, begging for a home and nowhere to put it.

Father stood on the ground roaring insults at Mark until he came down the ladder scarlet in the face with fury, and then they fought.

Mark Stephens was smaller, but he had boxed in the navy and he'd thrashed his employer in five silent panting minutes of thudding, punishing fighting, she could still hear the brushing of their feet shifting in the stubble as they circled each other – and her father's sobbing breath coming and going as the old sailor knocked the tar out of him.

When they got back home, at the farm, he'd washed and changed his shirt, and then beaten her with a strap till the blood came.

'You'd no call to watch, you bitch.'

He'd turned in the doorway, swaying a little, 'and if I hear a whimper out of you when I get back I'll beat you again, do you hear me?'

Her three younger sisters lying in the other beds in the room stared with enormous eyes in the twilight through the twisted iron bed ends, and the door slammed shut. Then they cried, from fright and misery, but she was too proud.

Her mother came later, tight mouthed, carrying a basin of cold water and sponged her back, dressing the oozing welts from her neck to the backs of her knees.

They could neither of them breathe a word to each other for fear of breaking down.

She couldn't remember if she was twelve or thirteen that year, but she could remember the feel of her father's hand holding her by the thick of her hair, in where the round of her skull ran into her neck, and the whistle of the leather belt in the darkening attic bedroom.

93

But it was all quite fresh to Walter, he had no wet or fine harvest memories and it all seemed pleasant enough to work in the sunshine to him, recalling summer holiday happiness at seaside places.

'You know I sometimes wonder if I didn't make a mistake in my vocation – there's something awfully attractive about farming. I mean of all ways of life it's the one that seems to have survived the beastliness of these times best – it's a man's work and it's decent work . . . do you know what I mean?'

'Mmmm, yes – it looks terribly hard work though.'

'You aren't afraid of hard work are you?'

'Yes. I don't see how you can't be really.'

'Oh, Anne, it makes you strong and hard, and keeps you from getting flabby. It's what's wrong with most people, they don't work anything like hard enough.'

'You don't know how lucky you've been.' She wanted very much to tell him about work that was so hard it blunted people, calloused them so that silk and fake silk, butter and margarine, stone and cement, wood and plastic were all one.

She wanted to ask him to think of touching her, or anyone else with hands and senses as blinded as that; or to think of being always so tired, dog-tired, that you couldn't take in anything but the simplest, and the most direct, sensations.

But she knew she could only tell it in terms of nightmare, as the hard luck story of her growing up. And that was walled off, like a burning gallery in a coal pit, because the cornfields were beautiful and there was another truth about them which her own story poisoned. She felt that some time she might come to know what the other truth was, and that then she would be able to talk to him, to anyone who was interested.

Perhaps she might find it out by running a farm with Walter, there might be some land of the twenty acres that went with the mill that they could farm.

They were buying the mill, the deposit was paid and the slow process of searching the title was going on, the solicitors working up their fees by writing each other fantastic questions about points that bygone generations of solicitors had prudently obscured.

Meanwhile they felt the place was theirs, and they used to go

94

to it every afternoon when Walter's work on the drawings was finished.

They swam now in the slowly stirring waters of the mill pond, among the rubbery waterlily stems. They got to know the summer birds and insects of the place, spying on them along the flat table of the water as they swam.

After they'd bathed they nested in the tall grass under the apple trees, lying still, talking softly so that the hush of the place shouldn't be broken, and often saying nothing for half an hour or more, just lying looking up through the leaf roof to see the fat summer clouds sailing slowly above them in the blue sky.

Anne used to watch them drifting and think, suppose he'd met me on the farm with those awful red hands I used to have from washing those damned nappies, and the washing up, wearing those frightful limp cotton dresses – yes, with a couple of sweaters pulled over the top, and my bare legs stuck into wellington boots, carrying a couple of pails of chicken mash down to the arks in the long meadow – would he have known I was his woman?

Or if it had been when I was in the A.T.S., in that awful hat – and if he had met me then he wouldn't have had the two children – but then that Margery would have been a young woman then, and I would have been a lumpish country girl still. . . .

'Darling, what are you thinking about?'

'Oh, nothing, just how nice it is being here.'

'Do you know the place is nearly ours? The lawyers wrote this morning asking if I'd have the money ready in about fourteen days, they want the money on tap because they're getting ready to complete the sale. I've written telling them to sell some stock and get on with it. So the place ought to be ours in a fortnight.'

'Oh, that's wonderful,' she rolled over onto her elbow and looked down through the orchard at the friendly mass of the mill, slowly turning into home, 'that's wonderful.'

But there was an answer to Walter's letter to the lawyers.

Dear Mr. Jackson,

I have your letter of instruction of the twenty-eighth, dealing with the disposal of the 1954-56 Melverhampton Corporation Stock. Under the terms of the marriage settlement it is only in your power to dispose of stock named in the settlement deed with your wife's consent. It will be necessary, therefore, for me to have a note from her agreeing to the sale of this stock before I can carry out your instructions. All that is wanted is a line stating her knowledge and approval of your intention to sell, with a witnessed signature.

Yours sincerely,

Edgar Lawrence.

The letter was there on the breakfast table with the morning post and the West Country edition of the London morning paper. Walter read it, while Anne read the paper, the special page with items of interest to West Country readers. A man at Weston-super-Mare had caught a flat fish with a profile of George VI on it, there was a big photograph showing the man peering round the fish smiling, and inset a coin with the royal profile on it. In the next column there was a headline: Schoolboy Batsman will Play in Crucial Test. On the opposite page there was a special feature article on the high cost of running a grouse moor.

'Who are these papers supposed to be for . . . ?' she asked in bewilderment. 'Who's supposed to care about this stuff?'

But there wasn't any answer. Walter had put the letter down on his plate and gone silently out of the room, without touching his coffee or eating anything.

She read the letter several times while she had two cups of coffee, bacon and eggs, toast and marmalade. There didn't seem to be anything so terrible about it – he'd just have to get the money some other way.

When she had finished her breakfast she went to look for him and found him on the riverside lawn. She stood on the veranda under the wire baskets of geraniums watching him for a while, wondering how long it would take him to come to enough to notice that she was standing there watching him.

He was pacing up and down, up and down, on the lawn.

To the river, turn at the top of the bank, back to the house, turn at the saloon bar window, and back to the river; to and fro, to and fro.

His brain was ticking like a clock with money, money, money, money.

Current account at the bank two hundred and ten pounds – deposit account, level three hundred. Two thousand pounds to raise in fourteen, no no, eleven, now, days.

I might do it on a mortgage – threes into twenty-five, eight near enough, and the third of the odd hundred is thirty-three.

Wanted, then, eight hundred and thirty-three pounds to lay beside the mortgagors sixteen hundred and sixty – then say another hundred and fifty for those damned lawyers – and we've got to have something in hand for living expenses – and furnishing the mill – and then there are next term's School fees for the children, and Margery has to feed and clothe them – and I still want fifteen hundred to be safe.

The competition for the new town isn't judged till the new year – I won't know about that – I haven't a chance anyway – and the Waldegreen job is held up for the permits, and the Phillipson's contract doesn't call for another payment till the end of the job in late October.

I've nothing to do but go to Margery. I haven't got security for an overdraft that big – what the hell else can I do?

And every time he worked the figures out he had the same answer. Go to Margery.

He was boxed in his own worry, it didn't occur to him to speak about it to the fair girl in the neat linen dress who stood watching him from the top of the lawn. He was miles away, wondering just how he could get Margery to sign that essential letter. She must do it, he wanted that mill. . . .

Anne became bored with standing up watching him and moved back to sit on a table swinging her legs. She was a little disturbed that he didn't see her, and didn't think of simply asking her 'have you got this money?' She became increasingly interested in the problem, just how long would it be before he would remember her?

8

ANNE thought about money while she packed at the Carp, about it in her usual calm and deliberate fashion. You had a plan and you had so much money, if you hadn't the right amount you either gave up the plan or waited until you had enough – it was simple.

It was a surprise to her that Walter could go ahead and make an elaborate plan without securing it first, it was an idiotic way of making yourself sick and desperate, she thought.

It was something of a shock to her, too, finding that Walter was like her, one of the people without money.

She could see that he had been shaken by the idea of raising two thousand pounds fast, it took him too close, too close to his margin of safety – perhaps beyond it, although he hadn't said so.

She had placed him, as a professional man, with a family, a house in London, and an income, among that class of property owners and solid, substantial citizens with whom she had been at war, had envied, and had loathed for the very security and certainty she had envied.

Perhaps that is why we can love, she thought, because we are after all on the same side, and I'm not different, or another breed – we're the same kind.

She wondered if the people who employed him as an architect treated him with the same poisonously good manners that made courtesy worse than disregard, and if he also had that poisoning sense of 'not belonging' when he found himself in one of their places, like the hotel lobbies, resorts, and pleasure places – like the dancing club Ross took her to – where she . . .

She looked out of the window across her open suitcase, down the garden to the stone bridge over the river to the hills behind the fluttering grey leaves on the willow boughs. 'Where I sponged on them, and sold myself.'

She said it in a hard voice that was meant to be a steady and dispassionate one, as if the blue hills were accusing her of something, and she was justifying herself.

'If what you want is on the other side of a muddy field you just have to get mucky, that's all – and it was the only way . . . it was.'

Again she spoke aloud, and again she could hear, in the echo from the walls, in a thin timbreless quality in her voice, her own utter lack of conviction.

Oh, god forgive me, yes, she said but silently inside herself, I got the money in a filthy way from filthy people, but I came from filth, and there it is . . . thank god I've got it anyway because now I can do more for him than his wife will.

She began to plan it out, she'd give him the money – no that wouldn't be the best way – she'd raise the money and give it to his lawyers, without saying anything, with no fuss, no signing this or that, no questions. It would just be love, and Walter would suddenly find one day that the mill was his.

The question was had she the money?

She went, mentally, over the contents of her safe deposit box in the bank in London, and worked it out, just how much she had got.

The oil shares Freddie Lautremont had given her, Mark Cerny's South African stocks, the National Defence Loan that Charles Addit had made over to her – she didn't know how the market was running but it was somewhere round about three thousand five hundred pounds, a bit more or a bit less.

There were the bracelets Ross had given her – they might be worth five hundred, perhaps more, they ran heavily through one's hands when they slid into a drawer.

The emerald ring from, now who? Well, it was worth two hundred or so, that makes more than four thousand.

And then there was the blue diamond hoop with sapphires, and the heavy Victorian gold jewellery from that arty boy, and the platinum link bracelet.

It would run somewhere between four and five thousand pounds.

It would be nice to be rid of it all, because while it was in that form it had people's names attached to it and bad, disturbing ideas came from it.

There was no getting round it, it was dirty money.

When it had been turned by love into Walter's mill the curse would be off it, everything would be all right, then.

As she slowly constructed her fantasy of purification Walter lived, mentally, through a couple of crowded days. He reached London in a fast train that stopped at no stations on the way, saw Margery and convinced her, in a scene of sweet reasonableness, devoid of ugly passion or resentment, that she could do no more in common decency than sign, took the note round to the lawyers, and saw that the purchase was going forward satisfactorily, signed a few papers, and returned to the Carp. It would be, he thought, rather wonderful being in London with Anne just for that time – they would look at places they had known when they were desolate and unfilled with each other, wondering how they had lived.

When Anne at last came downstairs with her bag packed and they set out for the station actuality was lagging so far behind his dreaming that frenzy began to eat him.

It mounted as the train carrying them towards London crawled along the single line from Lemlade to Oxford through the blue heat haze, and became desperation as they spent three-quarters of an hour waiting there for the London bound fast train to come in.

In the branch line train Walter sat in his corner seat hating the other people in the carriage for being easy and gossipy and in no urgent hurry; Anne looked across at him, and seeing his face twisting with bitterness and impatience, longed to be able to smooth it, to rest and ease him.

But when she leant over and touched his hand with a murmur of his name, to draw him out of his angry dream into talk, he twitched his hand away impatiently and withdrew firmly into himself. After staring fixedly for a few seconds too long out at the slowly retreating landscape he swung back to her and then gave a slow stare round the carriage, pausing at each face, as if to carry her round with him on a tour of inspection, demonstrating the impossibility of talking, either casually or intimately, in the presence of such dull, foreign minded deadheads.

It burst out of him while they waited in the station at Oxford, as they walked up and down the platform among the decayed, obsolete, railroad machinery and the slack disorder of milk cans, packages, and trolleys. He streamed with lonely, furious talk about the swinish ugliness that industry, that people, in their brute beastliness, had dumped down on Oxford's grey and violet loveliness, people like those wooden headed clots in that carriage. . . . She let him run on, amazed at the complete divorce that money had effected between them so abruptly and wondering how it was that she still, undoubtedly, loved this drunken stranger.

To break the even flow of his scolding she made him take her to the station buffet to get something to eat.

He made a scene with the waitress because she was slow in coming to them, and grumbled while they ate because the beer was warm, at body heat, and the sandwiches dry and old.

When the waitress came to scribble them the check there was another scene because she made it out for the wrong amount – she couldn't see it, and there was a wrangle over ninepence in hushed tight voices which made people look round and stare.

Some people were amused, others despised Walter for trying to teach an Irish girl that there weren't ten pennies in a shilling, he'd lose the silly cow her job.

Anne went quickly out when the manageress, breathing heavily, came over to straighten out the little misunderstanding. She felt very much alone standing there on the platform, even after Walter had come to join her.

They stood side by side in silence until the London train came in.

Anne recognised now that Walter was for the time being mentally sick: he was in a grip of a new crisis of desperation and anxiety akin to that in which he had so violently taken possession of her.

The dazzle of her bright gold had then obscured everything, now the shining light of the mill had made everything else a meaningless black.

She began to see the pattern of his life as a series of such critical storms – there must have been just such a storm when he took possession of Margery – he had lived by progressing from one obsession to the next. Each new storm of possessiveness devastated the past, and razed it.

She was suddenly frightened, badly frightened, that she might find herself like Margery, a badly scorched piece of debris in such an area of devastation.

She began to revise her fantasy in new terms: she would not just give the mill to Walter in loving compliance, she would get the mill bound to herself so that he could not have it without her.

But what lay beyond that, would he go on? Would there be another crisis beyond this one?

She looked at him, and loving him saw her wishes written on his face: he was a late developer, at the moment he was going through the crisis of his maturity – when it was over he would be sane and adult, ready for happiness and sanity with her, at the mill.

But she would all the same have to fight hard to see that the crisis did end that way, with his maturing.

If he was thwarted, and failed to get the mill, or if he got the mill in a crisis which involved the abandonment of his dreams of living with her he might go on, a passionate child, till his dying day.

When they at last reached London they went straight to Anne's flat in Beaumaris Street.

It smelt fusty with disuse and every polished surface was clouded with a film of dust and smuts. Anne fussed about, cleaning and housekeeping, for the hour and a half which Walter spent trying to get Margery on the telephone.

The telephone produced no Margery; though Walter got through to the operator and scolded her, saying there must be someone there, I know, there are children in the house – they couldn't just be left alone – there must be someone there . . . but the telephone just stayed dead, interminably making the whirr, whirr, of the ringing tone.

Walter went at last to the house in a cab, and faced the locked front door, the closed shutters, and the dead look of an empty building. Trembling he tried his own key on the front door, he had an odd feeling of being a housebreaker, or a rightless stranger, and passed in.

Everything was smothered in dust sheets, or covered with sheets of already discoloured newspaper, the clocks were all stopped. He looked about for some message giving a forwarding address on the telephone pad in the hall, or in Margery's desk, or in the kitchen drawer where they occasionally left messages for the help – but there was nothing.

He went back to Anne and with shrinking fury put through a call to the Bannerman's house. After a long time the housekeeper came up from her snug sitting-room in the basement and answered. She had hoped that if she took long enough the caller would ring off.

Grudgingly she admitted that the Bannermans were away, grudgingly admitted that she knew where they were, grudgingly gave the address, and under pressure agreed that there was a telephone and that she knew the number.

She had it written down.

She would let him have it if he really wanted it. She would have to go and fetch it. She shuffled off down the corridor leading to the stairs, and down the stairs, and along the basement corridor; Mr. Big in such a tearing hurry could wait, she wasn't going to put herself out . . . she shuffled back: Tregennor 9–44.

Long distance were busy, and a long time answering. When Walter got them at last the lines with Cornwall were all blocked by talk, and it was three-quarters of an hour before the call went through.

'Hallo?'

'Is that Tregennor 9–44?'

'No, this is the Dolphin – Tregennor 9–87.'

Another half-hour.

'Hallo?'

'Is that Mr. Bannerman speaking?'

'Yes, who's there?'

'Walter Jackson. How are you? I wonder, could I speak to Margery?'

'Oh, I'll see.'

There was a long pause.

'Hallo?'

'Yes?'

'Margery doesn't want to talk to you, Walter, I'm sorry.'

'Will you give her a message, please. I want to discuss a matter of urgent importance. . . .'

'Look here, my boy, she won't talk to you. You'd better write. Good night.'

'This is perfectly ridiculous. I want to talk to my wife. . . . Hallo? Hallo?'

Mr. Bannerman had hung up on him.

Walter turned to Anne, white with fury. 'These damned relatives of hers – first they interfere between you and me – now they try to force themselves between me and Margery – it's loathsome – loathsome.'

He walked up and down the room. 'The meddling swine – I don't believe they've any right to do it – she's my wife. . . .'

'What are you going to do,' said Anne, laughing at him inwardly. 'If I were you I'd go and see Margery. I'd make her see you.' She thought that if she could get him down there in that mood there would be an end of any hope in that quarter, and the mill would certainly come to him through her.

'Yes, that's the idea. You're a fighter, Anne, we'll make those bloody people square up to the facts.'

'You could catch the midnight train tonight, and be there in the morning.'

'Fine, fine – I'll do that.'

'It's nearly eight now, we'll go round the corner to the Greek place for some supper, then we'll come back and you'll get some sleep before you set out.'

He came and took her into his arms and kissed her on the mouth, passionately and ardently. But she wasn't deceived, he was not kissing her, he was kissing compliance and acceptance of his will – he was not even kissing a woman. Anne was used to that, but Walter was the man who had destroyed her tolerable way of living as acceptance and compliance and made it utterly intolerable and loathsome. The time when she could be just as much and as little as any man wanted her to be was gone: Walter had breathed life into her atrocious, dead clay, and there was now a need in her for recognition and acceptance. Any man who was unaware of it was her enemy, a lover blind to it was untrue.

She caught sight of herself in the looking glass on the wall, standing there in his arms in the middle of the room. She had so often given herself a quick glance of appraisal, standing there mechanically in similar circumstances, in old anybody's arms, that the sight of her there with Walter gave her the full measure of the change he had made in her life.

She stepped away from him, ashamed to be caught in that glass eye which had seen so much of what was – to its impartial surface – the same thing.

It mattered so much that Walter should be there with her, and unaware of her, and it was terrible to be told by the cold glass that it would always matter now that she had forsworn the magic world of indifference, life would never be easy like that again.

When they had eaten and Walter was trying to catch a few hours of sleep before he caught the night train to Cornwall the feeling grew.

She had given herself there on the bed where he lay, limp and relaxed, when she knew the sexual act as just another of the body's functions, along with sleeping, eating, breathing, seeing and hearing. The animal innocence was gone, and now she knew that she had betrayed herself there in that ignorance.

She felt an acute grief that she had lain there unloved, that anyone other than Walter had lain there. She couldn't bring herself to stay there near him, and sat over by the window on the far side of the front room until the change in his breathing told her that he was asleep.

Then she came back to sit at the bed end, loving him while he slept.

His face, smoothed by sleep and dramatised by the heavy shadows cast by the shaded bedside lamp, looked remote and wise, the unease of his transient greeds were gone for the moment.

She wished she could make it like that in all states, by all lights, and banish that unease for ever. But what permanent and serene thing had she to give any man? In the past she had given away everything she had to faceless men who didn't matter, there was nothing left now except doubt of her own value.

The world could give her a name and value, and once that was attached there could be no giving of everything worth while, no removal of difficulty and perplexity, there could only come more doubt and self contempt.

How could she keep him from the doom that had come upon him when he fell in love with her? If he had been in search of disaster he could not have contrived a more deadly situation for himself. She ought to go away, to slip out of his life while he was under the spell of this new obsession with the mill. He would forget the whole thing in half a year. . . .

But it would be even worse for him to feel himself abandoned in the middle of this crisis. Perhaps getting the mill for him, helping him to free himself from this Margery woman, and giving him what he wanted, was the atonement she could make, which would finally wipe out the past. And perhaps standing up to the raw mouthed world with her past would harden him and make him a real man at last.

She looked more closely at his face; she judged, rightly, that he favoured his mother in his face, there was something feminine in his good looks. The word pretty drifted into her mind. She wanted him to fasten onto one of his obsessions, to make him adhere to some single purpose, so that virility and maturity would banish the prettiness and make him handsome. And after all, no one in his world knew anything about her past or what she had done with it; they could both make a fresh start in that magically remote place they had found together. He had rescued her, and it was perhaps only fair that she should now rescue him.

It was a quarter-past eleven and time to wake him if he were to catch that midnight train; she stretched a hand out towards him to wake him, but he was in such a deep sleep that she could not bring herself to do it.

Half her motive in suggesting the midnight train had been to bring him up against Margery fresh from a night of discomfort in the train, irritable from exhaustion, so that he would be sure to make a mess of his brutally mercenary return.

She snapped the lamp out and stood for a moment in the dark, but no, she couldn't lie beside him there. She went through to sleep on the sofa in the front room, but lay there wakeful, hating the fat, heavy, shapes of the furniture. It was beastly-overstuffed and ill designed, the worst sort of chi-chi moderne. She had bought it from the fashionable decorator, and it had been confirmed as the right thing by the price. But now the things seemed gross and bloated, like jungle toads, or prehistoric, experimental animals.

Her mind drifted off to an extraordinary expedition to the Crystal Palace with the arty young man. 'My dear we simply must – it's London's only Park of Culture and Rest – I take all my Soviet Friends there – and besides they have the most divine fireworks.'

They strolled about in the gardens waiting for it to get dark enough for the fireworks, a little high after a good early dinner, finding the concrete reconstructions of dinosaurs scattered among the sooty laurels.

'Don't they look divinely wicked with those great fleshy bodies and those tiny heads – imagine little black eyes gleaming under those horny brows – wouldn't you be terrified by them! My dear, I'm frightening myself, I must hold your hand, really I must – I had a book when I was a child by that wonderful Nesbit woman, all about a park like this planned on improving, educational, positively Wellsian lines and all the prehistoric terrors came alive at midnight. Mustn't it have been too utterly frightening to be a little teeny weeny cave man, with nothing but a really rather hopeless stone axe, or a wooden club or something terribly handmade, hearing those great monsters crashing their way through the bush or whatever it was one lived in. And as for seeing them – it's lucky they're extinct isn't it – it must be marvellous to be extinct don't you think – absolutely nothing to worry about – I'm looking forward to it more than I can say. To be bourgeois, what bliss, to be about to be swept away into the dustbin of history – to perish with one's class – oh wonderful – and being typical of it is what's so doubly wonderful. We're a wonderful pair. . . .'

He suddenly turned his white strained face towards her, and it turned purple, red, and then green as the first splendid rocket of the evening filled the dark sky with a succession of coloured stars.

'We're a wonderful pair to face this reptile's memorial, me the epitome of everything that's weak, and decadent, and feeble, in my appalling class and you the epitome of every corruption it creates . . .'

'I'm not, I'm not,' she cried.

'Yes, you are, yes, you are,' he sang, 'yes, you are, that's why I adore you so unspeakably.'

Another wave of rockets hissed up through the sky, the flickering light of their bursting made the dinosaur seem to lurch towards them, and they turned and ran. . . .

She started up, she must have dozed off. It was three-thirty and the stale London air, breathed in and out of four million lungs, laden with the waste of who knows how many fires and kilns, lay still and sent not the least draught to freshen the dust-scented air of the unused room.

She tried to sleep for an hour and then went and sat by the window, smoking slowly through a packet of cigarettes until towards five the dawn began to whiten the sky. The daylight that would take Walter back to Margery had come.

She welcomed the chance to get rid of her past alone, and took comfort from the aspect of their parting when the Cornish express had at last swept out of the station on the gleaming curve of railroad track. She looked for a moment at the steel rails glistening in the sunlight, thinking of them running ahead of him all the way down there to that other woman, wondering a little what she was like.

There was something terrifyingly nice, when she came to think it over, about her letters to Walter – but there was also a cloying resignation. Self sacrifice of that kind was deadly, like walking on one of those horrible movie theatre carpets that yielded so much and were so kindly to your feet that it was a relief to get off them onto something hard and self respecting like marble.

She left the sooty glass cave of the station and went about her business.

The bracelets ran heavily through her hands, and fell with a slight clatter onto the velvet tray the jeweller pushed towards her. He lifted his head from them sharply and looked at her gloves and shoes for an instant.

108

'These are real diamonds – they are extremely valuable. . . .' His eyes took on the glassy film that clouds the eyes of smart men covering themselves. 'Or so I should say at a rough guess. I would like to keep them till tomorrow morning, so that I can have a proper valuation made.'

It was clear that he meant he must have time to check them with the list of stolen property circulated by the police, time to check up on anyone doubtful as she was.

'They were bought here,' she smiled at him, 'four years ago – as a present for me by Mr. Ross. I expect you have some record of it. They were sent to me so I expect you have a record of my name. Miss Anne Horne. You see on the clasp there, it says "to Anne from Charles".' It went on 'I was very happy' in neat engraved italic script, and the jeweller read it silently with a slight change of expression.

A kept woman, down on her luck, his alert air was relaxed by contempt and his manner softened to one of patronage.

'I daresay we can help you in that case, madam.'

Just the smallest hesitation over the word madam; a little gobble of spittle jerked out onto somebody helpless and defenceless, to make up for all the bought civility and obsequiousness to the other customers.

'I have some other things I'd like to sell,' she said, tipping out the rest of the things onto the blue velvet tray to lie cold and deadly, like a hoard with a curse on it in a fairy tale, or the proceeds of a robbery.

The man touched them with his fingertips, sorting them into an even layer, calling softly over his shoulder. 'Oh, Mr. Stephens . . . what do you think?'

Mr. Stephens came and stood close to him, pretending not to be sizing Anne up, touching the jewellery with his fingertips, ranging the articles into groups.

'We're not buying much just now you understand, madam, there isn't the money about there was two, three, or four years ago. It's what they call a buyer's market, why I don't know since it means that nobody in the market buys – not a seller's market any more. I can see you're not a dealer, madam, and in your own interest I'd be inclined to advise you to hold on for a time – I'm

109

willing to handle it for you mind – but this is my candid advice. Hold on until times get a little better. After all, what you have here is as good an investment as you can have in these times, and what's more there's no way of collecting a capital levy on it, or taxing it – you've got a very nice nest egg there that many people would envy.'

He flashed a look up from the jewels into her eyes for a moment to see how she was taking it, and saw nothing but faint disbelief, a placid attention.

'Well now, madam, I'll show you exactly what the position is. We're carrying a very heavy inventory just now – you know what that means? I'll show you. You see these bracelets of yours – they're good, they're as good as we knew how to make them in the days when we had real craftsmen in our shops. They're first class merchandise. They'ie real flawless diamonds too – they were cut and set in the great days. I'd like to pay you a great deal for them, what they're really worth. But look here, madam, let me show you this. . . .'

He led her to the back of the shop, into a little room, furnished with an admirable discretion in dark red and silver grey, and drew from wall cupboards tray after tray of such bracelets.

He shrugged, and spread his hands wide, at each new lovely thing he showed her. 'You see, you see, you see how it is . . . we've just got too many of the things, and there aren't the people to buy any more. You see I want to do business with you, and I want to be fair to you, but if I do business I can't be fair – do you see it? You see how I'm placed? You see why I tell you to hold on if you can?'

'I see,' Anne smiled, as cold as the stones themselves, 'I'm buying a house. I don't want these things any more – I want the house. If you don't want to buy my things please say so.'

'Mmmm, I see how you're placed,' he stroked his chin with his hand, staring into the trays of unimaginable splendour. 'You couldn't raise a mortgage, borrow on the security of the stones from the bank? Couldn't do anything like that?'

'Really . . . I'll leave these things with you until Thursday – when I come back you can tell me if you want to buy or not, and what you're willing to give. I'll call back then if you'll give me a receipt for the things now.'

'All right, if that's the way you want it . . . but do admit that I warned you. And if you ever regret this transaction, please don't blame me.'

It was the same with the stocks, Charley Oliphant, in an office urbanely furnished in dark wood, with early nineteenth century sporting prints on the walls, and a lingering smell of very good cigars, sat back in his chair smiling, asking her what he could do for her. Only the lines round his eyes gave away the fact that he was badly scared to see Anne in his place of business in broad daylight, and that he was trying to work out what the hell she could think she had on him. He came forward with a long sigh of relief, the front two legs of the chair hitting the ground with a bump, when she'd told him she wanted to sell – it was not blackmail, thank god. His smile became quite sunny, but his language was bleak.

'I'm sorry to hear you're selling on this market, Anne, honey, this is no time for selling. I could put you onto bargains, but I won't be able to do any profit taking for you. Believe me, I don't have to look at what you're offering, I can tell you we're going to lose money if we sell now. This Government has made a nice mess of things from our point of view. . . .'

She watched him as he ran on, rather amused by the change in him that had been effected during the last few years. He was one of those men turned out for commercial life by the second rate public schools who used to spend their whole lives carefully choosing the kind of tie, the kind of phrase, and the kind of mannerism that would suggest that they were regular army men of good county families – now he read *Time, Newsweek,* and the Paris Edition of the *Herald Tribune,* got his clothes, slipping through the sterling dollar barrier with god knows what expense of ingenuity, from New York, cultivated a loose limbed Texan sprawl in his chair, and a certain ambiguity of accent in his speech, and dreamed that he was born or raised no longer in Hampshire or Dorset among nice people, but among rugged ones in the Finger Lakes country, or the Valley of the Moon, still farther from the end of the trolley bus line in Beckenham.

The emptiness of his dreams made him seem not altogether real, and drained the air in his room of its vitality, so that when Anne came out again into the roaring street the hot town smell struck her with nauseating strength.

She walked down through the crooked little rat runs and alleys of the city towards the river, listening to the clatter of type-writers, adding machines, and calculators coming out of the open windows.

Here and there on the site of a bombed building huge blocks of Portland stone squatted inanely among parked cars, signs of the giant scale in which the city had once been conceived and built, in which there would be no rebuilding.

She stood at last on Tower Bridge and watched the water sluicing out on the ebb past the solid masonry piers, water some part of which had not long before run past the end of the garden of the Carp at Lemlade. Over on the beach under the Tower, mudlarking children, black legged to the knees with sooty mud, picked about to see what the tide had left them. They dodged in and out of the twisted ruins of a big steel lighter sunk there where it lay by a flying bomb years back, finding an oil browned swan half eaten by rats, a swollen dog, with a collar on it that was worth salvaging, and a variety of bottles that would fetch tuppence or a penny each from the rag, bone and bottle man.

A voice that was new to her suddenly sang in her head, clear, shrill, and true, like the voice of a boy soprano, on the edge between beauty and agony – 'suppose Walter never comes back. Suppose you find yourself alone – here. . . .'

She looked at the fouled river penned between the mud banks, the blackened wharves, and the shapeless masses of the factory buildings, at the poor little castle that had once dominated its town and been the seat of power and authority.

'This is the paradise I was determined to win, this filth and pollution is what I was determined to have; I see what it is now because I am in love at last. Love can't, love couldn't, bring me back to it – not now that I know what it is.'

Instantly the singing voices answered. 'You are here, and alone.'

She turned in panic from the parapet and began to walk northward off the bridge, she would take the afternoon train back to Lemlade, she would not stay a minute longer than she had to.

But before she was off the bridge she slackened her pace remembering the half sold jewels, the half sold stocks, the half made break with the past. She was still held in the city by a few last threads.

She saw days ahead of her, stretching away, and away, like the grey street in front of her, and for a moment her courage faltered. Just for a moment she joined the grey mass of defeated beings drifting, at other people's urging, for other people's purposes, along the pavements. They no longer believed in their dreams, perhaps they would come true, at most, in a few years, if their luck changed. Meanwhile they accepted, as a substitute for the farm in the Scotch islands, for the western plains, for a schooner pointing seawards round the world, the pleasures of a late suburban rose, a triumph on the municipal bowling green, and fortnight late in summer by the sea. Sometime they would get out. Sometime she would get out. For a few seconds she shared that flat sometime with them, and then she shook it off. She really was going: she had found her mill and she was going there, everything really was all right.

9

'I T's a perfect day for a fishing trip – it'll be wonderful in the sea cave,' said Mr. Bannerman, 'there isn't a ripple on the bay.'

He was arranging life so that it was full of distractions, to prevent Margery and the children from missing Walter. Every day there were picnics, picnics on the moors, picnics in the mysterious lunar landscapes round the china clay workings and the old abandoned tin streamings, trips in the fishermen's boats – it all made Margery and the children tired and nervous, but at least when they fell out in the evenings and bickered it was only a question of trifles. The distractions did postpone the sadness of facing deeper griefs.

While they all finished breakfast Mr. Bannerman fussed about, marshalling the expedition, telephoning Morrissey the fisherman and arranging for the boat, arranging with the servants to put up lunch, and darting into the coat room off the hall for the wicker picnic basket.

The children hated the sight of that basket for various reasons. It was certain to have pasties in it in the first place. They hated being told how nice Cornish pasties were – Mr. Bannerman was sure to open a box they were in and say 'Pasties, by jove, we're in luck again! I always say you can't beat a Cornish pasty on a picnic!' The children thought they were just a swindle, an unholy marriage between pudding course and meat course, with a frightfully unfair amount of dull pastry to be eaten before you got to the meat and apple. Besides there was no telling from the outside of the things which end was going to be pudding and which meat – you always got the wrong end first.

And the square wicker basket from the Army and Navy Stores stood too for the sort of picnic they didn't like. It had chromium boxes to put things in, plastic drinking cups, and an arrangement of straps on the lid that held plates, knives, forks and spoons in the right places: there were even salt cellars and mustard pots

with patent, foolproof screw tops. It brought all the stuffiness
and stiffness of indoors with it wherever it went, with please, and
thank you, and sit up straight, dear, and killed any picnic dead.

At home Margery's picnic basket was a big round orchard
basket that would hold a bushel of apples into which food was
put in a more or less unprepared state, a loaf and a bread knife
being the usual foundations.

The children wanted picnics where they could pretend they
were Tom Sawyer, Huck and Joe, on the island in the Mississippi,
or coffee coloured south sea children who had never worn shoes.

When Mr. Bannerman finally got his expedition under way
and they were all trekking down the cliff path to the cove where
the boats lay, the children came last with dragging feet, following
the beastly wicker basket like disinherited heirs following a
coffin. Deep down they knew there was something wrong, that
something hateful was lurking round the corner for them, and
they crystallised their feeling of unease on their muddling grandfather's good will as represented by the deadly basket; they
blamed him and it for making their life wearisome, perplexing,
and confusing.

But when Mr. Bannerman and the fisherman, rowing a short
sea stroke with the oars, that seemed no more than dipping the
narrow bladed sculls in and out of the water, cleared the cove
they began to enjoy themselves.

Francis called the point out at the end of the cove Java Head
and cleared it with a three masted full rigged ship. He had learnt
all the orders out of a book he'd been given for Christmas, and
sent up the sails in correct sequence, keeping the men on the hop
so that people watching her leave from the quay commented on
Cap'n Francis's stylish way of doing things. And when they cast
off the tug, the first possible minute after clearing the dreaded
Rip Raps off Java Head, the tugmaster was astonished by the
neat way the thing was done, and the speed with which the great
tall ship gathered way and slipped from them. 'I believe 'tis only
because of the insurance people that Cap'n Francis do ever use a
tug. They say he can find his way in and out of any port in the
world in the dark . . .' He squared himself solidly to the freshen-
ing wind and stood there, as impressive as Captain Ahab, but

not a bit dotty and immensely popular with his crew of picked men.

Jeanette lent over the other side of the boat, feeling the sun warm wood against her bare legs and arms, half thinking about the colours in the sea, the purple forests of kelp, the darker blue over the rock reefs, and the greens over the sand, half thinking about a poem she didn't quite understand which rolled round her head like a pebble.

'But Thomas, you must hold your tongue, whatever you may hear or see, for if ever a word you should chance to speak, You will never get back to your own Country. He has gotten a coat of the even cloth, And a pair of shoes of Velvet Green And till seven years were past and gone True Thomas on earth was never seen.'

The boat rose and fell gently on the fading Atlantic swell and she gently wondered what had happened to True Thomas really during the seven years and what it had been like waiting for him at home in Ercildoune for seven whole years. It must have been very nice when he came back – until the silver hart and hind came out of the forest to call him back to Elfland. . . .

So she dreamed softly and quietly on while a little breeze came up and ruffled the surface of the water with ripples, clouding its exquisite transparency to an even blue.

'Now we shall catch some fish,' said Morrissey, 'we wouldn't have caught nothing with the sea mirror calm like that.'

'Why not, Mr. Morrissey?'

'You wouldn't pop a mite to eat in your mouth if it hung down out of the sky on the end of a string with a hook in it would you, Mas' Francis?'

'I suppose not.'

'Well with the water like this they don't see the lines. I puzzle over what they do see sometimes. When the water's like this they'll even take silver paper. I see you don't believe me but you shall try and see if I'm joking.'

He twisted some of the outer paper off a tobacco packet in his brown hands and showed the children how to bait their hooks with his utterly unconvincing twists. They felt idiotic trailing them over the boat sides, and kept darting looks at the grown

116

ups to see if they were suppressing smiles. It looked like the idiotic practical joke in the book about eccentrics and jokers, where Cole or someone got two people to hold the ends of a piece of string round the corner of the Adelphi and the Strand. But suddenly, unbelievably, the first beautiful silver and green fishes came flip-flapping in despair into the boat on the end of the tarred line with the papered hook firm in their bloody mouths, Morrissey grabbed them, stunned them with a quick rap on the gunwale, nicked the hooks from their mouths, and handed back the still baited hooks for another play of the monstrous confidence trick.

The fish were always a tremendous surprise for the children. Fish to them was something limp and dull eyed, lying wetly in newspaper in their mother's shopping bag, or slackly on a tin plate in the larder, but here they were dancing muscle, vigour and love of life personified. They were terrified by the wholly unexpected strength, and the snapping mouths; far too frightened to tear the hooks out of their flesh. Morrissey had to do it for them.

The children were scared by the hooks, too, they handled them with grave thoughtfulness, taking great pains to seem calm and cool though their stomachs misgave them as they handled the harsh barbs with their soft pink fingers. Margery watched them while they did it with a queasy stomach, agonising inwardly about the horrors of getting those double points back out of the dear warm flesh.

I could not, could not, do it, she thought, gripping the thwart of the boat, and shrinking, shrinking down into the cool depths of the sea.

Her father thought she was in an unhappy daydream about Walter and pitied her, but she was despising her own weakness and wanted no comfort.

When they had three dozen mackerel in a slithery heap in the fish-well they hauled their lines and turned away from the bay parallel to the long line of cliffs which stretched away westward. Morrissey took the wooden housing off a small paraffin engine, primed it and after a moment had it merrily teuf-teuf-teuffing them along.

117

He beckoned Francis aft and sat him down holding the tiller, giving him directions about what point on the coast to steer for. The boy began to swell quietly with his little male importance and competence, like a little frog.

'She handles beautifully, Mr. Morrissey,' said Francis.

'She'm a handy little boat, sure enough, Master Francis.'

'How fast does she go?'

'She slips along fast enough for me, Master Francis.'

'Do you think we're doing six knots?'

'We might be doing that.'

Mr. Bannerman quickly cocked up his Leica and snapped the shutter on Francis unaware, catching him looking fierce and proud under the heavy responsibility of his first command.

Margery saw it, winced a little, and really began day dreaming of Walter. There was about the small boy's unformed face so much of Walter – Walter at his dear worst.

She remembered when he had gone out to close a deal on a sensible, practical, secondhand family car, and had returned after being talked into switching to an open six and a half litre Bentley, a fine car for road races which did twelve or fourteen miles to the gallon. He showed it her with just that fierce, proud, little boy's look, that was a crust over an inward state of being a little bit frightened. She laughed to herself on the edge of weeping and Morrissey the fisherman caught her eye.

He was not looking at her, but at some point that had its significance for him on the iron shore. His hands were lean, hard hands, bare, polished, and his face had nothing soft or poor about it. He had the nobility of a peasant or an aristocrat, the look of fortitude and calm strength that comes from a life lived on a consistent pattern. Morrissey followed the line of his choice from its start through to its end; there was no need for him to look fierce or proud, or defiant.

He glanced at her wondering why she was looking at him so intently, and then, undisturbed, looked away again to the cliffs which were related to him.

He began to read the book of the cliffs aloud to the children. There was Treberners Point, where the Stanmore Castle had gone ashore with all sail set, trying to be first home in London with the new season's China tea. Every man of the crew was drowned.

That was where the derelict battleship, on her way to the ship-breakers, went ashore and broke up.

Over there was Mouse Rock, where his father, Mike Trevannis and Artie Rowse were lost.

That greenish patch of water over there was always a good place for mullet, and when you brought that grey patch, that grey scar, on Merran point in dead line with the white washed barn on the brow a mile inland you turned seaward a mile and came to a hole where lobsters always were and always had been as thick as sheep at a sheep fair.

'Many's the fight us chaps have had to keep the froggies from shooting their pots out there, and many's the frog lobster pot I've lifted and emptied in my day on that ground.'

'Not fighting with guns and sabres, Mr. Morrissey,' said Francis, thinking of pirates and schooner decks slippery with blood.

'No, we'd scrap around with our fists, and give 'em a bit of a drubbing and send them off home to France. There weren't no real harm in it,' he sighed, 'things is different now.'

'What happens?'

'There's a cutter comes out of Plymouth, that watches over us all with Sonar, and the frogs don't come here no more. They sails out to the west, round the end of Ireland and they buys their lobsters from the Irish – good luck to 'em. They don't trouble us no more . . . now you steer straight for the cave mouth, Master Francis.'

The boy peered anxiously ahead towards the land, and saw nothing but the walls of rock towering out of the water. He faltered and made a bewildered half turn before wobbling back onto his old course. Jeanette giggled, and Morrissey looked puzzled for a moment.

'You must see it, Master Francis, there, there, 'tis near on sixty yards wide – big enough to slide the parish church into tower foremost – there. . . .'

Poor Francis looked at the brown and the grey and the olive green rock, and the beaches of white sand, and the tumbled boulders, and the dazzle of the sea, and saw no cave mouth filled with shadow.

'There, there now, Master Francis, put your helm up a bit farther. Now, now you see it.'

'But I can't see anything,' he yelped desperately.

'I can, I can, I can,' sang out Jeanette, 'I can see it as plain as anything – as plain as the nose on your face – as plain as the sun at noon, as plain as *plain* . . .'

'Well, you'm had better take us to 'un then,' Morrissey said, pushing Francis forward and holding the tiller for Jeanette to take over. When she had it firmly in her hands she stood very proudly there in the stern holding the bow of the boat onto a patch of shadow on the cliff face where the rock slid down sheer, like a wall of a house, and the sea heaved lazily up and down with no jagged buttresses to cream it into foam.

Morrissey looked along the line of the course she had chosen, and eyed this dark wall for a thoughtful moment; then he looked across at Francis who was sitting pouting opposite him, thinking him a beast for setting his sister over him just when the trip was getting really interesting. He nodded and slightly cocked an eyebrow in the direction of the boat's prow, then turned and gave Jeanette another long thoughtful stare. Francis looked at her and then at the cliff, and then at Morrissey.

Margery was amazed to see the way it was done; the boy and the man wordlessly became friends and fellow conspirators. It was poor Jeanette who was going to make a fool of herself – Francis hadn't been, after all, humiliated, he had been spared humiliation.

Jeanette, alight with pride, missed it all and steered on for the blank wall of the cliff.

Francis from time to time darted an ironic look at her, and then covertly turned back to the cliff and made a desperate effort to find where the cave really was for himself, so that he could enjoy the triumph of saying, 'There it is' when the time came.

Morrissey saw that the two children were absorbed and amused and suddenly withdrew, closing his mind to these irrelevant strangers, thinking of something of his own that would be with him, here, when winter had turned the sea grey and they were all gone.

Bitterly, bitterly, Margery envied him his ability to cross the boundary of his self so quickly, his ability to move into the world of these stranger children and out again so easily and so uncompromised.

If only she had been able to enter the world of that great child Walter so easily, and to come away again as freely, uncommitted and unwounded. But she and Walter were, alas, not strangers, and the price of knowledge was entanglement, she had learned to please and engage him at the price of being bound and involved.

Morrissey himself was probably helpless, confused, and miserable in some close webbing relationship at home – whatever he might be here on the sparkling water. . . .

She slid away from realities into daydream – walking on the beach in moonlight, along the sea cleansed sand, and Morrissey, or some lean brown stranger came silently out of the shadows, to vanish back into them when all passion was spent and appetite slaked. She walked back home through the maze of shadow and moondazzle, slack, soft, content, and free, sniffing the sweet scents of the aromatic cliff herbs hanging on the warm night air – absolute in her loneliness . . . she caught her father's grave eye on her, he thought she was grieving again and was wishing he could help her out of her sadness. Alarmed, she flashed him a bright smile, and to forestall any cheerful conversation that he might have prepared turned to Morrissey with a stream of prattle, about the fishing life, the winter's work in the village, and the sale of one of the local farms.

The children resented her attempt to remove him from their cave hide and seek, they obscurely felt that Morrissey was a cut above mummy's social talk. She rattled like that about nothing to local people at home who didn't matter but who couldn't be shut out of the house or disregarded; Mrs. Grant the president of the Women's Institute, Mrs. Crashaw the vicar's wife, people like that who weren't quite real. The children thought that if you hadn't anything to say talking to a man like Morrissey was much ruder than not talking.

And the chatter made Jeanette feel quite desperate because she, poor thing, was just beginning to feel that she'd lost the cave again. She'd been so certain – and now there wasn't a cave there at all.

She swung the bow one way and then the other slowly, hoping that she would pick up the cave, hoping that nobody would look aft and see the tell tale wavering in the wake – if only mummy would stop talking, and give her a chance! If she could only have a moment to think she'd see where it was. . . .

Morrissey suddenly bent forward and killed the engine, which spat once or twice fitfully and then died. The boat swung heavily on the small waves as it lost speed and became too heavy for Jeanette to control, she was badly scared that it might slide on and smash into the cliff ahead which now towered above them.

'Oh, Mr. Morrissey . . . ?'

'Why, Miss Jeanette, don't you know where you've been heading all this time?' He looked at her in shocked surprise, and then in amazement at Francis. 'Well surely you can tell her?'

'No.' Francis darted one last look round, and then owned it.

'Well, to tell the truth it is one of the most difficult caves on the South Coast to find – even though it is one of the biggest – you can't be blamed – even though we are within eighty feet of her now.'

A great arm of shadow which had been breeding under the cliff as the sun travelled westward now darted out and took them, breathing a cold breath on them that was a shock. The sharp teuf-teuffing of the engine had blunted all the other sea sounds, and this little shock brought them all back, with a hard clarity, as if enlarged. When the engine was first switched off they had felt the quiet, now, with the cold, they heard all they had been missing.

The waves made their own faint rustlings as they moved, a sound quite independent of the fat chuckling of the wavelets and ripples under the boat, and of the more active movement round the rocks. And there were the other noises, of the oars dipping into the water and coming out of it, and the heavy dripping of the oars ran forward for the next stroke. There was, too, the murmur and squeak from the leather pads on the oars where they worked and turned in the wooden pin rowlocks, and the rhythmic creak of the floorboards as Morrissey shifted his weight. And over and above everything else was the wild chorale of the gulls, each single bird of its own making an ugly mew, the whole chorus creating a chanting beauty that changed subtly from second to second.

Suddenly a quite unexpected re-entrant cove opened before them, and there they were under a great black arch, a mysterious breach in the shadowy secret wall.

Its night blackness threatened an icy chill; far above, up the sheer cliff, beyond the dancing cloud of gulls, the blue sky gleamed brilliantly, and far behind them the sunlight glinted on the dancing waters. They felt almost afraid to be going out of beauty into the dark.

Francis drew close to his mother's side, and took her hand.

Jeanette snuggled against Mr. Bannerman for a second and then dropped her head into his lap as they rode forward on a wave right in under the cliff. Then there was a moment of terror for her, that fetched her upright, screaming.

The chill breath of the cave, and the darkness brought a wild hope of life back to a mackerel in the fish-well. Touching its tail to its head, now on one side, now on the other, it skip-skipped out of the well, out onto the bottom of the boat where it flung itself desperately about. Before anyone could recover from the momentary paralysis shocked on them by Jeanette's scream it made one last terrible effort and was out over the side of the boat.

They all felt an immense relief and sat motionless listening to the scream travelling about the vaulted cave roof like a bird lost in a darkened church, Jeanette with the others listening to her voice's echo, open mouthed and breathless.

But no silence followed – the scream's dying fall was washed out by a jumble of middle-aged sounds, of huffing, heavy breathing, and clumsy heaving movement.

It was as if they had thrown some clandestine chamber of commerce or rotary club into a panic with their intrusion.

'What . . .?' said Francis and Jeanette, while Margery gripped the boy's hand fearfully, but the end of their question was drowned out in a confusion of splashes, as if the panic-stricken mob were taking in desperation to the water.

'The seals, the seals,' cried Mr. Bannerman and Morrissey, both pointing with shadowy arms to one side of the cave.

The children's eyes were getting used to the dark now, and the cave walls were no longer a uniform black to them, but purple and pink with sea magic. Where the men were pointing one black shape after another was scrambling and jostling to the front of the shelves and ledges to plunge into the sea.

'Look down! Down over the side of the boat!' called Morrissey, his voice echoing and booming like a cathedral preacher's. The children peered over the gunwales. The water that had seemed black was now palest green, like mutton fat jade, and across it fled one seal after another. Some shot right under the boat itself, trailing a stream of air bubbles dragged in at their plunge. Then at last there were no more sleek fugitives and the water grew still in the silent cave.

The children amused themselves for some time, calling to the echo, and then Morrissey began rowing out towards the sunshine, the visit to the sea cave was over.

Jeanette thought of True Thomas coming back from the dark halls of the Queen of Elfland, and mixed the thought with a wonder about the clumsiness of the seals on the ground and their darting beauty under the water. They turned from dogs into cats, she thought, right in front of us – you can believe in magic if you want to.

Francis wondered about the mackerel that escaped, had one of the seals gobbled it up, or had it gotten away? He slid down into the sea and took part in a life of perpetual pursuit and escape, darting through seaweed jungles with a squadron of fast young mackerel to rescue that crippled one by throwing off his pursuers.

They went farther along the bay to a beach of silvery white sand, inaccessible from the cliff top, where they spent the rest of the day picnicking, searching for cowries and painted top shells, bathing, exploring two or three small caves, and gathering armfuls of wooden debris cast up by the sea for the tea bonfire.

They started home late, under a sky no longer brilliant, but powdery, and less luminous for the moment than the sea itself.

When at last the boat slid softly towards the landing steps, in the smooth pool under the protecting granite harbour wall, everyone in it, except perhaps Morrissey, to whom the day's outing was a day's work like any other, felt a drowsy happiness. They were filled with delight, full of the feeling that comes when a run of good luck begins that promises to last.

They climbed out of the boat and up the narrow steps leading up onto the quay as Walter arrived in the bus that had brought him four miles from the inland railhead.

The children came up the steps first and saw him standing there a bare ten yards away, looking doubtfully about him, his hair a little rumpled, his night case in one hand, and his overcoat draped over his arm.

He was looking about and wondering about the next move: rule one in any tactical or strategic problem was to secure a base, but the Tinner's Arms looked dingy and inhospitable, and Ye Merrie Maquarelle was a wheel back chair and gingham affair. His eye fell on the local post office, newsagents, and general stores. He might inquire there about rooms.

For a moment his eye was held by the newspaper posters on the shop front. N.U.R. Ultimatum, Cabinet Meet, said one, Railmen's Final Threat, said another, Total Transport Stoppage in Seven Days, a third.

In the window above the posters drowsy wasps grazed on trays of synthetic looking ice cakes. A grown woman came and stood in the shop door licking an ice cream cone, talking to someone back in the shop without turning round and sizing up his possibilities as a pick up. Walter turned away from her steady cow-like stare towards the harbour, he would get a room for the night in one of the fishermen's cottages and steer clear of the holiday makers.

He saw the two familiar faces looking at him at once, and before he had given the meeting an instant's thought, broke into a delighted smile.

The children flung down their baskets of fish and ran towards him; oh, it was he, at last, and glad to see them, this was the day's glorious crown.

When Margery came to the head of the steps she looked across the cobbles and saw her two dear loves dancing on each arm of their father, pulling him towards her. 'Daddy's back, daddy's back,' they called and Walter's face split with his guilty, charming, unsure smile.

He had left his other woman, he was back, there in front of her, they were all four together again – everything was going to be all right after all. With a great lifting of heart she ran across the little space between them and was taken in his arms.

Mr. Bannerman came up the steps, the damp rucksack full of bathing things on his back, the heavy picnic basket dragging on his right arm. He stood staring and staring – he couldn't believe what he was seeing.

By god, if he'd run out on his wife – and then come back without a word of notice or apology – he wouldn't have been taken back as easily as that. A spasm of hatred shook him, he would have liked to have thrashed the dirty little swine, thrashed him till he begged for forgiveness and mercy – everything came so damned easily to him.

Jeanette looked curiously from him to her mother and father. What had twisted his face into such an ugly mask? And why did tears run down mummy's cheeks although she looked so smily and happy? She thought again of True Thomas and the Queen of Elfland – 'But Thomas, you must hold your tongue, whatever you may hear or see, for if ever a word you should chance to speak, You will never get back to your own Countree.' Would there be some milestone she would pass while growing up, would she come to and cross some barrier that lay between her and the grown up world, after which she would understand what went on in that strange magic place?

'Well, hullo, Jackson, I didn't expect to see you.'

'Oh, hullo, Bannerman. By a bit of luck I managed to get away after all and come down.'

The two men shook hands and exchanged a sight of each other's teeth in what were supposed to be smiles.

Jeanette watched them and understood what hatred was for the first time: and understood, too, that whether she held her tongue or not, she would never get back to her own countree.

10

PENHARRAD HOUSE was not a happy house, and it never had been although a great many people had, one way and another, been happy in it, at one time or another. Children were often happy in it – until like Jeanette they stepped out of a charmed circle and began to take notice. It was hard to say what of, but there was always something.

Jeanette used to lie in bed at night wondering about it. Daddy was back, mummy was gloriously happy again, and the weather was wonderful, day after day; and yet there was something terribly wrong. Whenever you came into the room where granny and grandfather were you found yourself listening to – Jeanette didn't know how to describe even to herself what it was. It was talk that wasn't real, that didn't join on to anything. When you put your hand on the door knob outside the room the people inside chopped off the natural flow of whatever it was they were doing and pretended to be up to something else, so that what they were saying when you came in wasn't joined onto the atmosphere or the tension in the room, it was unrooted, unconnected with anything that mattered.

And what was wrong with the conversations was what was wrong with Penharrad House.

It was a holiday house – built on the cliff edge where no sane, sea respecting Cornishman would build anything but a lighthouse, to be lived in for six weeks in the year. For the other forty-six weeks it stood empty, looking out of its black double windows over the heaving sea.

Everything about it was impressed with the mark of those weeks of waiting. The inside walls of the rooms had a refined roughcast finish – a modification of the treatment of the outside walls – so that they wouldn't be affected by damp and condensation in the winter. The stairs were made of Cornish slate, and so were the window seats, only the upper floors were wooden – it was a house built to stand empty.

127

The Wincklemanns had bought Penharrad from the specu-
lator who had built it, so that it wasn't their own idea of a house;
and they'd furnished it with odds and ends that wouldn't matter.

Half the furniture in the house came from Phil's father's house
in North Oxford after the old man died – solid Morris chairs
with uncomfortable but weather resistant cushions, lumpy craft-
work tables and chairs in the English compromise with the art
nouveau style.

The other half of the furniture was from Heals, bought in the
twenties when the Wincklemanns were an advanced young
couple making their way. When they began to arrive they began
to get less and less advanced and finally, when Phil's young
redness had turned into the middle-aged pink of junior minis-
terial responsibility in a Labour Government, the house in
Hampstead was furnished with good genuine antique pieces and
the Heals stuff was standing up to the climate in the empty house
in Cornwall.

It all had that indefinable air of unchosen furniture, and it
stood about in the rooms as if it felt its position acutely, looking
awkward and embarrassed.

Even the books had a curious pathos. They were mostly
children's books that had been grown out of, and abandoned by
the young Wincklemanns. Some were novels that had been
holiday reading at best, not worth taking back when the holiday
was over. The sad ones were the good books from the North
Oxford house; unreadable late Victorian editions, *Romola*, *The
Egotist*, that had been sent down with the furniture because one
ought to read them some day, and since there never was time for
that sort of book in London there might be at Penharrad – and
in any case while they were too good to throw away as rubbish
they were quite unsaleable – so what else? They smelt of dust
and their pages were discoloured – Francis and Jeanette, who
could read anything, found them impossible, even when house-
bound in the wettest weather.

And it had all become much worse in the last four or five
years; now that Phil had really got to the top he was always
either off on missions abroad, or taking his holidays in the
Italian lakes or in the south of France, and he lent the house to

People. It might have been better if they were his friends, but he ust lent it to people without any particular feeling about who they were.

He had had an affair with Mrs. Bannerman when they were both at Oxford, and later after they had both married other people, had shared with her an elaborate friendship that had been platonic, had been passionate, had become platonic again, and had then become a dead bore. At the end of it all he had felt it wrong to drop old Bannerman because he had, well, rather done the dirty on the old boy, and unkind to drop Mrs. Bannerman – because after all . . . anyhow tossing them the house for the summer was a large gesture which eased his conscience and – since he didn't give a pin for the place – didn't cost much to make.

The year before it had been lent to his brother, back from Burma as a result of the Government's generous and conscience saving gesture to world opinion, with no job and no pension at fifty-four.

The year before that his ex-Parliamentary-Private-Secretary had been given it as a softener for a blow that hadn't then hit him. It was only when the poor man got back to London late in September that he'd found out that he wasn't to have the big new appointment as Permanent Secretary to the Ministry of Fine Arts.

So the blankness of the house was utterly unsoftened by affection and love, even in the short periods when it was in use. There was moreover something indefinable about the place that Jeanette couldn't identify, which was in fact a sense of unhappiness.

Indifference had stripped the house of the warm and friendly associations built up while the young Wincklemanns were growing up, and evil was filling up the vacant space. It was about the place night and day, the invisible extra person in the room that everyone was conscious of, an unspoken word on the fringe of every conversation, the weight in the silence that kept the room still no matter how the sea wind blustered outside.

Jeanette lay in her bed at night and knew it first as the stillness that held the curtains motionless while the branches of the fuchsias moved in the wind a few inches beyond the frame of the wide open window, the unease and doubt about her father's absence.

When he came back she thought it would go, and had faced the dark happily after Walter and Margery had kissed her good night – everything was all right.

But as she lay there listening to the faint buzz of grown up talk in the drawing-room downstairs, and the clattering of knives and forks as they later ate dinner, the generalised thing had come back into the room, now compact and personal, something that had chosen her out of all the people in the house as a man might chose a woman, or an axe. She felt it settling into companionship, into a terrible intimacy, with her.

She sat up in bed and whispered to it 'Who are you?' But, in spite of her feeling of being heard, there was no answer. She sat upright, shivering a little, listening, straining for an answer, and knew that it was straining to hear her next words.

She heard the wind stirring the bushes in the garden outside, and farther off the murmur of the sea.

She saw the beam of the light on Penharrad Point swing its triple arm across the black sky. She watched it, counting the seconds, knowing she was awake and not deep in nightmare: Flash, one second; Flash, one second; Flash, one second; one, two, three, four, five, six, seven, eight, nine, ten, eleven, twelve, thirteen, fourteen, fifteen seconds; and flash, flash, flash, again. The Trinity House light was guarding the coast, downstairs they were moving through to the drawing-room again for coffee, and there was this thing in the room with her, watching her.

She lay down very quietly, dead awake, with all her senses sharpened unendurably; and lay so while the grown ups talked themselves out, played bridge for a while, and took themselves to bed.

She lay, so, listening for it, with it listening to her circling thoughts, until silence fell on the house. Then she could bear it no more by herself and slipped from the room and across the passage into Francis's bed.

He woke when she came to him and put her arms round him, but only with some surface area of his mind.

'What . . . who . . .?' He wasn't really frightened.

'It's me, Jeanette, do you mind?'

'Dear Goosey-pussey . . .' he said, dredging up a forgotten nickname of five years back, sliding back into sleep, and leaving her alone.

She lay beside him with the comfort of his warmth and slowly the presence left her. She relaxed and dozed, but presently snapped wide awake, someone was going through the garden with a light which flickered to and fro on the ceiling. With a stone heart she went to the window, and called out:

'Who's there? Who is it?'

'It's me, miss, Moorhead.' He held the light to his face, and showed himself with an overcoat pulled on over his pyjamas. 'I thought there was a heifer, or a big dog, in the garden and come out to see.'

'Oh, I see. Well, good night, Mr. Moorhead.'

She went back to bed, her own bed, and fell fast asleep till morning: that the thing was real enough to fetch a grown man up out of bed made it seem so inescapable that remaining on guard was clearly futile, she might as well sleep.

In the morning grey clouds were driving in from the sea, practically level with the cliff top, and gusts drove rain against the windows, rattling like spent shots. A day for indoors, they would be cooped up together in the house all day, and it would be hard on the nerves.

At breakfast Jeanette looked white, with big dark circles round her eyes, but Margery was too happy to notice it. Mrs. Bannerman asked her if she was feeling well, and she answered that the wind had woken her in the night, and that she hadn't managed to get to sleep again – she was quite all right.

'Well, luckily, we'll be having a quiet day today,' said Mrs. Bannerman.

'I expect she was reading late last night, with a flashlight under the blankets, I know I did at her age,' said Walter smiling at her, like a great sleek, satisfied tomcat, across the breakfast table.

She just looked at him with eyes that seemed much darker than he had remembered them, and said nothing; he turned away, thinking, well, it's an awkward age, and began to talk about the rail strike to Mr. Bannerman, an explosive, ill chosen subject.

131

'Yes, I see that it's not the time to have chosen, but you must admit the men have a case. They're . . .'

'What case? I don't see any case? The railways have an income, and it won't stand an increase in the wages.'

'I'll grant you that. But they're miserably paid . . .'

'What's that got to do with it, they aren't doing work that brings in any more money. What right have they . . .'

'Ah, that's the point, they have a right to a living.'

'They've a right to be paid for the work they do.'

'Exactly and it's vital work for the community. So it's up to the community. . . .'

'Oh, you want another subsidised industry. . . .'

'If the work's vital to the state the state must pay for it. . . .'

'But they're only pressing this wage claim because they want extra money to have to pay in income tax already to meet the food subsidies – next year they'll want another pay increase to pay the extra tax they'll have to pay to subsidise this year's pay increase – it can go on for ever.'

'That's rather over-simplifying, isn't it . . . ?'

'Well, you're over simplifying when you pretend the strike's over these wage claims, you know it isn't as well as I do.'

'Well the men have got a case there too . . .'

'Well if you believe in worker's control . . .'

'Certainly I do.'

'What! Any damned fool out of a job, who comes round cap in hand, qualifies the minute I take him on for a say in the management of my business.'

'That's not fair is it – I mean the technicians who run the railways are trained men and they know what they're doing.'

'Most of them are louts like porters, unskilled men, with no more notion of management than flying to the moon. Why you'll be saying next that your charwoman ought to have a say in your architectural designing – what's the difference. . . ?'

They were both red on the cheekbones and cool voiced; Mrs. Bannerman watched them tight lipped, and Margery wished men wouldn't be quite so fierce and awful about things that weren't really important.

'What really gets you is this business about the dividends on the railway stock – isn't it?' said Walter.

'It's robbery – simple theft. They guaranteed the stock – and now they want to evade paying out on it. . . .'

'Oh, come now – they only want the stock to share the risk with the railwaymen. You say the workers have no right to their pay if the income isn't being earned – but you're ready to insist that the shareholders get their whack, income or not. It just doesn't make sense.'

'Oh, it's no use talking – if you can't see the harm that defaulting on what's as good as a Government stock would do, well, it's just not worth talking, that's all. . . .'

'When I was a girl,' said Mrs. Bannerman, 'there used to be a rule against talking about money, politics, or religion at table – it always led to ill feeling, and was better avoided.'

'What can you have talked about?' asked Margery.

'Oh, there's so much, the theatres one had been to, what one had done, what one was going to do, horses, oh, all sorts of things – and gossip. . . .'

'What's gossip?' Jeanette's voice was as clear as a bell.

'Oh, just amusing stories about people.'

'It isn't saying what you really think of people is it?'

There was a slight pause in which the grown ups didn't look at each other.

'No, dear, it's just all the latest news about what your friends have been doing. That's all.'

'Oh.'

After breakfast Jeanette slipped away and sat on the window seat in the library, the sad room with the telephone in it and the two glass fronted book cases full of the forlorn, dead books that nobody read. She tucked herself in behind the brown velvet curtains close to the glass, watching raindrops course down the panes, and beyond their tracery the cold grey breakers running into the bay.

The library was an extra sitting-room that nobody ever sat in, people slipped into it for a few moments to telephone, or for a few moments' talk there if there was something private to be said.

The Bannermans came in, they didn't see Jeanette in her hiding place.

'I've a bone to pick with you, Courtenay.'

'What have I done now?'

'It was absurd the way you rowed with that boy at breakfast.'

'It's not my fault that he's an opinionated ass.'

'A young man can be excused for being a cub, but you're old enough to know better.'

'If the silly fellow doesn't know anything, and won't think about what little he does know, why should I have to sit quiet and listen to his nonsense? Tell me that?'

'Anybody but a fool would know – can't you see that his marriage is in a rather ticklish situation – and that the small chance our daughter has of being happy again with him isn't going to be improved if we jump down his throat whenever he opens his mouth. I should have thought even you could see that.'

'Margery's a fool. She's been shot of him once, and she'll be sorry she wasn't shot of him for good.'

'You're absolutely heartless – she's been breaking her heart for months – ever since he walked out – she's a changed woman since he's been back. How could you have wanted it to go on the way it was.'

'Oh, don't be sentimental. She would have got over it. She would have found some decent fellow and she would have been happy, much happier in the long run.'

'She loves him. She doesn't want anyone else.'

'That's only one side of the story. Doing your duty by a woman is a damned dull grind, and I don't think that young rotter has the guts or the strength of character to go through with it. He'll bolt again.'

There was the smallest pause.

'Guts or strength of character! My dear Courtenay – you flatter yourself – the guts and strength required by a rather dim regular army man to stick to a wife with just over two thousand a year aren't very considerable. If it came to it I should think that boy could manage just as much.'

'It's rather late in the day for us to fall out about whether I married you for your money or not. And that boy, as you insist on calling him, is a pretty dim architect if it comes to that . . .'

'He was a pretty good soldier.'

'A bloody chauffeur. They took a marching regiment and put them in tanks – he didn't know any more about warfare than a dirt track racer. He . . .'

'. . . fought in some battles that our lot won. And they gave him lots of medals, and pushed him up from second lieutenant to full colonel in five years. And you came out of the army with the same rank at the end of thirty years. Have I ever told you that you make me sick?'

'Never in so many words, my dear, but I've gathered a pretty fair idea in the past fifteen or twenty years.'

'And yet we've stuck it out. . . .'

'That's why it makes me sick and sorry to see Margery and that young fool letting themselves in for the same dreary let down. That's what'll happen if things "go right" for them – and if things go wrong he'll bolt and she'll be hurt all over again.'

'I can't make head or tail of what you mean. What are you trying to say?'

'Oh, I don't know – I saw that woman – I talked to her. He'll regret giving her up for the rest of his life . . . it's a mess. . . . Margery and he were finished – just the way we were finished years ago – they're no good to each other, they ought to make a clean break.'

'I don't know. I hadn't the courage . . . and when I'd found the courage it was too late.'

'Is it too late for them – they seem so happy, now. . . .'

'It's too late, and anyway she's one kind, and he's another kind – they can't be happy in the long run. . . .'

'Isn't there anything we can do. . . ?'

'We couldn't do anything for ourselves – what use can we be to them.'

Silence; the little girl sat behind the curtain with her knees drawn up close to her chest, her hands on her ankles feeling the knobs of bone, looking out with her dark eyes at the endless procession of grey waves coming in from the south-west to spend themselves on the shore. She did not seem to be paying any attention to the people in the room, no more than they gave to her, hidden away out of sight, but the words were sinking down through her mind to lie there close to her heart as part of her knowledge of the world.

'Oh, Courtenay. . . .'

'My poor old Dolly. , . .'

'I think I'll go and lie down, for a little, say I've a headache – anything. . . .'

Mrs. Bannerman went out. The colonel paced up and down for a time, smoking his pipe which filled the room with a pleasant, nutty scent. Prince Albert in the blue topped tin, hard to get in these days of dollar shortage, and somehow more delicious for that.

Well, there seemed to be a break in the rain, it would be a good thing to nip down to the village while it lasted to pick up the papers and get some fish. Nothing like a blow and a bit of exercise after a bit of a row – women didn't understand that – they went in for this business of lying down and cooking their discontent in a frowsty bedroom. He looked at himself in the looking glass over the fireplace and spoke to his grey, handsome, upright image; without fear or favour.

'You were the biggest dam' fool in the world when you married that woman for her money.'

He held his own gaze challengingly for a moment, and then turned away ashamed, leaving the room in an almost hangdog fashion as if the image in the mirror were still there looking back at him with its hollow good looks and its rather bogus charm: he had in his day stood in front of mirrors and smiled, working on that charm; and the remembrance came back to him as he went out.

Jeanette thought of going too, for a minute after the door clicked shut and the footsteps died away. There was a small wind deformed plum tree behind Penharrad House that bore early plums, of the greengage variety, and a bowl filled with its first picking lay on the kitchen dresser. They were very sweet fruit, with pale golden, almost transparent flesh under a yellow green skin that was flecked with brown – tiny little flecks, like freckles on a beautiful skin. Jeanette sat, without moving, thinking about

136

the crispness of the flesh and the sweet juice spurting into her mouth. It would be quite nice to stand by the big white dresser, eating one plum and warming another in her hand.

But it might be nicer all the same to stay where she was, hidden and secret, thinking about her great discovery. The thing was finding out what it was – discoveries were very puzzling – she knew that much. Colombus ran his boat up onto the beach and thanked god when he stood on it for letting him discover the short sea route to India; he thanked god for letting him come to that tired, old, old, continent with its crowds of people sick of their own history, and its temples full of twisty six armed gods, and all the time he was on the innocent soil of a new world. You could make a fool of yourself like that, easily.

She had found out something about love, something that was much more important than anything she had yet found out about the world.

There was something that men and women did together, that was never quite explained to you when you asked about it, and which was always silly rubbish when they whispered about it at school – that was love.

And then there was something that was talk; 'I love you my dear darling daddy; I love you, mummy, ever so much,' and Simon and John at school running up in the playground and kissing you, a wet smack on the cheek, and saying, 'You're more than a friend, you're a love,' and behind that was the vast something on which she had made landfall.

She had asked mother once what the word meant and her mother had locked her fingers in hers and said, looking away, out of the window and through the houses on the other side of the street to a far distant country: 'It's being best friends, and always together till the day you die, and having no secrets, and making niceness and letting horridness go; it's two people living together to make each other happy.'

She now saw that far distant country for herself, and it was not like that; that was how one would like it to be – a safe, well lit place and it was neither safe nor light.

'I love you,' you said, 'I love you,' and you ended up like grandfather and grandmother too sick of each other even to hate each other much, two old worn out people who could only say of their lives together that 'they'd stick it out.' That was easy enough to understand because they both looked worn out, their skins were whitened, with a transparent waxen look in the smooth places as if they did not have much blood in them, and they were creased, like apples at the end of winter, on their necks and round their eyes.

You could see how they would be unable to sustain love.

But with mother and father it was different, they were not tired or finished. And yet 'I love you' for them meant something else, too, daddy regretting 'that other woman' for the rest of his life, and the two of them living together in a way that was in the end worse than the pain and shock of parting. 'They're no good to each other.' And yet they said it to each other, 'I love you,' just the same.

It was all very queer and mixed up, like the sea – which was fun, and beaches, and rock pools with beautiful shells and plants in them, and blue, and sparkling and warm, and with the passing of a few hours, a shift in the wind, hideously cold, and hideously strong, breaking ships into pieces on its deadly margins and killing sailors with its chill before they had time to drown.

She looked down onto the grey desert in the bay where they had been so happy on the way to the sea cave, only four days before; it would be sheerest misery to be there now.

A squall drummed against the walls of the house, shaking the windows, and as it slackened the rain began teeming down again, blurring the panes. She sat on, motionless, quieter than ever, her breath hardly stirring the air behind the heavy curtain, for Walter and Margery were in the room now, standing lip to lip, in each other's arms.

'Oh, darling, it's so wonderful having you back. It's been such a long time. But I knew you would come back.'

'It's wonderful being with you.'

They were for a moment wrapped in a thick silence which was broken by Walter.

'We must get out of this unendurable house – your father can't stand me.'

'We could go back to London.'

'I don't want to go back to that house – it was living there that was so wrong for us.'

'Do you think that was it – that you wanted to get away from London – not from us?'

'Yes – I think so – now I've had time to think I see it like that. I made a mistake about what I was escaping from. It was that dingy second rate pall that's fallen on London since the war – I don't know – it's like a provincial town now.'

'It's been terribly gloomy without you.'

'Poor Margery.'

'But if we don't go back to the house, what shall we do?'

'I want to live in the country.'

'I've always wanted to, and it would be so much nicer for the children. It will be fun looking for a place – it'll have to be a proper house, not a cottage, though, because we'll need a room for your drawing office. Where shall we look?'

'Well . . . I've found a place – I think – I'm sure you'll like it – and it isn't madly expensive. It's a mill.'

'Oh, how lovely, I'd love to live in a mill – where is it?'

'It's . . . just on the edge of Gloucestershire and Oxford, near Kelmscott, on the Thames.'

'That's near the Carp – isn't it? Where you stayed with that . . . she thought she was going to live there – Oh, Walter – but it can't possibly matter – if it turned out that she wasn't important?'

'She wasn't important.'

'You went away with her, and fell in love with a mill – poor girl . . . wasn't she nice after all?'

'She was very nice – but I had to come back to you, and the small people.'

'They're nice, the small people.'

'We made them.'

'Oh, it's so nice, thinking that now, and it was so terrible when you were gone. I used to think poor small people, what shall I do for them? They need a daddy you know.'

'I'm sorry I hurt the small people.'

'Don't be sorry, now you've come back. We'll make them happy. Will it be a nice mill for them?'

'They'll love it. There's a big orchard out at the back. And paddocks they can keep a pony in – and a mill dam to swim in – oh, everything they could want.'

'And we'll be happy there?'

'I think so, if we want to be.'

'There won't be a ghost there, of a poor blonde who was left . . . did she see it?'

'She saw it.'

'But it doesn't matter, does it?'

'No, I don't think so. I know you, and I don't think it will.'

'Shall we go there soon. . . ?'

'As soon as we can. Before I murder your father . . . and we have to raise the money to buy it – we'll have to sell some of the stock in that marriage settlement of ours. You'll have to sign a paper saying you allow it. I'll post it off tonight and then it won't be long before we have our mill.'

'All right – it'll be rather an adventure for us – for me and the small people, going to live in a mill we've never seen. . . . Are there water lilies? Jeanette would like water lilies.'

'Yes, and dragonflies, and fish that make plopping noises, and wild duck hiding in the reeds – and a waterfall under the kitchen window – oh, everything.'

'It sounds lovely. It isn't terribly damp is it?'

'No, you goose . . . now -write me a line to say that you approve my selling some of our stuff for the solicitors so that I can catch the post with it – then we'll soon be off to our mill and out of this.'

'Mummy and daddy mean to be kind.'

'I think your mother does – I'm not sure about the colonel.'

'Don't call him "the colonel," it's too unkind. . . . What shall I say to the solicitors? It's too vague to say just; Sell some stuff . . . I ought to be more definite.'

'They just need a line saying that you approve of the sale of the Melverhampton 1954-56 stock held by our trust. I'll show you what to say . . .'

'You're being masterful. Oh, it's nice having you being masterful again . . . let's go and write this thing so that you can get it off. . . . It's so lovely having plans with you again. And knowing something about what's going to happen.'

'You're nicer to me than I deserve. . . .'

'My pen and paper, and everything; they're all up in the bedroom. Come up and tell me what to say. I love doing it for you because you're my love.'

Jeanette heard them kiss and go, and wondered about the girl who had seen the mill they were to live in – where was she? They had said 'I love you' to each other and then he had come back to Margery and the small people, and the girl was left alone, somewhere, saying what? She remembered looking through a door at her mother lying crying on a bed in the house in London. Was this other woman now lying that way because mummy was happy?

She jumped as the telephone started ringing, and for a few seconds panic filled her. The jarring call seemed to search the room, and she felt herself on the brink of discovery for the first time. Mrs. Moorhead came unwillingly from the kitchen and answered it while Jeanette steadied her fluttering heart.

' 'oo? 'oo? O! 'im . . . ol' on, jus' a mini'.'

She went out and was heard calling for Misser Jacks'n in the hall, and then he came to the waiting instrument, pausing for an inexplicable moment after he'd shut the door, standing there not picking up the receiver.

'Hallo? . . . Anne! Darling . . . of course not . . . of course I still do . . . of course I am . . . yes I'll say it, I love you very much. . . . I don't know – quite – I've got what I came for . . . . Yes, I did. . . . Yes, I had to be very nice indeed. . . . What, what do you mean? What sort of a surprise? Oh, don't be tiresome; I can't bear being teased. . . . Now, Anne, darling . . . . In a couple of days. . . . Yes, I'll be able to get away then. . . . No, not before. . . . Yes, I promise I really will come then. . . . No, I wouldn't let the railway strike stop me even if there was one. . . . Well, if I come at once she might cancel the letter before they'd acted on it, then there'd be no mill. . . . What do you mean, "that isn't important any more." Don't be so damned illusive and coy for god's sake. . . . No, I'm not angry. I do love you. . . . Yes, more than anything in the whole world . . . because you're beautiful, and kind, and – I don't know – because you're you . . . now we've cleared that up explain what you mean. . . . Oh, bother you and your surprise. I can't come until Monday. It would wreck everything if I did. . . . You don't understand. . . . Well, I give it up. I wish I could come and find out what the damned secret is today but I can't. I've got to stick it out till Monday for reasons I've tried to explain. I love you more than anything, but I just can't do it any other way, much as I'd like to be with you now . . . you know I would . . . no, after Monday nothing will keep me – not even Michael and all his angels. . . . Yes, I'm yours, altogether. . . . You know it, don't have to say it. I know it too, about you. . . . Yes, my love, till Monday night . . . all right if you want it that way, though it'll mean a madly cross country journey. . . . I think you're right. Things are better at the Carp than in London. But we'll have to go to London Tuesday to sign papers and all that. . . . Now don't start again. I know what has to be done. . . . Good-bye my love. If you can't understand business don't try. But look don't ring me up again, here, unless something urgent comes up – it's not too safe, anyone may answer the phone and anyone may bust in while I'm talking. So be patient till Monday . . . bless you, my love, good-bye.'

He put the receiver back into its cradle and remained standing silently over it for a full minute.

'Well, by god, it's what I really want to do,' he said at last, 'and the hell with anything else, and the hell with anything that stands in the way.'

But he walked up and down in the room for five minutes uneasily before he could go out and face the other people in the house. Jeanette listened to his footsteps, and to his muttering as he argued with himself half aloud, and revised her picture of Anne. She wasn't lying crying, she was somewhere gloriously happy thinking about living at the mill with Walter, just as mummy was upstairs thinking about living in the mill with Walter in glorious happiness. 'I love you, Margery,' 'I love you, Anne,' and 'I have a head on smash coming for both of you my own dear darlings.'

'I love you' was just a trick for getting people to do what you wanted, for getting them to take off their armour so that you could hurt them, for getting them to put themselves up onto a high place from which they could fall good and hard.

The door clicked and her father went away leaving her alone in the room. There was no one in the world you could trust.

Father would leave on Monday, though he would snuggle you in his arms today, mother offered you a future as insubstantial as a dream, the others buried ugly truths and lied out of kindness. It was all lies and concealment, and 'I love you' was the worst lie of the lot. Well she would never say it, never, not to anyone; and she would never believe it, whoever said it. And when it came to wounding and hurting she would always strike first, before they blinded her with their lies. 'I ought to cry,' she thought, 'now I know what horridness there is coming for us, but I won't.'

Mrs. Moorhead came into the passage and beat the brass gong which boomed and muttered through the house. Jeanette heard the sound fill the house and die away, and then she heard the trample and talk as everyone came down to lunch. Her name was called once or twice but she didn't move until they had all gone into the dining-room. Then she went and washed in a very full basin of the hottest water she could bear her hands in, one of her greatest pleasures.

Everyone was sitting down, looking fairly cheerful when she came into the dining-room. Mrs. Bannerman had finished with her depression, and Courtenay's walk down the lane under the dripping hedges to the village had blown his bad mood away; he was carving a plump roasting chicken with the generosity that comes of having two good birds on the dish. The delicious roast smell filled the room, a scent mixed with the oniony fragrance of the bread sauce and the herbs in the stuffing; they all looked up cheerfully when Jeanette came through the door.

'Hallo, Jeanette,' said Margery, 'where have you been all morning – I haven't seen you since breakfast?'

'I was in the library, reading,' she said.

Walter dropped a fork, and the Bannermans darted a quick look at each other and then at Jeanette.

'Were you, darling,' Margery went on, 'I looked in there for a moment in the middle of the morning – but I didn't see you.'

'Nobody saw me,' said Jeanette, 'I was sitting on the window ledge reading. I went there just after breakfast.'

There was a short silence.

'Do you want white meat or dark?' asked Mr. Bannerman in an odd, constricted voice as if he were being choked.

'White, please,' said Jeanette, looking at his scarlet face. She was not surprised when the knife slipped off the bird's breast bone and made a screech on the surface of the dish, nor by the silence which accentuated the ugliness of the sound. She gave her father a cool look before which he dropped his eyes, and then received her plate from Mr. Bannerman, remembering to say 'thank you' like a nice little girl.

'I wish I'd known you were there, I was bored,' said Francis.

'I wasn't bored,' she said.

The clock on the chimneypiece struck the quarter after the hour and it could have been that everyone was waiting for it to finish before they spoke. At least no one spoke until the mellow muted chimes had died away.

'I see in the paper,' said Mr. Bannerman, 'that the unions are going to make some sort of statement today. Apparently there was a conference yesterday of the railwaymen, the miners, the steelworkers, and the sugar people – all the nationalised industries – the rumour is they were talking about joint action. It looks uncommonly like a general strike again.'

'Oh, they can't,' said Mrs. Bannerman, 'do that!'

'I just remember the old one in 1926,' said Margery, 'I remember at school we all thought it was rather fun.'

Walter said nothing, he wanted to, but he couldn't. He just sat there looking at his daughter; from time to time getting a steady look back from her.

She seemed to be enjoying her chicken very much, and every now and then he tried to tell himself that children didn't understand things that weren't made specially clear and easy for them. But then he would find himself being looked through by her dark, steady eyes, and it was quite clear that she understood a great deal and that if she was missing anything it was not anything of great importance.

It was the look that girls gave you when they had decided not

144

to; something you said, something you did, something that happened in front of them, changed their minds, and they shut you out.

Looking at her gave him the same feeling that had settled on him in the empty house in St. John's Wood, the feeling that part of him had gone away and left no address, that the clocks were stopped, and that anything, anything, might happen. He looked at Margery, trusting and loving, and she gave him a slight lift of the eyebrows – she had no idea what had brought the tension and embarrassment into the air.

He wondered what would happen when his daughter's knowledge hit that loving trust? And what was going on with the Bannermans?

Mrs. Bannerman wasn't eating, she was taking little bites of this and that and dabbing at her mouth with her napkin and darting looks at Jeanette, in restless distress. And the colonel was eating doggedly away, staring at the child as if she was a snow-white tiger, or a talking dog, that had brought new and surprising information about the natural order into the house.

He looked back to his daughter, who was getting ready to say something, apparently to Colonel Bannerman, who stopped chewing with his mouth full to hear what was coming.

'May I have some more chicken, please, grand'?'

The colonel swallowed his mouthful, and gave a great sigh.

'Yes, certainly, dear.'

Jeanette handed up her plate with a faint smile. Walter suddenly knew that she was having a very good time indeed and he felt a slight crawling, stirring, sensation on the back of his neck. He knew the feeling, he had enjoyed it several times during the war; if he were a dog, or a fighting animal, it would be the hackles rising. He could see in his mind a big, ugly dog, scared, and filled with an excitement that was better than pleasure, walking tiptoe, stiff limbed, into trouble; bad trouble which it had looked for and found.

II

THE late August morning was hot and close and Anne woke unrested to an already stale day. The mail box was empty, and the telephone as dead as it had been since Walter's going. He'd been gone too long, she had waited too long, the town was closing in on her. She had breakfast round the corner in a big place run by Austrians, sullen because the place was going bankrupt, sullen at being caught in someone else's collapsing economy, resentful because the old world could not see that it was time they had a rest from hardship and disaster.

'This coffee is good, delicious,' Anne tried a smile on the dark waitress with the bad skin.

'Coffee, yes, coffee we can make. But everything else is not as we should wish it. All the time during the war I was dreaming of what would come after. We could have gay paintings of the Tyrol on the walls, and cheerful curtains and table cloths – very clean you understand, and crisp to touch. And for breakfast we would be serving good coffee, like this, but with whipped cream on top, and beside the coffee put a nice little straw basket with on a folded napkin rolls that you would eat with mountain honey. So it should be. It is very nice of you to smile when I bring slices of bread from a square loaf, margarine, and marmalade.'

'Oh, well, I expect things will get better soon.'

'So, better soon. When I am a little girl papa is a prisoner in Italy. Presently your father will come home and things will be better. After the war, presently there will be a peace treaty and things will be better. After the peace treaty someday they will do us justice and give our empire back, then things will be better. And so on, always presently it will be better.' She stood looking down at the dull utility china on the plain cloth that was not quite clean. 'Me, I can no longer believe that.'

'You mustn't be so sad.'

'No, it is silly – and not good for business.' She hung over the table without speaking for a moment, awkwardly picking up a thread of cotton adrift on the cloth. Anne thought irritably that feminism had never taken women into the undertaking business, and that this woman had missed making use of a natural gift; a nervous, hard-boiled, joking urban thought which sickened with its meaningless smartness as soon as it had taken the form of words. She looked up feeling a little ashamed and met dark brown eyes and a kindly smile which illumined the tired defeated face.

'I should like very much to be a golden-headed child and really believe that presently things would be better,' she said softly, 'and, who knows, for you it may happen.'

For a moment they stood looking at each other, then another customer rapped the edge of a cup with a coin, 'The service here is terribly slack – foreigners, I haven't patience,' her high-pitched voice complained, and it was over. Anne leant back in her chair and thought, 'Christ! I must be sickening for something – I'm getting gooey with sentimentality.' And then she felt at once the falsity of the thought. 'It simply isn't gooey, or wrong; for a moment we were in sympathy, in touch, and we gave each other a reassurance. It's this hateful town, and the idiot rattle of it, that makes us such cowards that we can't face the truth about ourselves and our emotions, and makes us hard, and smart, and loathsome.'

She left the place feeling much happier, but outside the great diseased mass of brick and cement lay on the earth brutally crushing any effort of will that might seek to deny its essential character. She escaped from it into Kensington Gardens and Hyde Park, thinking to find there an expatriate square of countryside that would bring her more comfort.

But the park was summer scorched; the trees prematurely autumnal over their soot-blackened trunks, and the grass threadbare.

She tried to reason her feelings about the place and the town away: to pretend that it was because she was strained and anxious that she noticed the terrifying ugliness of the people who lay sprawling asleep with old papers over their faces, old without

147

dignity, and animal without simplicity. And she tried hard to believe that it was for the same reason she saw the shabby litter of wooden spoons and ice-cream containers spilling out of the trash bins near the park cafés, that they were not really big enough to matter in the park's wide extent. She strolled on past poor Rima, grotesquely guyed in a passing fashion, down to the Serpentine, and there saw dissolving cigarette butts and sodden packets heaving on the lazy ripples by the cement margins of the lake. She stood looking at them, and at the cars parked along the roadway at the waterside, and she knew that really it was a noble piece of water in a well-landscaped park – that the misty lights at the far end of the water were pearly and lovely, and that the heavy violet of the lower quarter of the summer sky was beautiful – not just a haze of smoke waiting for a wind to lift it from the town. She walked a short distance over the grass and sat down on one of the spidery park chairs at a point which had at one time been among her favourite London places.

One looked south and saw beyond the lake and the bank of trees on its farther side a fantastic congeries of Edwardian roofs, of big hotels and clubs, which with their freakish turrets and pinnacles suggested Baghdad of the legends, or some even more promising city in which magic carpets, chest of diamonds, and birds or antelopes that proved in the outcome to be handsome and unmarried princes bewitched would be the commonplace of day-to-day living. She sat and looked, but the magic was gone.

The pinnacles and turrets still stood there, but they had an abandoned look. And indeed they no longer were above the playgrounds of the South African millionaires who had in the circuitous passage from Odessa and Warsaw to the Americas paused in Knightsbridge to give a golden tinge to a society in its autumn. The lavishly marbled halls beneath them no longer saw the silent passing of these exotic young ornaments of the Brigade, Krawinski, Sir Raphael, do Mondoro, and Moltifiore; they saw instead unestablished junior staff of a Ministry of which the Minister had not a seat in the Cabinet going to and fro with armfuls of dead files, or trays of tea cups, between one office and another.

The pinnacles and turrets now spoke no word of pleasure,

148

nor of enchantments; they scratched the sky like the dead bones of a steer in a salt pan.

Anne stood up, suddenly afraid. The rumble of the traffic was not loud enough. The air over the town was too still, lying there heavily, almost motionless.

There was an intolerable tension – it was as if the whole city was waiting, breathless, for a terrible explosion, or for the clear singing trumpets of the last judgment. She half expected to see the great mushroom-shaped tower of smoke that had been so long awaited, lofting itself over the horizon's rim, until she felt that the heart of the tension was waiting, and that whatever was to happen was still to happen.

It was the tension of the hour before disaster, created by the blunted telepathy of millions of uneasy minds – the human equivalent of that sharper force which sends shoals of herring and other fish milling in panic, or stampedes of herds of wild cattle and deer on an instant as if each member of the herd had received an order to run at that given instant.

She walked southwards, across the bridge spanning the lake and over the wide, flat space of playing-fields near the barracks. A thin line of people stood on the far side of the road from the barracks, staring, as if fascinated by the column of dark olive-green lorries drawn up outside the ugly, dark-red buildings.

An armoured car drove out through an archway, took its place at the head of the column, then moved off with the string of fat lorries behind it.

As each lorry grumbled off, changing through the gears as it got moving, the men inside under the green canvas hoods gave the thin crowd a long, steady stare as if they were something they had never seen before. They sat on the benches in the trucks in their battle-dress, with their green pipe-clayed harness on, and their neat, short automatic rifles held in their big red hands, men licensed and trained for deadly work. The pretence always was that it was for deadly work in defence of the community, against some external enemy; but now the pretence was falling away.

Anne met their eyes as they looked out of the wheeling trucks and they didn't look at her like men looking at female flesh;

149

they gave her the stranger look, at once curious and reserved, of troops looking at enemy troops for the first time, meeting a file of prisoners coming down as they make their way up to the line.

They were interested in her because she was one of 'them', but they looked at her through veiled eyes because they did not want any of 'them' to gather a hint of their anxiety or doubt.

The lorries vanished down the road and the idlers drifted away, leaving the roadway empty. There was nothing to see but the closed barrack gate, the wooden-faced sentry, and a few prematurely-fallen leaves lying yellow and brown on the ground.

Anne went out of the park into Knightsbridge, past the dignified Victorian mass of the French Embassy. A queue of worried-looking people waited outside the Embassy doors watching some of the minor figures of its staff pasting tricolour stickers to the windshields of the little flock of official Citroëns standing there.

Above, on the first floor, a man in a dark suit stood by one of the huge windows with his cheek against the cold glass, motionless and white faced, looking down at the diminished traffic on the street. He had the stricken air of a man who has been told to put his affairs in order because he has only so much time to live.

A man came and spoke to him, a shadow, barely-discernible figure, standing back in the room, and was answered with a single word; he spoke again, coming a step nearer to the figure in the window, who merely shrugged his shoulders, made the smallest movement with one hand, and uttered a laconic phrase.

A car flying the colours of a South American state with jaunty assurance drew up at the foot of the Embassy steps; a large, dark man, radiant with health, and with the knowledge that he possessed rather more good looks than are usually permitted to remain in private hands, descended from it, paused for a moment to warm the neighbourhood with his smile and then passed indoors.

The man at the window saw him come, and prepared himself for something manifestly disagreeable. He wiped his face, then the palms of his hands, with a wonderfully white handkerchief, while he moistened his lips with his tongue, and at last, squaring his shoulders, turned back into the room to greet the dear colleague to whom the crumbling of the keystone of the European arch was no more than the source of an idle-minded pleasure.

Anne stood watching the black space that he had left empty at his parting for a little while, realising with a frightened feeling the nature of the pleasure that had been so manifest in every movement of the South American as he had gone into the building.

Years before his President's wife, who had once been a film actress, and before that a taxi-dancer, had been told with brusque insolence while in the middle of a European tour which was to include a visit to England that if she came to this country she would be received unofficially and only by those people whose official positions compelled them to do so. She would not be, in any circumstances, received by the State or by those figures who were bred and born to symbolise it.

Anne had felt at the time that she had been somehow associated with that vast public insult, she had felt excluded by it from 'the others' with renewed force.

Senora Eleana de Viscaya might have, by force of character, by use of her intelligence, and of her gleaming beauty, have climbed rung by rung a ladder which reached from that little gilded pen on the edge of the dance floor, in which she had waited for custom, to the great marble palace in which her state housed its symbols of power and authority, but those who decided such things in our country decided that nothing had happened – they condemned her, so far as they could, to remain what she had been at her weakest, to be always what she had fought so hard not to be.

Anne had felt passing over her body the massive stone wheel of contempt which had been meant to crush the other woman, and had felt stinging in her veins the bitterness that the insult had generated.

She now glimpsed with a certain horror the long chain of consequences that led back link by link to that episode, through years of economic war, and realised that within the building the French ambassador, agonised at the beginning of the end of all

151

that he meant by European life was receiving the South American, whose only feeling was 'Well, we've brought off our little coup, we may not have done the trick altogether, but someone had to lay on the pile the last straw, and Senora Eleana is pretty sure that it was us – and that's all we've been working for.' He would be gloating inwardly in that fashion, and outwardly, in smooth language, asking the Frenchman as an older man, with more experience of Britain, his view of the situation.

Within a few hours the cyphered cable would be on the farther side of the south Atlantic and Senora Eleana's husband would walk through the big rooms, shuttered against the almost tropical sun, to tell her that it was all over.

'This time they're finished. Magnascas was with the French ambassador this morning; found him almost suicidal – it's his view that there will be some sort of revolution within the year.'

Senora Eleana would wait, and presently if events moved that way, offer the people who had insulted her asylum, as she had once despatched cases of cast off clothing to be distributed among the coloured poor of Washington's slums.

As she moved away from the Embassy, Anne abruptly thought of Ross sleeping, on the last night of her former life, in his defenceless loneliness, and of her cold hatred of him and his world. Thank God I have shaken it off, she thought, thank God my dear Walter has made me another kind of person. I would not do anything for hatred now, I would not hurt anyone or anything, if I could help it.

Her mind flapped like a flag in a fluky wind. And after all it might be just a dream, an ambassador may be calling on another merely to further some routine matter of international intercourse; there may have been a queue there for some reason that concerns only the French community in London; the soldiers might merely have been moving, as soldiers always are, from one place to another. If she were to go to Downing Street she would find no more than the usual single policeman, a cat on some steps watching a few sooty pigeons feeding on the roadway, and a few tourists from out of town looking with mild interest at the dingy houses which history had not succeeded in ennobling. It would be reassuring to find it so.

If it were so there would be an end to the dreadful feeling that things had become out of scale. She saw Walter clearly, and with sharp definition, in her mind, but dwarfed – it was as if she were looking down a telescope through the wrong lens, so that she saw the tiny image at the eyepiece end far away down a long brownish tunnel. Public affairs were crowding in on their private relationship. Nothing could be more important to them than their lives, and their future together, yet this crushing weight of doom in the air, utterly irrelevant, stole in between them, and robbed them of the central place in their own existence.

She took a taxi down to the Indian fortress at the corner of the Admiralty building facing St. James's Park; an odd stone age cliff dwelling which seemed ill at ease between the Regency elegancies of the north side of Pall Mall, and the sunlit eighteenth century expanse of the Horse Guards, a thick skulled savage from the present squatting among reliques of a gracious past.

It had been built during the second German war, at a time when menace had been something tangible, the actuality of aircraft ranged upon hostile airfields briefed for a strike, and of infantry climbing into troop carriers with their harness on. Then you could make defensive gestures like this – build forts, dig tank ditches, and get the guns and rocket batteries ready to sling a metal screen up into the sky when the enemy aircraft came.

But now the great gun ports of the fortress looked down, looked blankly towards the royal palace with no clue to the nature of what might come against it. Propagandists of one side or the other might say that the people were on the march, but there they were: Anne uneasy about her love, a woman with two children drifting down to find the pelicans in the park lake, three men knocking off work for a middle-morning bite listening to one of their number reading sports news from the first edition of the evening paper, and a thousand other figures walking and idling under the trees with jumbled personal thoughts private within their small heads.

That royal palace itself was bewildering; the heads it held wore crowns, at times, and ermine, and scarlet, but they were usually manifested in dark blue suits and discreet street clothes – as people with ration books, just like us.

There was in that the essential something that made the dark embrasures look so empty and unready for defence: the royal pair had long ago been given with their crowns the orb and staff of power, and had been associated with the sacred oils of divine kingship, but so soon as that formal pageant had ended they had become once again just like us. The crowns and symbols were returned to the museum as antiquities, and the divine king in his dark suit took the advice of his socialist ministers. The even English course from compromise to compromise promised to run on for ever, since, if it could accomplish that, it could clearly accomplish anything. It seemed sure that the kind of crisis which this great sand coloured lump of rock faced concrete was designed to weather could not be locally produced, it belonged on a borderland between two cultures, between two races, where blood was the argument.

As Anne moved on leaving it behind, reassured by its remoteness from anything that she could imagine in this setting, it winked at her.

A marine in a tin hat, with a slung tommy gun, moved across one of the embrasures and shut a heavy steel door which hid him from view. The sight was startling, giving the authentic chill to the blood that comes when a log on a river bank moves its tail, yawns wide a pink mouth lined with teeth, and slides off into the current as a crocodile.

Anne hurried on across the empty parade ground, and on up the narrow passage into the park end of Downing Street. She was terribly afraid now, filled with the feeling that something which she had never defined, on which she had unknowingly always relied, was crumbling away under her feet, as old stone turns to sand under too heavy a load.

There was a silence in Downing Street that made the four hundred or so people there whisper. They watched the doors of number ten with a settled attention, occasionally turning their heads to speak softly to their neighbours, but keeping their eyes fixed on the important door. They were like relatives in the corridors of a hospital waiting to hear news of the outcome of an operation, or parents waiting for news of a birth and like such people they had the self-effacing discretion of the unimportant.

They knew they could do nothing, they knew they were not wanted, they knew that if they were any sort of nuisance they could be legitimately packed off, so they were on their very best behaviour. The docility and the goodness were impressive in a way, and yet there was something dispiriting about it.

Anne thought how many of the men had bad profiles, sharp little doggy faces, and how many of the women looked tired. The men and the women looked white faced and exhausted, and as they stood with their hands in their pockets and cigarettes smouldering stuck to their lower lips, it was difficult to think that their good behaviour comes fairily easily to the devitalised.

Two women near her started talking in the wonderfully lazy board school London speech that has driven out cockney, and for a moment she thought they were foreigners.

'Go' a cigare'?'

'Mmm.'

'Ta, haven' go' a li'?'

'No metch's, 'm'awfli sorri.'

Speaking in the top part of their mouths, with the least possible movement of lips and tongue, they blurred on with the unlit cigarettes wagging up and down.

'Do you want a match?' said Anne.

'Ta eve' so.'

Anne struck the match and held it in her cupped hands while they sucked at their cigarettes.

'What's going on? Why's the crowd here?'

They blew out lungfuls of smoke, and shook their heads.

'Dunno, dunno 'm sure.'

'I s'pose i'something to do wi' th' Gov'm'nt,' said the second girl. 'You know th' cris's'n' all tha'.'

Anne felt a spasm of irritation before she reflected that she, after all, knew no more than that when it came to it. These were with a certain element of parody, fellow creatures.

'We never miss a crisis,' said the first girl, still dropping most of her consonants and clipping every word to its debased core. 'We seen them all.'

'Yes, we never miss anything big. We haven't missed anything since V.E. night. We've seen them all.'

'From Churchill to Bevan. Bevan's her favourite, though I tell her he's put on too much weight.'

'Weight! He's nothing to what Churchill was. She was balmy about Churchill. Who do you go for?'

'I don't know that I care about any of them very much. Who's there now?'

'All them, you know, the Government people.'

'But what are they all here for today? What's the matter?'

'It's a crisis, dear, you know . . .'

Anne left them, and as she walked away towards the group of reporters and pressmen standing just outside the Prime Minister's house she heard one girl murmur to the other:

'She' sof' in' she?'

'Ye' she's proper sof'.'

At the fringe of the group of pressmen there was a tall faded looking man wearing a dirty waterproof in spite of the heat, cleaning his nails with a file. For some reason she felt that he would know what it was all about, and would explain if she asked him.

'I beg your pardon. I wonder if you could tell me . . .'

'I'll tell you anything. It'll be a pleasure.'

The man straightened up and put the file away.

'What's the matter?'

'I'm middle aged. I don't earn enough money. I married too young. I don't like my wife any more. I have some children – ill mannered brats – who are too like my wife. I hate my work. Anything else?'

'No, please don't be silly. I meant why is this crowd here?'

'Oh, that. You're too good looking to worry about that. I mean if you did know you wouldn't understand. You couldn't look like that and have brains enough to understand politics.'

'Come off it. Please tell me.'

'Don't you read newspapers? Haven't you been told? Boys we've failed, here's someone who doesn't know what is going on!'

One or two of the other journalists and reporters looked round, gave a quick look at her hair, her bust, and her legs and looked away. One or two people round about laughed. Anne flushed.

'Now you've made an ass of me, tell me.'

'It's the union leaders. The tough boys. They're in there telling the P.M. that mines belong to miners, railroads to railroad-workers, sugar to sugarbabies. It's syndicalism V democracy. The final struggle for power. And do you know what happens then, baby? Do you know what comes next?'

'No.' Anne looked at him and realised that he was drunk, although it was still only eleven in the morning. She wondered idly how it was done.

'No more do I. I could have told you once – when I was a bright boy fresh from the university of Nottingham – but years of hanging around on doorsteps waiting for people to come out or go in had cured me of all forms of intellectual activity. All I'm fit for now is to give the enlightened electorate the information it needs to frame its opinion on great issues. Am I boring you? Don't give me the answer, I know it. I can tell from the way your eyes are beginning to glaze. It's something that happens to women when I talk to them. And you have such lovely eyes. Do you really want to know?'

'Yes.'

'We go bankrupt, that's all. Those bastards in there are just forcing the Government into doing something which means we go bankrupt. The Government are telling them so in words of one syllable, but they're too god damn stupid to understand it. They think that only bosses can go bankrupt, they think that working men and wage earners are somehow immune to the process . . . but I'm a lush labouring under grievous personal disappointments. I may be all wrong. And why should you worry? With what you've got . . . you'ld be all right even if the Russians came.' He brushed his mouth with yellow stained fingers. 'If you had a cigarette, and a match, I could have a smoke, and I'd be grateful.'

She gave them to him; he was like the sort of dog that follows you on a country walk, knowing its being false to it's owner, knowing you don't want it, longing to be one of the party.

'Thanks,' he said, 'I spend too much money on drink to be able to smoke in the ordinary way. That's an awful confession isn't it? But it's true. I don't care what happens anyway. I

157

couldn't be any worse off. I haven't dared to go home for the past two days. You know, you won't believe this, but my wife has brought my children up to despise me. They think I'm a failure. I can hear them thinking it when we're all in the house together. They used to think I was a real journalist. You know, our correspondent in Sofia, Mr. Jewson the famous foreign correspondent, like that. That was when they were kids. Now they know I'm just a reporter in a dirty trenchcoat, and I don't even work for a newspaper. Just an agency reporter. I write the sort of stuff that gets in the early editions of the evening papers, just padding for the racing news, about a cat in a tree in Lambeth, and about Bevan looking bronzed and fit when he arrived at London airport, and Sir Stafford looking dead, that sort of stuff. I'll use you in my story about this. "Smartly dressed women were among the crowd," that'll be you, smartly dressed women. I used to work for the dailies, I've worked for all the dailies, and then I was independent for a bit, free lancing, you know, looking for work, and now I'm an agency man. Perhaps my wife is right, do you think she could be right?'

'Right about what? I don't know, how can I know?'

'About my being no good. About telling the children I'm a bum and a deadweight on her and them.'

'Yes, I should say she was.'

'My god that's cruel. How can you be so lovely, and be so tough. It breaks one's heart.'

'But you wanted me to say "yes." You made it impossible to say anything else, didn't you? Why do you do it?'

'Oh, it's a line, it sometimes works. Another cigarette, please. A lot of women go for it.' He took the cigarette and stopped speaking to listen to Big Ben booming out the hour from the clock tower. Eleven. The last stroke died away into the traffic hum. 'You've got to be what you are to the top of your bent, you see, and I'm dim. It works up to a point. Match, please.'

'Do you want me to strike it for you?'

'Thanks.'

They stood silently watching the front of the house for a dragging minute, then the man took his cigarette from his mouth and nudged Anne with his elbow.

'Look at this crowd. The only things in sight that's new, well made, and decent, are the cameras my colleagues here are flourishing about. Look at that thing Eddie's waving about – cost him £250 quid with all the gadgets – and it isn't the least bit of use to a man, woman or child. You should see his underwear. . . . By god, it's a rotten world.'

'Oh, why don't you do something about it then. Instead of just slopping about in a dirty coat cadging cigarettes, cadging sympathy, cadging everything . . . you can't be so helpless.'

'Oh, me, I wasn't always like this . . . when I went away to the war I was a professional man, quite a good man by my lights. I was quite a good soldier, the army thought. And when I came out I got the old job back. But it wasn't the same. That lot in there were scared of the papers. They can't bear any form of power but their own. They've been starving us of newsprint ever since the war. You know what the damn things are like – four pages of snippets – the longest story I've had in print in the past five years ran to 250 words. What does that do for my self respect? What would it do for anybody's self respect? I tell you those bastards in there have whittled me away to nothing. Remember that thing in the Disney picture? "You're nothin' but a. nothin', you're not a thing at all. . . ." ' He lifted it loud and clear out of the crowd in a mellow barfly's tenor. People looked round and a policeman cocked his head up sharply and stared.

'That's enough, Jewson, you know better than that,' he said in correct Hendon college accents.

'Okay, sarge'.' Jewson shrugged his shoulders and looked at Anne. 'You see how it is, a wake, and no singing allowed.' He hummed it again, softly, 'You're nothin' but a nothin', you're not a thing at all. . . .'

'That's all rubbish. You're a man, a person, nothing outside can take your manhood away. Nobody but yourself can make a nothing out of you. . . .'

'It's been done, baby. Those people are deciding all about our future in there. They didn't ask us for permission. They didn't ask us what we wanted. They don't ask us now. There isn't a damn thing we can do about it. Just obey, suffer, die, as they used to write on walls in Italy. "All we like sheep," you know, or perhaps you don't – you don't look as if you had a hymnbook background.'

'It's all rubbish, nobody makes your life for you. You make it for yourself. They don't decide anything important in places like this.'

'Oh, no? You'll learn. Just because queues of chaps want to go beddybyes with you you get a comforting illusion that way, but you wait. You wait. . . . Here they come!'

The whole street gasped with him. The pressmen surged towards the door, which opened with breathtaking suddenness. Anne pushed up with Jewson, the crowd pressing in behind her. The policemen lent gently against the tide, solidly keeping it back. The flash bulbs flickered as the union delegates filed out and grouped on the steps.

They were beefy, energetic men, one would have taken them a few years back for successful contractors, provincial businessmen, or senior executives up in London to state the views of some chamber of commerce or industrial group. They wore the most expensive kind of suit you can get without making the upper class gesture of getting one made for you, their ties were the finest silk, shrewd gifts from people who knew that nothing was too good for power, and only their solid presentation watch chains hung with little medallions, and their solid signet rings, spoke of the lodges, chapels, and brotherhoods, which were the sources of their strength.

They had fought their way up out of the pits, the foundries, and the engine sheds, by being hard men who made hard bargains with the employers for the men. The employers could sign or could get out of business, our terms, not theirs.

It was the technique that had brought them up to the top, to unlimited expense accounts, union owned cars new every year, out on the front drive on Christmas morning and the rest of the year in the garage where you wanted it when you wanted it, into the union owned house with the union paid rates and taxes. All the bosses were out of business now, and there was no skin off their arses. There was only the state to deal with now; a new name, but still just an employer trying to hold out against that little extra something that was wanted. The old technique was good enough.

They stood solidly grouped on the steps with wooden faces looking over the heads of the cynical newspaper men – hirelings of the press lords, scum to be disregarded – at the little crowd, faintly anxious, faintly hostile, beyond. Its members were not union members and so of no importance, they were just the drifting, discontented, disorganised and voiceless mass whose discomfort when the strike came would force the bosses to give in. Their babies would want milk, their fires coal, their tables food, they would squeal when it came to it, and the opposition would collapse at the sound.

They knew where they were with the opposition, just as they had known where they were with the old bosses. The old bosses only existed as long as they could sell things to that feeble mob in the street, cut off the supply of labour that supplied the things to sell and they crumbled up. These new bosses would crumple, too, they were even more dependent on the mob than the old ones were, and they'd crumple faster under pressure.

The Prime Minister came out onto the step for a last hand-shake with the head of the delegation in front of the cameras, doing what he could to gull the crowd and the newspaper readers into believing there was still hope. He smiled and the flash bulbs flickered madly while the two men pumped out cordiality, look-ing sideways at the photographers, not at each other. The reporters jostled through the ring of cameras, calling for a statement. The Prime Minister held up the neat white hand of an educated man, and a local hush fell.

'We've had a very fruitful discussion. While no final agree-ment has been reached I think I may say that we have cleared the ground for a settlement. In the course of the next few days I hope the few remaining difficulties will be cleared away.'

The railwaymen's chief stepped forward before the Prime Minister had finished, and waved his hand, a slab of meat hardened by years of manual labour, in a curt gesture of repudiation.

'T'Prime Minister can say what he likes. The fact is we're at loggerheads. No agreement has been reached, period. No agreement is likely to be reached while the Government maintain their present attitude, period. Strike notices affecting the members of the five unions here represented will be posted tomorrow and our men will walk out on their jobs midnight Monday, period. That is all.'

He stopped talking and looked thoughtfully at the Prime Minister who looked at the floor, touching the little hollows on his temples at the end of the eyebrow ridge with a thumb and the middle finger of the same hand, shading his eyes with its palm in gesture of a tired reader who has been forced to lay down his book because the type has begun to swim under his eyes.

'No hard feelings, Mister Prime Minister,' the big bulky man full of confidence held out his hand to the slender, shrunken one who took it, clearly only because he could think of nothing else to do. This time they just clasped hands for a second and looked straight at each other without smiling.

Then the important man, who was power, and destiny, for millions of people, turned away, and carried the light with him, leaving the representative of the old order and the old certainties standing, the merest of spectators to his going, on the doorstep.

The big men who did not know what they were doing settled their hats on their heads, and started off solidly through the crowd looking more massive than the ring of policemen who made way for them.

The crowd went with them, goggling at their new masters; no one stayed to watch the Prime Minister go back into his house, to join the Cabinet. Anne saw Jewson and the pack of reporters sprinting ahead of the crowd into Whitehall, racing to get the news to their offices. Anne had seen all they had seen without quite understanding it. She wondered what people would make of it who got it through Jewson, through a rewrite man, through a written language, unlike their speech, which they had never really learned to use.

She walked out, in the wake of the crowd, into Whitehall and saw the fat black cars drive off, then turned down into Parliament Square. The funny spiky fake gothic Parliament building looked much as ever, dwarfing the old church that lay under its shadow, but the sense of doom weighed down more heavily than before, so that the familiarity of the scene intensified the unease. It looked exactly the same, but there was no comfort in that.

She looked up at Big Ben's clockface on its square graceless tower, and saw beyond it banks of woolly cumulus clouds sleeping motionless over south London. Perhaps that was it, thunder in the air. That gave you the feeling of unbearable tension sometimes – the building up of a really big thunderstorm, on a hot, still day. She strolled on towards Westminster Bridge, thinking a pool of cool air might lie on the embankment near the river, and that it was in any case nice to look down on running water and the business of the tideway. She found Jewson coming out of a phone box outside the teashop facing Big Ben, still green faced and trembling from his sprint.

'Don't say "Hallo, Beautiful," or I may slap you,' she said.

'I was only going to ask you for another cigarette.'

'Did you make it?' she said striking a match for him.

'The U.P. beat me to it. They had a man waiting in a car with a walkie-talkie. They had it on their tape by the time I got through to the news desk in my office. They were funny about it. Made a crack about if I'd had trouble catching a hansom cab. I'd resign if I had any guts – or any money. They like to humiliate you. They . . .'

'Please, don't. Let's talk about something else. What did that mean back there?'

'I forgot you were the one who likes information.' He paused. 'I don't know. It means a general strike I should say, like 1926 – but you wouldn't remember that. And on top of it the sort of crisis there was in 1931 – you were about four then I suppose – so you wouldn't remember that either.

'Christ, I don't know . . . it means all sorts of things that don't mean anything to you.

'It means trials of strength. Political demonstrations with lorry loads of armed troops out of sight round the corner. It means an end of the cosy British way. We're going to be European about our politics. Those union boys are just pulling the props out from under the whole stately business of constitutional Government. It's going to be a game between groups now, and the toughest group is the Government for as long as it can hold what it's taken.

'It means money going down the drain, and nobody being sure of what they've got. Oh, I can't explain . . . look . . .'

He wanted her to look out across the channel to the great cities of Europe as he'd seen them in the bad hours; with the electricity cut off through most of the day, with the queues outside the empty markets, with the armoured cars cruising through the wide empty streets, past the blank faces of the shuttered shops and bolted doors.

He could see, as clearly as if they were already in the street, the groups of men with armbands on the sleeves of their civilian coats and jackets, marching past the stalled streetcars and the silent factories.

He remembered looking across the empty park to the glassless shell of the university buildings on the fringe of Madrid in dead silence, he remembered the trivial rattling of small arms fire on the Place de la Concorde, the shells from the mountain guns bursting inside the upper floors of the big apartment houses in Vienna, the mortars and the rocket-firing aircraft going to work at first light in Athens.

He licked his lips, it was the silence that was worst.

He remembered lying awake all night in a Warsaw hotel, waiting for a phone call that never came, hearing the hours chimed off one by one, wondering where the clock was, and in the morning getting a cable from the London office telling him they'd heard from the agencies what had happened to the Social Democrats during the night.

Then another night of silence in Prague, working for another paper, going round all night trying to get a lead on the thing behind the silence, going from one house to another where they didn't know or wouldn't talk, and in the end shacking up with a girl and two bottles of plum brandy to keep the silence out of the room.

And in the morning, with a top flight hangover, reading the official announcement about young Masaryk.

Then two days waiting for the cable firing him, pretending it wasn't coming, going round pretending to be on the job, trying to find out what happened, interviewing frightened **people, and** people who cried, feeling his nerve going, and his blood turning into water inside him.

Masaryk! He'd interviewed him once or twice, a beautiful man with a sort of bigness about him that marked him off as one of the great ones of the earth: he'd met all manner of people in places of power and responsibility and had met few of those. It was terrifying to think of him pulled down and destroyed by the little people who thought of virtue only as a mask, and nobility as a sham . . . those were the worst days of all.

'. . . look,' he said again, 'I can't explain. But there are people like us who know about happiness, and want it, and are miserable about not having it, and there's another kind. Perhaps they were just like us once, and not being happy soured them – I don't know – but anyway they're different now. They've given up the idea of our sort of happiness, that you get from inside yourself by loving, and being kind – they've no use for it. All the dinginess, and the roar of the machines, and the complication of life – it's broken them down, swamped them, as people. They think of themselves as small, helpless things – they've no faith in anything inside themselves. They believe they can only do things by banding together till they're strong enough to take what they want, from their employers, from the state, from life. And once they've found that sort of strength, and had a taste of what they can take, they want to take and take and take until there's nothing left. They don't dream of putting anything back in because they don't believe they've anything to give. They'll smash anything that stands in their way, and when they've smashed everything, and there's nothing more for them to take, they'll start smashing people. . . .'

He put out a hand to steady himself, shaken with the effort of saying something he really felt and really meant, clutching at the door of the iron telephone box. An alcoholic queasiness stirred in him. 'You think I'm crazy.'

'No, no, I think you're tired and ill. I don't believe you've had anything to eat this morning. Why don't you come into this place and eat something. You'll feel better.' Anne tried to steer him towards the tea shop, but he shook her hand off his arm.

'I've got an ulcer. You'd kill me . . .' he stared into her face. 'You don't believe a word I've been saying; you cow, you lovely, lovely, stupid cow.'

Tears abruptly choked him, and ashamed, he turned from her.

She watched him go: she did not love him, so there was nothing that she could do for him, just watch him carry the burden of his own inadequacy off into the stream of passers-by. When he was gone she crossed over to the embankment and leant over the parapet watching the few weekday trippers filing onto river steamers, and the tugboats passing with their long tows of heavily laden barges.

Drifts of canned music blared over from the perpetual fun fair which lingered on in the exhibition grounds alongside County Hall, and its flags and banners were reflected in a thousand points of colour on the brown water.

It didn't look like smash and revolution, and yet there was that brooding unease tickling her spine. Behind the trees on the embankment she could see, looking over her shoulder, the red and white mass of Scotland Yard. What a strange building it was, to house the heart of a modern police force! A quaint handcrafty neo-medieval object, bedecked with little towers and arched windows, that might have come out of some fairy tale nonsense about the Teutoberger Wald, about a castle built by magic in a night to impress a greedy princeling.

Her mind's eye slipped between her and the police head-quarters an image of the Prime Minister, with his mild little mongol face shrunken with anxiety, being slighted, and brushed aside on the steps of number 10.

Suppose it was to come to a deadfall between the kind of power with which he had been threatened, and the kind of power that lived in that building, and could call on the marine in the Admiralty and the guards in their lorries? Would it really matter? Let those who like that sort of thing kill themselves that way, she thought, I'm one of the sort that gets down into a cellar, or out of the way, until it's all over. A plague on both your houses.

But suddenly she remembered the money she'd collected the day before from the broker and the jeweller. They had given her cheques, but the figures on them suggested great wads of notes to her, and that was the way she thought of them; things she could turn into the mill, and furniture for the mill and a future that she had dreamed into the most concrete of realities. . . .

Perhaps Scotland Yard was suitably decked out like a fairy tale castle because it might be the focus of a fairy tale event. She remembered the name-guessing stories in the fairy books she had had as a child, Tom-Tit-Tot, and Rumplestiltskin. The man with the secret name was full of magic and power, and could do what he liked to the captive princess. Or until the prince discovered the secret name; then the magician's spells lost their power, his doors flew open, his servants ran away, and the treasure chests in the cellars turned into bins filled with old leaves, waste paper, and rags.

The big bulky men had stood there facing the cameras like masters: they might have discovered words of power that would make the men in Scotland Yard hand over their elaborate apparatus, make the guardsmen hand their weapons to men in the crowd who reached for them and go home, and make all the paper in the city with promises written on it into paper and nothing more. All that money in the bank might turn in a few hours into nothing, something less substantial than the dreams it was to transform and realise.

She felt the terror close on her that had been stealing nearer all morning: those dreams must come true, she could not endure life if they did not. She turned and looked up at the great clock; it was only twenty to twelve. There was still time to do what she wanted, to give the money to the solicitors to complete the purchase of the mill, to get down to the country and buy things for the house, to get out into her private world of happiness before the big crash came.

12

ARGERY decided on action a few days later, on Sunday night. She and Walter had kissed the children good night and left them, but she was presently called back upstairs by a persistent voice. Jeanette had decided to let go with her torpedo.

'What do you want, darling?'

'Daddy isn't going to London tomorrow.'

'Yes, he is, he's going to do some business with his solicitors. He's found a lovely place for us all to live in the country and he's going to buy it for us. And he's going to sell the London house, and arrange to have all the London things moved down. Don't you worry your silly little head.'

'Is Anne going to live with us in the country?'

'Anne? Which Anne?'

'Daddy's Anne. The Anne he says he loves more than anything in the world. The Anne he's going to meet on Monday.'

'I don't know what you're talking about. You've had some sort of dream.'

'No,' the child looked up, pitying her mother's innocence, 'I heard them talking on the telephone. He's going to Anne tomorrow. He said Michael and all his angels wouldn't stop him.'

'Don't you worry. I expect you didn't really understand what daddy was saying.'

'Does daddy really love us?'

'Yes, of course he does.'

'Then why is he going to this Anne person at the Carp?'

'Oh,' she looked down at the pretty head and the shadowed questioning eyes – the truth was best, you had to know sooner or later. 'You can love several people at once you know. Like me loving you, and Francis, and daddy, there isn't anything very hard to understand in that.'

'But why didn't daddy tell us about Anne?'

'Oh, I knew about her, darling.' She took the small hand and kissed it. 'You needn't worry. There's nothing to worry about. Now I must go, or I shall be late for dinner. Good night, darling.'

'Good night.' Jeanette kissed her and let her get as far as the door. 'It will be horrid if daddy leaves us again, won't it?' She said it in a soft sleepy voice which her mother could hear or pretend not to hear. She pretended not to hear, so Jeanette knew that her disclosure had done the damage it was meant to do. She snuggled down in the bed and dropped off into a sound sleep.

Margery stopped at the stair head and leant over the banisters looking down from the unlighted landing into the brilliant hall downstairs. She thought the solidity of the banister rails was nice, but hated the hearts which had been cut out of each post at about two-thirds of their height.

She lit a cigarette and watched its thin stream of blue smoke sliding up into the shadows above her. She wondered how she could be such a fool as to love Walter.

She made out the case against him. He walked out. He found I had some sort of control over his money. He came back and got me to sign it away. Now he's got what he wanted he's walking out again. He's lied to me, about the house, about Anne, about everything. He's quite unscrupulously going to hurt me and the children. He just doesn't care. I ought to hate him. I love him. Is it just because I'm a sensual beast? Does my greedy body make me love a swine? He's not a swine. He's the nicest man I know, I don't want anyone else.

She thought how wonderful 'it' had always been with him, never like that with anyone else. And 'it' had been specially wonderful since he'd come back. How do I feel about it now that I know that the ecstasy covered betrayal and deceit?

She watched the smoke drifting upward. It didn't matter at all; and she wouldn't feel any differently about 'it' tonight, in a few hours, with the knowledge that betrayal and deceit was in his mind.

She thought with irritation of dinner and the evening of polite conversation that lay ahead, she wanted it to be over so that they would be together, even if it was to be the last time. Could it be

169

that he was getting something out of the sense that he was doing her wrong? That he got a kick out of her as his victim that he wouldn't get from giving her love and trust? Then was it important to him that she shouldn't know her position? Did his pleasure and delight depend on the secret that he thought he'd kept from her?

That was a tricky point to decide, and since admitting her knowledge might spoil what little with certainty remained to her she decided to say nothing to him about what Jeanette had told her.

She went to their room and dressed carefully in her black party dress, feeling strangely happy and adventurous, looking at herself in the mirror and talking to her image.

I suppose I must be a masochist, or I wouldn't be feeling like this. It's a contemptible thing to be, darling, you ought to go to a psychiatrist, and get whatever-it-is fixed. I've no intention of letting anyone into my mind to finger my thoughts, thank you, I'm very happy the way I am, really. Yes, but darling, you've got to be sensible. What about the day after tomorrow. Maybe tonight will be wonderful, and worth it, but it won't last the rest of your natural. What are you going to do?

She broke off the argument and thought about nothing but what she was doing to her face to make it as nice looking as possible, for Walter, for nobody else.

The soft night wind off the land whispered in the fuchsia bushes on its way out to sea, and the surf stirred gently on the shingle beach at the foot of the iron cliffs. The Penharrad light swung across the sky, and on the eastern horizon there was a blink where the moon would presently rise. She leant on the window sill and looked out. I'm still beautiful. I don't have to worry about sex. There are plenty of men in the world. Why shouldn't I just let him go? But all that's idiotic. I don't want sex, or a man, or men; I just want my dear Walter.

She took a turn about the room and several times caught glimpses of herself in the tall glass on the wall. A well made woman, with a handsome face, in a clever black dress. You can't just lie down and let things happen to you, she thought, you love Walter and you want to keep him. Yes, I do, I do.

One of his tweed jackets was hanging on the back of a chair and she gathered it up and snuggled her face to it. It felt rough but pleasant, and it smelt agreeably, strongly of tweed, a little of his pipe tobacco, and faintly, but certainly, of him.

I don't want to let him go.

A paper stuffed carelessly into the breast pocket slipped out and fluttered to the floor. I ought not to read it; if I was really well brought up, and a lady, I wouldn't read it, she said to herself as she read it.

It was for a moment disappointing, a list of railway stations and times, not a letter to or from that woman. But as she deciphered the wearisome complications of a journey by rail from St. Austell to Lemlade she was moved to pity: 'Oh, but my poor Walter, you can't, you simply can't . . .' and then another thought struck her. It was a long roundabout journey with changes that involved considerable waits. If she borrowed her father's car she could easily get there first. If he arrived and found the two women to whom he'd promised a future at the mill together he might be forced into being open and frank, and honest about what he really did intend, to one, or the other, or both.

And it might be quite a good thing for Miss Anne Horne to see that there was a third point to the triangle; Margery had an idea that Walter might have cut her down, aged her, and faded her a good bit, in describing her to his mistress. It was her experience that married men who were after women always tried to ease either their own or the woman's consciences by saying or implying that the marriage didn't exist sexually: either the wife had found someone else, or there was the grimmer tragedy of a virile male chained to a sexually dead female.

She dropped herself a curtsey in the mirror, 'You fell for it yourself once, darling, after all.'

For a moment her sense of well being and courage left her. She remembered the excitement of being loved by a mature and accomplished man, and of giving him something that life had cruelly conspired to deny him. And it had made her so proud that she, a girl of twenty-two – nobody – should have been able to give him what his wife, a successful, beautiful and extremely gifted, actress, could not.

171

She had pitied her, looking down from the dress circle in the darkened theatre, for being cold and frozen, and unalive inside, the mere appearance or illusion, the empty outward shell, of a woman.

And then the show had closed, because she was going to have a baby. There were coy little paragraphs about the blessed event in the gossip columns, and photographs of her looking adoringly at him, with the pig looking proudly back. And he had come round, sheepishly, and tried to explain.

She had an idea that it might be rather a good thing for Walter to have a little explaining to do to Miss Horne; he deserved it for doing what he had been doing, mentally, to her for the past week.

She leant towards herself in the glass, her elder sister this time, realistic and practical. 'Darling, do you really want to get into what may be an emotionally exhausting and humiliating scene with this woman and with Walter at the end of a long and tiring drive? Wouldn't it be much better to . . .' 'No it wouldn't, I've been quite tolerant and limp and feeble enough, lying about and crying and waiting. I'm through with all that. I'm not going to be just dumped. And if there's going to be any emotional hatchet work on this situation from now on, I'm going to do it.'

'But darling, all this tough talk isn't a bit like you. Do you think you can go through with it? You're really rather a nice person, do you think you can be as horrid as that? It's all going to be very undignified.'

'Yes I know. And I'm pretty undignified there in bed with Walter and I like it, and I was pretty undignified in the nursing home when the babies were born and it was worth it. And mummy was pretty undignified when I was born. And mummy and daddy were pretty undignified before that. Life is undignified. The only time you can be dignified is after you die, for a few hours, and even then it takes embalmers or a deep freeze to keep you that way until they get you underground or burnt. I'm for indignity and life.'

The gong boomed and filled the house with its fat noise, calling her down to dinner. She went down happily, feeling and looking lovely, and enjoying the rustle of her full silk skirt, it was rather an exciting business, being alive.

172

It was raining the next morning. Solid walls of grey rain came in across the bay, falling from a fairly high cloud canopy which stretched away unbroken over the land and the sea.

Margery drove Walter into St. Austell and put him onto his train, guiltily thinking of the five rainswept and bepuddled junction platforms on which he would be standing in the course of the day. It would be much kinder to take him with her all the way, and spare him his exploration of the west country railway network.

He said good-bye and kissed her in a solemnly sacramental fashion that made her want to giggle, she wanted to tell him to cheer up, because he wasn't going out of her life for ever, whatever he might think. But that seemed unwise. As unwise as letting on that she knew where he was going and was going there too; by an alternative route as they said in the guide books. She realised, as she stood on the platform talking to him, waiting for the train to start, that she ought to think of him as an awful cad, as he was thinking of himself. But she couldn't do it. She put her long slim fingertips down the line of the sinews from his wrist to his knuckles and loved him, cad or no.

A squall brought heavier rain lashing through the station and she ran for the shelter of the car; when she looked back the train was slowly pulling out under a blanket of puffy white exhaust steam. He was gone.

For ten defeatist seconds she believed it as she watched the line of carriages gathering speed and moving away from her. Then she sat up quickly and pressed the starter button, it was time to get moving.

She drove out of Cornwall across sour Dartmoor, and into Devon, past all the boarding-farms, the pixie tea rooms, and the pull-in camps for caravans. Somewhere she crossed a cultural frontier between Cornwall and Devon where the Piskey Tea Rooms became Pixie Tea Rooms, farther on into Somerset the pixies dropped out of it and the rain beat down on boards which just bluntly offered teas.

She went through Crediton and Tiverton, missing Exeter. She was sad about missing Exeter because of the big black and white cat that was always sitting on a chair at the west end of the nave when she visited the cathedral, the most regular and nicest church cat she knew of. She would have liked to touch it for luck, but it looked like too much extra mileage on the road map, so she just thought about it, with its nose covered with its tail, and hoped for luck.

She sang a little between Tiverton and Taunton, humming in the back of her throat:

> Oh it's only a cardboard moon,
> Floating over a cardboard sea,
> But it wouldn't be make believe
> If you'ld believe in me.
> Da de dada de dum de dum,
> Dedee Dedee Dedee,

Bother, I can't ever remember a whole song.
What's that thing, that other thing, that other tune.

> Strictly between us you're cuter than Venus,
> And what is more you've got arms,
> Oh let's go cuddle in a corner
> Toodledele oodle deetle ooo.

I just can't remember any more.

> A wumptum met a Bromide,
> Walking along Broadway . . .

I can't even get the beginning right.'

A vision of schoolgirls in gym tunics sitting round a portable gramophone and wanting to be grown up went with that one and silenced her. Who were they? Bertha English who married the man in the timber trade? Betty Stockfield, or Stockton, who was so mad about horses; I never saw her again. Lydia who? Now Lydia was my real friend, then. I ought to remember her name.

And come to think of it when I sing I ought to remember something better than this mushy American stuff. She started through what she remembered of Gilbert and Sullivan and

174

decided that on balance it was sillier than anything had any right to be that stuck in your mind.

I must have something better than that feeble stuff in my head. 'He threw the glove, but not with love, right in his lady's face. . . .' I got that one at school but I don't believe it's any better. Now Shakespeare's good. It's agreed, there's no doubt about it. If I can remember anything out of him I'm not just a low grade moron.

Through Glastonbury and on into Bath she wrestled out what she remembered of Portia's part in the *Merchant of Venice*, concentrating on the words through a film of more available recollections of the actual business of rehearsing and mounting the end of term show.

'Well,' she thought, 'I can do it. But it's no fun. If I were to tell the truth I'd have to admit that what gives the poor old merchant the only point he has for me is that I was Portia, and that being Portia gave my longing to show off and be the centre of interest a satisfactory run. Really what I like about that play is the fun we had putting it on. If I told the truth I'd say that it all seemed old and dead and the jokes as unfunny as you could make them. And all that stuff about the pound of flesh, and those idiotic caskets; it couldn't mean less.'

She began humming and ran through all the tunes from The Gay Divorce finally piecing together the whole of Night and Day and When We're Out Together Dancing, Cheek to Cheek.

'Why does that mean so much more to me? It's wrong, it's indefensible. Oh, no, it isn't. It means my first grownup parties. And my first terribly exciting evenings with my first chaps. And then Cheek to Cheek means knowing I belonged to Walter and that I was going to marry him, we called it our tune, it was the beginning of the best part of my life and I'll love it always.'

She sang it again, right through, before she turned herself into that wise elder sister again.

'My dear you're a barbarian. How can you glory in this contentment with second rate? Perhaps Walter has gone off because having the babies has addled your mind. Perhaps he couldn't stand talking to anyone with no intellectual life whatever.

Perhaps your shallow little teaspoon of a brain wasn't big enough for him.

'Oh that's all my eye. It wasn't anything to do with my brain.'

Her inner argument stopped then, and gave way to a confused puzzling. She had known since last night something essential about her relationship with Walter, but she didn't know what it was. It was an odd feeling, like having an exciting parcel in the hall waiting to be unwrapped. She was a little afraid of unwrapping it, and suspected that all the light trivial chatter that she had been occupying her mind with was designed to postpone the time for thinking about that. It was something to do with giving herself to him with that withheld knowledge of his plans in her mind; it had been terribly exciting being so close to him, and so utterly with him, with that one thing, like a diamond in her hand, held apart. She gave those sectors of her mind which were not occupied with driving up to that.

The clouds were breaking up over Bath, and its slated roofs flashed with the first gleams of sunshine of the day. For a moment she thought of taking lunch there, but it was still fairly early, and the stone houses, streaked with wet, looked sullen and uninviting. The gutters were full of racing brown water, and the streets in the lower part of the town were partially flooded so that the traffic moved through the slap and chop of a jumble of waves. When she came out through Batheaston she felt tired and for the first time, open to doubt. It seemed an unbearably long journey, and a foolish one.

She pulled the car up by the roadside and got out to smoke a cigarette and think about going back. She would arrive half dead, the girl would pitch into her and tear her apart with all the truths she didn't dare tell herself. Walter would arrive to find her whipped and would kick her out without any hesitation. She looked back down the hill at the sprawling city, thinking she'd junk her pride, go back there to eat lunch, and then drive on home.

She shook her hair out into the fresh wind and watched the clouds blowing away in rags and strips under the clear watery blue sky. What an odd place Bath was, hateful really, with its untidy sprawl out into the country, its dinginess, and its way of

176

turning its back on you. From wherever you were outside it you saw nothing but the backs of houses. When you were inside it you saw nothing but solemn, fraudulent, façades quite unlike the ragtag ugly backs. It was lovely when the sun was out, if the traffic wasn't too bad.

'There you are, dodging away. You're making up your mind on an important matter. Give your attention to that and nothing else.' She must have driven a hundred and forty miles, probably a little more. It would be idiotic to go back, idiotic.

She drove on with a new plan. She'd drive on for an hour, or thereabouts, get a good meal, sit over it taking it easily and quietly, and then when she was rested and fresh close in for the encounter.

That was the plan, but at the end of an hour there wasn't anything very much about and she began to hurry. She went through a big straggling village with a biggish public house in it, hurrying, forgetting that she was looking for a place to eat, then argued with herself about turning back until it was too late to do so.

And suddenly there it was, the plain white lettering on the blue board, The Carp, just over the hump of a bridge. She pulled up with a squeal of brakes, scared to death, feeling oddly that she was lost far away in some deep recess of her body.

In the dark front room she rang a little bell standing on a baize covered table, and waited for Anne to appear. But instead a nice fat woman, a plump, ageless, country person, looking like her old nanny, came and asked what she could do for her.

'I'm looking for Miss Horne, Miss Anne Horne.'

'I'm afraid I don't know her, ma'am. Leastways she's never been here that I know of.'

'Are you sure?'

'Why, yes. I'll ask my husband, if you like, but there's very few as comes here that I don't know of.'

'Oh, I suppose not. You're not expecting her? There's been no room booked?'

'I'm quite sure about that, dear.'

'I must have made some stupid mistake.'

'I'm very sorry I'm sure. Can I get you anything?'

'No, thank you, no. I'm sorry I've bothered you.'

She went out and stood on the wet gravel, looking through the thin tops of a bed of withies at the flat riverside meadows. What a fool I've been to come all this way, on the strength of an eavesdropping child's word, what an unbelievable idiot.

The Carp, the Harp, the White Hart; they might have said anything. She was surprised to notice how much of the sky was reflected in the puddles on the road, and how their clear inch of water caught and held the now intense blue of the sky. They may be anywhere, together already, or they may not even be going to meet. And then she suddenly saw it.

'I'm so sorry to bother you again, but just now I was thinking of my friend's maiden name – I'd forgotten she was,' the sour taste of lies in the mouth again, 'Mrs. Jackson.'

'Oh, yes, Mrs. Jackson. But she's gone on to the mill. We know Mrs. Jackson well. You should have told me you wanted Mrs. Jackson. Well now. She was here last night. The vans came from London with her stuff this morning and she went over to see them unload. I expected her back to lunch. But there, I suppose she'd got her stuff out and felt like christening her kitchen. She's delighted with the place, excited about moving into it like a child. But I expect you know her ways as well as I do.'

'Yes.' She hoped the smile was all right; it didn't feel quite good enough on the face. 'Is the mill far?'

'Oh, dear me, no. I'll show you.' The nice woman bustled her out through the front door into the roadway. 'First right, and then first left. Doesn't look like much more than a lane, and it isn't if the truth be told, but the mill's up at the end of it. You'll be there in five minutes. 'Tis a lovely old place, and Mrs. Jackson is that happy to be moving in. She'll be pleased to have a visitor on her first day, I know.'

Margery again hoped that the smile was not too obviously forced, said good-bye, and drove on. Anne must have something very nice about her to have charmed that friendly, warm hearted person . . . but then people who kept inns had to be warm hearted professionally, and I'd said I was a friend of hers, so perhaps that doesn't mean anything. First right; yes, that might mean

178

nothing at all, just the light touch of the professional greeter. But then my dear Walter loves her so . . . first left, goodness, I'm nearly here.

The roadway was lined with bushes and shrubs still bent under the weight of the storm; the rose hips and the hawthorn berries shone under a glistening film of water and the ripe blackberries looked like some new kind of precious stone. Everything was dripping, and the car flung sheets of water out of the wheel tracks into the roadside grasses. 'I'm stiff, I'm tired, I'm scared and I'm hungry. This lane isn't going anywhere, it's going to peter out in a farmyard or a bog in a minute. I'm going to get stuck, and it'll serve me right.' But she came round a bend, and there, breathtakingly, was the mill nestling into its countryside under its snug roof of graded stone tiles. She got out of the car not believing its grey beauty and its absolute rightness; it was the most wonderfully homelike house she had ever seen, sitting snugly there under the strong protective flank of the mill. Her eye ran up the great rose vine which clambered towards the mill roof, loaded with a heavy second blooming of big creamy-white cabbage roses. One of its branches ran out sideways towards a loft door, in which a golden woman was sitting eating an apple, swinging her legs out over the front of the building, looking down at her with dark violet coloured eyes. She was dazzled. Oh, yes, she thought, if I were a man. . . . I might just as well go home. . . .

'I hope you haven't come to look at the house, because I'm afraid it's already been sold.'

'Well, no, I'm afraid I really came to see you,' this was the bad moment. 'I'm Margery Jackson.'

'Oh.'

The girl swung her feet up into the loft and stood up, stared down for a moment, and vanished. Oh, heaven, what now, thought Margery, am I going to hear the lock grind shut? Am I going to have to try to persuade her to talk to me, speaking through doors, gesturing outside windows? There's no accepted procedure for handling this, and I've no idea how it's done. She took a few steps toward the door, and waited for what seemed an eternity, until it opened.

179

'How do you do, Miss Horne. I haven't come to be horrid.'
She offered her hand and it was a little reluctantly taken.

'How do you do? Do come in.'

They walked into a drawing-room, in which obviously new furniture stood about looking dazed and uncertain of itself. A fire burnt rather reluctantly in the grate, not doing much more than smoulder.

'Do sit down . . . I lit a fire because the rooms have been empty for some time – but it won't burn – the wood is wet because of the storm. Do you mind if I draw it up?'

Anne knelt with her back to Margery, holding an old newspaper across the fireplace.

'I expect the chimney's damp.'

The flames began to talk and whisper, glowing red through the paper until it began to scorch; Anne folded it up and set it down on the pile of logs by the fire.

'Why did you come?'

'I wanted to talk about you, and me, and Walter.'

'I don't want to hurt you, Mrs. Jackson, but can't you see that it's no use? Can't you see that it's all over between you and Walter? Won't you just hurt yourself and hurt him if you try and keep him now? I'm sorry, but I can't see what I can say that won't be cruel.'

While she spoke Margery looked into her eyes to see if she was speaking truthfully, and in pity, or if she was merely using a kindly form of words in order to wound more effectively. As she wondered and quite unwittingly, she put her hand to her shoulder and with her fingers touched, through her clothes, an oval bruise which she had seen there as she dressed that morning, as a blue and purple stain on her white skin. Anne let the words 'that won't be cruel,' die on her lips as the possible significance of this gesture dawned on her.

'I thought,' she said it in a dismayed whisper, 'that all that sort of thing was over between you.'

Margery shook her head and smiled; a smile which was, though she had no intention of making it so, deeply and richly sensual, filled with a recent content. Without her knowledge her body smiled.

Anne still knelt by the fire watching her over her shoulder, now she turned away and looked at the unenthusiastic flames, and the blue smoke sluggishly going up the chimney. The smile had shocked her deeply because it showed her how completely Margery wasn't the woman she'd been imagining, stale, used up, and dull. She'd imagined her as a woman pulled down by her children, who had become what can be accurately described as a housewife, whose imaginative and instinctive life was over. And she was much better looking, too, than she had supposed. She'd thought of her as one of that class of women who seem to be pretty because all the qualities of youth rest on them, but who have nothing left when the colour and lustre go. But she was instead one of that happier kind with good bones and good features, which reaches a definitive appearance round about twenty-four or five or so, and holds it for twenty years or longer.

'Could I have a glass of water, I'm terribly thirsty.'

'Oh, of course,' Anne looked at her again, 'have you had any lunch?'

'Well, no. But don't bother. . . . If I could have some cheese?'

'I haven't had any lunch either. I've been eating apples all morning. I've got some eggs and some bacon. Let's see what we can find in the kitchen.'

'I oughtn't to bother you, really. . . .'

'No, come along.'

Anne smiled at her and led her through into the big low ceilinged room, littered with half unpacked gear. Stacks of plates filled with dust and ends of straw, stood along the dresser, saucepans still in their shop packings were all over the floor, and jumbles of jars and jugs and packets of food stood in a rabble rout on the tables. They cooked their bacon and eggs on a calor gas stove that smelt of hot paint as it did its first work, and ate them out on the little terrace looking over the mill dam. Fifty yards from them a hawk hovered over the reeds on flickering wings, and then sailed easily away in a long glide. They ate apples, and drank coffee sitting on the balustrade looking into the waterfall which roared out a throaty boom as it spilt the morning's heavy rain.

'It's unbelievably lovely here.'

181

'Yes, we fell in love with it the minute we . . .' she bit off the 'we' and the delighted enthusiasm.

'I would have done too,' said Margery quickly, 'everything you've done, probably.'

They looked at each other and were conscious of the beginning of friendship, and they were both troubled by a feeling that this was wrong, or improper, and that they should be resenting or disliking each other.

'We haven't talked about anything important, yet, have we?' said Anne.

'No. I meant to think it all out on the way here, but I thought about everything else. The thing is that Walter has told me that he's buying the mill for us, and that we're going to live here. I'm not sure if he meant that or if he just said that to get me to let him have some money. I came to find out if you were forcing him to leave me, or if it was just that he felt he couldn't have us both, because women are supposed to be like that, and if he'd just worked himself into a state . . . oh, dear, I'm being incoherent.'

'I think I know what you're trying to say. You wrote it in a letter once.'

'Well I suppose it was too early then. I don't think Walter was thinking at all then, he was just feeling very intensely about you, and there wasn't room for anything else in his mind.' She stared into the crest of the waterfall, at that wonderful spot where the moving water seemed motionless, as smooth, and as hard as the finest rock crystal. 'When he came back after he'd been away with you, I loved him as much as ever, more perhaps. Everything between us went better and I was thankful to you. He was richer inside himself for having known you, and richer physically. He told me it was all over between you, and that it had turned out that you weren't important. I knew that wasn't true really because he'd have come back small and ashamed if it had been, and he was proud. When I found that he'd just come back to get the money I felt angry for a moment, but then I saw that couldn't be quite true either, because he'd made me so wonderfully happy for that ten days and I knew he'd been happy with me. And he likes the children, too. He felt bad about leaving us this morning, he was unhappy for the first time since he'd been back. I could feel it, and he looked it, poor darling.' She paused wondering how she could put it. 'You must have known . . . what would happen, when he came back to persuade me to let him have the money?'

'No,' Anne looked a little puzzled and upset, 'No. I'm not as nice as you are. I meant mischief, honestly. I thought he'd make a mess of it. I thought you'ld find out that he'd just come for money, and that would really upset the applecart once and for all. I thought you'ld be angry and kick him out. I thought you'ld send him back to me. You see, I had the money for the mill all the time. He didn't have to go to you. But he never thought of turning to me. I thought I'd teach him a lesson, that was it really.' She paused, as if thinking of an excuse, and then added, 'You're not in the least what I expected.'

'No one ever is,' said Margery, wondering if she was altogether justified in taking this as a compliment. 'The point is that Walter didn't make a final break with me.'

'My rather dirty trick didn't come off.'

'No.'

They listened to the boom of the waterfall, a solemn warning sound, thinking their own thoughts.

'What I'm trying to say,' said Margery, 'is that if Walter needs both of us to make him happy I want him to be happy. All I can't bear is the confusion and unhappiness there's going to be if he's going to be pulled to and fro between us, lying to us and pretending we're each the only one. I thought I'd come to you to say that. And if you can bear it we'll tell him when he comes that there isn't anything difficult, and there needn't be anything horrid. We'll tell him that he can have us both.'

Now I am utterly humbled and disgraced. Oh, Walter, my dear, dear, love, she thought, but there is nothing, nothing, I wouldn't do to keep that part of you that belongs to me, and to give you what happiness I can.

'All right. We'll tell him that. And he can decide what he really wants.'

It was on the tip of Anne's tongue to say that what she was most afraid of was that she had in a sense lost Walter already, and that he was now more interested in the mill than in her. She realised that the proposal which had been made to her was made in a determined effort to hold onto a fragment of Walter which this other woman still undoubtedly held. She thought that if she accepted it she would be doing quite a lot to secure her hold on her own fragment of his personality. Walter was a mosaic of irreconcilable dreams and it was worth having a place in as many of his dreams as possible. And this woman seemed friendly, unmalicious, and likeable.

'I'm sure we shall get along. I know this is a happy house, and it'll be our own fault if we aren't happy in it.' She stood up and patted Margery on the shoulder. 'I'm sure it'll be all right. Let's go in and get on with the unpacking. I'm expecting Walter about five, and I'd like to have it reasonably tidy when he arrives.'

She went indoors, carrying the tray with the coffee pot and the cups. She didn't stand aside for Margery at the door and wait for her to go through, there was no point in that hostess and guest pretence, after all, since they were now the women of the house.

13

WALTER arrived at the mill later than they expected. He had missed one of his connections, and when he had arrived at the Carp paid off the taxi before he went in to learn that Anne was gone to the mill.

He walked up the lane among the puddles tired and angry at being dragged up to be faced with a dream that was now an unrealisable gossamer. When he came in to the space before the house in the evening glow, and found Bannerman's car standing outside it, that was the last straw. It was bad enough having to swallow the financial pill that meant he wouldn't ever be able to have the mill without having that old idiot gloating over him. He imagined the colonel indoors trying some blackmailing threat or other unpleasantness on Anne, and swore he'd throw him into the mill pool after he'd beaten him up.

He went straight in through the front door and up the passage towards the kitchen, calling, 'Where are you,' fiercely, with his fists already doubled up to smash blows into Bannerman's face. He flung open the kitchen door and went in.

Anne was half-way up a step ladder and Margery was holding it steady. They had just been hanging a wall clock, one of those flat American clocks with a transfer picture of Saratoga on glass above the clock-face, and Anne was setting it to the right time and starting it. It had a full, mellow, bronze tick, and when it began pulsing on the wall they both felt oddly stirred, as if the heart of the house had started to beat. Then they heard the fierce cry, in the house – 'Where are you?' And Walter burst in.

They were frightened for a moment thinking his fury was focused on them, but suddenly the colour drained out of his face and the battle fury left him.

'What the devil. . . ?'

Anne managed to get down off the ladder and went and took him into her arms, kissing him.

'It's all right,' she said, but he twitched his face away staring over her shoulder at Margery who stood stock still holding on to the steps recovering from the violence of his entry.

'What do you mean by following me here? What has she tried to do to you, Anne?' He held her protectively.

'It's all right. We're friends. There isn't any horridness between us. We're friends.'

She half turned out of his arms, and with her arm round his waist led him up to his wife. She put her other arm over Margery's shoulders. Walter thought of an incident at school when a master had broken up a grudge fight and made him and another boy shake hands and forswear their quarrel, remembering the mixture of relief with a curious, troubling, shame. He ought to be on bad terms with Margery, he was in honour bound to be, and yet there she was – beginning, a little shyly, to smile.

'We thought we could, all three, live here quite happily together,' said Anne slowly, looking from one to the other of them feeling drunk with emotion, feeling that a great tide of love was flowing out of her, that she was a vessel charged with it, and that on her bounty any number of people could live in amity. There was no reason why it shouldn't be like that, none. Walter kissed each woman in turn with a grave bewilderment, listening to the rich tick of the clock, and looking about the room, filled with soft sunset light, believing that it could be so. Then he broke abruptly from them. He sank down into a chair on the far side of the kitchen table.

'Well, it's a wonderful idea, and I think you're two wonderful people – but it's all dream stuff. It just can't happen. We can't pay for the mill. I don't even see how we're going to get on in London.' His voice broke. 'It's unbearable to sit here, knowing that . . .'

'What do you mean?'

'Oh, hell, haven't you seen the papers? The stock market has gone to blazes because of this damned strike that begins tonight. The shares I was going to sell to buy this place are worthless – or nearly worthless – already if I sold everything I'd got we couldn't buy it. God knows what happens to our income.'

'But the mill's yours. You've got it. I gave your solicitors the money.'

'What?'

'Yes, I said it was your money. They told me they could go ahead and complete. I asked if you had to sign anything and they said, no. That was the surprise I told you about on the telephone. I expect you'll get the deeds any day now. The mill belongs to you.'

The clock ticked out the seconds as Walter sat frozen faced, motionless and unsmiling, astonishingly – it seemed to Margery – ungrateful. He gathered himself. 'How did you raise that much money?' He said it in a low, unhappy voice.

'I sold some jewels – I got a lot of money from them – and I sold some shares – I didn't get much for them. But there was plenty, and there's a good bit left over. . . .'

'Money you got by. . . .'

His voice died, and for a moment he and Anne looked at each other as if they were cut from the same block of stone, hard eyed. Margery felt wholly excluded from their relationship and wondered at the ugly intensity which money talk had brought into the room.

'As for income,' Anne went on in a harsh voice, 'I thought we'd use the money I've got left to buy a few cows and some geese and hens. You said you wanted to farm. The land that goes with this place isn't too bad, though it is on the wet side.'

'And we can sell the house in London,' Margery said, 'that'll give us enough for two or three years for sure, and we'll probably be able to pay Anne for our share in the mill as well.'

'For god's sake . . . you don't know what you're talking about,' he shouted it at her in exasperation, still staring at Anne with a stricken horror on his face. 'I can't take your money, that would make me . . .' his voice had dropped to a whisper again, 'beneath contempt.'

'There's no difference,' said Anne in the strange hard voice that didn't seem to belong to her, 'between me and my money.'

'You're being absurd,' Margery broke in on her, 'you didn't hesitate to take money from me when we were poor and you weren't earning much after we were married. I loved you and I was happy to help you. Anne loves you and I don't see why she shouldn't give you what you want. There's nothing wrong in

187

taking money from a woman if she wants you to have it. You're being stupidly proud. You ought to be proud that Anne should want to do such a thing for you, and very proud that she trusts you that far – I don't know what you've done for her to deserve so much.'

Walter turned to her with his mouth moving as if he was making a last minute choice between several words which were jostling to be out of him, but he said nothing.

She saw that he was looking at her with complete incomprehension – like one of Cortez' men looking at the carvings in an Inca palace, or a tourist staring at the figures on the Ankor Wat.

He got up and walked round the table to touch her on the shoulder briefly with a blunted gesture which was partly an apology, partly a caress, and partly an approving pat. Then he went and stood by Anne who was apparently intent on the spot where his head would have been if he were still sitting on the other side of the table; all the gentle beauty gone from her, driven away by anger, so that she looked like the priestess of some destructive hunting goddess.

'Forgive me,' Margery could barely hear what he said, 'between the two of you you've rather knocked me off balance.'

She did not move and he walked away from her to the western window to look out into the golden blaze of the sunset beyond the orchard. As he stood there silhouetted against the light, a dark, perplexed figure, Margery watched a miraculous return of the Anne she had first seen among the roses, she relaxed and softened into her natural undeadly self. She faced Margery and began to speak just as Walter spoke.

'Well if you two can stand it I . . .' he said.

She raised her voice to silence him.

'Margery, there's something I have to tell you. I'm not your sort of woman at all. I don't know if it would be right for me to ask you to try to live with me. I've done things I have to be ashamed of, everybody tells me I must – even Walter is . . . I ought to be honest with you. I . . .'

'For chrissake,' said Walter 'No.'

'It's all right, Anne,' said Margery. 'I don't want you to tell me anything you've done or haven't done. We all make mistakes.

I've made them myself. All I care about is that you're the Anne my Walter loves, that's enough for me. If you blurt anything out now I might not understand. . . . We'll get to know each other in time. I can tell from the look of you that it can't be anything that won't wait till we really do know each other. I'm sure it'll be better that way.'

'I think it will, Anne,' said Walter.

And so it was left like that; a coiled rattlesnake, drowsy in the warmth of love, that might be forgotten, and might never bite, but would always be there, not far off, with its sacs of venom.

Walter thought of it now and then with terror in the first days, now and then with guilty horror when he saw his children settling down to like Aunt Anne. Now and then his sense of the comic almost overcame him when he saw them all together at meals in the kitchen, a big family, odd by any standard that he was used to.

It was all easy at first because every stage of setting up house was a private victory against the great dead weight of the strike that was now pressing gloomily down on everybody. Anne bribed the owner of a furniture van to run through the pickets on the road to London, and brought back the contents of the St. John's Wood house, all the pretty and familiar chattels that meant home to the children and a good deal to Margery.

Anne won her way through one picket line after another in the role of a young bride whose marriage it was a shame to spoil for a drab political issue. The pickets looked at her beauty, watched her crying convincingly into a handkerchief, or on to the stolid vanman's shoulder, and let her through – 'just this once.'

When it got back to the mill the loaded van was chalked all over with hearts pierced with arrows, and joking good wishes rudely phrased, here and there linked up with a political slogan in a cheerfully nonsensical fashion. 'God Bless Our Home. May All Your Troubles Be Little Ones. Support the Strike And Defend Your Standards of Living', and so on.

Margery had a difficult journey down to Cornwall, and back, with the children, but her mind was lifted from its discomforts when the colonel discovered from some carelessly phrased remark what was going on at the mill. He tried to get Mrs. Bannerman to help him to hold on to the children for their moral protection; but she, although thinking the idea of the *menage a trois* was messy – it was as far as she went with morality – was rather exhausted after having such very young people in the house for six long weeks and secretly helped Margery to find a local taxi that would start her out on the road back to Lemlade.

'Trewartha will do it, I'm sure. Everybody says he was terrific on the black market during the war, and he's always willing to sell petrol. But not a word to your father, mind.'

Mrs. Bannerman dialled Trewartha's number, and listening to the dialling tone looked round Phil Wincklemann's house. Why did it seem so much worse, somehow, three people living together, than the idea of a man slipping away to his mistress's flat for an hour or two, or off for a weekend now and again? To her it was quite different, and she wondered that her daughter shouldn't feel it too. She couldn't imagine living with Courtenay and Phil simultaneously, indeed she'd made it a point of honour never to have anything to do with Phil under Courtenay's roof, or in any bed that technically or actually belonged to Gwen Wincklemann.

'I can't imagine myself living in a hugger-mugger with one of Courtenay's women,' she said looking sideways at Margery, as usual trying to see in her some trace of the little girl with whom she was once so intimate, wondering how she had become such a complete stranger. 'And it won't be very nice for the children, when they find out, will it?'

'It would be a shock, but it's better for them than losing their father altogether – besides, they need never find out.'

'Children always find out things.'

As she said it Mrs. Bannerman's heart missed a beat, because she remembered the terrible scare Phil had given her, a scare that she had given herself by her own carelessness. The only thing she had been able to think of at the time was to make Courtenay feel that it was possible for the child to be his, and to lie the whole thing through. And that was what she had done; and in the end Margery was born on an ambiguous date, so that she had never known, herself. She had never said a word to Phil, and never a word to Courtenay – there was no way of saying it – and Margery had never had an idea, not so much as an inkling of the doubt. It wasn't true that children always found things out. She resorted to the formula which always closed discussions in which they were bound to disagree before any point of real friction was reached.

'Well, you're a grown woman now, darling. You know what you're doing.'

The voice of Trewartha answering the telephone broke in on her private line of thought and she returned happily to the trivial surface. Trewartha it appeared, reckoned that he would be able to take the family as far as Exeter, and he had a friend with a garage there who would probably get them through to Frome or Bath. And they would be sure to find there – or in Trowbridge – some car hire man who would take them on for the rest of the journey. It was arranged that they would start at nine the next morning, Trewartha would bring the car up to the back door and Margery would slip away with the children while Courtenay was having breakfast. As they completed their plans the colonel was heard shouting in the house, 'Dolly, Dolly, Dolly.' He came and stood close to the door and talked to her in a loud voice which was meant to reach Margery.

'Tell that woman, that if she leaves this house to go to that man and his mistress she'll never come back into any house of ours.'

'Why don't you speak to her yourself, dear?'

'I've no wish to speak to her while she's in her present frame of mind. I don't know how you can. I'm in favour of thrashing her and locking her up till she comes to her senses, but the law won't allow that. Tell her that she is paining me more deeply than I know how to say, that I'm brokenhearted by the whole disgusting business, and that I won't hesitate to go to my lawyers when things are back to normal to see if I can get the children taken out of her hands. They're in need of care and protection.'

'Do you think we could give it them, dear?'

'Of course we could. We could give them a chance to become decent clean living people.'

'We brought Margery up, dear, and you don't seem pleased with the result.'

191

'We were too damned soft with her.' He raised his voice again so that Margery should miss nothing. 'Tell her I'd sooner she was on the streets than living in a mess like that. Tell her she's got no right to do it to the children. Tell her. . . . oh, dammit, tell her not to be a fool.'

He stamped away. He wouldn't eat with Margery and went down to Llaney Haven for his tea and his dinner.

The only places that you could eat at in Llaney Haven were for tourists and excursionists who had come to see a fishing village famous for crab and lobster and it was assumed that they wouldn't want anything else. The colonel had a five shilling Cornish crab tea and there was nothing but lobster to be had for dinner. In the morning he was liverish and irritable, and when he suddenly realised what was going on flared up into a raging passion. Just as Trewartha was starting up the engine he appeared in the back door, scarlet faced with a working mouth.

'Oh, look there's grand',' both the children cried together, 'we knew he'd come to say good-bye.'

O, god help me, thought Margery, I don't have to be afraid of what comes from inside our funny household, it's going to be what comes from outside that'll be horrid.

'The children will hear anything you say, you fool,' said Mrs. Bannerman quietly, smiling and waving to the children.

She tugged the colonel gently out of the way and then deftly swung the back door shut, so that the children saw him vanish as suddenly and unexpectedly as Punch dropping out of sight from the stage of a Punch and Judy show.

'Why was grand' shaking his fist at us?' said Francis, in a puzzled voice.

'I expect he was just pretending to be cross because he doesn't want us to go until the strike is over,' said Margery placidly.

'Does everybody get cross when they get old,' asked Jeanette. 'Will you be horrid and try to stop us doing things when we're old enough to have babies of our own?'

Trewartha laughed, reminding them that they were with a stranger and the car bumped off down the little lane to start them on their long journey.

When Francis and Jeanette were safely asleep in bed at the

192

mill, and Margery was telling the story with the three of them gathered in under the circle of lamplight in the front parlour, they were all able to laugh at the thought of the red faced colonel shaking his fist and vanishing. Walter threw another log on to the fire, sending a chain of sparks flying up the chimney and adding a reddish tinge to the warm yellow light from the oil lamp. They all at once became thoughtful.

'How do you think the children will take it?' said Walter sadly.

'I don't think they'll have to take it as a blow or a shock if we're reasonably discreet. In time they may realise how things are, but by then they'll have had time to get used to it.'

'I'm sure it'll be all right with Francis, he's solid and nice about things,' said Walter, 'although he's still only a baby. But I'm worried by Jeanette.'

'Oh, I'm not,' said Anne, 'we took to one another. As soon as she arrived she made me take her up to the end of the mill bank and all over the place. I'm sure we're going to be friends.'

'She's been very strange lately,' Walter said, 'and I am a bit worried about her.'

'Well,' Margery sipped her cocoa, feeling the warmth of it and the warmth of the fire stealing into her and changing into a delicious exhausted sleepiness, 'you left us at a bad time for her. She's just beginning to . . . oh, you know, we all go through it. We're all warned about it, and we're all upset by it. It's an awkward age for a girl – we'll just have to be specially nice to her for a year or two.'

Anne looked down and traced a line on the carpet with her finger, Walter stared into the fire. They were both a little embarrassed at the breaking of the great tabu, and they were both reconsidering the nature of the household. They had been thinking of it as made up of three people and two half-people of lesser importance in a fixed and established relationship each to each. And now one of the half-people was on the edge of changing from girl into woman. The agreement that had been made didn't mean anything, couldn't mean anything, since they were all involved in that pattern of change whatever they might undertake to immutably be to each other.

'I shall fall asleep here,' said Margery yawning, 'if I stop another minute. I must go to bed.'

She went off, dead on her feet, and left them alone in the warm glow.

'Do you really think this is going to work out, Anne?'

'Mmmm.'

'What's "Mmmm" supposed to mean?'

'Oh, I know you. You're a terrible male man. Nothing ever does work out with them. You eat us poor girls up, like lady spiders and gentlemen spiders, only the other way round. You were happy with poor Margery until she got used to you, and you got used to her, and she became a mature woman. Then you had to have something fresh, and young, and exciting. You'll want another woman soon – five years, ten years, perhaps sooner. Then you'll blow this nice place up.'

'Do you really believe that? Don't you understand at all?'

'Yes, of course, I understand, I was just teasing you a little.'

'You know I really love you, don't you?'

'Yes, of course, I do.' She leant her head back, shut her eyes and turned her mouth towards him. Then after a few seconds she nuzzled away from his mouth and whispered in his ear.

'You are happy, aren't you? Happy enough to stand it if I tease you just a little now and then, when we're alone?'

'Of course I am. Much happier than I thought possible, wonderfully happy, far happier than I deserve to be.'

'Don't say any more.'

She didn't explain, but it was in her heart to say that he sounded as if he were speaking the truth when he told her he loved her, and that when he added words about happiness they sounded like words and nothing more, sounding like the speech of an actor who does not understand or like his part.

As Walter sat there in the firelight, looking at the play of the flame flicker on her loving face, he left her and a part of his mind began to worry and consume itself in speculation about worthless things that weren't in his life at all. He had become a man living in a mill with two women, and his only hope was to live entirely with them, from the mill and its land. But he had a puppet in his charge that he was concerned to keep strutting, a professional architect with a London office, and he fretted and fretted in case the strike and the national bankruptcy which was going to come out of it should interfere with his efforts to keep this doll moving and looking alive. He couldn't face the thought that the world might see that the puppet was dead, a fabrication, and he couldn't face the freedom he'd have if he were suddenly to say to the puppet, 'look here, old boy, I can't keep you going, I'm not an architect, and I never should have tried to be one. I'm through with our partnership, it's a bore, and it's preventing me from being a man.'

It was rather dreadful and frightening to be a man, all on your own, without the protection of some kind of ticket, professional or otherwise. He couldn't quite bring himself to throw the puppet away, it was so much easier to shrink away from people and life and leave the puppet to face things.

And now these strikers, and their power hungry leaders, were smashing up the puppet theatre – though they didn't know it – and they were going to throw all the puppets out into the rain and the cold. The puppet operators were going to find themselves stripped and naked in the open and it wasn't going to be nice.

He tried hard to think about it, passing it off with a laugh: 'Well here I am in the buff, boys, this is what I am, take it or leave it.' Yet however he tried to convince himself that it would be a great relief when the whole pretentious fake of the State collapsed and vanished, the thought was inescapable that it would leave him and all the others like him looking rather a shrimpish lot.

He'd read too many newspapers full of news about foreign places he'd never seen, and human interest stories about people who weren't quite human. He'd whittled away his own personal tastes too much so that he could exist as an architect in the movement. He'd read too many books he didn't want to read because he'd been told they were the thing to read. He'd modified and toned himself down all the way round the clock to fit in, to pass, to be accepted. There wasn't much of a man left up there in the puppet loft to be a man when it came to it. If those strikers did the damage that the papers said they were going to do he'd be left with nothing apart from his professional failure, nothing in the world. Well, that wasn't true, he'd still be an adult male, and he could fool himself that he was something like a god by diving into Anne or Margery's devotion and wallowing in that.

He turned his face down to Anne's to kiss her and found her watching him with open eyes, waiting for him to come back.

'You've been away a long time.'

'I must have dozed off for a moment.'

'No, you left me. You went away somewhere and you didn't take me with you. It frightens me when you leave me like that. You aren't tired of me already – are you?'

'Of course I'm not, I love you, and I'll never, never leave you.'

They went up to bed and the dark of night settled round the mill as the last logs burnt out on the hearth.

The roar of the water going over the dam woke Jeanette towards one in the morning, and once she was awake the excitement of the new place kept her awake. She wrapped herself in her familiar eiderdown quilt from London and sat on the wide window ledge of her room looking out into the darkness.

She heard nothing at first but the roar of the falling water, then she began to hear other sounds through it, a faint quacking of wild duck among the reeds and the strident call of a night bird she didn't know. The sky was filled with stars which seemed brighter than she had ever seen them before, and she had never before, that she could remember, seen stars reflecting in water.

It was so different from Penharrad House, soft, gentle, and happy, that she couldn't understand it or believe it. And Aunt Anne, who ought to have been a wicked stepmother or a false friend from a fairy story was nice, nicer than any woman she'd ever met. Nicer almost than mummy. And mummy was nicer here, somehow, than she had been at Penharrad House, or at home.

It was impossible to make out what had happened, impossible.

An owl, a darker shadow in the starlit murk, drifted along the reedbed and swooped up to alight on the roof ridge of the kitchen just under Jeanette's window. It sat there for a minute or two turning its head swiftly this way and that as sounds inaudible to any human ear reached it. Presently it opened its wings and slid silently away.

196

Jeanette fell asleep, to wake in nightmare as she began to topple off the window ledge. She was swimming, drowning, in happiness, which was thick, and heavy, like treacle; she struck out for the surface, feeling that her lungs might burst, but she sank down, and down, into the sweetness. A piece of wood drifted past her and she clutched at it.

She found herself half off the window ledge, holding tight on to the window frame.

It was bright day and the ripples ran up the mill pond sparkling like diamonds in the morning sun. She watched their play for a few seconds entranced, then the feeling that she was stiff and cold rose up in her and joined the lingering terror of the dream.

She looked at her cold, deserted bed, and did not want to lie alone there. It was an occasion for snuggling in with mummy or daddy for comfort, a luxury she was occasionally allowed when nightmares or secret miseries woke her from sleep. On the first night in a strange house it would surely be granted her.

She tiptoed out, a funny little bundle wrapped in her patch-work quilt, past her mother's door to her father's: he was sometimes easier to wake, and more understanding.

She opened his door quietly and said 'Daddy' in a small voice.

He did not wake, but Anne did. She lifted her eyelids and saw the girl standing there without fully wakening, she smiled faintly at the absurdity of the quilt cocoon, shut her eyes again and went back to sleep.

Jeanette stood stock still for a few seconds looking at them. They looked like drowned people. Walter's shoulders were bare and he lay on his back with Anne's head cradled on his right arm; her left arm, looking oddly boneless, lay across his chest, her hair was spread in a great glinting pool over the pillow and his head looked richly dark against it.

Jeanette shut the door quietly and slipped back to her own bed, lying there in the cold sheets without warming them, as still and cold as a stone, until the house began to stir and it was time to get up.

The image of the girl in the doorway wrapped round in the quilt sank slowly into Anne's half dreaming, half waking mind, losing its sharpness, its reality, and its colour, until it began to acquire another strength among the unseen images of dreamland. Later in the day she remembered with amusement, as an odd thing, that she had dreamt of Jeanette – as a chessman, a castle, with her head staring out over the battlements and her pink feet peeping out at the foot of the walls. She wondered for a moment what could have made her dream of such a freakish, whimsical appearance and dismissed the thought as of too little importance to be worth bothering with.

14

MARGERY and Walter stood in the kitchen doorway, watching Anne and the children crossing the orchard with pails of mash for the chickens and gruel for the calves. It amazed Walter to see the way in which Anne had conjured a farm into being as a going concern all round them: he had bought some farm books at the bookstore in Lemlade, and was slowly beginning to understand how one set about the business, but he was a long way behind Anne who had bought two cows, a few heifers, some geese, and a hundred fowls, and was feeding them and collecting eggs and milk while he was still puzzling out what a balanced ration was. It seemed to consist of a very precise mixture of substances that they hadn't got and not to have much to do with the bales of hay and the sacks of black market oats which were in the mill building, and still less with the clumping dark red mangolds which had been shovelled out of a tractor trailer into one of the sheds.

'Surely the cows aren't going to eat those dirty great turnips, they're as hard as bricks?' he asked Anne, thinking she'd made a mistake buying them.

'Not till after Christmas, honey, then you'll see them eat 'em up fast enough.'

'What are they going to do till Christmas, then?' he said, picking up one of the mangolds gingerly so as to get as little mud as possible on his hands, and turning it round, eyeing it as if it were a Sung pot.

'Don't you worry about that, I've bought a stand of kale at Benning's farm over on the other side of the river. Good stuff with plenty of leaf on it – and it ought to be, seeing the price I paid for it.'

'Do you really know what you're doing?'

'Of course I do – I ask people and they tell me.' She lifted her voice to carry above the noise of the idling tractor and called to the farm hand shovelling out the roots. 'That's the way to feed cows, isn't it? Kale to Christmas, mangold after till the grass comes on?'

'That's it, ma'm. That'n hay. You can't beat it unless you get a bit of cake. Nowadays 'tis the best you can do.'

Walter listened to him with no pleasure in his voice, hay was high, and he said cike for cake; the ugly sounds jarred on his ear, and it humiliated him to know less about anything, even their own skilled trade, than these barbarians. The man was wrapped in bits of sack meant to save his clothes from the mud on the roots and the threatened rain, so that he looked like a tatter-demalion out of a Breughel picture. Walter threw down the mangold and turned away.

'Why does everything to do with farming seem so dirty and so heavy?'

'You can't get a living out of the ground without getting your hands dirty,' Anne said, 'it's hard at first but it gets easier.'

'Don't you believe it, master,' the farm hand chipped in, 'it don't get any easier. An' if you want to keep them hands of yours white and nice pick another trade.' He held up his own badger paws, calloused, and with the nails black with dirt driven up to the quick by mangold pulling. 'You can't stay nice farming.'

Walter went indoors quickly, sensing mockery in the man's voice. He imagined him in the bar of one of the local pubs getting off some piece of country wisdom 'th' old grey mare's the better horse up to the mill, if you asks me.'

He went across into the mill and began to puzzle away its machinery, finding out how much of it was still alive under the fur of dust which coated it: dredging in a tamer, more civilised dirt for his manhood, and for the feeling that he was superior to the boor – a skilled man, a technician, a man with a brain, not just a white handed passenger.

And in the end he had drifted up to the top floor, here and there on the way looking at a bearing, turning a wheel, and fingering a lever, guessing what the dusty, mysteriously shaped tools were for, settling at last into a dream of making this his workshop and designing room. He stayed there, dreaming, at tree top level, until Margery rang a bell on the kitchen terrace and he knew it was time for lunch. It startled him out of his reverie and he realised that he'd been hiding from his work up there, hiding while the two women carried the day.

The thought recurred to him as he stood beside Margery in the doorway, and he felt jealous of the children because Anne was so much with them, and so happy to show them all the tricks and dodges of animal keeping.

'Where are they all off to now?'

'Anne's teaching them how to feed the calves. They love it. They love every minute of it here. It's wonderful for them.'

'Doesn't it worry you at all – I mean, she seems to run them like everything else round here. Aren't you afraid she'll turn them into muddy little farm brats?'

'Walter! I believe you're jealous of the children – it's too absurd. She's wonderful with them, and for them too – you can't begrudge them the fun they get out of being with her.'

'Oh the hell with it, it isn't that at all.'

He stomped indoors and stood looking round the kitchen, now warm and alive as he had imagined it with Anne in the days when it stood empty. But the murmuring clock, the gleaming china on the dresser, and the glinting pots and pans, all spoke of work and told him that this was Margery's domain.

Outside the animals and the raw earth turned up by the plough announced Anne's domain. The children ran happily between the two. He only had no place in the scheme of things, except as a male animal, the lover of the two queens.

He thought of a bull he'd seen on a farm near Brescia, munching hay with a sort of contented insolence, rakishly crowned with flowers. He could see the trail of hay hanging down below its dark muzzle, being slowly drawn in as it munched away. It was quite happy to be just maleness waiting on call in a shady barn.

Margery came in and stood by the stove, skimming the fat off a chicken soup she was reducing, pouring the spoonfuls into a bowl, intent and apart. He felt idle and purposeless and she was aware of his aimlessness, it was like a bluebottle in the room – an annoyance.

'You know, it worries me a little the way we've been carried by Anne since we came here. She's done far too much for us . . .'

'Oh for god's sake . . . as if I didn't know it.'

'I'm sorry, but it worries me a little.'

'I know, it worries me – but when the strike's over – and things get straightened out, we'll sell the London house and we can pay her back. And I can get my equipment down from the office and I'll start work.'

Margery was silent for a little too long.

'I don't know anything about these affairs but – judging by what they say on the radio things are going to be pretty bad when the strike does end – do you think a country district like this is going to give an architect much business in a slump? Apart from anything else you'll be a stranger . . .' Her interest in her work became a little theatrical, there was too great a deliberation in the way she did not lift her head and look towards him. 'I don't mean to be horrid, but . . . well, we've got to think about all that sooner or later.'

'You aren't,' he said it with the ill-tempered control of someone picking a quarrel, because in this case it would be easier and pleasanter to have a row than to put the facts of the situation into words, 'hinting delicately that I'm Anne's kept man, and that I'd better find a honest livelihood, by any chance?'

'I would say something like that if I hated you and if I was rather a nasty person,' she faced him now and he had to drop his eyes because the tenderness and love in her face exposed the ignoble nature of his words, 'but you know quite well that I love you. All I mean is that the income we used to rely on for our bread and butter isn't going to be worth much from now on, and that it looks as if your professional earnings aren't going to amount to much for a long time to come. . . .'

'Now you're saying I'm a failure.'

'Oh don't be tiresome. You heard the Prime Minister the other night saying that the new towns and all the other projects like that have been shelved indefinitely. He said there wasn't going to be any building up a new Britain, there was going to be a fight to salve something worth having from the wreck – I don't see a private architect making money out of that situation . . .'

'He was just trying to frighten the strikers back to work.'

'Oh, Walter you're hopeless . . . you know all I'm saying

really, I can tell by the way you listen to me. You know that when you left me for Anne in the first place you were kicking your old professional life to pieces. The mill's something quite new and quite apart – it's no use hanging about dreaming that your old life is going to reassemble itself and come after you.' She shook his sleeve gently. 'Wake up, darling, and come and live with us, it's nice here – it really is.'

'For Pete's sake . . .' he twitched away and went off into the mill house, slamming the kitchen door behind him.

He stole through into the mill presently, and spent the rest of the morning brooding over the silent, dust-swaddled, machinery. At the end of the week they all had the idea, he was cleaning up in the mill and getting everything in running order, greased, oiled, and trim. The children began to be excited about the thought of seeing the great wheel turn under the foaming weight of water from behind the dam.

'We'll be able to have our own electricity,' said Francis, 'we won't have to bother about the current being switched off except for an hour in the evening.'

'We could crush oats, and grind up meal for the farmers round about,' said Anne, 'they'll be glad of it if things go on as they are. I'll talk to one or two and see what they think.'

'It's early yet,' said Walter, 'it's a long job. The plant's been idle for years.'

He did not look up as he spoke, and Margery and Anne both looked quickly at him, then simultaneously introduced fresh subjects. Walter noticed and winced. Damn it all, a mill is a complicated affair, it takes a bit of mastering, it's not as if it was just a question of finding a lever and pulling it to set the place working.

Anne dropped her conversational diversion, and let Margery talk, wondering as she listened why she couldn't bring herself to tell Walter about her father's farm. Even now she was completely back in that world she was still afraid of calling up ghosts from that particular place and time. She felt that it might make it much easier for Walter to lean on her if he knew that she had been bred to the work, and didn't think that she'd performed some miracle of adaptation. She had grown to mastery of a way of life by living it for sixteen years, acquiring its techniques and skills unconsciously day by day; she couldn't understand why it made Walter sick and ashamed that he couldn't step in and lift that mastery as if it was a ready made coat in a few days.

She looked lovingly at him, wondering what made him so desperate, so greedy, and so ashamed of unimportant things. He felt her eyes on him and was sure that he was being despised, 'by god I'll have that mill rolling before the end of the month . . .'

But he couldn't do it. He had every part of the mill as clean as new, he had all the moss and dirt off the big wheel, he had the hatches that would close the spillway and send the water running down the conduit on to the wheelhead in working order, but he still hadn't grasped the links between all the parts, and he couldn't find how you put the big wheel, or the various machines in and out of gear. He had nightmares of the water crashing down on to the locked big wheel, stripping it, making matchwood of all its buckets; and of the wheel beginning to spin and transmitting its power on to locked machines and stripping out their gearing. And the bright and clean machines seemed to mock him, because he couldn't tell what, ultimately, they were for, or how one controlled them if one knew that.

He became more and more the curator of a museum, keeping a number of mysterious exhibits in perfect condition in a timeless, lifeless, vacuum.

Once the back of the cleaning up work was broken there wasn't much to do. He sat about with an oil rag and an oil can, watching the motes dance in the sunbeams, ready to start moving about if he heard footsteps on the stairs. The others didn't intrude on him, sensing that it was something he wanted to do alone, waiting to rush in with joyful excitement when the wheel began to turn and a dull rumble announced that the mill was as alive again as the Mill House.

But the waiting ran on, and the water ran on over the spillway with the familiar steady roar.

The leaves on the trees were late changing colour, everyone spoke about the way they held their green until they went a dingy brown with the first frost that finished the flowers and made the dahlias look like boiled cabbage. Then one sunny morning all the trees seemed to have turned yellow overnight, and the air was filled with leaves drifting diagonally to earth.

Hundreds fell into the mill pool and sailed down like golden boats, languidly at first, sliding by the rushes and the lily pads, then racing faster and faster as they neared the spillway, where they were swept down and under, to be transformed into black river silt somewhere far away.

They all ran out after breakfast to catch their twelve happy months. It was a family joke of Margery's and she was happy that Anne knew it too, you have a happy month for every falling leaf you can catch before it touches the ground. They leapt and pounced about in the fresh morning sunshine, delighting in the crisp air of autumn, and soon each had a handful of leaves – the year's happiness, sure and certain.

Francis and Jeanette ran off, bright faced, to see if there was anything on the night lines they had set up at the head of the pool. They believed there was a big pike up there, they had seen a grey shape sliding in the black shadow under the alders and they meant to have him. Margery went indoors to make beds and Anne and Walter were left alone. Walter threw his handful of leaves down with a laugh, and they walked over to the little railed bridge below the mill wheel. Anne let her leaves fall down on to the dry stone channel bed under the wheel, where they rustled and circled in an eddy of wind.

'It'll be funny,' she said, 'when the water comes through this way, over the wheel – we'll be living in a house with a stream running through the middle of it . . .'

'It'll look pretty from here.'

'When's it going to happen . . . ?' She didn't look at him, she just watched the circling leaves on the dry stones.

'Next week, or the week after. . . .' He didn't look at her, either, but also watched the leaves dance – in and out, and round about.

'Good.' She touched his hand. 'Two or three of the farmers have said they'll be glad of some grist for winter feed, and it'll be good to have some cash coming in. My money's pretty near gone . . . it didn't last long did it? Still, it got us what we wanted, and we've made a pretty good start.' She straightened up. 'I must get to Bennings after a load of kale – I can't loaf about all morning.'

She went off to harness the horse. He heard the cart go down the lane a quarter of an hour later as he stood with an oil rag in his hand staring at the silent, motionless, hammer mill on the second floor.

When he heard the iron tyres of the tumbril wheels grinding over the gravel again, he came to with a jerk, he was sitting on the flight of stairs leading up to the top floor, not standing up any longer, but he couldn't remember when he'd moved.

All he was sure of was that he hadn't done a thing while she'd been over the river, while she'd cut a square of kale, loaded it, and come back behind the slowly pacing horse. It was no use, he wasn't ever going to get the mill working, it was beyond him, he had to face it, and tell her. He ran down the steps and out through the door into the sunshine.

Anne was just jumping down from the yellow blue pile of kale on the tumbril and a little wizened man with greyish hair was steadying her. They left the horse standing cropping on the grass verge, and came towards Walter. Anne smiling, and the man smirking a little as he touched his hat brim with an uncertain finger.

'Walter, this is Mister Barnard, Dusty Barnard from Jubilee cottages down the lane. They call him Dusty because he always used to be dusty from the mill . . .'

'That's right, mam. Pleased to meet you, Mister Jackson. They isn't much you can tell me about thick yer mill. I worked 'un best part of eighteen years in Mis' Templeman's day – before he shut down in the bad time, thirty-four I think it was, before the war. I'd like to have a p'un' note for every sack I've run through the old mill, I'd be as rich a man as you could wish if I had. I hear you're talkin' of getting the old wheel turning again. So Missus Jackson here tells me.'

'Yes.'

So Anne knew without being told that he couldn't manage the mill on his own.

'Well 'tis good news to me if no one else. I was sorry to see the wheel stop, and I'll be happy to see 'un start again. I likes to see the old things go on, and I likes to see a job o' work done.'

'It'll be a great help to have somebody on hand who knows the ropes. I haven't really tried her out yet. I've just been cleaning up and getting her ready.'

'I expect you've had a job of work.' He spoke with the slightly derisory tone of a professional who has scented an amateur. 'My word, you done a smartish job of tinkering about,' was what he said when he had inspected Walter's clean and gleaming surfaces inside. 'I never seen the place look so much like one of them farm engineer's showrooms in all my time in th' ol' place. Still there's no harm done what I can see.'

He took Walter up to the top floor and showed him how a sack of wheat or oats started down the chutes up there and travelled to floor level undergoing various treatments and becoming one or another kind of feed on the way. 'That one does kibblin; run the wheat through there and you'll get a coarse ground whole meal, they likes it for the poultry and that, you got yer various settin's – that's the one for crushing oats – you don't get oatmeal – it rolls 'em and splits 'em – that way you get a cow food. If yer wantin' oatmeal you runs it through that mill back there, where I was talking about the wheat meal.'

He went back to that mill and pushed a lever which lifted the top half of the machine so that Walter could see the stones.

'They got pretty good faces, yet.' He ran his hands across them, 'You can feel the ridges, see? 't always used to make me laugh back along when they was talkin' about that healthy wholemeal loaf. Doctor Matewson in Lemlade was always on about stone ground wholemeal, said people as ate that stuff wouldn't want no physic to loosen their bowels. Had quite a lot round here eatin' it, and put ol' Templeman in a tidy way of business with "health flour." What'd 'e call un. Templeman's 100% Wholemeal Flour, Guaranteed Stone Ground, and then underneath in curly writin', eyetalic they calls it, or somethin', "Nature's Royal Road To Health and Fitness." Nature's Royal Road Scrapin's more like, and I often told Doctor Matewson what I thought – now you feel them ridges. They're real enough ain't they? You feels em strong and hard under your fingers, eh?

Well run wheat through there for half a year, maybe a deal less if you run five days a week – and them ridges 'll be gone. Those there stones 'll be worn down as smooth as that part of the famous baby. Every six months you can count on having them stones out, then its chip away chip away miller's man ridge up me millstone as quick as yer can. Tweren't quick work neither with a cold chisel and a maul, that stuff was no more kind than charity, hard as granite. Ol' Matewson caught me at it onct, sittin' in the sun out there in front of the mill, when he comes to see Missus Templeman over a new baby or somethin'. "Whatte doin' there, Dusty," he says, "you 'ent settin' up for a sculptor." "No," I says, "I'm a chemist's boy today. I'm fixing to work up some o' that grit you uses to scour out the insides o' your patients with," I says.'

He gave himself up to a silent inward heaving.

'You mean to say we could mill flour here,' asked Walter.

'I daresay you could, though 'tisn't much of a trade fightin' them big mills at the docks – that's what bust Mist' Templeman. The flour mill's on the floor below – there's an art to that one – we used to make a real nice flour if you could get yer mind off the grit in it.'

He rubbed his hand over his face.

'You ent really thinkin' of settin' up for a miller are you, Mist' Jackson?'

'Well, yes – things are bad – transport's all over the shop. I thought a local mill might be quite a sound business proposition.'

'Well, I'm glad to hear it. I warnt sure from what Miss' Jackson said – I thought you might just want to see if the wheel would turn for a curio – or to grind up a few sacks of yer own feed. I'd be glad to give you any help I can.'

'That's very good of you.'

'You got a few bags of oats down below, we might christen the new management by running a few on em through the crusher. What'd'y' say?'

'Fine, that'll be fine.' Walter took the hand which the old man held out to him, and they pumped hands up and down for a few seconds in the excessive formality of rustic bargaining. His genuine thankfulness at having found on his doorstep all the knowledge and knowhow that he lacked, was mixed with another and more powerful feeling – now that the expert had arrived it was clear that all his work in the mill had been the merest fiddling; and it would be clear, when his arrival brought the mill to life as rapidly as the sleeping princess on the arrival of a prince with sense enough to kiss her, to everyone else.

Dusty moved purposefully about the mill rooms for twenty minutes, and although Walter watched him intently and asked several questions as he worked he was aware that he was missing most of the essentials of the old man's craftsmanship. He would, he recognised, be bound to Dusty in a long apprenticeship before he was Jackson the miller or even Jackson who could work the mill.

When the mill wheel at last began to move, under a silver glaze of foaming water, he was standing on the bridge with his arms round the shoulders of his two children, between Anne and Margery – one of the spectators.

The oats began to slide down the feed chute and a deep rumble, a happy sound, filled all their hearts with excitement.

They went inside, and feeling the dry whitish dust which filled the air settling on their tongues and their noses, saw the crushed oats running into a first floor bin. The boards under their feet trembled with the vibration, and the oats ran like a liquid, not like dry stuff at all. The children darted about, asking Dusty this? Dusty that? Dusty how? Dusty led them all down to the bagging platform on the ground floor and showed them how to control the flow, shifting the stream of grist deftly from one outlet to another as the bags filled, deftly tying their necks with a trick knot and getting them swiftly out of the way before the next sack was full.

The ton of oats was through the mill and bagged up in no time at all, less than half an hour. Dusty was delighted.

'You done a good job with that pretty little ol' oil can of yourn,' he said, 'there aren't a hot bearin' as I can find, and the whole outfit seems as sound as ever. I'm doubtful of the inwards of the flour mill, though. What d'y'say I comes up tomorrow and has a proper look at 'un?'

'That would be very kind of you,' Walter tried to keep any hint of bitterness out of his voice.

'You know one thing,' Dusty pushed his cap on to the back of his head and looked seriously at the children. 'When that ol' mill started rumblin' and grindin' and boomin' away I'll bet every rat and mouse for miles away sat on's hunkers and said to hisself "They's workin' Paradise Mill again." An' those that didn't hear un'll get the smell of the grist pretty soon. They'll all be movin' this way presently. How many cats do you have?'

'We have pussy from London,' said Francis.

'One poor London pussy!' Dusty looked very sad, 'he'll be run off un's feet. You mun keep cats if you'm going to keep a mill. One cat by hisself won't have a chance. Now if your ma's agreeable,' he said darting a look at Anne, 'I got a mess of kittens down my place that the old cat's eager to be rid of – they'm just about ready to leave home.'

'Oh, yes, please, we'd love some kittens,' cried the children tugging at Margery's hands. Margery looked to Anne, questioningly.

'Oh, I don't see why not,' she said, smiling at Francis and Jeanette, 'we've got more milk than we know what to do with.'

'Well, then, what d'you two say to coming down to my place after a pair of kittens before dinner, can't be twelve yet. What d'you say, eh?'

'Oh, yes we can, can we please, mummy, please?'

They went off happily, completely captivated by Dusty.

Dusty returned the next day with a canvas bag full of his tools and took over the mill, too.

Now when the children weren't looking after Anne's animals they were in the wonderland of the mill listening to Dusty's talk. Talk streamed from him, pent up in years of living in a tiny cottage with a woman who didn't much interest him and wouldn't be bothered to listen to what he had to say. He bewitched them with anecdotes of another world, so strange to them that it was as if they had encountered True Thomas himself, the traveller who had been off to the homeland of magic.

His first job had been with a blacksmith who had a contract with the county council 'to make them big iron rakes the roadmen used to pull the flints and stones into the cart ruts in the roads.'

He conjured up a strange England in which the railway was

the only familiar thing, with iron tyred horse carts the only
traffic on the roads.

'I remember ol' Mr. Ross up to the Hall, sold a stand of timber
he didn' expec' to some time along ninety-three or ninety-four.
Got a thousand pounds for 't. T'were a windfall and it put him
in mind to have a bit of fun.'

'Anyroad the cheque came from the timber merchants one
breakfas' time, and before noon Mr. Ross was off for London in
his smartest suit, with a camelia in his buttonhole, and his flat
topped hard hat, like a bowler hat, only fawn coloured and with
a style to un, jammed down over his eyes, and a little manila
cigar on the go.

' "Expec' me when you sees me," he says to the coachman who
took un to the station and the train goes out.

'Nobody sees or hears ought of him for ten days, then I'm out
up the Swindon road, takin' a pair of horses that'd been new shod
back to Stacey's Barton, and I comes up with Benson the carrier
comin' the other way, 'e cracks his whip cheerful like: "Watcher,
Edwin me boy, the conquerin' hero's back again," he says, "look
in over the cart tail, and you'll see a sight worth seein'." '

'Well there 'e was – Mister Ross, in all his glory, his hat gone,
his trousers split at the knees, some shabby no good had switched
coats with him, and he was dead to the world, stretched out on
a bundle of straw with his legs swinging down over the back
of the cart.

'It turned out some London gal had put him on the Swindon
train the night previous, she bought his ticket, he hadn' a copper
left in his pockets.

'One of the Swindon porters recognised him and got the
carrier to take him home. Gaw, I thinks, there's the gentry goin'
home, and I lifts me hat properly respec'ful.'

He ran on and the children listened, entranced by these
glimpses of the adult world and by the picture of a sunlit rural
landscape behind it. It was a world of abundant delights as well
as of strange characters.

Dusty transformed a hard winter which had settled down when
the riverside meadows were flooded, into a wonderful thing of
skating on limitless expanses of ice, hissing across a mirrorlike

surface, day after day, down the valley as far as Oxford and back again. He filled their dreaming eyes with the vision of a wonderful night spree, with hundreds of skaters twirling and waltzing to the music of the best silver band in the district by the light of a bonfire which consumed eight waggon loads of faggots during the evening.

Then there was the whole day's journey southwards over the downs to the Marlborough Mop Fair, a journey made by a dozen smart young chaps in a horse drawn brake with their instruments, and a banner saying 'The Thameshead Aeolian Society Silver Band.' Dusty with his cornet the smartest of them all – 'I could ring tears even from judges at the band contests with that cornet.'

And there were the Cotswold fairs to the north, some of them running to two and three day sprees. 'A day o' business, selling the fresh broken horses, or the sheep, or the fat stock, or whatever you taken up ther', and a day of dancin' and fun to round off. Them was rare times, and I had the cream on 'em till I fell foul of Mister Ross.'

'What happened, Mr. Dusty?' said Francis. 'Did you fight him?'

'With me hands tied behind me back. 'Twas getting along towards Christmas time, and I was a bit short of money.

'Well, I knew where a good many pheasants roosted in the woods back of my place and I had the thought that a bag of pheasants, ten or twelve brace on em would be just as good as money if I took 'em into Swindon. The thought took a hold of me and presently I were out there with a bag and it was fillin' up nicely with birds when I was caught.

'They took me up before a magistrate for poachin'. I'd never been caught before. I'd never been up in front of the beaks, never, not for being drunk or fightin' nor nothin'.

'The beak sittin' up there lookin' at me like some sort of ullage, like I was somethin' raw and sour, was that same Mister Ross I seen on the cart tail that mornin' a year or two back.

' "Young man," he says, "this is a clear case and you deserve to see the inside of the county jail. I'm strongly minded to send you there since I hear most unfavourable reports on 'ee." He natters on, about how I don't seem to stick at nothing, how I'm always trapisin off to fairs and such, and how I'm gettin' to be a notorious scoundrel.

' "I'll give ee one las' chance," 'e says, "as you're technically a first offender. But I warn ee if I ever see you here in the dock again it'll go hard with thee." I goes home, an I thinks it over for a bit, and the more I thinks of it the more it riles me. After a day or two I'd got so worked up about it I decided I'd go an' tell the old rip what I thought on 'im.

'I waited outside his mansion for the best part of a morning, then when he comes strolling out I goes strollin' up to him and asks if I could have a word with him.

' "I've got no work for you," he says sharpish.

' " 'Taint work I want," I says, "I want to tell ee somethin'. I want to tell 'ee I haven't drunk away hundreds of acres of timber, and I haven't let London women twist me out of money that the roof of me own house is crying out for, nor let dozens of farms moulder away for lack o' paint and repairs, and no man's seen me boozed silly riding home on the tail of no carrier's cart. And I'm tellin' you," I says, "that you ain't in no position to call anybody a notorious scoundrel."

' "You're asking for a touch of the whip you young lout," he says squintin' at me sort of ugly, "but there's other ways of dealing with your kind."

'I knew what he meant, the old brute, he'd had quite a few boys with a bit of spirit run out of the district – he'd tell his tenants not to employ' em and if they found a house and job near at hand on another estate he'd tip the landlord the wink, tell him he'd got a notorious troublemaker on the place, an' that did the trick.

'I could laugh at 'un because I'd already been into Swindon to sign articles with a Captain Manning who was recruitin' skilled men for a venture he was startin' up in Patagonia.

'I was there seventeen years, tamin' and breakin' horses, helpin' ship them all over the world. . . .'

He paused for a moment gathering his memories of another life, and then took the children across the Atlantic to take part in wilder adventures. His Spanish second language returned to him, and its richness filled the mill and stirred the hearts of his listeners. His silver cornet rang out loud and clear singing through his repertory of bland Victorian ballad music 'I dreamt that I dwelt in Marble Halls', 'The Minstrel Boy to the Wars was gone.'

The music stole out of the mill and echoed out across the South American plains. Francis heard it with half-closed eyes, imagining it travelling off in the twilight, he thought of Patagonia so far under the curve of the world as in perpetual half light, across the paddocks filled with wild, unbroken horses, which flung up their heads to listen to the unfamiliar voice.

'They were men out there,' said Dusty. 'Real men. There's always men where you get Spaniards, they've got a proper pride.'

He whipped off the mouthpiece of the cornet. 'If that there Ross had been a Spaniard he'd of killed me for talking to him like that. And I would have gone round for no argy bargy with him neither. I'd have gone round to kill him. We're more like pet pussies than men in this country, we don't know what pride is.'

'Did you ever kill a man?' asked Jeanette, drawing a grass stem from between her teeth.

'You don't want to trouble about what I done or 'ent done,' said Dusty.

He looked at her, suddenly embarrassed by her sex and her curiosity, remembering she was a person and not just a listening ear. ' 'Spect I've talked too much already.' Then he saw Francis sitting watching him with the wide, open, defenceless look of an enthralled child and he was aware of the absolute difference between the boy and his sister.

'It's true what I tells you about them Spaniards,' he said. 'A man's got to have something in himself he respec's no matter what. When you're beat out and in rags, when you 'ent got a penny nor a hope you got to be able to talk with the grandest, like you was their equal. You got to think of yourself as a cabellero, a horseman ridin' by stiff and proud across your life. You want to tek good care you don't go through life on the cadge, Master Francis, some men got an idea they 'ent men unless they can get women to give 'em something. . . ."

Jeanette sniggered with a suddenly hot face, and Francis

looked at her wondering a little, conscious of the loneliness he felt more and more often when he was with her.

'You'm a knowin' little piece ent you?' said Dusty and laughed, winking at Francis. 'Girls is all right until they becomes women, then they gets foolish. That's another thing you wants to remember.'

'It isn't true, it isn't true, it isn't true,' cried Jeanette, 'we know all the important things that silly old men never guess at. . . .' She ran out of the shadowy mill through the sunlit doorway.

Dusty rolled himself a cigarette silently as Francis watched him, and behind him the motes danced in a shaft of daylight.

'What did she mean, Mister Barnard?'

'She meant more women remembers they're women than men remembers they're men.'

He drew on the cigarette and blew thick coils of grey smoke into the shaft of sunlight and watched them lie there on the draught until they lifted and disintegrated.

'You can't go and grab anything up anywhere in the world that'll make you more of a man than what you are. Mister bloomin' Ross talkin' to me in court dishonoured me because I was a soft sort of man. I thought he'd properly shamed me and I ran off to Patagonia to hide myself if the truth be told. But he hadn't no power to take nothing away from me, and I weren't any more of a man for travellin' three thousand miles. But it was worth it in the end 'cause of what them Spaniards taught me.'

He paused and looked at Francis.

'You don't understand what I'm saying, do you?'

'Not really,' said Francis. 'Tell me more about Patagonia. I could understand about the horses, and the round ups, and the horsebreaking.'

'Another time. Me mind's running on man-breaking at the moment.'

He sat quietly polishing the silver cornet for a few moments.

'There's an owl's nest in the roof,' said Francis.

'Always has been ever since I known the mill,' said Dusty. He took up the cornet and launched into 'My Heart's in the Highlands.'

Walter appeared in the doorway grimacing at the noise. He

was tired out with bicycling round the neighbourhood drumming for custom for the mill. Everywhere they had been suspicious of him as a miller, and everywhere he had been forced to say that the mill was being worked by Dusty Barnard. Then they said 'Oh, yes, Dusty knows the old mill like you know the back of your hand.' After that they thawed out and confessed they'd heard the mill was being opened by a London man – 'an artist or an architect or some such' – and of course they'd been reluctant to send corn to a miller without any sort of feeling for the job, or qualifications for it. 'But if Dusty's there! Well, there's no more to be said.'

He looked across the mill floor with loathing.

'For Pete's sake I can't hear myself think . . .'

The tune broke off as his lips moved. 'That's better. There are three loads of corn coming in tomorrow from Watchett's, Cummin's, and Benson's at Kelmscott. They reckon to have them here before ten. They want the meal before midweek. Here are the details.'

He tore a sheet of paper out of his notebook and handed it to Dusty.

'That's all right with you, isn't it? You'll be able to manage by yourself won't you – I've got to do a fencing job tomorrow morning. Those blood-damned heifers have knocked that fence down at the bottom of four acre again. But you'll get along, won't you, Barnard?'

Dusty took the sheet of instructions and read the front of it before giving the blank back a steady look; Francis held his breath because he knew there was something wrong – Dusty seemed to have become wooden in his clothes, a hard and hostile automaton.

'I expect I'll be able to manage, Jackson,' he said thoughtfully, giving the remark an unaccented, unstressed delivery that brought it right home. Francis saw his father change colour, and saw one of his arms jerk in a brief involuntary nervous reaction.

'Well, come along, Francis, or we'll be late for tea,' Walter said, riding it. 'I leave you to run things your own way in the morning, Mister Barnard.'

He went out of the mill without a second's delay and for a

space neither Francis nor Dusty moved. Then the man patted the boy on the shoulder and sent him off. 'Run along or you'll be late for that tea.'

'Can I come along and help you tomorrow, Mr. Dusty?' asked Francis.

'Yes, you come along, and I'll teach you the proper knot for tying a bag of grain, you'll be a help I daresay. Now you run and catch up your father.'

He was learning the knot the next morning when Walter was down in four acre driving fence posts and nailing ash poles to them to make a fence.

The old wire was as rotten as string, and there was nothing to be done with it but fling it into the hedge out of the way. The ash poles had to be cut out of the hedge timber; Walter felt he was doing wrong in using green wood on any sort of work, and he had an idea that the ash was not the best of woods for fencing. He had some recollection that its period of life in the open without treatment was short.

He was suspicious of the fence posts too. He'd found them, ready cut and pointed up, stacked in the old cart house at the back of the mill, and had been grateful. But now as he drove them into the ground with the applewood mallet he wasn't at all sure about them. They had a tendency to split, and cushion out, under the blows of the pightle, and one or two of them split when he nailed the fence poles to them.

As he neared the end of the job he began to feel that he was clobbering up a patch that would hold the gap for eighteen months or two years at the outside, then the work would have to be done all over – and probably with indifferent materials again.

He drove another post rather enjoying the sensation of hitting its top so that the flat face of the wooden headed pightle struck it true, feeling he was doing it pretty well. One more tap and it would be home. The mallet hit the outside inch of the post top and it split to ground level. The sudden appearance of the clean white splinter was startling as a scream.

Walter set the mallet head on the ground and resting himself easily on its handle swore for a full minute.

'That's fancy language.'

The voice came from just behind him on the other side of the hedge. A corduroyed man looking like a game keeper stood there with a gun over his arm watching him. His gun dog worked along the hedge.

'The post split . . .'

'You're using poplar wood, by the look of it – it's all right for making matches – it's no use for anything else that I've ever heard of.'

'I know it's the wrong stuff, but it's all I could lay my hands on at short notice.'

He felt about for something that would keep the man talking to him. 'Are you having much sport?'

'I had a couple of duck up the stream . . . are you the new man at the mill?'

'Yes, my name's Jackson, Walter Jackson.'

'Glad to meet you. My name's Ross, Charles Ross.'

They shook hands over the fence.

'How do you like it at the mill? When the Templemans were my tenants they were always complaining about this and that, but it seemed a pretty decent sort of place to me.'

'Oh, you used to own the mill did you?'

'Yes. Last bit of the old estate left. And I'm damn glad to have it off my hands to tell the truth. I'd been trying to sell it for years. I believe my father was hawking it about for a long time too – we used to own all this parish and most of the next – all I've got now is the shooting rights over a few farms, and believe me I'm a sight better off. There's no curse like a landed estate these days.'

'Then you're not my neighbour – I thought perhaps you farmed this next piece of land.'

'Oh, no – I gave up work years ago. Found it didn't agree with me . . . I live over there . . . about four hundred yards beyond that clump of trees. Come along and have a drink and a bit of a yarn some time. I'm generally not far off.'

'I'd be glad to.'

'Well, drop in when you feel like it, or the weather's bad or something . . . I'll be getting on.'

He pushed two fingers up to his hat brim and went off up the hedgerow in the wake of the questing dog.

The fencing was soon finished and Walter flung unused posts, poles, the pightle and the can of nails up on to the cart, clucked to the horse, and sauntered home.

The autumn rains had saturated the ground and as the weight of horse and man bore on the crowns of the narrow plough lands which ridged the fields water oozed on to the surface in a circle a few paces round about. By Christmas, if the rains held, the farm would be a sea of mud.

The trails of kale and hay which were spread across the pastures for the out-wintering young stock were already marked by belts of poached ground where the animals had stood and jostled about. A third of the kale and a good deal of the hay was being wasted, trodden into the gumbo before it was eaten.

It all looked sordid, disgusting, wasteful and inefficient.

Presently Anne would be pestering him to clobber up racks for the hay, so that the animals could pull it out without walking over it and trampling it into the dirt. It might be a good idea to forestall her by getting the racks made first.

He figured out a way of fixing racks under a roof on the bed of an old waggon, then they could feed two or three days' hay at a time and still have it out of the mud and out of the rain. But the steady squelching and oozing underfoot made him think that the racks. would be surrounded by such a wallow if they were left in the same place for a day, let alone two days, that there wouldn't be any point to it. Well, let Anne think up something, if she wanted to.

He came through the gate into the home pasture and as usual the geese made a demonstration in force against the horse, advancing with their heads aligned like the legs of a beauty chorus, hissing in mock fury. They moved Walter to the pitch of heaving clods of earth at them – it was so utterly silly. Every time you came into the field with the horse in the cart there was this frightful fuss and outcry. Fifteen minutes later, when the horse was out of the shafts and out of harness, they wouldn't even look up when he was turned into the fields.

One of Walter's clods hit the chest of the leading goose,

knocking him off his feet: he collapsed into an ungainly flounder, beating the ground with his wings. The flying wedge broke up, and the other geese grouped, hissing indignantly, about the casualty.

'Perhaps that'll teach you a lesson, you bloody fools,' said Walter, red faced and a little scared that he might have damaged or maimed the goose.

He hated the geese for their idiotic hostility towards the horse-plus-cart, and was determined to teach them to abandon it. The stricken goose suddenly found its feet again, and staggered off to join the others in their protest meeting, apparently all right.

Walter went on through a clump of alders and came in sight of the orchard.

Anne was up a ladder picking the last apples, and the children were sorting the fruit and grading it into storage trays on the ground beneath her. Margery was taking in some washing off the line. Dusty – Mister Barnard, thought Walter bitterly – was kneeling above the mill dam clearing the metal grille that kept dead leaves and sticks from being swept down on to the wheel. A busy little crowd, a mob, a horde of greedy emotional dependants waiting for the chance to make more demands . . . he suddenly thought of Ross's offer of hospitality in the house out of sight beyond the trees.

He decided not to say anything about it – it might be very pleasant to have a place to go that none of these people knew anything about, where he could be out of sight, out of mind, and unloved.

15

WALTER found Charles Ross's house easily enough, standing in the small decayed remnants of a park and an overgrown formal garden, just where he had been told it would be.

All the same he was taken by surprise.

The butt end of an avenue led up to the house; sixteen huge oaks, twelve of them deadfalls, in two lines of eight, faced each other across a tumbled sea of intertwined blackberry vines. Out of the blackberries reared gateposts crowned with huge urns loaded with fruit and flowers, and the upper parts of an elaborate screen of iron gates, some of which had been forced off their hinges by the exuberant growth of the bushes, and were now supported by them at tipsy angles. That approach was impassable.

Walter worked round to the right under the dark shade of a dense thicket of Portugal laurel forty feet high, until he came at last to a moss covered path, marked only by a few bicycle tracks, which led him inwards.

This was the entry through the formal gardens. Walter knew he was in a formal garden when the path swerved to one side and made a detour round a moss covered statue of a woman holding an urn which lay like a fallen tree across the direct route.

The woman had been naked but was now clothed in a skin tight suit of green moss, of chemical brilliance, which suggested something between a very lush velvet and a very delicate close growing fur.

A few paces farther on the path went up a flight of steps that had been split and fractured by seedling sycamores and ashes whose grey muscular fingers were still tearing the masonry apart.

Among the wild plants and the self sown trees a few tough survivors of the old garden fought on; Walter recognised a bay tree, towering up some twenty five feet above him, and saw at its base, half overgrown with bark, two bands of hoop iron. He stared for a second and then realised that the splendid dark green tower had once been a poor clipped thing carried about in a wooden tub, set out for the summer, and taken to hide from the frost in winter. It had been left out to fend for itself, and instead of perishing miserably had driven its roots down through the bottom of its tub to tap the rich blood of the earth for its nourishment.

He passed on and came to an open space, covered with rank grass and here and there a degenerate rose bush, grazed by a couple of tethered goats. Beyond this, the house.

The east wing was a reasonable eighteenth century building, well proportioned and level headed. The main block was an argument between an inaccurate memory of Indian architecture, and the colourful Victorian perception of the later Renaissance in north Italy. The west wing was a verdict in favour of the Renaissance, a huge ballroom which filled Walter with an uneasy sense that he had sometimes – of having heard a remark before, or seen a face before, in a dream. He could have sworn that he had seen that façade somewhere else. . . .

It came to him at last with a rush – these were the top two floors of the Palazzo Rezzonico in Venice, detail for detail. And very queer they looked, too, with the bottom story shorn off and replaced by a mingy parapeted terrace; not a pane of glass left, the window frames out, the light inside showing that the roof was gone.

There was a steady tapping from within this shell which excited Walter's curiosity. He went forward, giving the goats a wide berth, to find out what it was.

Ross was on his knees in the ballroom chipping away at the parquet floor, already half gone. He was throwing the parquet slabs into a sack as he lifted them. He looked up and saw that he had a visitor.

'Oh, hallo, I'm just getting a bit of firing. I'll be done in a minute. Hang on.'

Walter saw mosaic pomegranate bushes, laid into a gilt background, on the walls; saw a fantastic fireplace supported at each side by not quite life sized naked women with butterfly wings, looking grotesque cut from carrara marble, their hands folded modestly over their plump breasts.

Ivy, elder bushes, willow herb, and ragwort had already found a footing on the upper parts of the walls.

'What a fantastic place. . . .'

'Grandfather built it for my father's twenty-firster – not bad as a gesture of paternal pride was it?'

'Magnificent I should say.'

'Well I daresay you could, in your detached position. The fact is, though, old man, that it didn't quite come off – as you see . . . not that I'm ungrateful for these nicely shaped slabs of oak, which fit into my stove a treat.'

'What went wrong, or is it rude to ask?'

'It's rude, but there, I'm garrulous.

'Grandfather mortgaged what little of the place was left unmortgaged to pay for the thing and for a colossal party for my father's coming of age. God alone knows what he did but something happened at that party and father had to go abroad. He got to like it, too, and he didn't come back till grandfather had a stroke. That was eight years before he died. Father had been abroad forty years all but six months then . . . there's nothing quite like family life in Britain, I always say, it's what made the British Empire so far flung. I mean it seems perfectly natural about Australia being the place to go, doesn't it – it's as far as you can get . . .'

'You've got something there . . .' he was puzzled about one thing. 'What happened to the roof? I should have thought it would be down here, but it seems to have just vanished.'

'Oh, that. Well you see when the onion dome on the main block – a lousy thing, half Indian, half Russian Orthodox, like the Brighton Pavilion up to a point – fell in in 1943 or 44, building materials were pretty scarce so I sold the lead and the timber off those roofs.

'There was a clever little fellow in the squadron who had an understanding with a building firm. He sold that stuff to them like a fox taking chickens. They were doing flying-bomb repair work.

' "I've got what you want!" he said, "imported timber, real good stuff, Oregon pine, I think, matured, been under a roof since before the war – are you keen?" The buyer was keen too –

I had a couple of pretty good parties and a lot of good times out of those roofs. Well there we are, this sackful'll hold my little stove for a day or two. Come along to the bar.'

He swung the sack up onto his shoulder and led the way off through a doorway into the main block.

The floors were out and the roof was off there too, the only fittings left were the mid-Victorian French fireplaces, and the huge main staircase of white marble, flaked and pitted by exposure to frost, which swept up to the first floor in a double flight. Heavy brocaded wallpapers hung in tatters from some of the walls. Leaves rotted into earth mould on the stone flags of the ground floor rooms where they had been drifted in by the wind: Ross showed Walter round as if the place was in the state in which he had first known it.

'That's the billiard room. Full sized table. Landseer over there on the wall, highland scene with dogs being noble at the edge of a brook. There were two big silver candlesticks over on the table by the window – used to fascinate me – Highlanders chasing Indians round palm trees, place for the candles up in the top of the palm tree – something to do with the Mutiny or Lucknow or something. This was grandfather's room, fancy I can still smell cheroots in it sometimes, had a lot of Ettys on the walls mixed up with hunting scenes. Hell of a mixture, busts, glistening thighs, dogs, horses, and foxes. Father took a high puritan line about it, but he used to buy Tuke.'

They went through another empty doorway into the drawing-room.

'Father made it over – had out all the old brown mahogany and horsehair, had it redone – all grey and pink in the French manner, and six Tukes. Smashing boys bathing in the buff, pink bodies and green sea, hot as Etty in another line. I thought they were worth something, the old man paid enough for them, but it was all I could do to raise a fiver apiece for 'em – tricky business selling oil paintings. I believe I made an ass of myself on that deal.'

He paused and threw his head back calling 'Oh, Charles, Charles, hallo Charlie.'

He pointed upwards.

'I was born in that room up there, the one with the fireplace that looks like brawn – look there's Charlie.'

A white owl appeared in the fireplace, blinking at them with enormous eyes, hissing irritably, ordering them out.

'He thinks he owns the damn place. You shut up, Charlie, you can have it when I'm gone, but you'll have to share it with me till then.'

The owl hissed as intransigently as ever, and went on scolding them until they went through a dark corridor into the old part of the house.

'Why the hell they ever wanted more than this I can't think. You'ld suppose an Emperor could be happy here, he'd have room enough.'

He flung open a pale yellow door.

'Library.'

Walter looked in at an oblong room lined with empty shelves, uncurtained, the shutters half closed, dust thick on the floor.

'A double cube, forty by twenty,' said Ross, 'too poky for grandpaw.'

He shut the door and marched on into an oval, pillared, central hall round which an honour guard of gods, crowned and epauletted with dust, stood white against dark blue niches.

'I tried to sell these dummies, but they're a drug it seems.' Ross scowled at Diana's dusty dingy chiton.

'I'm glad you couldn't,' said Walter, 'it's one of the finest things of its kind I've ever seen. Whoever painted those niches blue was a minor genius, and all that flashing gleaming colour above – it's marvellous – it's the best thing of its kind – after the chapel at Wardour – that I've ever seen.'

'No,' said Ross, 'don't come the man of culture and refinement on me. This stuff is no good. Look at it, the secondhand at second hand – the eighteenth century English architect groggy with admiration for the sixteenth century Italian, thinking the sixteenth century Italian is classical Roman. And the classical Roman behind all that, though the sixteenth century wops weren't onto it, was a phoney, tasteless, rich-bitch, contractor's style meant to put the eye out of the Greeks. You can have it.'

'It's all made of duff material too, compo of one kind and another, the marble's not real marble and the pompous stuff up in the roof is made of exactly the same material as those ruddy wedding cakes you see in shop windows. It would be all right if you could eat it. . . .

'Even the old galoot who built it was a sort of compo man, a stuffed and mounted Roman hero.

'There's a stack of his letters around somewhere in one of the rooms. He called himself the Victor of Chuprassy, he won some footling little brigade show in India, and called himself by that laurelled title ever after.

'Used to write letters to his wife in the third person: Ross never can, nor never will, see the sun set without turning a thought tinged with the deepest affection to that wife and those tender babes so far away, they are ever present in his heart.

'This architecture is fine for that style of writing, and of affection, and of thinking about yourself . . . count me out on that though.'

'There is a whiff of bank architecture about it, I suppose.'

'Architecture for a bank with no funds, old boy. When you think what a bit of spit and muck a man is, and what a yeasty, stinking affair family life is – well damn all this toga-ed up splendour as a silly life. And if you want to argue the toss, do it somewhere else, I can't take it.'

'Well I know it's a lie about life, but it's pretty good fun all the same. Like a leg show, or the ballet, or something like that . . .'

'If you think what a noble piece of work is a man, how like a god, etcetera, when a lot of well trained chicks waggle their legs and bottoms at you I don't. And what I think when they wag the old apparatus at me hasn't anything to do with Corinthian capitals or marble gods in marble drapery. There's only one bit of this building that comes to grips with reality, and that's the can.'

He pushed open a door and went out, leading the way down a stone staircase into a shadowy basement dimly lit through ivy and nettle screened windows sunk in area pits. They were in a long passage which seemed to run the full length of the house.

The roof was festooned with pipes and wires, now useless relics of vain endeavours to modernise the building in the past.

'Here we are, thank god, now we can do a bit of drinking and stop this bloody talking, my throat's as dry as a limekiln. I never met such a fellow as you for talk.'

He showed Walter into a shadowy kitchen where a huge fire was roaring in the stove, filling the room with a pleasant reddish glow. There were a couple of chairs each side of the fire, and in the middle of the room there was a table loaded with dirty plates, the remains of a pie, a couple of cold birds under an old style meat cover, a battered milk can, an oil lamp and several bottles of whiskey. Ross fished about for a cleanish plate and glass, put one of the birds on the plate and handed it to Walter, then put the glass and a bottle of whiskey beside his chair.

'Now you've got food and drink, let's have silence for a bit.'

He fed more of the parquet flooring into the range, adjusted the chimney draught, and sat himself down in the chair opposite Walter with the same provisions.

The pheasants had been roasted to eat cold and were plump too. While Walter was finishing the breast he thought he would probably leave the legs, but when it came to trimming the last of the white meat off the wishbone with his teeth he found that this finicking business had given him fresh appetite. When the legs were gone he undid the top two buttons of his trousers and poured himself another glass of whiskey.

It was dark now and the only light in the room was the red glow from the fire. The room was scented with whiskey and pipe tobacco, the only sounds were small clinkings of their glasses, smaller stirrings in the fire, and an occasional bump or scuffle behind the skirting boards or under the floor as the rats went about their business.

'I begin to like you, Jackson, at first I thought it was going to be jaw, jaw, jaw, when you were around – bad as having a bloody woman on the place.'

'Why did you ask me over?'

'You looked like a killer, cursing out that split post. Gave me a fellow feeling – I suppose.' Ross paused, looking into the fire. 'Were you in the war?'

'Yes.'

'Ever got around to being honest about it?'

'No.' Walter thought for a long time. 'No.'

'I was flying, driving an aircraft, from early on. I began to get worried during the famous Battle of Britain, found I was having the best time I'd ever had in my life. Pace, excitement, it was like the best part of sex lasting for a month. I loved it. I'd get on the tail of a bomber, kill the rear gunner, and then finish the aircraft off. I shouldn't say it, but when those crates dived as flamers or broke up in the air there was nothing like it.

'It was the same with a fighter – better, really – the terms were more level, you were in a more personal relationship with the other fellow. He had the same sort of ship and presumably had the same sort of feelings, and you knew exactly what he felt when his crate started coming apart under the six-gun treatment.

'I caught myself thinking it, clear and open, when I got some poor bastard where I wanted him, "this is it, chum, there's not going to be any more flying for you, you're going down with that thing." I'd feel cheated if I saw the fellow bail out.'

He drank, and thought.

'Let's face it, I enjoyed killing those bastards. First time I ever let go with the full armament of a Spit I had the biggest thrill I ever had in my life, I thought, by god, I'll be letting that go in earnest – and I couldn't wait.

'I had to go in for all that RAF stuff about the dim view, and the bit of a party, and being scared, and going for a Burton, and being permanently grounded, and pretending to take a poor view of bloody mindedness.

'But it didn't come natural.

'And when the rockets came in. I wasn't happy about them at first, they looked so bloody messy on the aircraft, but soon after they came in we had to shoot up a building in the Le Mans neighbourhood, and the way that elegant white house came apart convinced me. After that I was for rockets.

'After V.E. day, the only thing wrong with war for me was the long spells of boredom between killings.

'I was brought up on books like *All Quiet on the Western Front*, and *Her Privates We*, and Barbusse and all that stuff, Hemingway's

228

doctor getting the nurse into the family way and doing a bunk into neutral Switzerland was my war hero. And here I was having the hell of a good time.

'I worked hard on being glad the Germans had folded up, but that surrender announcement was as hard to take as being told that sex had been abolished as from today. The only hope was getting out into the Pacific theatre quick, but that folded before I could get into it, and they handed me a bowler before I could turn round.

'I had a nervous breakdown, had to get into one of those godawful rehabilitation centres and get worked over by a psychiatrist.

'I used to wrestle with that damned fool daily, he'd tell me I felt guilt about the fellows I'd killed, and ask me if I'd ever killed any puppy or kitten or anything when I was a kid that had shocked me. I told him my father gave me a gun when I was six and gave me half a crown for every flying bird I killed with it in the next two years.

'I kept telling him my problem is having guilt about not having guilt.

'He gave me all the clippings on the Neville Heath murders and asked for my reaction. I said you've got me wrong, what I like is killing men in combat conditions.

'He said what do you like doing with women, don't you ever have any phantasies of that kind? I said I didn't dream of food when I had a full stomach. He said, what did I do with women, so I told him. Then he said, ah, your relationships are fundamentally fugitive, unsatisfactory affairs. I said they're free from slop, and they don't lead me into a love nest full of nappies and squalling babies, all I want from a girl is a damned good wriggle and a lot of laughs.

'He kept on trying to crack me like I was a message in code, looking for that unhappy childhood, those frustrations, the adolescent shock. We traced everything as far back as we could and all we dug up was Maisie Walgren, the keeper's daughter, who used to live with her father in Black Tom Wood.

'Maisie gave me the first good wriggle and the first lot of laughs.

'I came down here and dug her up, she's a fat married woman out Swindon way, and I said "do you remember anything queer about us? Were we ever caught or anything? Was I shy or ashamed of anything?"

'She said: "Lord no, you was as cheerful a little cocksparrow as I ever wish to meet, Mister Ross, you was always cheery at it, and grateful for it; proper polite and kind at the right time and proper manly at the right time. You gave me me first you know."

' "Crickey," I said, "I never knew."

' "No," she said, "nor didn't nobody else except me husband. 'Twouldn't have been fair not to tell him. Howsomever he was keen on me and agreeable to take the baby, you was away at school at the time, and least said soonest mended I thought. My hubby was quite proud of the little fellow, said you could see the old squire's blood all through him. He's done very well for himself in the electrical trade since the war. We all looks up to him."

'Like a fool I told the psychiatrist all about it, he was delighted, said he'd unearthed the secret well-spring of guilt.

' "I never knew a thing about it," I said.

' "Ah," he said, " ah, my friend, the psyche knows more than it tells the conscious mind!"

' Before I knew what I was at he had me under deep narcosis, and when I came to my nerves were shot to pieces, my appetite was gone, and in a few months I was in the thick of the only unhappy love affair I've ever had in my life. Knocked me endways.

'When I snapped out of it I beat it down here, and I've been living here like a bloody fox ever since.'

He swallowed down some whiskey. Walter tried hard to recover what he had thought at times in North Africa and Italy: grinding along on tracks was rather different from sweeping through the air at three or four hundred miles an hour – but there had been moments. Ross spun the liquor in his glass and went on talking.

'I could kill that bloody psychiatrist any day of the week. When my great romance blew up in my face I went back to my favourite playmate, the nicest, most beautiful girl you ever saw, a damn good wriggle, good for more laughs than anyone else I ever played around with. When I went to her for the old treatment all I wanted to do was cry. I wish to god I'd never let that bastard mess around with me. I wish I was still an honest-to-god killer. Why the hell can't they let a man alone, to be the way he is?'

'The pursuit of happiness you've got to go for it, security you've got to want it, the four freedoms; you've got to enjoy them,' said Walter feeling pleasantly muzzy. 'There's no place in society for a man like you.'

He considered it.

'If you can't fit into the welfare state you've got to have your odd corners ironed out. If you don't want to be happy, stands to reason you're abnormal. And then there's the democratic view – greatest good of the greatest number – you've got to make compromises.'

'Up the alley with your compromises. Take a farmyard: the hens will outvote the others, they'll vote hen happiness and hen welfare. What's to become of the horses, the cows, the pigs, and cocks come to that. It's all a crock of the well-known article.'

He spat onto the hob of the stove and the little gob of spittle hissed and vanished.

'Happiness lasts as long as that, you can't plan for it or arrange it. It's different for everybody. For me it was in tension and excitement, in killing, and in getting a woman. I'd be a liar if I ever said anything else.'

'I don't know. . . .'

Walter wanted to say that it couldn't be so, that there must be a fallacy in what Ross was saying. But he found himself wondering why he had grabbed at Anne, and why he had thought that a girl passing in the street should have something that would last for him for ever. He wondered too why Anne, and Margery, and the children all uniting in a common effort to find happiness in the wonderful Mill House should make something so hateful that he was already desperate for escape.

This moment of near drunkenness in the firelight was a bliss greater than anything he had recently enjoyed, apart from the actual physical pleasures of sex, and a large part of it was the certainty that no woman was sitting waiting anywhere upstairs in the vast emptiness of the house, and that no woman would come on tiptoe to mess with the dirty plates, get them clean glasses, or badger them with devoted attentions.

He went back to what Ross had said about the war and tried to work out hitherto evaded sections of his own feelings. The desert had been better than Italy. There was no tail and no family life between Alex and Tripoli, just country that might have been made·for having a war in.

If there had been anything incongruous and wrong-looking out there it was the presence of the model Italian colonial settlements, those desperate efforts to force an urban culture that depended on lushness and fertility for its existence to take root on sand and rock. The tanks, the guns, the ugly, lumpish lorries, looked more at home there, they seemed kin with the horned lizards and the warped twisted plants that were natural to the sands and the flaking rocks.

In Italy it had been all wrong, and the machines intruded into an established pattern like a dirty word dropped into drawing-room conversation. Children darted about between the brutal vehicles, fragile and tender skinned. When you looked through a cranny in the wall split by an anti-tank shell, you looked into outraged family life, at a marriage bed with fragments of the plaster ceiling on the covers, at a wedding group cockeyed on the wall, at a crucifix face downwards on the floor among shards of broken china.

And the tail, hoisted up high on top of great cork platform shoes, got all mixed up with the army.

It was better to have it all a long way apart, so you could get away out of the fighting and clean yourself of the smell of death in a woman's body, and then take yourself a long way back and wear off the stink of women among the cold metal parts of Mars.

He tried hard not to think about Naples and Rome in the full splendour of liberation, when half the people in both cities seemed to be living on what they got out of the Allied armies in bed.

He'd get into the vehicle going down for leave thinking good thoughts, about the cultural centres of the ancient world, and about the noble and famous buildings which he as an architect ought to go to see in order to renew his professional strength and virtue. Perhaps it was the way you had to sit bunched up on the hard seats in army vehicles, perhaps it was the way you had to wrap up in thick, heavy clothes to keep out the knifing Italian mountain air in winter, but whatever the reason his thickening blood began to make him itch for sex long before the cities came in sight.

He would climb out, easing his stiff, cramped legs to the ground, saying, you'll walk this off, in a few minutes, it's going to be different this time. This time I'm going to spend my money on buying and sending home some of those marvellous books on architecture they have in the antiquarian booksellers, they've lasted three hundred years and they'll last me my life. This time I'll track down that Andrea Pozzo, and the Vignola. This time I'm going to look at Santa Maria in Trastevere, and San Martino a Monti. This time I'm going to go from sight to sight and I'm not going to look at a bloody woman until I'm out of Rome.

In the first or second church he'd stand wrestling with it, loathing the incense for catching him in the nose like the smell of a woman. He'd suddenly spin round and make for the door, striding down the aisle with his back to the altar, his metalled heels clanking on the marble, heading for the streets crawling with women, the maggots on the body of the army, on the carcass of Rome.

And there was always a woman among them who answered. If you looked you found beauty – of a kind. When you talked you found decency – of a kind. And when you had built up the illusion of pleasure and love you took it to the usual lousy room and smashed it to pieces.

Now he was far enough away from it he could see it. It was self disgust that he had been seeking in the corruption of Rome and Naples. He wanted the disintegration of any noble dream about himself that might have smuggled itself into his mind. The need had always piled up on him in any lull in the fighting, when the Brigade was not being used in the actual business of war but was being reformed and re-equipped, trained to use new techniques, or just rested. When the Brigade was on the move or in business it was different. The need was met in a different way, then. He could call back the map reference of any villa garden, or olive orchard, or a group of buildings, he didn't like the look of, and have it dowsed by time on target from supporting artillery. Or he could get his own close support to take the front off a suspicious looking house. Or he might catch a soft column of enemy transport with its pants down. And when German infantry, so deadly good at their job, when they had the jump on you, so bloody neat and soldierly, even in defeat, came running forward with their hands up, there was no need to accept their surrender.

He remembered the protest that had come his way after that particular incident – 'aren't you getting the least bit bloody-minded, Walter, shooting those chaps, looked pretty bad if you ask me? After all they'd packed it in.'

'Sorry, Jock, but we aren't in that sort of business. If the PBI had been about they could have held their hands, we hadn't time, and they'd probably have changed their minds by the time the PBI arrived. Then we'd have had a rocket for leaving uncleared pockets behind us. You can't stick to girls' rules fighting AFVs, you know.'

That had been another of the rewarding excitements, treading the hair line between being a good officer and a bloody-minded four letter man. Many officers wooed their men with a soppy paternalism, like scoutmasters in a slum settlement. Indeed there was pressure from the war house to make you like that. At O.C.T.U. they talked about democratisation. It was meant to make the Labour Ministers and the T.U.C. happier about the army. But he had decided early on that the soppier you were with the men the soppier they became, and the more resentful; they liked to be let alone. He let them alone, and was as cold as possible in his relations with the sergeants and N.C.O.s, treating them as trained animals of another breed than his own. The only concession he made to them lay in being very good at his job, so that in his only point of contact with them he was beyond challenge.

The unit resented his coldness but knew it could rely on him. And because he let his men alone to be men his conscript unit achieved the morale of an old time regular army formation, they acquired the wiry, independent manliness of the old fashioned Englishman.

It was that achievement which he had to make worthless by being brutal and unnecessarily destructive in action, and privately in the bodies of bought Italian women where he could prove his manhood worthless and the pretensions based on it shams.

The whole basis of his relation with the unit and his grip on it was a fake, and what had given meaning to his life was making it as big a fake as possible.

He thought of the great pillared hall above built by the Victor of Chuprassy and envied him for the power that had enabled him to leave such an enduring monument to conceal his frailty and lack of substance. He would give a lot to trade his vision of Rome for that eighteenth century gentleman's picture of it, perhaps out of the exchange he would gain another vastly more agreeable picture of himself.

'Gentlemen, I give you the Victor of Chuprassy,' he said, raising his glass.

'Chuprassy, and his keg of diamonds,' answered Ross and they drank. 'He brought back about seventy-five thousand pounds worth of diamonds he looted from some rajah's tent after the famous battle. Founded the family fortune on that and some smart dealing with quartermaster stores. He had no problems . . . What do you do about cash, Jackson?'

'I don't know. The mill brings in cigarette money. We live on milk and eggs mostly, and things we grow or raise, we've been running on what we had. The problem hasn't come up, yet. It's going to though.'

'Same here,' Ross put some more wood on the fire. 'I put most of the money I had when I cleared out of London into whiskey, I've got enough here for a couple of years. And I can shoot all I want to eat. But things like sugar and tobacco, and parties, bother me a bit. . . . When you want to get a girl to play you can't get her into a place like this and give her a leg off a bird and a tumbler of whiskey. I've been wondering about financing the odd visit to London.'

He lit a fresh pipe, and his face looked more lively in the flare of the match.

'I was thinking of going into trade,' he said.

'What?' Walter stifled an impulse to laugh. 'Not the best time, with everything rockbound by this strike. . . .'

'I don't mean that sort of trade. . . . I don't know what you've heard, but I've heard all sorts of things that aren't in the Government bulletins. They say there were food riots in Bristol a few days ago. I met some people walking down the Swindon road who'd left Oxford because it was too hard to get to eat there – they'd been turned back outside Swindon by some sort of regional authority which had check points on the roads to put a stop to food scrounging. They'd picked up all sorts of wild stuff on the road about what's happening in London and up north . . . haven't you heard stuff like that?'

'Bar talk in the Carp. Someone in the bar had met a man who'd met a man. That sort of thing. There was a yarn about a scrap between some soldiers who'd been sent down to unload a couple of food ships at the docks and the dockers. And then there was another yarn about some General – Mackinder or some such name – trying to arrest some union leaders – I didn't believe a word of it. But whatever the rights or wrongs of the situation it seems absolutely the wrong moment for setting up as a merchant adventurer. You're a fugitive from the nineteenth century. The common man is here with his uncommon mess. This is the time to lay low.'

'I think you're wrong. If you ask me this is the time for big returns on smart deals, and a lot of fun bringing them off. The whole business of distributing food is gummed up. The docks are gummed up. There's only food in the country for fifty in every hundred people. In the towns they must be frantic.' He drank thoughtfully. 'My bet is they'll give what they've got for food. Anything you ask.'

'Black market stuff?'

'Well . . . I'm no pea-green incorruptible, and if there isn't any white market any more – call it black market if you like, but I'd rather dirty my lilywhite paws than lay me down and die.'

'You could lie low and live.'

236

'It's too tame, the quiet life is not for me.'

He stirred the fire with a poker so that it glowed red between the fire bars, lighting his face more dramatically than the flaring match had done, showing Walter once again his curiously blurred good looks.

He had a fine face, but it had been made of the wrong material; it was a work of art that deserved a bronze eternity, but being of a synthetic plastic material had lost in softness all touch with reality and so deserved nothing.

He thought about the lovely young R.A.F. faces, with clean bone under firm flesh, and the strong hard hands of the good men; and about the way these men were burnt out, so that they abruptly became blurred and soft like this, more pathetic than the used up material of any other service. He did not know any old army men or navy men who radiated this peculiar sense of being cheated, of waking suddenly to find that something was gone. Perhaps it was that they lived so near death in their youth that, when they came to be grounded by middle age and death went off a long way, waiting for it to come again weighed on them more than on those others.

Ross on his side of the fire felt its livelier heat on his face and wondered if he would say anything about the rumour that had reached him that food smugglers feeding the London black market were being shot out of hand, by armed road patrols, and that it was the adventure of risking his neck that was drawing him like a moth to a light.

He remembered moments in London in the last days of terror, when the flying bombs were snoring into the town night and day, moments of wonderful pain when the snoring stopped and there was a dead silence while the machine stalled and dived.

That moment when he was alive from head to toe in the presence of death, so acutely alive that he knew with every muscle, every vein, every nerve in his body what the difference between life and death would be, was what he was going into trade to get. For it he would barter any honour, any dignity, and any reward.

'I'm taking delivery of twenty-five pounds of butter and twenty-five pounds of pork tomorrow, got it off one of the farmers hereabout. I thought I'd make a reccy into Bristol with it and see how it went. If I can make some contacts I'll make a regular thing of it, bigger quantities, too. And if we can work out a system we might try having a crack at London.'

'We?'

'Yes. You and me.' Ross slumped back in his chair. 'Don't come the good citizen over me, please. If you wan't to hand out any of the civic uplift get back to that mudhole I found you cursing in, and curse away. I think this might be a lot more fun than squashing about in gumboots among the mangolds. Take it or leave it.'

Walter considered the ethics of it, and thought, no. Then he thought of mud on his boots, weighing him down, mud on his hands, and on his clothes, the seas of mud spreading round the gateways.

'All right. I'll take it.'

'That's the boy. That calls for a drink.'

They drank to their partnership, to free trade, to brotherly love. Walter fell asleep in his chair. Ross finished his bottle and went and slept on his camp bed in the corner of the room, snoring. The mice came out of their holes and began working on the carcasses of the pheasants on the plates which had been left on the ground by the armchairs.

Anne and Margery lay wakeful in the mill, waiting to hear Walter come in. Dusty had told them that a farm on the other side of the river had been broken into the previous night, by Londoners some said, others said by R.A.F. deserters from stations in the west country making their way to their homes in the north. There were a lot of nondescript bands of people drifting about the country now the bus lines and the railroads were not running, trying to get home, and growing hungry on the way.

16

I T wasn't the last night that the two women lay wondering where Walter was, sometimes they wondered for two or three days at a time.

When he was at the mill Margery had the strange inadequate feeling that had often possessed her when he was on leave during the war. He was stronger and harder than the man she normally lived with, and to a certain extent a stranger.

There was not much to talk about, his interest was in something outside, that had more interest for him than his life with her. The thread of all their private associations was cut by this outside thing, so that their conversation lacked warmth and even material. She would find herself making conversation with him, raising topics and abandoning them one after another as he failed to respond.

There was even a break in their physical relations, so that she seemed to be giving herself to a stranger who did not know her body or her body's rhythms.

That had been the worst thing in their wartime meetings, when they had such a short time together, and they had become, physically, strangers. There was an assumption that they must have been missing that part of each other, and an assumption that it was the quick way to get back to each other, and it wasn't, it was just a demonstration of apartness.

It had been, several times, on the tip of her tongue to say, 'Look here, this isn't the important thing for me – you don't have to . . . if you don't want to. . . .' And then there was the impossibility of saying that it wasn't important. There was, she guessed, probably nothing more wounding to the male self-esteem, than that statement. She suspected it to be the most wounding thing a woman could say to a man. And when there **was** plenty of time, and they were together free of the pressure **of a** limited number of hours to train time and parting, then it was important, and right, and very much wanted, and the statement that it wasn't important was a lie.

She wondered how many marriages had broken up during the war on the physical strangeness that comes of being apart. She could remember, herself, sitting down and writing a letter, when she was overtired and underfed, and worn with fear of the bombing.

'Oh, darling, I am so sorry about how beastly I made everything by being so cold and unresponsive yesterday. I did so want to be anything else. I don't know if I'm getting too old for you or if you've found a new woman or what, but I know I'm spoiling it for you and when you come home you expect something I can't give. Please, please forgive me, if you can, and if you want to go to someone else don't come to me out of duty or obligation. I don't know what makes me so cold and dead. If it's something wrong with me I haven't the right to hang onto you like an old man, I suppose I ought to say woman of the sea, and spoil everything for you. I'll go to Dr. Rickaby tomorrow and see if there is anything wrong and see if he can be any help. . . .'

Luckily she had torn up the letter and not sent it.

If she had they would, for sure, have drifted into an arranged divorce. Several of her friends had broken up their marriages for no better reason than that there was a strangeness after being parted for a month or longer between every forty-eight hours of common life.

But now, but now, Walter was a stranger all the time. When it came, it was this terrible cold contact with a body that had left its mind elsewhere, this curious hurried loving from a body interested only in a quick release from itself.

Sometimes he would just drop dead asleep beside her, afterwards, without a word of tenderness, or love. Sometimes he would lie awake for an hour, smoking, then suddenly get up and go.

Sometimes he would come to her, at two or three in the morning, from Anne, waking her with a sudden brutality that carried through into her nightmares, so that she could not be immediately sure if he was with her in reality or in dream.

He was not always sure himself, and felt ill at ease in the mill just as he had felt ill at ease in the great churches and among the noble monuments of Rome.

This was what endured, this was what was solid, worthwhile, and worth making – and he could not bear it. He wanted to turn his back on it and stride out to find what he burned for.

He would sit in the mill in the evenings, listening, perhaps, to Margery reading to the children, with Anne listening too, while she ironed some clothes, seeing the lamplight falling on their nice faces, seeing that what was under his eyes was happiness, seeing and hearing all the time the other thing outside, where he wanted to be.

What made such an evening full of anguish was the impossibility of breaking through it with the declaration that it was no longer happiness for him, the impossibility of declaring for that outside which was essentially nothing you could declare for. How could he say to them 'I don't any longer love you, or cherish you, or care one way or the other for anything which concerns you, what I care for is the shine on a rainwet back street, the half-open warehouse door which may be the way into a trap, the road block where the phony papers may be questioned, the look in the eyes of the people who are afraid of me, the tension and the squalor of our racket?'

He would lie in bed beside Anne smoking, not able to touch her, knowing she wanted him to touch her; silent, knowing she wanted him to talk to her.

'Can't you tell me about it?'

'About what?'

'What it is that makes you so unhappy and knotted up. . . .'

'I'm very happy.'

'Well, why aren't you sleeping. You aren't eating. You go off for days at a time . . . there must be something.'

'There's nothing I want to tell you.'

'Oh, Walter.'

He would feel the faint movement of her silent sobbing and move away from her. If she stopped he would stay, if she lost control of her tears he would say, 'For god's sake . . .' and go to Margery.

If she stopped crying he would lie quietly beside her, still not touching her, feeding on her anxiety and wakefulness, thinking, and planning new extensions of the other life. He knew that the activity of his mind was intolerable to her in these night hours, and that her consciousness of it was like the exasperation of too bright a light, or too loud a radio, shining in her face or blaring in her ear.

He would lie there acutely, poisonously, awake until in desperation she forced herself to take from him the barest minimum that she could get, the pure automatism of the thing itself stripped of all humanity or tenderness. Then he would fall dead asleep, like a dog, released at last.

In London troops had been called out to work some of the vital services, the docks, the meat markets, the power stations, and the postal services. At the East India dock pickets stoned lorries bringing guardsmen in to unload a ship full of meat that was going bad because its refrigeration system had broken down. A brick crashed through the windshield of a six ton truck. The driver took his hands off the wheel to shield his face from the brick and the knives of flying glass. The truck swung sideways and sheered through the crowd of dockers, ending up against the dockyard wall with two screaming men pinned between the brickwork and the front bumper of the truck. The crowd swung back from the swath of injured men lying on the ground, stunned for a moment, and hushed. There was no sound but the pattering of their feet on the pavements, and the crying of the hurt men. Then there was a roar and the crowd rushed in on the stationary truck. It was overturned and burned. Four of the guardsmen were killed, twelve badly beaten, and the weapons of all of them seized, spirited away into the roaring mass of men. A company coming to the rescue and clearing the street had two men killed and killed eleven.

That was the beginning. The next day there were more soldiers killed, and more strikers, in accidental, unplanned outbreaks of violence.

The day after that a crowd of strikers tried to rush the big power station at Chelsea on the south side of the river. A local group of strike leaders had made a plan to wreck the automatic gear that unloaded the coal ships lying at the riverside wharf.

The sailors working the power station tried to beat them off with rifle butts, but the crowd came on, brushing the cordon aside, breaking it up, beating the men, and taking their weapons. A small group of sailors penned in a corner shot their way out. Strikers began to fire at them with stolen rifles. A sailor, seeing a friend go down, shot through the neck, switched his bren gun over from single shot to burst firing, and fired on until he had emptied a magazine.

The sound of machine-gun fire echoed out across the river, and later that day the soldiers used mortars for the first time. During the night martial law was proclaimed in the London area, and General Forrest Marshall made a surprise raid, arresting all the union leaders he could lay his hands on.

A civil war had begun.

All over the country the union leaders and the socialists formed committees of public safety and tried to take over the big towns. In the north of England they succeeded, in the south they were too weak, and the soldiers established control. The southerners were first to issue a proclamation claiming that they were the Government, then the northerners proclaimed a republic. An Independent Socialist republic was proclaimed in Wales.

The soldiers had been preparing for the situation for years, ever since the big scare of the Russian Revolution in fact. All their armour, most of their artillery, and their most effective divisions were stationed in the south, in the agricultural counties south of the Thames. They cleared the socialist strongholds in Southampton and Plymouth quickly, and then moved on Bristol. When they had cleared the southern ports they planned to move north on the industrial centres.

The Republicans in the north appealed to the Russians for help, but the soldiers thought they could win before Russia could do anything to profit by the situation. At the same time they appealed to America for help, just in case.

While all this was happening Walter and Ross had parleyed their original deal in fifty pounds of butter and pork into operations that were getting to be of major importance in the lives of hundreds, of thousands, of people.

Their first dealings in Bristol had been easy. In the confusion of the collapsing strike, and an inept communist attempt to take over the port there was no difficulty in finding the way to hungry people and taking what they had in exchange for food.

But when the Republican administration took control, and established a stable authority, the roads became difficult, and a makeshift security police net began to work. Running odd lots of food in by bicycle was risky and, although it paid off from two hundred to three hundred pounds a time, or in tobacco worth far more than that in the countryside, it allowed them to take only a fraction of the possible return.

Ross would walk about his kitchen cursing, trying to think out some way of getting trucks onto the road, of cutting a larger slice of the easy money. The opportunity came when the soldiers moved on Bristol.

The military cordon round the town, and the defences, seemed to put an end to operations for good and all, but it turned out otherwise.

Walter and Ross tried all one night with the heavy packs on the backs of their cycles. They tried all the back alleys, the cinder tracks across the vacant lots, and the devious approaches that they could trace on the inch to the mile map, but in turn everywhere they found the soldiers. Good as the Republican police net had been it was nothing to the close mesh of the army radio net, in which every platoon was in touch with every other platoon and with company all the time.

They spent some hours lying penned in a backyard eavesdropping on a command post the other side of a board fence, listening to a search which was being made for them.

They had been glimpsed and lost, but the searchers were close on them and within a few minutes of their first being reported an area that would take them hours to leave had been warned.

From time to time a candelabra flare dropped from a patrolling aircraft drifted down over the town shatteringly dissipating the security of the dark; they only got away by dumping the loads and later the bicycles. They reached home three days later, tired to rags and three hundred pounds to the bad.

'Well, Ross, it looks as if we can't go on with this.'

'I think we can, Walter. It's just an occasion for reorganisation, for renaming the concern. I think I can solve the transport problem now.'

Ross was rooting in his trunks in one corner of the room.

'Ross is going to become the wing commander once again. And a good citizen. I hope Mister Jackson is going to come along and play the colonel.'

He found his old uniform and pulled it out of the tin trunk.

'Look at all the pretty ribbons, mustn't I have been a brave boy!'

He rapidly changed his clothes and then with a jaunty air finished his conversion by producing his uniform cap and putting it on.

'There now, every inch the birdman. Do I convince you, Walter? Do I look genuine? Will I pass?'

'Yes, you look pretty good, but I'm not going to try to bluff my way through that cordon on the strength of a fancy dress outfit, even with you to do the talking. You're underestimating the military if you think you can do it.'

'No, you're doing the underestimating, of me and of the military. What we're going to do is organise something in the name of humanity and mercy.'

He reflected for a moment.

' "Non-Partisan Relief." You want a good undramatic, drab sort of name that they'll be able to initialise – N.P.R. I'll go and see the general running the attack on Bristol – Mackinder's his name I think – Some of us, sir, are rather gravely concerned at the suffering the fighting is inflicting on the defenceless sections of the communities involved. I am not making a sentimental appeal for women and children, many of them, I'm well aware are giving their full support to the disaffected elements. I am referring, sir, to the hospital population, the women and children in maternity homes, and the aged in institutions. N.P.R. is a non-party organisation that is interested solely in feeding these classes of people. I want your authority, general, to negotiate with the Republican authorities in Bristol for the passage of a convoy with food for the hospitals, the maternity homes, and the institutions for the care of the aged. Etcetera, etcetera, lay it on the line drab and factual as possible.'

'You'll never get away with it, soldiers aren't fools.'

'That's what I'm counting on.'

And Ross was right. The general sanctioned the negotiations, giving the code word Trojan Horse to all correspondence dealing with it. He did not at first sight care much for the look of Ross, but the other members of the committee who called on him – the Lord Lieutenant of the county, the Conservative candidate for the old Parliament, the Mayor of Bath, and Colonel Jackson in a neat pin stripe suit, did the convincing. Ross cancelled the effect of his appearance by knowing the relevant facts, and laying a sound operational plan on the general's desk. When the general had considered it for a few moments he looked up.

'This is a much sounder scheme than I thought it was going to be. Did you frame it, wing commander?'

'With the help of Colonel Jackson, sir.'

'Hm.' The general brooded over it for a moment. 'I'll sanction it and arrange for you to have a parley with the Republicans. The food situation in the town is bad and I imagine they'll jump at it. Try to get guarantees that it will go to the right people, but if it doesn't there isn't much harm done, the quantity I'll permit will be nine tons daily – that won't do much more than whet their appetites. And if the wrong people get it, it'll only annoy the people who don't. We'll hope of course that the sick and the mothers do get it.'

'I'll do my best to see that they do, sir,' said Ross smartly.

'There's another point,' the general looked thoughtfully at the committee. 'The art of running armies successfully is largely a matter of keeping them free to do their proper work. When Bristol falls to us we will have a large hungry baby dropped in our lap, and we'll be anxious to get rid of it. I don't want to tie up my supply columns on relief work if I can help it. There are other tasks on which this force will have to be employed at the earliest possible moment.'

He hesitated for s second, uncertain if he should tell this group of civilians that the first big drop of Russian arms, supplies, and technical advisers was expected to reach the midland and northern forces in twenty days, and that he desperately wanted his freedom of action to take part in a drive to forestall that. He decided to leave it alone.

'I would be most grateful if N.P.R. could prepare a scheme for feeding the entire city when military operations come to an end. I am prepared to allot trucks and petrol, if you will on your part produce food, and drivers for the transport.'

It was the decisive moment, all the members of the committee turned to Ross, and the movement of their heads drew the general's clear grey eyes in that direction.

'I should want special powers, sir, to requisition food and enrol the necessary drivers.'

'Yes, I see that. The area's under martial law. I'll give you authority as food controller, Bristol area, and we'll give you power to make requisitions in Gloucestershire, Somerset, and Wiltshire. I should like to see your plans in three days' time. I hope to drop the hungry baby in your lap in five days at the least and ten days at the most, you'll have to be ready. I hope you gentlemen will give Wing Commander Ross your fullest support. I must ask you to excuse me.' He gave them his charming smile.

When they were almost gone from the room he called Ross back.

'Just one thing, let me know how this immediate project goes. And if in your negotiations you give the impression that you've got a number of food convoys waiting to come in to the town as soon as they let us in, well, it wouldn't be at all a bad thing.'

He smiled again and Ross smiled back at him.

'I won't let you down, sir.'

The negotiations were bad, endless talk in an unheated room, with people who hadn't eaten or slept properly for too long. They were badly scared at finding themselves up against a situation that looked like coming to fighting uglier than any mere exchange of small arms fire, well aware that their material was trifling compared with that lined up against them. They couldn't understand why the soldiers didn't come in behind their armour or use their guns, they feared that some annihilating blow was being prepared with cruel deliberation. They were deeply suspicious of the convoy idea.

'Why should these damn fascists do it?'

'I think you've got them wrong altogether,' said Ross, 'certainly they've done everything they can to make things easy for N.P.R.'

'The Welsh sent us a message saying they were going to get a food ship into the port last week, and the Midland Army Group said they were going to strike through to us in a few days, but nothing happens.'

The man in the dirty mackintosh, who seemed to be the chairman, rubbed his eyelids, he seemed hardly aware that he was talking aloud.

'We had eight hundred people die of malnutrition last week. You can pay too high a price. . . . What's the use of nine tons of food to our maternity hospitals, they've no light or heat.'

'Well,' Ross shifted on his feet. 'It's no part of my job to make propaganda that might influence you one way or the other, but our convoys are waiting to come in the minute you recognise the central authority.'

'What's this? What's this?'

The Republican military commander arrived, in a black leather coat worn over Home Guard uniform, with his binoculars and his Sten gun, the conventional type of romantic left wing military failure, still dreaming its dreams of defeat in Spain.

'Why wasn't I informed that enemy delegates were here, comrades?'

He spoke with a manly rasp which dropped out of his voice when he wasn't concentrating on it, and left querulousness.

'What credentials have these men got, comrades, where do they come from?'

He stepped up to Ross and plucked at the black armband with white letters on the airforce blue sleeve. 'NPR, eh, NPR, what's that? Why haven't I been told?'

'Non-Partisan Relief,' said Ross, 'Milk, eggs, and butter for your hospitals and maternity homes. Nothing military about it.'

'How did you get in here? Who the hell are you? Who passed

248

you through our lines? I've a good mind to order your arrest.
You may be a spy.'

'Now steady on, chum. We gave you twenty-four hours'
notice. The battalion commander on the sector gave us procedure
instructions and we came in, as arranged. We're no surprise
packet. Or shouldn't be.' Ross looked wonderingly at him, so
did the civil members of the Republican committee. 'Colonel
Jackson here will show you our passes, signed and counter-
signed by your battalion and brigade commanders. Everything's
in order. Aren't you in contact with your front line troops,
Comrade General?'

'I must check this story at once.'

He dialled a number on the telephone, and got no answer. He
dialled another number and got no answer.

'The phone isn't working, Comrade General,' said a member
of the committee.

The man in the creased leather coat dialled again, and sat, with
the dead 'phone in his hand, on the corner of the desk, waiting
for nothing to happen. Nearly three thousand of his men were
absent without leave, there were no rations, the enemy were
closing in, his commanders were no longer reporting to him,
and his own incompetence stared him in the face.

'You've done everything that was humanly possible, Comrade General,' someone said nervously. 'We must face the
inevitable.'

'They've let me down,' he said, 'they've no faith. We've been
betrayed. There are saboteurs everywhere.'

No one listened to him.

'Can you,' another member of the committee spoke, looking
down at the finger nails of his right hand, 'promise us that there
are food convoys actually waiting to come in, and that Mackinder
will let them in if we surrender?'

'I can promise you that,' said Ross, 'and if I can take any
message to General Mackinder when I go back that might bring
a speedier end to the fighting I'd be very glad to do it.' He
paused. 'I want to assure you that I'm absolutely neutral in this,
I'm only interested in getting on with the humanitarian work of
distributing relief supplies at the earliest possible moment. It's

the women and children I'm thinking of, and I hope you'll think of them too.'

The chairman rubbed his eyelids again, then picked up his gavel; he tapped on the council table with it. The first time he opened his mouth he made no sound, he coughed, and then his voice burst out, surprisingly clear and strong. 'I move,' he said, 'that the offer of these gentlemen to act as intermediaries be accepted.'

At the end of the month N.P.R. was the official agency for distributing food in the region, and when relief began to come from the United States under the 'everything short of war' programme, N.P.R. was the chosen instrument in the south-west.

Ross installed himself in a number of commandeered houses in Royal Crescent in Bath with a magnificence worthy of the Victor of Chuprassy, and enrolled a large volunteer staff from the well-bred, well-mannered, and civic-minded middle class inhabitants of the town.

Two admirals, a brigadier, and two lieutenant-colonels served voluntarily on their operations staff, and a large administrative group served for poverty line salaries paid out of a grant from General Mackinder's funds. Ross as Director-General passed all the projects drawn up by the operations staff, and gave careful considerations to the reports of the economic research wing which provided information about the location of surplus and shortage areas.

Privately he referred to this second organisation as 'our market research chaps.' There was business to be done in the shortage areas. Legitimate convoys took food there. Ross issued directives that they should go there, his operations staff working from the directives drew up the projects for collection, routing, and distribution, and submitted them to Ross for approval. He read them with care and made a rapid note in his private diary of their exploitable points.

The bulk of the convoy would go through, and its badly needed food would be distributed where it was wanted. Somewhere on the route one lorry, or two lorries or a half load, would vanish into thin air.

Walter waiting at a cross roads, or on a corner at a suburban street crossing, or outside some easily recognisable building, in his N.P.R. car, would collect the money from some anonymous figure who would walk up out of the shadows, ask him for a light, and slip him a case full of notes.

When he was not out trading Walter was to be found in his splendid office on the first floor of one of the houses in Royal Crescent, behind a door labelled Security Officer.

'We couldn't have done better if we'd set the thing up in Kensington itself,' said Ross. 'They're all dead keen and they've been brought up so well that a nasty thought never comes into their heads When they hear about lorry loads of stuff being stolen or just vanishing they think how horrid and lawless the lower classes are. And to think we were peddling the stuff on a two bicycle basis a month ago.'

'The whole thing's going to blow up in our faces, any minute.'

'Well, that's your job – seeing it doesn't blow up. You're not Security Officer for N.P.R. for nothing.'

A secretary came into the room with a file of papers, and put them down.

'This is the file on that convoy that was jumped outside Southampton last night, isn't it Miss Willert?' said Ross.

'Yes, sir, it's terrible the way our lorries are always being stolen. One of the poor men was quite badly hurt. We ought to have guards riding with the convoys. The stolen food has gone without a trace, but the Southampton police recovered the trucks near Warsash this morning.'

'That's a very good idea about guarding our convoys, Miss Willert. As a matter of fact I'm thinking of sending Jackson here up north to put it up to General Mackinder.'

'Oh, I'm so glad, Colonel Jackson.' She gave him her fresh pleasant smile, 'it's terrible to think of those poor boys being dragged out of their lorries and beaten up by these racketeers. I hope you'll manage to persuade General Mackinder to give us some of his men for escort duties. It's only fair to the drivers.'

She went out; a nice sweet breathed, sweet minded girl with a well washed, well exercised body and a kindly mind. It was horrid for the truck drivers to be hauled out of their cabs and beaten up, it was rather exciting that General Mackinder's armour should be moving north somewhere near Liverpool, and that General Forrest-Mitchell should have liberated Lincoln – that was war and different.

'What's this armed guard idea? It's the last thing we want isn't it?' said Walter.

'No, we've got to have it. This is the third slip up, this Southampton effort. Stanislavsky had it all arranged, he'd made the advance payment in dollars, everything was laid on, but the convoy was jumped ten miles before it got to Stanislavsky's rendezvous. Stanislavsky's man was here this morning, much put out. I had to hand him back twenty-five thousand dollars. That hurt. I like real money.'

'But if we'd have had a lot of soldiers on our hands we wouldn't have been able to let the Poles have the stuff, even if it had got through to the rendezvous. It's a crazy idea.'

'No, child, trust Ross. Ross knows best. When you get to Mackinder's H.Q. you will find an atmosphere that will carry you back to the happy days of 1940–42. That attack of his is back on its starting line, and there is talk of disengaging to regroup. I don't think the general will detach any of his armed might for light duty in the back areas just now. What you will get is authority to arm N.P.R. security squads, and take good care you don't get anything else. See what I mean?'

'I see what you mean.'

The security squads materialised quickly out of the big towns, the debris of the Bristol comrade-general's assault guards, the debris of a short-lived Republican riot squad from Southampton, veterans of the speedways and dirt-tracks of the old days.

The men were already possessed of a species of uniform when they were enrolled. Boots lacing to the knee, black leather knee breeches, leather jackets, and crash helmets. Walter was amazed at the ease with which, by the addition of shoulder flashes, standard armament, and a standard motor-cycle, they were transformed into a unit.

He paraded them at the end of a week for Ross's inspection and was horrified at the impression they created. Their faces had a curious pared away look as if they had been shaped by a sculptor at pains to work out a symbol for a generalised garage-minded type, cleared of irrevelant individual traits **and** characteristics.

They had been, it was true, conditioned to similarity by their obsessions, few of them had thought much about anything not concerned with either girls or motor-bicycles since their release from school at fourteen, and for most of them there was not a tolerable noise between hot jazz and the jarring roar of a well tuned engine. Talk was only tolerable, as cards were tolerable, if there was a background of the one noise or the other. Now the collapse of the order that had never meant much to them except an irksome restraint had brought a new, even more exciting music into their lives, the stammer of automatic weapons.

They were all between seventeen and nineteen, and they had all missed the war. They were conscious of it as a deprivation, and this time they did not mean to be left out of the party.

Walking down the lines of the parade, with each man rigidly at attention, Walter felt a pang of terror as he passed one empty, loveless face after another. They had really scraped the bottom of the urban well in assembling their ambiguous unit; what they had got was bad enough in itself, what frightened him was that these faces seemed in some way to mirror his own, not as it had already become, but as it would become when stamped with linaments of satisfied desire.

'We'll have to keep this bunch out of sight as much as possible, Ross. Nobody who gets a look at this outfit could trust N.P.R. an inch.'

'They scare me to death. I didn't know you, Walter, really I didn't. You've surprised me. I ask you to organise a police group, and you raise up the wiriest batch of thugs I ever set eyes on.' He laughed. 'They're magnificent.'

'They'll give the whole show away.'

'If they scare other people as much as they scare me, they'll do all right.' He laughed again, throwing his head back, and Walter noticed with a certain envy the natural grace of his movement.

He was no longer drinking heavily, the softness of his flesh was gone, he was now lean and hard, filled with a sinister concentrated life.

'We can do any mortal thing we like with that lot, as long as we keep them moving, well fed, and happy. You made it. You've got to keep it. If you don't, it will take charge. And then I would be scared. Think of Charley Snow in charge, hooh, you keep tight hold on Charley Snow.'

It was no easy charge to undertake. Snow had been ace rider of the Port Charlton Tigers and was prepared to speak freely, and show photographs that confirmed his stories, about that chapter in his career. The photographs were all very much alike, with Charley ploughing the cinder track with one leg or the other, on the inside of a turn, out in front of a closely bunched pack of motor-cycles.

'That time I lapped Stan Wallis.'

'That night I was on the beam, got four firsts and we piled up a twenty-four point lead on them fellows from Wembley.'

It didn't look like much of a sport to Walter, and as he looked at the deafening photographs, it seemed to him that whoever won the sprint to the first corner of the oval track and arrived there with the inside berth, had the race.

Charley looked at him. 'That's right.'

He seemed genuinely puzzled that Walter should expect more to be in it than that, and a look of anxiety came over his face as he sought the right answer that was not purely automatic.

'You got to get out in front, and then you got to stay there.'

He looked uneasy, something was escaping him that he couldn't explain, or put into words. He abandoned the research and put down a formula that acknowledged the difficulty and excused him from any further effort to come to grips with it.

'There's an art in it.'

There was indeed, as Walter recognised when the men staged some team races later in the week, to show him what they could do. They understood the capabilities of their machines so completely, and they managed their own bodies with such masterly combination of their instinctive and controlled resources, that they reached the breathtaking parody of art that ice skaters, bare foot dancers, and athletes achieve. A mindless perfection that dies in the instant of its achievement.

Walter could see why Charley valued this momentary perfection, no one who thrilled to it could imagine the deeper layers of his character, the chapters in his life story which he did not discuss; the discharge with ignominy from the Airborne Division, the sentence for receiving a stolen typewriter, the sentence for taking a car, the acquittal for lack of evidence on a rape charge, the two paternity orders.

He could see still more why it meant so much to some of the others, who were recordless, who came from streets, from families, where the idea of perfection or its possibility must have been as unimaginable as daylight on the deep ocean's floor. On their machines, the centre of attraction for a great crowd, they swept through into another world in which anything was possible, leaving their frustrations and their feeling that life was on top of them, so far behind that they could be forgotten.

Now that the world of everyday life, which had once seemed so solid and unchangeable was seen by the flickering light of civil war and social breakdown, these moments of possibility, of mastery, seemed to offer themselves more and more often, and in even more exciting forms.

Some instinct brought them into N.P.R. security squads despite that organisation's bland facade. Another kind of man reading the descriptions of their duties would have imagined hours of watching and waiting around thievable goods, ending with an arrest perhaps to be crowned later by a conviction – the dullest kind of industrial police work.

They saw it less realistically, more dramatically. They saw the wharf rats stripping out a truck or lorry by the dim half light of a naked bulb swinging high up on a gantry in the gusty estuary wind. They saw the thin light reflected back from the shiny black tarpaulins flung off the load, from the dockside railroad tracks, from the steel wheel rims. They saw themselves jumping the thieves, rushing on them from dark corners in a moment of dynamic adventure. When the wharf rats bolted for it, used to baffling unarmed police by dodging among the dockside lumber in the dark, the tommy guns cut them down chattering through quick tongues of flame.

When Charley and his men were boys the films had nourished this secret dream, it was one of the things which life excluded and denied them. Now they imported the dream into life.

When the dock police and the civil police came, shocked, to take the wounded into custody, and to dispose of the dead, they were no longer the law and the authority which had once seemed so powerful and so terrifying, because incomprehensible; they were merely the weak and inhibited who had power and did not dare to use it.

The squads stood about, exhilarated mentally, relaxed physically, despising the police who, with their papers and documents, knitted a formal fabric of legality to throw over bodies which they would have thrown into the nearest dock or onto the nearest piece of waste ground.

The chief of the Southampton Dock police called Walter down from Bath in the middle of the night.

'I wanted you to see what sort of things these . . . men,' he gave it an emphasis that indicated his ironic use of the word, 'of yours are doing.'

It was four in the morning when he reached the port.

The dock area was brightly lit by the lurid light from two burning American tankers which had been hit during an air raid in the earlier part of the night.

The police inspector disregarded that altogether and led Walter to the dock where his men were waiting. They were sitting on a stack of timber watching the fires across the water, they looked like a winning football team who had been honoured by a torchlight procession on their return home after the big game of the season. There was a contented, sated, youthfulness about them. They were completely indifferent to the police, as to a lower order of creation, but as soon as they spotted Walter they sprang to it, and fell in with an impressive smartness.

'What's the trouble, sar'nt?'

'We caught some men working on this shipment of ours, sir, and now there's the usual flap about shooting, sir.'

'I see. Tell the men to make themselves comfortable, we may be some time clearing this. Did you hurt anyone?'

'We knocked off two men, sir.'

'Try to bring them back alive, now and again, for the record. It looks better.'

Walter turned back to the inspector.

'Well, my men seem to have been doing their duty. It hardly seems an occasion for calling me down here in the middle of the night. If your police can't see our shipments through the docks we have to protect them. We've General Mackinder's mandate. Our stuff goes to women and children and the sick, we can't be sentimental about thieves.'

'I'm not asking you to be sentimental, I'm asking you to get your men to show some slight awareness that there is such a thing as law, and common decency. Look at this.' The inspector twitched back a sheet.

The two men must have been running elbow to elbow. The security squad had apparently brought their eight tommy guns to bear simultaneously at kidney level, each man had been hit by twenty or thirty shots between the shoulder blades and the buttocks.

'These men are petty sneak thieves, neither of them ever stole more than ten pounds worth of stuff in his life. This man, Mutty Evans, was apparently trying to get away with two tins of condensed milk, the slowest and oldest of my special constables could run him down in fifty yards – he's nearly sixty. And your young gunmen do this to him. They can't have tried to make a pinch. I tell you it's disgraceful. Absolutely disgraceful. It makes me ashamed to have anything to do with law enforcement. . . .'

His mouth opened on another word, but all sound was smothered by the roar of one of the tankers blowing up. A huge column of fire, of heavy smoky flame that seemed quilted, stood up over the docks and a hot blast tore at their clothes. A silence followed in which everyone stood rivetted by the sight of the heaving smoke, and by the intense brightening of the light at its base which spoke of a lake of blazing petrol spreading out round the split carcass of the tanker.

In the silence an appalling scream, tiny, but sharp and hard so that it scratched the ear drum like a diamond, travelled to them from the zone of flame. It went on and on, as if it were produced by a machine, and then abruptly stopped.

Walter looked at the inspector's face, sullen with hatred, reddish orange in the light of the burning.

'Your methods are all right in a law abiding world, inspector,'

257

he said, 'but they aren't related to the conditions of civil war. You used to be able to allow every dog one bite, we're so weak from loss of blood we have to shoot when the dog looks like biting. Your methods are too luxurious, we can't afford them.'

The inspector let the sheet fall back over the mess of splintered bone, burst bowels and torn flesh. He said nothing for almost half a minute.

'One day,' his voice was toneless, 'they'll do this to you – and to me, too, because I let you do your dirty work in my territory. There's no end to this.'

He walked away into the shadows, spoke for a moment or two to a sergeant of the Dockyard police, and then vanished. Walter felt briefly, an impulse, to go after him in order to tell him all about the monstrous fraud of N.P.R., to confess, to break up the whole hideous machine. This shipment was destined for Stanislavsky, and since he was paying in genuine dollars again there was, this time, to be no slip up. That was why Mutty Evans and his friend had been shot down.

The wind backed from south to south-west and a low cloud canopy came in from the sea, bringing with it a steady drizzle. The orange red glare of the fires was reflected sadly down from the weeping clouds so that dawn broke unnoticed. Walter waited about until Charley Snow came in with the special squad that was to see the lorries through to Stanislavsky and to relieve the men who had been on guard all night. By then Mutty Evans and his mate were gone, there was only a memorial patch of sawdust, clean and resin scented, masking the bloodstain on the dock.

'Your boys are getting trigger happy, Charley, pin their ears back. We're unloved here and we can't afford it. We must keep on good terms with the dockyard people.' He yawned. 'Keep out of trouble, and see the loads get through to Mister S. I must go off and get some sleep now, I'll meet you at the rendezvous at 2200 hours. You'd better leave here at dusk, say 1630, or 1700 at the latest, I don't want you getting tied up if the northern air comes in again. Well, I'll be there.'

He drove out into Southampton to look for a bed.

The town was all brown and silver under the drizzle, and the people going to work were hunched against the wet and the morning cold. Their faces were white and exhausted after the raid broken night, and they looked at Walter's warlike uniform and brown painted car with an expressionless resentment.

The town had never recovered from the big raids of 1940, it was now overwhelmed with hopelessness at the sight of the great black smoke tower rising up into the clouds behind the dockyard walls.

Many of its people were with the northerners politically, and the thought that their friends were ready to bomb them filled them with anguish. When the tanker went up during the night many of them thought the Russians had intervened with 'it', they walked to work, sick with apprehension, pursued through the daylight by nightmares of guilt for Hiroshima and Nagasaki.

They did not lift their eyes to the crude daubings of Peace, Peace, Peace, and the hammer and sickle which the party paint pot crews had splashed across a hundred walls in the night. The town major's propaganda units were out effacing the signs of that activity with equally meaningless posters, black lettering on red, Keep Britain Free. Keep Britain Free.

Queues were already forming outside the foodshops, most of the others were shuttered, and their dead fronts were encrusted with layers of Communist paint and right-wing posters. The gutters were full of dingy refuse and waste paper; the leaflets dropped by the raiders in the night shone whiter and fresher than the rest, but they were already sodden with rain and beginning to melt into the slime.

Fate was plastering the town with its own unmistakable slogan, expressed in the flaking paint, the unreplaced broken glass, the smokeless chimneys, the dingy clothing of the boys and girls – No one can win, No one can win, No one . . . and it was the only slogan that was credible.

Walter could not bring himself to sleep in or near the great dead sprawl, and drove right out into the New Forest before he could bring himself to stop.

He found a bed in a guest house near Fordingbridge but after two hours found he could not sleep there. He dressed again and walked about the garden watching the Avon sluicing past the end of the lawn, thinking of the quieter water behind the mill dam, and about Anne, and about Margery and the children.

After lunch he felt calmer and suddenly hungry for sleep. He lay down fully clothed on his bed and pulled the old gold and niggerbrown eiderdown over his body just as a chiming clock struck two, he glanced down at his wrist watch and saw that the guest house clock was four minutes fast. He shut his eyes to see if he could sleep, fearing that now he was offering his body what it asked his rebel nerves might refuse it, independently.

When he opened his eyes again it seemed that he had only been asleep for a few seconds; and although it was dark, his watch confirmed the impression that he had not slept long, when he snapped on the bedside lamp he saw that it was only five past two.

He lay untroubled for a space and then suddenly realised that he had slept for twelve hours, that he was four whole hours late for the meeting with Stanislavsky.

He startled the night watchman sleeping with a shot gun beside him in the downstairs hall, waking him into fear. The man stood up shaking with his hands over his head, licking his lips.

'You won't 'urt me. I'll show you where everything is . . .'

'No, no, man, I just want to pay and go.' He was angry and suddenly abashed by the inhumanity of his anger. 'I'm sorry I startled you.'

'I'd just dozed off . . . you never know who's about these days. I should of known you were all right.' He let Walter out through the chained and locked front door. 'We have to be careful with all them deserters about – they'll do anything – anything.'

Walter reached the rendezvous towards half-past three. One of his own men was waiting for him, stamping up and down in the road, to keep the frost from his bones.

'I thought you was never coming, sir,' he said. He kicked his stone cold motor-cycle into life and went ahead to show him the way.

They turned off a main road just south of Whitchurch, up a farm service road, into a yard surrounded by shadowy black buildings. A roller shutter door slid up and they drove straight into a dimly lit barn, as big as a church in the dimness.

When Walter stepped out of his car the quiet of the place swept up to him, the hush of downland country with its great open sweeps.

There was a clinking sound of spades and shovels from the other side of the barn. It sounded like the only noise in the world.

Charley Snow came to him from the far end of the great building, walking with his quick grace. When he saw that Walter was listening he cocked his head up and listened too. He smiled.

' 's our chaps. They're digging a grave.'

'You ran into trouble?'

'Not more than I expected.' He smiled again. 'I had my doubts on this from the first. From when you tol' me Mister S. was one of them Poles.'

'What do you mean?'

'Come and have a look.'

They walked through into a garage at the far end of the barn. Bare electric light bulbs hurt the eyes as they shed an unkind glare over the concrete floor with its scatter of dark oil stains.

A massive lorry stood mountainously on the far side of the room near the open door of a toilet. Over the can there was a well lettered sign, 'Leave this Place As you Would Like to Have Found it.'

The back wall of the garage was scarred and pitted with bullet marks and at its foot lay seven men, already stiffened in death.

'What the devil have you been up to?'

'That one, the one at the end there, is Mister S.'

Walter went over and looked at him. He had been a tall well made man, a little too good looking, a little too clearly a woman's man. He looked just like Mutty Evans now. Looking at him, and thinking that, Walter remembered that he had been envious and a little jealous, quite a bit jealous of this man. His grasp on life had been firmer than his own, had done what he wanted with fewer qualms. Now he was rubbish like Mutty Evans.

'Didn't you understand, Charley: Stanislavsky was in with us. You were only meant to get tough with anyone who tried to take the stuff before he got it.'

He spoke quietly as he would have spoken to Francis or Jeanette if they had by carelessness broken something valuable,

261

the value of which they couldn't be expected to understand – ↲
and as if it was partly his fault for not explaining before that the
thing was precious.

'This is a bad mess.'

'You don't get it, sir.'

Charley was being patient with him, he realised with surprise,
and tolerant of his innocence.

'Mister S. found it much cheaper to take your stuff in a way
that he could get out of paying for, if you follow me. The lorries
was picked up six miles short of the meeting place by his own
men.

'You can't trust them sort of people. You don't know who to
trust these days. I was quite took aback when I saw we'd got
him. He offered me ten thousand dollars to rat on you. But I
wouldn't take it. I knew he'd do the dirty on me if I did.'

He touched Stanislavsky's body with the tip of his boot. 'It
was the only thing to do, really. If he'd of turned nasty the whole
N.P.R. business would of been up the spout.'

The nausea that had overwhelmed Walter at the docks
returned, intensified a hundred times. In this closed space the
bodies gave off a slaughter house reek. He remembered the
inspector's words 'they'll do this to you' as if it was a curse that
had been competently laid on him by a magician, and wondered
when he would come to a wall.

'This may put the whole business up the spout, if it comes out.
And anyway Stanislavsky was our chief contact . . . we had to
work through him. I don't know how else it's to be done. Oh
damn this for a mess . . .'

'Oh, Mr. Ross'll think of something I daresay, sir,' said
Charley. 'And I don't think this'll be found out. The boys have
shifted the dung heap out in the farmyard. It'll be back in place by
first light, and all this'll be under it. No one'll know we had
anything to do with it. And we aren't losing anything on
tonight's work. Mister S. had a hundred and ten thousand dollars
in his safe – that's mor'n three hundred thousand pounds. We
done well out of it.'

'How did you get into Stanislavsky's safe?'

Charley looked at the dead hands, and Walter looked at them

too. Something had happened to the finger nails. They neither of them said anything, there wasn't anything to say.

'I thought we might split it, sir, fifty for Mr. Ross, thirty each for you an' me.'

'Oh, god, no . . .' Walter spoke without thinking.

And then he saw an avenue of escape, with thirty thousand dollars he could make a fresh start in America. He could leave it all behind, and build, real buildings, on uncontaminated soil.

'All right, we'll do it that way. But this may be our last job, Charley. We've gone altogether too far over this.'

'Oh, I hope not, sir,' said Charley.

They walked over to the farmhouse under the starry sky, breathing the sweet country air, and in the looted office, littered with old bills, love letters from girls, ambiguous business correspondence, and the literature of a Free Polish Democratic Party, they divided out the money.

As he took it Walter pretended to himself that he was taking his journey money for an escape, but he knew that he was making a contract and that when he put out his hand towards it something was settled forever.

Not between him and Charley, although in the division he acknowledged him as an equal, but between him and some vaster external force – the natural order, or fate. He saw briefly before his inward eye the bearded figure at the centre of a Romanesque altarpiece – God.

Charley's short, square tipped, fingers leafed quickly through the thick wad of hundred dollar bills for one last check, and then held them out. Walter reached over and took them.

He knew what he had done, he had reached the end of a journey, he had not embarked on one – with all this money he acquired what he had been looking for all his life, the irremovable stain. He would never have a moment of doubt or uncertainty again, he was lost beyond all hope of finding his way back.

For an instant of time he thought he saw all the angels in heaven silently turning their faces away from him, but before they had completed their slow turning movement he wondered at the fancy – he did not believe in any of that stuff, he was lost, alone, in the dark.

He slapped Charley on the shoulder.

'Didn't you find where Mister S. kept his drinks, Charley? Thirty thousand dollars calls for a drink of something good, lead me to it.'

'I'm glad to see you're yourself again, sir.' Charley looked enormously relieved. 'You seemed proper upset back there in the garage. But believe me we've nothing to worry about.'

They went through into the farmhouse dining-room where there were drinks and glasses on a sideboard. In the centre of the table there was a glass jug filled with dark violets, still fresh, picked that morning and put in water by one of the men in the garage; their heavy scent filled the room with a gentle sweetness, the soft memorial of another world.

Part Two

17

WALTER reached Bath early the next morning and found Ross was up north conferring with Mackinder: it was not known when he would be back. He spent two full days mooning about the city, waiting. The atmosphere had undergone a subtle change. The excitement of the first days of the civil war, and of the thrust northward had gone. The one sheet daily papers from London had big blanks hacked out by the censors from their headline stories, and nourished rumours.

Forrest-Mitchell underestimating the strength of the enemy air and overestimating his own cover had been caught in the open on the morning of his attack on York.

What had happened then no one, with any precision, knew, but there were various stories to choose from: Miss Willert had heard that Forrest-Mitchell was surrounded somewhere between York and Lincoln.

One of the lieutenant-colonels had an optimistic story that though things had gone wrong in the opening hours of the attack Forrest-Mitchell was slowly fighting his way into York, according to plan, but with heavier losses than he'd bargained for.

A tipsy civilian in the bar of the Empire hotel had heard from 'someone who was there' that F-M had got away by leaving everything behind, including his headquarters unit. He'd reached London with a staff car, three armoured cars, and two requisitioned buses full of officers. His drunken talk was sober truth. All along the east coast the roads were swarming with Russian armour, and the air was full of Russian aircraft. Pockets of southern troops were holding one or two places, but most of the men had surrendered after the first few hours of real fighting.

Walter heard him elaborating his history of disaster to a drunk woman who wasn't listening to him, he was the only person talking in the fairly crowded bar; everyone else was sitting round drinking slowly, without enjoyment, and listening. They didn't believe what he was saying, they didn't believe anything, they just knew that it was all pretty hopeless.

The drunk woman every now and then said, 'shut up, shut up, you'll get yourself into trouble.' But the printed notice on the wall threatening all manner of severe penalties for careless or defeatist talk didn't mean anything any more.

No one cared.

Towards mid-afternoon Walter took up an enquiry into the disappearance of two trainloads of food that ought to have reached Rugby three days earlier from the west country, occupying himself with that to break the boredom of waiting.

They were at Westbury, partly pillaged, in the goods yard. The engines were stone cold and there was no coal in their tenders, there was no coal anywhere at Westbury. The traffic manager showed him the whole jampacked yard with its motionless trains and dead engines.

'The only traffic through here for the past two days has been military stuff, and not much of that. We've got one diesel car moving for civilian traffic, and that's the only thing we can move. Since this morning the only line clear through to London has been the up line, it's been single line working all day. There's a train, run out of coal, standing on the down line somewhere near Savernake. The military said they'd send an engine to haul it out of the way this morning, but they haven't. It's my belief they can't.'

He stopped talking and drew a picture of a girl on the blank form in front of him, doodling to pass the time, it was a curly haired girl with a snub nose.

'Those bloody yanks,' he said, 'if they won't come and fight the Russians for us, they might at least send us some coal.'

Walter checked up on his story at various stations on the way back to Bath, and found it the same everywhere. No coal and no traffic.

At one place he passed an infantry battalion marching north on foot without a single truck in sight, moving at the pace and in the manner of a Roman legion.

When he reached Bath it was twilight and the bite of frost was in the air. Hundreds of people, wrapped in thick clothes until they seemed ungainly and pillow shaped, were going back into the town with perambulators loaded with firewood, or bundles of it slung over their shoulders.

Looking across this stream at the roof tops of the town Walter realised for the first time how few of its chimneys were smoking.

He drove down into Bath station to make one last enquiry about the coal position and found its waiting-rooms and offices crowded with campers, some of them had been waiting there on the off chance of getting a train for two or three days.

The station staff had all gone.

Walter opened door after door and intruded on family life, brothel life, and plain suspended animation. The old parcels office was filled with sleeping deserters, girls of thirteen to sixteen, old tramps, old women; they lay stretched out on makeshift beds of brown paper, shavings, and corrugated paper from ripped open packages, indifferent to each other, to anything, to Walter standing in the open doorway most of all.

Even the deserters didn't bother to stir at the sight of a uniform. They knew that the eye of authority was already glazed and unseeing. Whatever happened they couldn't be worse off in the glasshouse or anywhere else.

Night settled on the town and the street lighting didn't wake. The few windows that showed a gleam let out the soft yellows and oranges of lamplight and candleflame.

Walter locked the car into the N.P.R. garage, and went up to the Crescent to leave a message with Ross's secretary to say that he'd be spending the night at the Empire and wanted to see him on a matter of urgency the minute he returned.

When he went into the hotel he found it filled to overflowing with southern officers having a last spree. Drink had given them a temporary freedom from the weight of the darkness outside and the knowledge of defeat. Sober in the middle of it all, Walter felt lonely and left out.

He went back through the revolving doors of the hotel and picked up one of the hundred odd girls standing in a silent parade along the parapet of the public gardens facing the Victorian building. He chose more or less at random – he just wanted someone to talk to and drink with.

He had a moment of malaise when he stepped back into the brilliantly lit lobby, fearing that she might look too much what she was, but it was all right – she was a decent enough looking Kensington girl in a tailor made with a single row of cultured pearls, and a velvet cap-like hat with a regimental badge on it.

'Rifle Brigade, isn't it?'

'Oh, the badge. Yes, it was daddy's regiment, and my – a friend I had was in it, too. Let's not talk about it.'

She pulled her lips back off her teeth. It was a smile of a kind.

'You need a drink, let's fight our way through to the bar.'

'Well, it's a terribly nice idea, but actually, if you don't mind I'd much rather eat.'

'You look blue with cold. A drink would warm you up.'

'Well actually, I'd be sort of afraid to have a drink, because honestly I haven't had anything to eat yet today, and I'd get hopelessly tiddly if I did have even a little drink.' She pulled her lips back off her teeth again. 'It's silly, but, actually, I'm much more interested in food than money or anything else.'

'I'm sorry, we'll go straight in to see what we can get to eat.'

'That would be marvellous.'

They had brown Windsor soup, roast turkey, and apple tart. They had a bottle of wine but she wouldn't drink any. She sipped a little water and ate, and ate.

'You oughtn't to eat so much,' he kept warning her, 'if you've got an empty stomach.'

'I know it sounds silly, but I don't know when I'll get another meal.'

'I can get you a case of tinned stuff tomorrow.'

'Oh that's big talk,' she was sickly white with dislike of him for a moment, 'I hate men who go in for big talk. I've got to go through with this now I've eaten your food, but please don't promise me a lot of things to make yourself feel big. I know what I'm doing. It won't make things better if you tell me a lot of lies.'

'I'm sorry, but I'm in a position to do it.' He showed her his N.P.R. flash and explained it. 'If you give me your address I'll see to it.'

'I don't know. You might expect too much for a whole case

of tinned food. Actually, I mean, I'm upset at the idea of being under such a colossal obligation to anyone.'

'Very well then, we needn't talk about it any more.'

They were at the only table with any empty places left when four members of the United States Military Mission came into the room. The head waiter looked round and began to steer them towards their table.

'Oh, god, I hate Americans,' said the girl, 'I hope they're not coming here.'

Walter looked at them, envying them their height, their physical magnificence, and their healthy faces.

'Why don't you like them?'

'They're so vulgar and awful, and they're so terribly noisy and immature, they're like people who aren't grown up.' She looked at them with loathing. 'They always let us down.'

'What on earth do you mean?'

'They stay out of wars as long as they can making money, and then they come in and claim all the credit for winning them. And now they aren't doing anything.' She suddenly began to look green. 'I feel terrible.'

'You're going to be sick. It comes of cramming yourself with all that stuff when you're really hungry. Look, I've got a room on the second floor with a bath, here's the key. You go up and get it over with, I'll come up later and see how you are. Don't worry. But run along, or you won't make it.'

She left, rapidly, brushing past the soldiers.

'I hope we didn't scare your guest away, colonel,' said one of the Americans sitting himself down after they had formally introduced themselves.

'Not at all, she wasn't feeling quite the thing.'

'It's very courteous of you to let us share your table.'

'Oh, it's nothing.'

'We really appreciate it, all the same.'

Walter sensed that they were all deeply embarrassed by the girl's flight, and wondered how to put them at their ease.

'I'm afraid you're not seeing Bath, or Britain, quite at its best.'

'Ugh, well, no I guess not.'

They all looked uneasily at each other, and rather curiously at Walter. The youngest of them opened his mouth as if to say something and then clamped it shut. But after an inward struggle the suppressed remark burst out, as if it had a will of its own.

'How the hell can you talk like that, colonel, giving us that small talk stuff about "not quite at its best." Don't any of you people know how bad things are?'

'Now Don,' said one of them. He turned to Walter. 'I apologise, colonel. Don, here, can't get used to the British attitude. "I couldn't care less," and all that. He's from Texas where they don't grow understatements. They go after the naked truth barehanded down there, and shy the lumps at each other, crude and raw when they've caught up on it. Don't let it worry you.'

'I made a damn' silly remark as a matter of fact,' said Walter. 'I don't know why we do that sort of thing. I know as well as you do that the military position here is hopeless. But then if I told you so frankly I'd be sort of fouling my own nest, there's the off chance of you people turning the scale and I don't want to do anything to spoil it.'

'For heaven's sake,' the Texan jumped in again. 'That line we get everywhere. "When your aircraft come," "when you get coal through to us," "when your petrol arrives," "when you decide you've got to beat the Russians to it " . . . we were at an airfield here this morning finding out what had happened to forty jet fighters that were sent there before the fighting began. The damn things were still crated up, the way they came off the ship. The C.O. at the field gave us a lecture, what we ought to have done was send maintenance crews, pilots, and fuel, with the machines. He wanted us to fight his war for him. It's worse than Greece. Nearly as bad as China. We've wasted millions of dollars on shipping in stuff that's never going to be used. What's the matter with you people? How can you just let go of life the way you're doing?'

'It's hard to explain.'

'I'll say it's hard to explain. . . .'

'Now Don. You've no right, no right at all . . .'

'That girl who left the table just now. She was going out to throw up. She was outside the hotel offering herself to anyone who'd buy her a meal. I didn't realise how hungry she was, my guess is she hadn't eaten probably since sometime early yesterday or the day before. Anyway her reaction was typical of starvation. She was cagy but I gathered her father was a regular army man, and her husband is either in the army or has been killed with it. I may be wrong, but I have a feeling that she's the end product of the heroism you're asking for. People have been being heroic all over Europe since the Napoleonic wars to fill the streets of the big towns with women like that.' He paused, adding inwardly; 'and to fill the luxury hotels with people like me.'

'What you say, colonel,' said the senior American officer, 'is profoundly interesting, and if I may say so profoundly distressing. It is entirely characteristic of the attitude we have encountered almost universally since we landed in Britain.'

He spoke rotundly, like a politician, and with a slowness intolerable to a European ear.

'We are acutely conscious of some deep seated social sickness which has robbed most of your people of their self confidence and their faith in any form of social organisation. Now what, would you say, was at the root of that sickness?'

'I don't know. If I could say, if it was common knowledge, we wouldn't be in this pass.'

The Americans leant back, they had been leaning forward, confident that he would make some pronouncement that would reveal a point of view, a philosophy that could be reported on as the property of a typical British colonel.

'That girl was angry, and bitterly resentful, when I offered her a week's supply of food. I'm not sure that I know why, but I suspect that she can't trust anyone who offers her anything above an irreducible minimum.

'All her life she's been promised things, by her society, by the politicians that run it, by the people who brought her up.

'And here she is on the street, existing from meal to meal.

'I was brought up in a progressive liberal family which believed in progress – if everybody was sensible everything would go on and on getting better and better. We thought we were taking part in a continuous, creative revolution.

273

'I began to practice as an architect in the thirties, and I built very little because capitalism was collapsing. . . .'

He caught the Texan's eye fixed contemptuously on him.

'It may not have seemed like that to schoolboys in Texas, but it looked like that over here.

'I never thought I'd look back on that time as a period of opportunity and promise.

'I've had eight good contracts since the war, only two got as far as building, neither of those got near completion. They had to stand aside for state schemes.

'That would have been all right if the state schemes had been sound, but they weren't. They weren't a stimulus to the country, they exhausted its resources. There wasn't anything to complete them with. There was nothing left for the independent builder when they were abandoned. All over the country you'll find the steel frames of great structures that haven't been worked on for two or three years. You'll find new towns laid out on the ground and abandoned. You'll find new state plants for this or that which exist as dreams, as concrete foundations, as stacks of building material among the drifts of nettles.

'That's what it's like in my trade. It's like that all over – everyone you know is involved in the collapse of too grand a dream, doctors tied up in the half completed, half abandoned, health scheme; teachers trying to work a huge educational reform that can't work unless an impossible school rebuilding scheme goes through; businessmen pushed out of production by a trade union dream of short hours and big pay. . . .'

'You're getting into a drone like Longfellow in Hiawatha with all that stuff. Whyn't you say the hell with all this, and scrape up some party to take over with a sensible programme?'

The Texan leant forward, waving his hand in pantomime of someone waving away a fly or a nasty dish.

'Why do you Europeans all lie down and wait for death when things go wrong? Why do you sit around telling each other hard luck stories from dawn to dark? Why the hell don't you make a try at making do with what you've got?'

'That's what you Americans can never realise. We haven't got anything. We gave up individualism for something called the General Good, and when we'd sold out to it, it died on us.

'We're each of us alone now with its stinking carcase.

'We don't believe in God, we don't believe in Marx: Freud taught us we couldn't believe in ourselves . . . you don't make defiant gestures towards the fates in that state of mind.'

'Now, Don . . .'

The senior American officer pitched in quickly to forestall a monosyllabic comment which had already imparted a recognisable shape to his subordinate's lips.

'We as Americans find your attitude on this a little hard to take because we exist by continually reviewing our beliefs and our values.

'We're acutely conscious of all sorts of shortcomings in our society: we're very troubled for instance by the race problem. There's social schizophrenia there, the actual pattern of behaviour of the majority group to the minority doesn't square with the majority attitude on the human rights question.

'It seems to us that Europeans in a similar situation would just lie down and abandon their belief in human rights.

'They'd say that the failure of our society to reach a solution of the race problem indicated that our ideas on human rights were unrealistic dreams.

'We don't, frankly, understand the prevailing mood of defeatism. We're eager to find some hint of determination, or even of a mere desire to survive, on the part of our European friends that would justify further military aid.'

He paused and looked about him.

'We are in process of framing a report that will recommend cutting our losses, as we cut them in Asia. We find you British in the south, here, even harder to understand than the Kuomintang. There's even a noticeable air of festivity about this place tonight, though it's been clear all day that your military position is deteriorating very rapidly indeed.'

'You're catching this British speech habit, Chan,' said one of the officers who had been silent so far. 'It's my guess that this southern junta is finished. If it can do any more deteriorating in its present position I'd be surprised.'

'So would I,' said Walter. 'So would I.'

The Americans all sat very upright, leaning a little back and away from him in their chairs, deeply shocked by this exhibition of European decadence, this naked admission of failure.

'You see, it's like this,' he said. 'Once we were a simple little agricultural economy, poor but honest. We ran off with a beautiful coloured girl who told us she was going to give us hatfuls – or is it hats full – of rubies.

'We had a wonderful honeymoon with that Empire.

'And then it turned out she wanted more money than we'd got. We ran off with a great big golden girl who was going to set us free from the drudgery of farm work, and make us cities paved with gold. When we came to we found ourselves stuck with places like Manchester and Birmingham, where the rain leaves a black stain because the air's so foul, and with the biggest bankruptcy in the world.

'Then we ran away from that mess with a red head – she said she knew that our golden girl had hidden a great big treasure away in some bank or other – it was just a matter of finding where it was, then we could have a wonderful share out, and everyone would be happy.

'She made us feel so good we had the share out. We never found the treasure.

'It had been spent already on the spree before last. That's how we got this hangover.

'And we haven't much confidence in you because you're with the golden girl now, and flirting with the red head. We know how that sort of party ends. We're through with optimism for the time being.'

'I see the outline of your case, colonel, but I don't like it. It's a hard luck story that won't stand up.

'As we see it your individuals are abandoning themselves to the welfare state out of sense of their individual inadequacy. And as we see it your state is abandoning its international role in a very similar way.

'We see your people welcoming – that's what appears to be happening – welcoming a complete disaster. Being taken over by the Russians doesn't seem to mean any more to them than a

276

release from responsibilities and burdens they find too great to think about.

'They've hit bottom, nothing more can happen, they seem sort of happy about it – that's how it seems to us.'

'That's about how it is,' said Walter.

'I don't know which would be worse,' said the Texan, 'to be rotten and not know it, or to be rotten and like it that way.'

A party at the far end of the dining-room broke up, and its nine tipsy men and women were leapfrogging towards the swing doors, along the narrow alleyway between the tables. Near the door one of the frogs keeled over under the weight of the jumper and they both went sprawling into a trolley laden with silverware and glass.

Laughter spread across the room as the jangling smash died away, people stood up to see what was happening.

One of the men wanted to fight the head waiter; he was carried out backwards by two of the others, making threatening gestures as he went, like some mechanical toy that there was no way of stopping until its clockwork motor was run down.

The hot band in the nearby ballroom started up for the first dance of the evening. Its rapid pulsing floated cheerfully into the dining-room mixing with the clatter of knives and forks and the roar of laughter and talk.

'You see,' said the Texan, 'they're happy to be licked. They're excused further effort . . . good grief, what a state of mind they must be in.'

'I hope you never know it, major,' said Walter. 'You may though. When we sold out and went Socialist we accepted a materialism more complete even than yours.

'When you go materialist you limit yourself to two things, success or failure.

'After the torment of not achieving success there's a sort of happiness to be found in adjusting yourself to failure.

'You'll realise in a year or two you'll never be a four star general.

'In time you'll maybe have to realise you were cut out to be the oldest major in the Army Air Forces.

'You may even find yourself being happy in that position.

'I'll come around then and tell you you're happy to be licked.'

'Well!' The Texan put his hands on the arms of his chair and pushed it back sharply as if he were about to rise.

'Colonel,' said the senior American, 'Major Macarteney, here, has the full confidence of the commanding general.

'His efficiency rating is *superior*.

'He is the younger brother of Senator Macarteney. His prospects in the service are more than excellent.

'Your remarks are entirely unjustifiable.

'Adjustment to failure is not one of the problems that face Major Macarteney.

'I think you should withdraw that suggestion.'

'I withdraw without reservation,' Walter stifled an impulse to laugh. 'I regret even putting forward the hypothesis that anyone from Texas could fail, let alone our friend here. I apologise, Macarteney.'

'Forget it.'

There was a pause that lasted an instant too long, then one of the Americans spoke.

'You know the two critical dates in Anglo-American relations?'

'No?'

'Bunker Hill, and the New York opening of *Journey's End*.'

Walter drank listening to them talking among themselves, they had in some way extruded him from their party.

'I don't get it.'

'Why Bunker Hill made us believe in something that never existed, and *Journey's End* showed what the hell of a mistake we'd made.'

'Well now, he's going to make the British Empire disappear under a napkin, hey presto. I bet you can't do it, Nick.'

'I boned up on the Empire once. It never was. They didn't even have a General Staff till round about nineteen hundred. They didn't count for the snap of a finger in Europe from 1840 to fat Edward's time. When they had some showdown with France over the Sudan in the nineties – that Fashoda thing – they found they hadn't enough artillery to support a brigade overseas. The great power we think we fought against in the War of

Independence only came into being during the South African war....'

'Guns aren't everything,' said Walter.

'He's still here,' said Texas.

'No,' said the historian, 'we know guns aren't everything. It takes sterling virtues, moral ruggedness, and all that, to run a great Empire. We had a look at that side of the British in *Journey's End*. We're onto you, colonel.' He lifted his glass. 'Here's to the Empire, chaps, all fifty years of it, from sunrise to sunset.'

'You've forgotten something,' Walter stood up.

They all looked at him with a barefaced eagerness. From the second in which he had admitted that the southern military position was hopeless they had been working steadily to find out just how much he would take, and they were interested now to see if he had just come apart under pressure, or if they had got him angry to the pitch where he would stick up for himself. If he had come apart under their ribbing then they would know he was no good. If he was in a mood to fight he was all right. They would climb down then, as Texas had made him climb down, and admit that he was a man.

'Generalisations about states and groups aren't worth a damn. They don't mean anything. They aren't about real things. The only real things are people. Take them one by one and you'll find out something worth knowing. Take great issues and great states and you'll just get a bellyful of wind, approximations that won't mean a thing. Find out why Texas here is so aggressive and so touchy, and you'll find out something worth knowing. Find out what happens to people and you'll have the answer to what happens to communities. . . .'

The four faces looked at him, carefully noncommittal and blank. The historian and the senior officer had an intent look in their eyes. Walter knew that they were rapidly filing the material they were getting for future reference. He could see it taking shape on a card, the sort of card you could process through a machine.

Nationality: British. Status: Middle Class, Colonel, Middle Aged. College Education. Remarks. Weakness of character and

Defeatism, functions of the bourgeois situation in society. Typical symptomatic thought patterns. Overemphasis on the importance of the individual, corresponding loss of belief in Society (agency depriving his class of its privileged position).

They were looking at his flesh and blood, and his tormented emotion, and making it into a ghostly, negotiable abstract.

Only the Texan saw him in human terms, and then from no vantage point of sympathy but only as a warning of what might happen to him if his will broke, if he resigned himself, and gave, limply, up the struggle to reach the glittering stars at the top of the trees.

'Communities which stake their future on success, and sacrifice . . .' the words were campaign oratory, abstract, dead, unrelated to life, they were poisonous coming out of his mouth, 'individual rights, and make families and natural associations less important than communal duties commit suicide. When they run into failure they've no reserves left. They've just got crowds of broken people on their hands, people who'll turn on the community that has failed them and tear it apart.'

Walter shut his eyes, momentarily dropping the lids so that he could shut out the irrelevant dining-room and in a moment of dark clarity find the phrase that would take what he was trying to say out of the foggy realm of abstractions, through the defensive outworks of psychiatrists' language into the hearts of the men facing him.

As soon as his eyelids met he found himself in the glare of the naked bulbs on the dockside gantry, of the naked bulb in the farm garage, looking down at the broken bodies on the concrete. He had forfeited all right to speak.

He opened his eyes again instantly, and flinching from the uncomprehending eyes fixed on his face, turned with a helpless gesture and left them.

'I guess he was drunk.'

'Are we stuck with his check?'

'I guess so.'

'You've got to hand it to the British. In some lines they have talent.'

'That brown Windsor stuff is terrible. I guess it's the food

280

they eat. Think of being reared on this food. You'ld reach twenty-one longing to find the way out.'

'I'd give a lot to know why they are the way they are.'

'We never will, thank god.'

Walter went up to his room and was for a moment puzzled by the faint smell of puke that reached him as he stood in the doorway. Then the girl sat up in bed and lit the candle. He'd forgotten about her.

'I'm sorry, I've been terribly sick in your bathroom.'

'Oh, bad luck, I was afraid you would be.'

'I've done my best to tidy up. I'm terribly sorry.'

'Don't be sorry.'

'I was so angry with myself. I hated to see all that lovely food go to waste.' She lay down and began to cry.

'There, there.' He sat down on the side of the bed and patted her shoulder. She rolled over and dabbed her tears away with a corner of the sheet.

'I kept trying to stop myself. There, that's all now, I said, but I just kept on and on, until it was all gone.'

'Poor kid.'

He patted her hand, got up and went with some reluctance to the bathroom. She had made a good job of cleaning up considering her condition. She'd even washed out her blouse and hung it up to dry, and she'd cleaned off the front of her skirt and her jacket. The clothes were all neatly and sensibly on the towel rail, along with the towel she'd used for the cleaning job, that too washed and rinsed out.

The tidiness and the practicality conjured up a nice background where some clean and orderly woman had brought her little girl to be neat and good, training her to be a good wife and a good mother.

He came out of the bathroom and found her lying stiffly in the bed staring at the ceiling. He looked at her face and saw that she had her underlip clamped between her teeth. When she brought herself to look at him and saw that he hadn't been undressing in the bathroom she slowly relaxed. She tried to smile, but her shoulders were drawn in together with disgust. Her body was shaken by a shivering fit.

281

'I've got some cans of a chocolate flavoured milk drink the Americans sent in, I'll warm one up and see if you can keep that on your stomach.'

He took his camp stove out of the bottom of the wardrobe and heated the can in a pan of water on its roaring ring of flame. While he waited for it to warm up he rang through to the office but there was still no news of Ross; he told them to call him the minute they had any and rang off again.

'Now drink this in little sips, make it last as long as you can. If you bolt it you'll throw up again for sure.'

'I don't believe I can touch it. It smells so sickly sweet.'

'Don't be difficult. If you don't get back into the way of eating you may die of it.'

She took a few sips, fought nausea for a moment, held them and then began to drink again. When she was done she lay back again letting the warmth of the drink spread through her.

'I wish I wasn't so scared of dying. It would be so much easier than anything else.'

'You're about twenty, aren't you?'

'Twenty-two.'

'What happened to you?'

'Daddy was chief of police in Charport, he stayed in office when the Republicans were in the town.

'He said he had a duty to perform.

'Then Mackinder's people came.

'They had some sort of a court martial. It was secret. Then they shot him.

'I don't know where my husband is. Mummy sort of collapsed after what happened to daddy.

'I brought her to Bath because Aunt Jessie lives here. Now she's ill too.

'I tried to get some sort of work, but I couldn't. We had about a hundred pounds when we came here, but it's all gone.

'Aunt Jessie eats and eats. She's terribly fat. She puts her fingers right into her mouth when she eats and licks her fingertips for the crumbs.'

She looked at the ceiling as if everything she wasn't saying was written on it.

'It's a terrible thing to say, but when I go home I pray that I'll find them dead. It's all so hopeless.'

She ran out of words again.

'You didn't see me steal the rolls off the table, downstairs, did you? I'm getting good at that sort of thing. They're in my bag, now. To take home to mummy and Aunt Jessie.'

She sat up in bed and imitated Aunt Jessie eating a roll.

'She takes off the crust bit by bit, and then she picks away at the crumb, putting the little pieces bit by bit onto the tip of her tongue. Then she dabs at the crumbs on her lap with her finger-tip, like this.'

She licked the tip of her finger and dabbed at the bedclothes. She lay down again.

'I couldn't get them anything yesterday, or the day before. Mummy just lies there. . . .'

She thought for a long time.

'That's what happened to me.'

'You poor child.'

He picked the only thing out of her story that really interested him.

'Are you sure your father was shot by Mackinder's people?'

'Yes. They shot everybody in Charport who had anything to do with the Republicans. It was the same in Bristol.

'One of the girls was telling me about it her brother was shot. She knows who did it. She says it was the man who cleaned up Charport for the generals, too, and Plymouth, and Wolverhampton. A Major Fergusson.

'She said we all ought to get together to make statements about what happened when the Reds come, then they'll kill Major Fergusson.

'She said she'd found out a lot going with the officers here, some of them work for Fergusson.

'Actually, I can't see any point in it, it won't bring daddy back. It won't bring her brother back.

'I suppose it makes it easier for her to keep going if she can think about getting Fergusson killed. All I think about is food, really. And I hate Aunt Jessie much more than Major Fergusson.

It's much worse for her to be greedy and fat, than for him to have killed daddy.'

Walter didn't say anything, he was surprised that he hadn't thought before that Mackinder had a Charley Snow on his back, was certain to have in the nature of things. The northerners would be sure to have one too . . . there would be someone in the end to tap him on the shoulder and ask him if his name was Walter Jackson.

'I believe I've shocked you. I know it's terribly wrong of me, to feel the way I do about Aunt Jessie, but I can't help it.

'I'll tell you something worse.

'I was nerving myself not to go home any more tonight. Mother hasn't recognised me for a week now, she never speaks. It might be much better for her if I let her alone. . . . I mean she isn't really alive the way she is, it might be a sort of release really.

'And I think Aunt Jessie is only pretending to be ill, if I didn't go home she might get up and look after herself. She's got some silver hidden somewhere. She doesn't want to sell it. I've tried to find it, but I can't. If I just didn't go back I'm sure she'd manage. She could sell the silver and manage.

'Do you think it would be right if I didn't go back?'

'I can't say. If you feel it would be right, then it would be right.'

'No, it wouldn't be right . . .' she dissolved into childish tears. '. . . it could never be right. But I can't do anything else. I hate them so – for being so helpless.'

He watched her as she lay weeping with the feeling of impotence that sometimes had overwhelmed him when Francis or Jeanette disintegrated under an unfathomable baby grief.

You can't cry, he remembered, with a toffy, or the kind of sweet that has to be sucked, in your mouth.

He had some glucose sweets in the wardrobe, they'd come from America and they were supposed to be specially virtuous for the nearly starved, they'd do her good as well as stop her crying.

She took one, and presently quieted down to an occasional snuffle; lying there with tear stains round her eyes, and her cheek bulging with the boiled sweet, she looked much younger than twenty, hardly a woman at all.

He read the medical spiel on the label, about how good the glucose was for her condition. What she wanted was milk, eggs, and plenty of protein foods, fish, chicken, and, later on, butcher's meat.

What could he do for her? Nothing, probably.

The candle flame began to flicker and he deftly nicked quarter of an inch off the elongated wick.

'You could live here for a bit, if you wanted to.'

'How could I? It's fifty pounds a day, isn't it?'

'I keep this room all the time. I live in the country, but I have to be here three or four nights a week. You'ld have it to yourself half the time.'

'You'ld go away, and I'd be landed with the bill.'

'I promise you not.'

She stared at him with terrified eyes.

'What would you want me to do?'

'Nothing.'

'Oh, no. It's never like that.'

He felt uneasy with the bottle of boiled sweets in his hands. It was like the things you read about in the *News of the World*: furtive old men hanging about the gates of the schoolyards; 'come into the bombed buildings, come-out onto the waste ground, and I'll give you some sweeties, little girl.'

He got up and went away from the bedside into the shadowy part of the room outside the circle of candlelight. Behind him an enormous black shadow travelled across the wall. Her voice came thin and small from her wispish shape in the middle of the big bed.

'They always want more than you bargain to give. And if you give it, they cheat you . . . I can pay for the dinner you gave me. What I'm ready to give you won't pay for anything more. I won't take anything more than I can pay for. It wouldn't be decent.'

He walked about while his images marched and counter marched across the looking glasses on the dressing table, and on the wardrobe door, multiplying at their bevelled edges, brightly flashing across the movement of his slowly swinging shadow.

'I don't want to owe you more than I can pay back. I don't want to owe anybody anything. I'll only take what I can pay for. I won't be dishonest.'

'You won't have to be.'

He waved his hand round the room.

'I'm offering you the emptiness of this room when I'm not here, the part of it I'm not using when I am here. I'm offering you food I wouldn't eat, and money I'm ashamed to have. I'm offering you nothing, and I don't want anything for it.'

'I don't want you to pretend to be in love with me. I don't even want you to be interested in me. I just don't want to be alone. A dog or a cat might do, but the dog wouldn't be able to look after itself while I was away, and the cat wouldn't be here when I wanted it. Just be here, that's all.'

'I won't,' she said it stubbornly, 'take anything I can't pay for. It wouldn't be fair.'

'I've told you how you can pay for it.'

'I'd owe you too much.'

The candleflame guttered up, down, up, down, as the wick drowned in melted wax; darkness, while he stared stupidly, rushed in on the down beat and possessed the room.

He groped for a fresh candle with his eyes tight shut to shield them from the blackness, but not finding one, panicked. He heard footsteps and laughter in the corridor and made for the door meaning to let light into the room, but ran into the end of the bed.

He'd no idea where the door was. He reached out across the covers towards her heavy, scared, breathing, and found her hand held protectively in front of her face.

She gave a little gasp as he grasped it, of pure terror.

'You don't have to be afraid. I'm afraid. Say something so I'll know I'm not alone. I'm afraid of the dark, now. That's why I want you to be here.'

'I can't think of anything. . . .'

He laid his head on her breast and listened to the beating of her heart, feeling the warmth of her body.

'I knew you'd want more than I can give,' she said. 'There isn't anything anyone can do for anyone else.'

286

'Just be here,' he said, 'that's all I want.'

She thought about it, with less terror. He heard her heartbeat slow down to an unhurried thumping.

'If that's all you want, I'll stay. I'll be here.' She put her hand on the back of his head and gently moved her fingers in a minimal stroking movement.

'You're no worse off than anyone else.'

He barely heard her, and before he could say 'No, no worse,' he was asleep.

She thought of slipping away, but her blouse would still be wet – and he might turn nasty if he caught her. She held him in her arms, drowsed, and dreamt that he was her husband, come back. When the telephone rang and she felt him trying to go she held tightly onto him.

'Don't ever leave me, never leave me again . . .'

'For god's sake.'

He twisted away, desperately.

'Hallo? Ross? Thank goodness you're back. I've got to see you right away. . . .'

She listened hopelessly to the wrong voice talking in the dark, and then in the near silence to the tiny quacking of the metal plate in the earphone. She could hear his breathing. It was one stranger listening to another, to talk from far away.

The connection was bad, and Walter had to strain to hear the thin voice through the crackling.

'All you want to worry about is getting out of here, old man, get out before morning. It's all over bar the shouting.'

'What?'

'Mackinder is finished. The Reds have licked him. They broke through along his whole front yesterday. They're on their way. I've been running like stink to get ahead of them. They'll be here by midday.'

'Are you sure?'

Walter fought hard to clear his mind of the mists of sleep, it was hard to discard his anxieties about the Stanislavsky killing for something that might be worse even than that in its consequences. 'I've heard a lot of rumours about the eastern front. Are you sure this story isn't . . .'

287

'I was there. The rumours can't be worse than the truth,' Ross broke in. 'They had me once for a couple of hours. I've come from Mackinder's H.Q. I know what's what. And those fuggers aren't playing the game in the gentlemanly way. I helped two blokes from the Dorsets get away. They're shooting everybody they find in uniform over the rank of sergeant. Take my tip and get going: get home and into civilian dress. Leave no traces behind.'

'What about N.P.R., all the papers, the organisation . . . ?'

'I'm arranging a fire, old boy.'

'A fire? I don't understand. . . ?'

Walter thought of the whole widespread structure of the relief machinery. How could you burn it like a letter?

'Hell, don't be so slow on the uptake.'

'I can only just hear what you're saying . . .'

'Look, I'll tell you what. I'll pick you up on my way to Lemlade when I pull out – oh, in an hour. Then I'll put you in the picture and we'll cook up a cover story together.'

'In about an hour?'

'Yes, will you be ready to come?'

'Yes, I'll be ready.'

'You'd better. We'll be cutting it quite fine enough as it is. I'll be seeing you.'

'In an hour then. Good-bye.'

'I'll be seeing you.'

It didn't matter, then about Stanislavsky, he thought, standing in the dark fumbling for the base of the telephone, nothing could matter very much in the face of chaos.

When he had hung up he stood fingering the badges of rank on the shoulder of his battledress jacket: they were rewards of duty faithfully done in a war worth winning. It would be bloody funny to be shot for having them up after tearing his conscience to pieces for all that he had done since.

He was surprised to find that he wasn't alone, that there was someone with him in the room.

'It's always the same.'

'Eh, what's that?'

'It's always the same.'

He found a candle and a match at last and rediscovered her face, she spoke flatly, without looking at him.

'They always try to make it more than they can buy. And when they've got it, they cheat.'

She brushed a lock of hair off her forehead with a small, beautiful, hand.

'All that stuff about always being here, and wanting not to be alone. You're going to turn me out in an hour.'

She sat up glaring at him, furious with him for not being her husband, for being part of the crushing and pitiless flow of meaningless events.

'Not that I care, not that I expected anything else . . .'

'Now, listen. . . .'

'Don't try to get round me again.'

'I've got to go now for a little while. I'll be coming back. I want you to be here.'

'You'll never come back. I'll be left, in trouble with the hotel. They'll go to the police. I know.'

She swung her legs out from under the covers and stood up in her shift, a gawky schoolgirl in spite of her make up and her age.

He watched her looking for her stockings and shoes in the seat of the big armchair at the bed end. He stepped up to her and took her hand.

She stood quite limply waiting, it wasn't worth defending herself, whatever he might mean to do – blows, love making, abuse, it would make no difference.

Momentarily the thought of all three chased through his mind, anything would be worth doing that forced her into making some acknowledgment of him as a person, but that was not really what he wanted. The trace of a rooster's pride still in him wanted that, he wanted this intimacy of indifference that hadn't taken them even to the point of exchanging names, and wanted it to go on like that.

'Let me get dressed, please, I'm getting cold.'

'Go back to bed,' he let her hand go, 'you can't go tonight . . . and there's no point. I'm going. The room's paid for up to the end of the month – that gives you eighteen days. There's a stack of tinned stuff in the wardrobe . . . and here's a thousand dollars to cover anything that comes up. You'ld be a fool to go. I don't see how this can add up to trouble for you, whatever happens.'

'You're a fool,' she found her handbag and pushed the money into it. 'I may go the minute you've gone, with all this. I'd be a fool not to.'

'I know you won't.'

'You can't know.'

'I do. That's all.'

She shrugged her shoulders as if excusing herself of all blame for the consequences of his idiocy and putting her bag down went back to bed. She did not speak to him again, but lay watching him as he gathered up his coat, his webbing belt, and a few documents which he crammed into his brief case.

He settled his cap onto his head and looked into the glass on the wardrobe door to see if he was properly dressed for the outside world.

As usual the N.P.R. cap badge surprised him by not being the right badge, and its absurd character gave him a twinge of panic, as if he had found himself on the brink of going on parade in fancy dress. He eyed it, N.P.R. in a laurel wreath above an inscribed ribbon, 'Mercy to All, Favour to None.' What an unutterable swine Ross was. He paused in the doorway, looking back at her candlelit face.

'Good-bye. I don't know when I'll be back.'

He waited for a few seconds for her to answer, but she made no sign. When the door was shut he stood just outside it wondering if he should go back and ask her name, or if he should tell her his own. He heard the pudder of her bare feet on the floor on the other side of the door and the click of the bolt driven home. He went off down the stairs to wait for Ross in the almost deserted lobby.

18

ANNE came in from the milking shed with just short of eight gallons of milk and set most of it in the wide skimming pans standing ready on the cold purple slate shelves in the dairy.

It always pleased her to fill the blue-white enamel pans with the creamy warm yellow-white milk. The richness of the milk from the demure dark eyed Guernsey cows never ceased to surprise and delight her in comparison with her memories of the thin chalk white stuff that her father's scrub shorthorns had produced.

She poured the dregs from the two milking pails into a saucer in the kitchen under the sleepy cat's nose, rinsed the pails with cold water, and stood them to drain in the scullery.

When she came back the cat was standing up yawning, stretching its legs, as it stood over the saucer preparing to drink. The coffee percolator chuck, chuck, chuckled on the stove and filled the kitchen with a pleasant smell, reminding her of breakfast.

She went into the larder and chose eight eggs, four white for herself and Margery, four dappled brown ones for Francis and Jeanette. On first thought she meant to boil them, but on second thought she decided that was lazy – they'd had boiled eggs the day before, it would be nicer to have them scrambled. She put a pan on the cool side of the stove with a walnut of butter slowly melting on its bottom and broke the eggs into a mixing bowl, added two tablespoonsful of cream, and scattered salt and pepper on the surface; all ready to beat up and cook while the children ate their porridge.

The sun lifted clear of the drift of willows on the far side of the mill dam and flooded the kitchen with sunlight. The children burst into the room with it. They stopped in disappointment when they saw Anne.

'Oh bother.'

'What's the matter?'

'We meant to have breakfast ready when you came in from milking this morning,' said Jeanette.

'For a surprise,' said Francis. 'Look! There's the kingfisher.'

The bird flashed past the window and they all ran to watch him fly on up the edge of the reedbed out of sight.

'Gosh, he's beautiful, isn't he?' said Francis as they all leant over the window ledge hoping he would come back. He turned his head a little closer to Anne's ear, 'nearly as beautiful as you.'

She rumpled his hair, fondly, loving him as much for being himself as for being Walter's child. It was extraordinary how like his father he was without being a copy of his father, exciting to see how happiness at the mill had added to his beauty since he had arrived.

'Come and eat your porridge.'

They sat down over their big bowls of oatmeal, sugar and cream while Anne beat up the eggs and put them on the fire. She stood over the stove keeping the eggs moving with a wooden spoon. Two rounds of buttered toast were waiting ready in the cool oven on hot plates.

Waves of heat came up from the stove into Anne's face, and hot and cold flashes dashed over her body. The room seemed to sway like a boat as Margery opened the door, coming in with a smile and a good morning.

'Oh, Margery, can you finish the eggs, please? There's toast in the oven.'

She wiped her forehead which was inexplicably wet with beads of sweat. 'I don't feel well. I must just lie down . . .'

She ran out of the room.

Margery went up to see if she was all right as soon as she could, and found her still white and shaky, but already feeling better, lying on her bed.

'Oh, I feel so terrible.'

'I expect you do. I always did.'

'Do you know,' Anne looked unhappy, 'what's the matter?'

'There isn't anything the matter. There's nothing wrong with you, it's all quite natural . . .' she pressed her hand. 'Please don't worry. I'm not upset.'

'You can't be so nice. You make me feel terribly ashamed.'

'It isn't that you don't want the child – that it's an accident. . . ?'

'Oh no . . .'

'I didn't really think so. I saw you looking at Francis the other night after tea in the lamp light, and it crossed my mind then that you were thinking . . . about something like this, about what a child of Walter's would look like.'

'You're not angry?'

'I'm a little bit jealous . . . but I knew it was bound to happen sooner or later, and, really, I'm glad for you.' She smiled. 'It's all mixed up like everything else, but it's worth it, I know it is.'

Anne sat up with her colour coming back and they looked out at the sunlit landscape. Their field of winter wheat shone brilliant green on the dark earth, the withies were beginning to blaze with orange and crimson, and the other trees glowed at their twig ends with purples and dark reds.

'Mother had so many children, and she hated it so . . . I'm scared of it, Margery.'

She took hold of herself.

'And father hated mother for it . . . that's what I'm afraid of really.'

'It isn't the same for all women,' Margery disregarded Walter's feelings for the moment. 'Some women hate it, and have a bad time. Some women manage the whole thing without much trouble. I had an easy time and I rather liked it. Honestly, it was the most tremendously satisfying thing I've ever done. I'd always felt a bit ashamed of being a woman until then. It's difficult to explain, you'll understand when it happens . . . it's making a new person, a new life, out of your love, out of an emotion, out of pleasure . . . out of nothing. I felt so rich and creative when the children were born that almost everything else except love seemed rather small and trivial, and unimportant. . . .'

They sat side by side looking at the sun bringing the earth back to life after the winter. Margery remembered that Walter hadn't been able to touch her from the time he knew she was pregnant until the time the babies were weaned, it had cost him an effort of will to pretend to be interested in the children until they were no longer babies.

He had once confessed to her that the smell of the babies and the sweetish milky smell that had come from her while she was feeding them had disgusted him more than anything else that lay within his experience in peace and in war.

He had told her this to explain and justify a period of indifference and neglect that had wounded her, she could remember still the shock with which she realised that he thought he was clearing up a misunderstanding with reasons as clear as daylight which anyone in their senses would understand.

Though she could envy Anne for carrying a child of his, she could not envy her next fourteen or fifteen months of relationship with him. The first part of it would not be too bad, her body would manufacture its own subtle narcotics to keep her from worry during that time. But it would be hard when she woke from her creative dream to find that she had somehow committed the gravest of offences.

A memory of the very beginning of her marriage came suddenly to the surface of her mind. They had been driving into London on a Sunday morning and as she had idly looked at the numbers of working class fathers out with their children or with their charged perambulators he had turned to her with a smile of amused contempt:

'I wouldn't be seen dead pushing a pram.'

'Why ever not. . . ?'

'A man looks such an ass pushing a pram, so hopelessly unmanly. . . .'

She hadn't understood how it could be unmanly to do anything that proclaimed a man's fatherhood and was surprised by the vehemence with which he stuck to his point.

'Don't ever ask me to push a pram for you – that's all . . .'

Anne thought of the way in which her father's time out of the house, down at the pub boozing, had drawn out with the progress of her mother's pregnancies, until towards the end he merely came to the house to sleep. As the child grew away from its mother she became tolerable to him again, until once more the tenderness that grew up between them betrayed them into a physical relation and the cycle began to roll round towards its climax.

Father would suddenly realise that her body was thickening, or would detect her in some necessary preparation which she would be furtively making.

'Why, you ain't that way again? You stinkin' animal, tell me you ain't breedin'? You creature, a man's only got to put his hand on you and you're in pod. Tell me you ain't that way? Tell me you're doing it for sis, or that cow down the road. Don't tell me we got to go through all that again.'

'Hush, you, Ned Hanson, the children. . . .'

Anne could see her mother in the low ceilinged kitchen, dead pale, pretending to be unruffled and getting on with the household work, pretending the children weren't crowding the room, silent, scared to death. Her father sat in the big armchair bawling out his filth, scarlet in the face, with his blue eyes popping out of his head, leaning forward with his strong, cruel, hands on his knees.

She saw the doctor bending over him in that same stuffed chair the evening his last child – so far as she knew – was born. He had passed out and was lying snoring with his head flopped over onto the fat padded arm of the chair, his mouth open and the pupils of his eyes rolled up under the half closed lids. His waistcoat was unbuttoned, his tie loosed, and his shirt, open down to the third button, showed a triangle of scarlet flesh glazed over by a gold fuzz of curly hair. His breath filled the room with the reek of secondhand whiskey.

The doctor, so clean, and so much harder and finer, that he seemed to be a different kind of animal, leant over him and tried to shake him back to consciousness.

'Wake up you carcass,' he muttered, 'your wife's blessed you with another daughter . . . poor bitch.'

As she had helped the doctor into his coat she had sworn she would never, never, be tricked into bearing any man a child.

And now she was longing for this Anne-Walter person, to have it in her arms, to see it turn day by day from helpless pink slug into a fine Walter-Anne boy, or an Anne-Walter girl. She dreamed of seeing whichever it was to be growing up in the quiet and security of the mill to take possession of life at last, unscarred, unwounded, rich in love, ready to make more love.

But the old demons that she couldn't leave behind, as she had left the old farm behind, presented her with a picture of Walter leaning forward in a chair, his face twisted with fury, a parody of her father, shouting his loathing of her fulfilment and liberation, disgusted at the realisation of his virility, at its incarnation.

'I'm scared of what will happen when I tell Walter. I wish he was here. . . .'

'He . . .' Margery started, 'he came back late last night – or early this morning – between three and four – I think – I didn't think that you wouldn't know. . . .'

'Oh . . .' Anne's eyes widened. 'I wonder if he knows. He's been so strange lately – as if he hated me – at times – I wonder if he's, somehow, guessed. . . .'

'How shall I bear to live if I've already become loathsome to him,' she thought.

'Have you noticed anything? Has he said anything about being angry with me? He hasn't said anything about wanting me to go away? Has he?'

'No,' Margery said, 'or rather I have noticed . . . I don't know what . . . but I was going to suggest that I should go away. My being here has been rather a failure – it's just spoilt the you and him thing, and it hasn't done the me and him thing any good. He's been so strange to me . . . I thought I'd have to go . . . but it's so lovely here, and the children are so happy, and we get along so well . . . that it does seem a horrible thing to leave. . . .'

'Please don't talk about leaving . . . I need you – I've been very happy with you and the children. . . .'

She wanted to go on to explain how far away she had been from this happiness which Margery had helped her to regain.

'Promise me that you won't go – or think of going. . . .'

'I'll promise. . . .'

Walter came downstairs at midday, but Anne could not get

296

him alone until after lunch. Margery contrived it, even then, taking coffee through into the front room and leaving them there together with some excuse.

Walter was silent and his eyes seemed lightless. Anne feared that he was sick with some incurable illness – that fear momentarily drove out everything else.

A log dropped in the fire and sent a train of bright sparks streaming up the chimney. Although Walter was staring straight at it he made no indication that he was aware of it. His pupils remained motionless, fixed on something else, far away.

When he blinked his eyelids moved across motionless eyeballs, he drank his coffee down like an automaton, still staring ahead of him.

'Walter,' she said it three times and drew him back into the room. 'Is anything the matter?'

'Oh, everything. . . .' He was bewildered to find that she wasn't in his own state of abject hopelessness.

'Have I done something wrong?'

'Good lord, no. It's just that . . .' He shrugged and swept one hand round in an embracing gesture. 'It's all over, everything's finished. There's no point in going on.'

'But . . . I love you, and so does Margery, and the children are wonderfully happy . . . and there's the mill . . . and the farm . . . what more can you want.'

'Don't you understand anything . . . the war is over, Mackinder's been beaten . . . the Republicans will be here any day, there's nothing to stop them. . . .'

'But, darling, the cows will go on giving milk. The wheat and the oats will grow just the same . . . and more and more farmers are coming to the mill. . . .'

'They'll take everything away from us. You don't understand. They hate us.'

'They can't hate us for growing things, and for grinding corn. We're useful . . . and besides you've been doing this relief work. Nobody can have anything against you. They won't bother us.'

'You talk like a child. Everything's finished.'

'It's only just begun.'

'There won't be anything but bitterness, starvation, and vengeance . . . don't look so smug, I can't tell you what it's like in the towns already . . . it's all going to spill out over the whole country now. It's the worst mess there's ever been. . . .'

'Can't you stop thinking about politics, and all that dreariness? Can't you remember the mill for a moment, and all of us? Can't you see how much we've got?'

She reached out and touched him.

'Walter, I'm going to have a child.'

'What?' She saw from his face that it was bad news. 'Are you sure?'

'Yes, of course.' She lifted her head proudly, 'I'm very glad.'

'You can't be – you can't want to bring a child into this filth and mess. You can't . . .'

Now that he had been brought back to concentrate his thoughts on her he was appalled by her, by her gross vitality, her abundant health, the generous golden glow of her whole being; she had no right to be like that, she should have been like one of the grey faced, hopeless people in the town queues, like the girl in the hotel; she ought to face reality.

'It wouldn't be fair to the child. We've nothing to give it.'

'Oh, Walter . . .'

She opened her arms and let them fall, with a gesture resigning him and his absurdities to the immensity of the world that lay about them.

'You can't have it. . . .' He looked at her. 'How long have you known? There's probably still time. . . .'

'You're mad.'

'Don't be a sentimental fool. I'm just trying to think of some way to protect you from this disaster.'

'It isn't a disaster. It's the greatest happiness for me. I won't get rid of the child.'

'I'm sorry – I've put it crudely to you. You don't realise how bad things are. . . .'

He dropped his voice, maddeningly treating her as a sick, nearly deranged, person.

'In time to come you'll see why I have to take this line, and you'll be thankful. I know it.'

'You don't know anything at all . . . about me, or life, or anything.'

'I wish I knew something about the local doctors – we'll have to find the right man.'

'You can't mean what you're saying.'

He went over to her and patted her like a horse that was being restive and giving trouble.

'I know it must have been a shock for you to find out what's happened to you. I realise I can't ask you to be reasonable at once, but just think it over, and I'm sure you'll see that I'm right. . . .'

'I'll never agree to murder my child. . . .'

'Please don't prejudice the issue with words like that. I know it's an ugly thing to think about, but it's common sense – you must try to think about the difficulties. We can't always do what we want. . . .'

He felt a great pity for her welling up in him, it was heart-breaking that she shouldn't be able to realise the futility of her defiance of fate, or her determination to colonise the lost future.

'I'm sorry, darling, it would be wonderful if things were all right – but they just aren't and we must face it.'

He paused, pulling at his underlip, facing it, and she looked at him wondering how it was possible to love him as much as ever – even now. He thought, Ross!

'I know a man who may be able to help us – he knows every-one round here – he'll be able to put us onto the right doctor. I'll go and see him this afternoon.'

He looked importantly at the clock on the wall, the man of action to the rescue.

'Now don't you worry, everything will be all right.'

'Nothing will ever be right again between us if you do this. . . .'

She looked at his white, strained, face unhappily. Something from her farm knowledge stirred in her, the recognition of outward signs of disorder that would make her pick out one animal from a herd with a half spoken doubt – I don't like the look of that one.

'Walter, you're tired, you're run down . . . sleep on this before you do anything, before you make up your mind. I've

299

not been "caught"; this isn't anything I want to get out of . . . for me it's happiness, the most exciting and wonderful thing that's ever happened to me . . . can't you try to see it as what I want most in the world?'

'You're out of your mind. . . .'

He moved a little farther away from her, appalled by her blind, animal faith in the future, by her blindness to the unspeakable realities. The dock rats, Stanislavsky and his men, gibbered at him; he could not let another child come into the world, either to be a killer or to be killed, to take its unbearable portion in the endless cycle of painful birth, suffering, and death.

'There's only one thing to be done. . . .'

He went out through the back door, and, standing by the window, she saw him go off through the orchard out into the mournful fields.

The morning's sunlight was all gone, clouds had been driving south from the northern sky on a cold wind all day and were now banked solid from one horizon's rim to the other, dark green, light absorbent, packed with snow.

If I believed the sun would never show through again, if I believed it would always be like this, if I believed those black, glistening trees in the orchard would never set leaf or fruit again, if I believed the mill would never have ripe grain to grind again, then I might do what you want me to do, she thought. ·

She saw him farther off now with his head down against the cold wind, a hunched up, twisted, figure, moving rapidly across a faraway field, searching for death for her child.

She went out quickly and called after him. 'Come back, come back, Walter, come back. . . .' There was no answer, he was too far away.

Walter did not find Ross although he called up and down the empty house and through the wild garden. A kettle simmered on the hob of the range in the empty kitchen, and Walter sat waiting in the wicker chair, lured by this promise of an imminent return, for more than an hour before he gave up and went back to the mill, leaving a note on the table – 'Must see you on a matter of greatest urgency. Will come again tomorrow about ten. W.J.'

Ross heard him calling, and lay hidden till he saw him go drearily away down a walk nearly closed by overgrown Portugal laurels. The first snowflakes fluttered down, like white moths against the dark green bushes brushing his shoulders, as he passed out of sight.

Ross went back to work angered at the waste of time. He had spoken plainly about the unwisdom of Walter's coming near his place by daylight in any case, at the moment it was doubly inconvenient. He made his way through a tangle of bushes back to the old church where he'd been when he'd first heard Walter's call.

The light was nearly gone inside. The stained glass robbed the dark green glow of the snowy twilight of its last brightness – it was a mere softening of the darkness when it had filtered through the Pre-Raphaelite reds, purples, and arsenic greens. The winged stunners, and the armoured saints, of the Burne-Jones heaven held the church as an outpost of night.

Ross wondered for a time about lighting a hurricane lamp. If anyone should see a light they'd be bound to take an interest in it, any local would know that nobody had had any good reason to show a light in the place since . . . he couldn't remember when.

He could dimly recall going to morning service there once in a blue moon when he was ten, eleven, thirteen perhaps, with his hair slicked down and his best clothes on.

'I don't want to go to church.'

'My dear boy,' said his father, 'nor do I, but it pleases the servants, it pleases old Coggins, and it does us very little harm. You should always try to give pleasure when you can, and if it pleases Coggins to see the old squire and his son and heir in the ancestral pew when he's running through his rigmarole, that's as good a reason as any for going.'

'But I don't believe in God.'

'Good gracious nobody asks you to swallow all that mumbo-jumbo . . . it's just a matter of form.'

'Then it isn't important and I needn't go.'

'On the contrary, there's nothing, absolutely nothing, more important than good form. . . .'

That was about a year before the last service had been held in the church, old Coggins had died and the new incumbent had been allowed to shut the place. Nobody had been near it since.

Ross thought he heard the boom of guns to the north and went out to listen, but it was only the wind buffeting the louvres in the belfry. Nobody had been near the place for years, after all, it would be rotten bad luck if they should happen to come tonight of all nights.

He went back inside and lit the lamp. The light conjured up Lord Chancellor Ross on his tomb in his white marble full bottomed wig, between baroque pillars curled like barley sugar. Admiral of the Blue Ross appeared in elegant basso rilievo profile in a medallion above another relief of the battle of Las Cuevas.

Ross walked down the nave towards the altar, and turning into the north aisle, set the lamp down at the feet of Lady Margaret Ross who lay on the table tomb there beside chain mailed Sir Hugh, whose body had been brought back from the Holy Land after the first crusade.

Above them on the wall the Rifle Brigade badge cut in white marble stood out stark on a black marble slab with white inlaid letters. Frederick George Leopold Ross, beloved son of . . . died of a fever at Williamstown, in the Island of St. Mana, in the West Indies. . . . In the chancel, ghostly white, three marble fates wept as they severed the thread of the Victor of Chuprassy.

They were life sized girls whose lavish pagan charms had always embarrassed poor Coggins and interested Ross, they caught his eye now and he gave them the high sign – if they were the fates, fate was all right. Hollywood had nothing better to offer. Still there was no harm in taking care of your own future.

He bent to his work, picking away with a knife at the mortar that held one of the side panels of the table tomb in place. The joint in the stone work was fine and it was slow work loosening the slab, but it was nearly done.

He worked for another hour and suddenly felt the slab move freely, all that remained was to lever it out. It came surprisingly

302

easily, with a rush of dank air from the tomb that made the lamp flicker. For an instant Ross fancied horrors, but there was nothing to be seen when the flame steadied but a square of darkness. When he held the lantern in the opening he saw no more than a slot in the ground with two collapsed coffins and a few brown bones lying there quietly as they had done for centuries. Ross saw with contentment that the dead had indeed become dust, and that the grave was dry as the Gobi.

'It's as good as the bank,' he said.

He went back to the nave and leant over the door of the family pew, groping for the suitcase he'd put there a few minutes before Walter's arrival. It was surprisingly light to handle. He had been prepared for a greater weight, and in the pool of lamp-light he snapped it open with his heart in his mouth. Suppose that while he'd been out trailing round after Jackson some swine had slipped in . . . but it was all there.

The hundred and twenty-seven thousand dollars, the four hundred thousand pounds, snugly wrapped in medical looking oiled silk, in tight wads of ten thousand pounds. He eyed them narrowly, startled as always by the foreign look of the hundred pound notes that came out after the third devaluation. But they were all genuine Bank of England stuff for all their vivid reds and greens – he'd made sure of that.

He patted them, with a feeling of content. Even if the pound went down the hill for another mile the dollars would see him through; whatever the next year or two held, he would see his way on the far side of the hill fairly plainly. Getting out might be tricky, but if you wanted anything you only had to go after it, and there it was.

He shut the suitcase again and eased it in under the effigies of the knight and the lady. Before he could turn the case inside the opening he struck the coffin end. It disintegrated and slid away round a skull which swung sideways with a gleaming grin and a dark look from long abandoned eye sockets. It stared on with its amused look until the stone slab was back in place, and even then Ross felt it watching him through the stone with the same irony.

He squatted back on his hunkers working mortar into the crack round the slab, and tried to talk it down.

'You've been in there long enough, Sir Hugh, to take a detached view of money. I will some day perhaps, but you've got to excuse me meanwhile. If you never handled a gold coin in your life you've got a right to grin at me, if you ever gave your purse a shake to feel the weight of it you've not a leg to stand on.'

He was glad, for all that, to get out of the church.

A thick skin of snow was on the ground and he walked to the house through a steady fall of tiny dry flakes. The snow was drifting hard, whirling about his feet like a fine powder. Ross felt he was being followed and faced sharp about twice before he got indoors; he felt watched even when he was behind the shut door and in the firelit kitchen, the dark look was still on him.

He stood in the glow reading Walter's note. He'd told the fellow not to come by daylight and here he was proposing another daylight visit already. What did the windy toad want with him?

He heard a step in the corridor and darted out, flashing his torch this way and that on nothing. It would be a long night alone; it might be a good thing to get out and see a bit of company. He banked up the fire, and went.

Death went with him, three paces from his right hand and a little behind him, leaving no track in the snow, but enough there to make him turn his head constantly to catch a proper sight of his dark figure.

19

ANNE recognised Ross as she opened the door to him and let him into the bright kitchen, but pretended not to know him. He started, knew her, and thought of claiming her, but then, as she looked impassively at him, allowed himself to become doubtful.

'Don't I know you. . . ?'

'I don't think so . . . sir.' She had decided in a flash to pretend to be the servant while he was in the house. He had never been there before, with luck he might never come again – he might just have dropped in, having lost his way and needing directions. 'Is there anything I can do for you?'

'I wanted to see Mr. Jackson – or he wanted to see me, anyway tell him I'm here.'

'I'll see if he's at home, sir.' She bobbed, parlourmaid fashion. 'Will you wait here, please.'

At the door she caught herself, and turned to find him looking at her with a certainty of recognition in his eye.

'What name shall I say, sir?'

'Ross,' he dropped his voice to a whisper, but one certain to reach her, 'as you very well know. . . .'

She pretended not to hear it and he knew for certain that it was her, and not some freakish pseudo-twin thrown up by nature in her pattern. Presently she came back, showed him through to the front room, and then went away, heavy hearted, to hide until he should be gone, back into the dark in which he belonged.

'Pretty girl, that maid of yours, Mrs. Jackson,' said Ross making small talk after he'd been introduced.

'Maid?'

'Yes, Anne Horne . . . the girl who let me in.'

'Do you know Anne, Mr. Ross? How exciting. It will be nice for her to have a neighbour who's an old friend. . . .'

'Well I used to know her well enough in the old days. . . .'

He laughed. Richly, a laugh with a dirty thought in it.

'It's bloody funny to see her trying to go straight with all this parlourmaid stuff, bobbing little half curtsys and saying, "come this way, sir, Mr. Jackson will see you now, sir . . ." '

He was angered by her pretence of not knowing him, and out to make trouble.

'Anne? Trying to go straight, I can't think what you can mean . . .' said Margery in bewilderment. 'She's not a maid.'

Walter sat with a dry mouth, wordless. Ross! And now the bitch wanted to saddle him with a child.

'She's not exactly a maid, Ross,' he said in a harsh voice. 'She's a sort of friend of ours . . . she's in trouble just now and we're anxious to help her. I though you might know someone who would be useful . . . you must know all the doctors round about here. . . .'

'But, Walter,' Margery looked at him, with anger all over her face, 'how can you talk to a stranger about this, about Anne, as if she were an animal or a piece of property . . . without consulting her. You know very well she wants the child. . . .' She turned more temperately to Ross. 'You must forgive me . . . but Walter has cheated by bringing you in on a family row.'

'You're a fool, Margery. Ross knows more about Anne than you do . . . he's one of her family if not ours, unless I'm very much mistaken . . . you don't know what you're talking about. . . .'

'I won't stay here . . . if you want to accuse Anne of having an affair with this man, speak to her about it. It's nothing to do with me.' She stood up. 'Anne, Mr. Ross, is my best friend. You owe her and myself an apology.'

Ross stood up furious in his turn with Margery for not knowing what he knew, with Walter for dragging him out through the storm, with Anne for pretending not to know him, with death for looking him in the face.

'That's a lot of crap, Mrs. Jackson . . . you've been made a fool of, either by Anne, or by your husband.'

She went quietly to the door and opened it.

'Good night, Mr. Ross. I hope you won't have to remain in

our house any longer than is absolutely necessary. Good night, Walter.'

She turned to go. Ross shouted at her back, all he knew about Anne, hoping she was hovering in the dark passage, listening. A stream of ugly words ran out of his mouth. Walter sat and listened with his head bowed, fearful even of looking at Margery's back.

Anne was not in the passage, she was in her room, sitting by a candle placed on the window ledge, watching the snowflakes whirl by through its circle of light, small in the large dark of night.

Jeanette had heard a strange voice in the house and had crept along the upstairs passage to the staircase head to listen to its burring murmur rising up through the dark.

The drawing-room door sprang open, letting a bar of light out across the dark hall, her mother appeared framed in the blaze of lamplight; and as she stood there Ross's angry words ran out past her, eager to be heard, with the knives of their meaning ready in their hands. They stabbed Margery woundingly enough as they rushed past, but the real murder was done at the stairhead where Jeanette leant motionless, fascinated, over the banisters.

Margery pulled the door to, chopping off the end of the crude stream and stood for a moment gathering herself.

'How could Walter have brought such an unspeakable man into the house. . . . He must have been drunk. . . .'

She marshalled her reasons for not believing a word of what he had so violently and unforgivably said; but while the reasons clanked rationally and mechanically into place her instincts and intuitions counter-marched.

The inward secret part of her that had resented their liberal 'civilised' arrangement as an outrage against her relationship with Walter, her natural possessiveness and jealously, believed every vile word that had been said. The air in the mill was poisoned.

Jeanette tiptoed away down the passage and slipped into her room, shutting the door. Margery heard the door latch click and went quickly upstairs. Had Anne been eavesdropping? Had she heard the whole thing in acquiescent silence?

Margery looked along the dark upstairs corridor and saw the thin bar of candlelight under Anne's bedroom door. She imagined her standing just inside the room, with her back to the door, straining to hear if any more was being said about her, terrified at being exposed, afraid of what was going to happen next, breathing like a hunted animal. She went to the door and opened it.

Anne sat there, quietly, still at the window, looking out through the panes at the snow. Each square of glass had its narrow white frame of glinting snow.

As Margery looked at her Ross's words lost their power, they had no relation to this; but there was a tenacious bitterness in her that wanted them to remain true and ugly.

'Is it true . . . ?' It burst from her.

'It was.' Anne spoke softly, 'but you know what I am now.'

'Why did you hide?'

'I am ashamed of what I was . . .'

She looked at Margery's face and saw disgust there.

'Don't mistake me, I am not ashamed of what you think . . . I was ashamed of not loving, of wanting so little, and giving so little . . . I was ashamed to look at him because . . . I was like that. That's all.'

She suddenly knew something more deadly than anything that could come out of her past.

'I am afraid of him, because Walter turns to him, and not to us. I am afraid because I know now why Walter wanted me and turned from you to me. I am afraid because I know why Walter turns to him from me. He wanted me because I was love turned to dirt, because I was love turned sterile, because no one man meant anything more to me than any other, because he thought or felt that I was certain to be false and untrue . . . almost all the men who used to come to me were married. They used to sneak away from love, and home, and happiness, and come to me to buy disgust, a stain, guilt . . . or sex that was nothing but themselves . . . and I was happy enough to be what they wanted. . . .'

'How could you be . . . how could you . . . Oh, Anne . . .'

308

'Because I was born to a parody of love and marriage which made it seem worthless and loathsome – I ran away from it and made myself as safe from it as I could, as far from it as I could get . . . I was such a fool.'

She looked at Margery with eyes round with horror, and Margery looked wonderingly back at her, not understanding what depths lay out beyond her zone of knowledge.

In memory Anne was back at the farm; her mother was ill now, all the time, broken with child bearing and hard work. Anne listening heard her mother use some last treasured strength to fight the huge man off. She heard him grunting and fumbling along the passage towards her door. As he came in she slid out of the far side of the bed. She stood holding her breath in the blackness while he groped for her. The iron bedstead creaked as he felt for her, and knowing where he was she darted for the door, grabbing up her slippers.

They played hide and seek round the sleeping house while she gathered up, coat, scarf, and bag.

She couldn't find her shoes in the dark, and had to be content with her silly carpet slippers with pom-poms. .

He heard her shoot the bottom bolt of the back door, and dashed for her. She ducked under his arms, smelling the hot waft from his body as she escaped, brushing his jacket with her cheek.

He stood there by the door waiting, breathing heavily.

She slipped away into the parlour. She was half an hour lifting the pot plants off the window ledge one by one, trembling with a hundred fears. At last she slipped out through the little window, feeling earth spilt from one of the flower pots gritty under her bare knees as she crawled out.

She ran down the farm lane, the mud striking cold through the thin imitation leather soles of her slippers, the puddles soaking them.

Round the first bend she stopped, shivering. The cold air cut through her coat. She had nothing under it but a night-dress. She struck matches, and counted her money. A ten shilling note, four and six in silver, fourteen pennies.

She came out onto the metalled road and began walking slowly

309

towards the nearest town, thinking only, I'll never go back, never.

The road went a long way, too far. There was no coming back, even if one wanted to.

'What are we going to do . . . ?' Margery asked.

'I am going to bear a child that will never be afraid of love or life or birth . . .'

'But we can't just go on . . . I shall never be able to forget – what that man could call you.'

'I don't ask you to forget it . . . I shall never forget anything . . . have you never done anything that you regret? Isn't there any part of you that is left behind for good? Isn't there something you've been that you will never be again . . . ?'

'Oh, nothing . . .' Margery cried, 'like that. I have never . . .'

Her voice died away, drowned in a rapid flood tide of memory that could not be denied. All that she could add with honesty was '. . . been found out' but she said with venom in her voice, 'sold myself.'

Below them the back door opened and a shaft of light flashed out across the yard, a passage through the night. Down it Ross lurched away from the house turning his collar up against the wind and the whirling snowflakes.

Walter's shadow appeared and fell over him, the shadow gesticulated and something was shouted after the retreating figure. Ross spun round and replied, out of a twisted face. '. . . bloody fool . . .' was all they heard of it upstairs.

The door slammed shut and Ross vanished like a lantern slide.

'Perhaps Walter will come to his senses now . . .' said Margery firmly. 'We'll go back. . . .'

The dark window was illuminated again by far away flashes, like lightning through the whirl of the snow, followed by the rumble of gunfire.

'. . . to our real home.'

'The mill?' Anne said, 'you'ld leave the mill, just because I've been a fool – before you knew me . . .'

The guns roared, off in the distance, telling Margery in their deep voices that there was nowhere else to go.

'We were happy here. I haven't changed. The mill hasn't

changed. I don't understand why a few words should change everything . . . please try to accept what I was, what I'm not any more. Take me back as I was. I'm still exactly the same.'

'It's easy to say,' said Margery, 'but how can one forget what one knows?'

'It's not a matter of forgetting, it's a matter of knowing what's important and what isn't. . . .'

The guns spoke of death to each other again, sounding farther off now, blanketed by a heavier fall of snow.

'It was such a little time ago that I promised you that I wouldn't go. . . . I don't know, now. . . . I've lost track of everything . . .'

Margery hesitated. She liked Anne's determination to bear her child; she liked the happiness she had made round the mill; she liked them so much more than Walter's sour sickly fury at life and his inability to trust himself or his future.

And what in the end did the ugly words amount to – that Anne had once thought more about money and things than about life and living. So many people grovelled in front of the golden calf and asked it to accept their minds, and – in other ways – their bodies – giving up their whole lives to money grubbing and property grubbing. Why should that form of servitude and indignity be so much worse than any other?

Yet when she thought about it she squirmed inwardly and knew with all her senses that it was something much worse.

But there was Anne before her golden, kind, and gentle, and carrying a new life. No matter how vile a man or woman has been, they can turn their back on their vileness and walk back into happiness if they only want to do it enough. Love for Walter had made her want to come back and here she was. How could it be right to try to push her back into the darkness?

'I've been very stupid – I've allowed myself to be upset – perhaps I'm over tired . . . for a moment something ugly in me wanted an excuse to dislike you . . . I'm sorry. Forgive me – I'm sure everything will be all right between us. Don't be angry with me for having said silly things . . . it was just a fit of jealousy.'

'Let's talk about it in the morning – perhaps we shall both think more clearly then.'

A few dove grey clouds rode like feathers in the green sky as the sun rose, and they dwindled away as it cleared the horizon. The sky became an intense eye scalding blue. The ground round the mill was padded and masked with a foot of snow, and the mill pool stretched away like a white roadway. The water raced over the dam with a muted sound under a curtain of ice. Everything glistered and sparkled in the clear air.

Francis woke early at the sound of guns opening to break up a dawn tank movement off to the north. He ran out as soon as he was dressed, delighting in it. He took the shot gun and went off round the hedges hoping to catch a pheasant or a partridge dazed by the white glare and the clogging, powdery, snow.

Anne heard him fire twice as she finished milking, and wondered what neighbour was shooting so near at hand so early. She was surprised when Francis appeared in the cow house doorway, flushed with cold and pride, his breath making a silvery cloud about his mouth, holding the big gun and two copper brown and bottle green cock pheasants.

He held them high and his young arm trembled under their weight.

'Oh, Francis, how marvellous . . .'

'One with one barrel, and then the other with the choke. I didn't believe I could. I sort of didn't think, and it just happened. Oh, it was wonderful. He was flying over the hedge, and I thought he was gone, and then he went flump, into the snow. I'm terribly excited.'

'You're getting a frightfully good shot. I don't know how you can hold that great gun, let alone shoot with it. I'm awfully proud of you.'

'I'm proud of myself. Dusty says it isn't boasting to be proud of doing things well. At school you had to pretend to be not specially good at things. If you were good at something you had to pretend you were lucky. I think that's silly don't you?'

'Dusty's a very sensible old man – in most ways.'

312

'He showed me something the other day. He made me put my hand into a sack of wheat and bring it òut full of grain, and when I'd counted it, thirty-five grains, he said, "do you know what you've got there?" And I said, no, and he said, if all the other corn in the world were destroyed you could plant the world over again with that handful. I said you couldn't and he said I could and I'd better always remember it. Do you understand what he meant?'

'Yes.' Anne finished running the milk through the cooler. 'Let's go up to the house. I bet you're going to eat an enormous breakfast after killing those two pheasants.'

'Can I have sugar with my porridge?'

'It's terribly short.'

'Two pheasants ought to be worth a spoonful of sugar. I might take them into Lemlade and sell them or swap them for something perfectly useless. I'm offering you a bargain. . . .'

'Oh, all right, flint heart.'

They walked up together. The boy with the heavy gun and the two pheasants, the woman with the two buckets of milk. Anne idly noticed her tracks down to the cowshed, a single line.

Someone else had come out since she'd been down, walked about half-way, and then branched off for about ten yards, turned, and gone back into the house.

There was something written with a stick in the snow at the branch off, and the lines of the scored letters were filled with shadow so that it looked like dark blue writing on the whiteness.

The pheasants fell limply into the snow, dropped, and the shot gun teetered off the other way to bury itself almost out of sight. Francis sprinted forward, ahead of Anne, his feet kicking up white clods.

He began madly scuffing and tromping about along the line of writing. It began 'Anne is a . . .'

He came back scarlet faced, his breath labouring. He picked up the gun and brushed the snow from its blue black barrel.

'Why did you do that?'

'I just felt frisky.'

He picked up the birds and shook the snow from them by jerking them up and down. A few drops of blood fell from them.

313

'Don't be unhappy, Francis, it didn't matter.'

'It was ugly.'

'It didn't hurt me.'

They walked on in silence past the trampled spot where the writing had been.

'I'll never forgive Jeanette for that. It was the rottenest thing ever. I'll hate her for always for wanting to hurt you.'

'Please forget it, Francis, don't quarrel with her, and don't say anything more about it – to me or anyone else. . . . Promise me.'

'All right. But I'll hate her inside.'

'I'll be unhappy even if you do that.'

She tried not to think about it, not to wonder why Jeanette should want to insult her. How could she know that that word would wound her or could be applied to her?

When they came into the kitchen Jeanette was sitting eating her breakfast with her back to the door; she didn't look round or speak. When Anne spoke to her a little later she didn't answer, and after a few seconds spoke to Francis as if Anne wasn't in the room.

Francis answered with a rudeness designed to show that he was altogether on Anne's side: he was furious, killing two pheasants in the snow had made it a wonderful morning and now it was all spoiled.

When Margery came down the room was filled with misery, the electrical feeling emanated by people over-conscious of each other. The words they spoke to each other sounded thin and false, the cups clinking in the saucers, the spoons and knives touching their plates, sounded like loud noises. Margery had come down in an easy frame of mind for which she had fought during the night: it was not for one human being to sit in judgment on another – she was lucky never to have had to withstand the pressures that had weighed on Anne – and she lived with the Anne she knew and not with information about her from a stranger. But now it all seemed changed, the knowledge stank in the room. There was no disregarding it.

'I'll go and give those heifers down in Willow Acre some hay,' Francis said.

He went round the table and kissed his mother fondly on the

314

cheek, hugging her about the shoulders. Then he gave Jeanette a quick angry look and went and kissed Anne.

Jeanette watched him with a basilisk look fixed just over his right shoulder. He went out and they presently saw him going away across the home paddock with a huge mound of hay over his shoulder on a fork, looking like a haycock walking away on two legs.

The guns were going harder now, nearer, and the windows chattered a little to their vibration.

Jeanette left the room in silence.

'She knows, all about it, somehow . . .' said Anne, despairing.

'Oh, no, she can't . . .'

'She does. I can't think how.'

Anne pushed her hair back off her forehead.

'She wrote something beastly for me to see when I came back from milking, in the snow by the path. Francis came back with me. He saw it first, he tried to scuff it out before I saw it . . . so he knows, too.'

'She must have been awake last night, listening – when that horrible man was here . . .'

'I don't know how I'll ever make up to you for the hurt I've done you, and the children. . . .'

'It's not your fault, it's . . .'

Margery couldn't name Walter. He came swiftly into the room at that moment.

'Go on, you were going to say it's all my fault.'

He poured himself a cup of coffee, and did his best to look bold and defiant, like Ross, but looked sullen and uncertain.

They looked at him and forgot all blame and hatred in love, in their longing to give him a quiet happiness that would last out his life and theirs. It was his fault, but it didn't matter, the future in which it would all be straightened out, and in the end forgotten, was what mattered.

'Oh, well,' he said. He misread their silence as contempt, or a disguised statement that they did blame him, 'it doesn't matter.'

He took his cup with him and went to the back door, and stood there looking north across the snow listening to the battle. The

315

noise of the gunfire was moving round from north to north-east. He could just make out the muted clinking rumble of tanks, heavy tanks moving fast along a metalled road, only a few miles away. The battle was swinging away down the Thames valley towards London. That meant that the northerners had as good as won.

'It doesn't matter, it will all be over soon.'

They didn't bother to argue the point. They knew well enough that nothing can be finished quickly, or by that sort of agency. Everything important was worked out over lifetimes. What was happening at the mill would decide what shape the lives of Francis and Jeanette would have, what shape the life of Anne's unborn child would take. Anne, Margery, and Walter, had been brought to the mill by their parents' loves and griefs of long before.

'For god's sake, can't I get a word of sense out of either of you bloody women this morning?' he said. He could not bear their silent love. He wanted bitter language, and resentment, charge and counter-charge bandied to and fro, warfare in the heart. The clock that Anne and Margery had hung together while they waited for him on their first day at the mill struck, and marked the passage of another hour.

20

WALTER stayed at the mill for another fifteen days, less and less there in mind each day. The silences and tensions between the two women and the girl, the blind stupidity of Francis – who always spoke as if the working of the mill was the most important thing in the world – irked him and sickened him. He felt, too, that Anne's condition was becoming physically manifest, and every time he looked at her felt that the child was claiming him.

'I didn't ask for the bloody child – why the hell should we be saddled with that on top of everything else?'

He spent most of his time lying on the single bed in the spare room, smoking, as if he were already in prison waiting trial and execution, numb minded, neither reading nor thinking, just letting different patterns of reverie drift in and out of his head. He did not go out until after dark, and then kept close about the buildings, his farthest point being a spot on the mill dam, about half-way up its length, where he could stand and look across the flats to the dark clump of trees masking Ross's house.

Once or twice he took a few steps in that direction, then the thought of seeing him again – one of Anne's men . . . turned him back. He saw him often enough in his daydreams, Anne and Ross together; small, brightly lit figures which sharpened in definition when he shut his eyes . . . they whispered and laughed, or jeered at him, and wherever he rolled his head there they were in the centre of his vision. He could only blot them out with reveries fashioned of other material. . . .

He would dream through a marriage with one of the girls he'd known before he'd married Margery, through a life in which he never married. More and more he dreamed of the girl in the hotel.

They slipped aboard some rust caked steamer at the docks and waited, hidden, until they felt the engines come alive and settle into a steady rhythm. Then they would hear the deck movement, and the footsteps die away, and presently hear the woodwork creak, and feel the ship nose into and over a sea . . . she would put her hand into his and they would go up on deck to look back at the alien land.

They would get to America, to Spain, to the Argentine, somewhere where they would be two anonymous foreigners, alone in a crowd that meant nothing to them, in which they would meet no one who could have any claim on them. She walked beside him in very plain linen dresses, cold and indifferent even under the tropical sun, her faded, exhausted, good looks all the more precious in contrast with the blaze of that warmer, richer, world.

They would live together in hotels without the killing responsibilities of housekeeping, without ties. When they were bored they would move on to a new place, to another hotel. They would be absolutely free. . . .

He heard a car drive up and went to the window and looked out. It was the brown military police car he'd been expecting.

He watched the police getting out, big, red faced, men in British uniforms with familiar red M.P. armbands, but with red stars on their shoulders. He thought of making a fight of it for a second. Then remembered he'd thrown his revolver into the mill pool for fear of an arms search some days earlier. There was nothing in the house but Francis's shot gun. The M.P.s all had pistols and the driver had a sub-machine gun of Russian pattern.

He opened the window and asked what they wanted in fair Russian. They all looked up, it seemed to him like dogs scenting game.

'What dost' t'booger say?' said the officer.

'Ah canna rightly say,' said his sergeant in broad Glasgow. 'He'll be some sort of foreigner.'

'Pardonny moi,' said the lance jack, 'Nous sommes des agents de sceuritay militaire ill sagee doon cherche poor Mackinder's fuggers and, ay I mean, ay poor days armements defendus ay der voir vos papiers de identity and all that, Comprenny?' He ended scarlet with embarrassment.

'I'm sorry, I'd got the wrong end of the stick,' said Walter. 'I thought you were Russians. I'll come down and let you in.'

'Now we'll never know about how good the Corp is at the parley voo stuff,' said the sergeant.

'Come on down, fast,' said the officer.

They searched the house quickly and efficiently, and made a quick check of everybody's identity papers, matching their names against a black list. Walter couldn't at first believe when it was all over, that they had nothing against him, or N.P.R., only a slight coolness towards him for having sat on the fence. Well, they'd find out later. . . . Anne gave them tea, and they sat gratefully drinking it in the kitchen with their flat topped caps upside down on the dresser like a row of sitz baths.

'It's all over then?' asked Walter.

'Been all over for near on a fortnignt. The last of the fighting was hereabouts. The southerners broke here and that was the end of it, thank god.'

'How are things?'

'None so bad as they might be, considering.'

'I mean are there restrictions on movement, martial law, all that sort of thing. I mean would I need a pass or anything if I wanted to get into Bath,' he groped momentarily for a reasonable excuse, 'to see if the N.P.R. business needs any tidying up, or anything?'

'You can go where you like, providing your papers are in order . . .' the big north countryman looked at him curiously. 'But if I were you Mister Miller I'd stick to my mill.'

Walter left the mill a few minutes after the police car drove away, Margery just caught a glimpse of him cycling off down the lane, weaving to avoid the potholes.

They thought he'd probably gone to Lemlade to see if he could raise some lamp oil, sugar, or cigarettes and matches. They were surprised that he wasn't back when night fell, and uneasy all through the night waiting for him to return.

But he never came back.

Charley Snow was in a new uniform, plain blue, with a flat peaked cap with a black leather visor. As soon as the Republicans came in he reported as a member of the Bristol Assault Guard who'd been in hiding through the Occupation. He was taken on, with back pay, by the political police and now had a new set of silver letters on his collar. R.P.P. He was in a patrol car looking out for officers from Mackinder's defeated army trying to filter back into Bath to join their families, trying to get westwards and southwards to the ports. When they were caught they were shipped to re-education camps in Scotland and Wales, and held there while the Republicans tried to find out who had been responsible for what.

There was a brisk rivalry between the political police, the military police, and the civil police over the hunt. The civil police fought hard for the old local organisations; the political police tried to establish themselves as the cadre of a unified Western Regional Police Force which would absorb all the town and county forces. The military police were out to rope as many suspects as possible into its own camps.

Charley Snow cruising through the streets of Bath in his big black Wolseley squad car, with three men, had a certain amount of pleasure out of poaching under the noses of the Bath city authority. The politicals said the Bath police were unreliable, too sympathetic to the fugitives. They were making a point of arresting as many suspects as possible inside the city limits so that they could put up a case, backed by statistics, for removing the senior officers of the city police and replacing them with their own men. It was work Charley enjoyed.

The car slid up Lansdowne Road slowly, towards Springfield Place, with Charley at the window looking at the faces of the men on the pavement, watching for anyone who turned away at the sight of his police uniform. Men on the run always served themselves up on a dish.

'On up the Gloucester Road, sarge, or shall we get back into town?' said the driver pulling up alongside the first house of Springfield Place.

'On up . . . .' said Charley, looking past the drivers' head, out over the offside wing of the car, along the Charlcombe turning. There was Walter riding easily on his cycle freewheeling down into the town. Why the hell was he in Bath? He ought to have been lying low, anywhere else. He was sure to be recognised, and if he was picked up he was sure to talk. He'd been bloody queer the night when . . .

320

'I want that man on the bicycle, quick, get after him, Reilly.'

Walter was far ahead, freewheeling down the slope. They couldn't catch him before he was up the steps and into the hotel, leaving the revolving door turning slowly behind him.

Charley hesitated, there would be one hell of a row about jurisdiction if he took a man inside a building in Bath. But if the truth came out about N.P.R., and the Bath people could track him into the politicals there'd be an even nastier row, a much, much, nastier row for Charley.

He climbed out of the car, there was only one thing he could do about Colonel Jackson.

'Wait here, you chaps, I'm going in to get him.'

He walked slowly across to the hotel doors making a rough plan. He had one official gun that he was supposed to have. He had another that he was fond of, that he wasn't supposed to have. It wasn't recorded anywhere. No one would know, if it was found in Jackson's hand, that it had been put there. Jackson wouldn't say how it had come there.

Charley began phrasing his report. '. . . behaving suspiciously. I followed him into the Empire Hotel and found that he had not got the necessary papers. I said, "you will have to come with me, I am afraid." He did not reply but drew a pistol and backed away saying "leave me alone." I said "That will not do. . . ." '

He came to the now barely moving revolving door and set it spinning briskly.

Walter went straight across to the reception desk and recognised the usual man standing there in his cage, behind the bank-like bronze grille and the desk top litter of blotters and registration forms. It was like coming home. He smiled. The man looked back at him, his eyes betraying him, his face pretending ignorance pretty well. He leant forward when Walter was right up to him and with the automatic smile that he would have used to greet a stranger, said in a whisper.

'Get out, get out, get out. Don't ask any questions. Get out.'

'I . . .' Walter steadied himself. 'Is the girl still in my room?'

'Yes. But get out. You can't do anything.'

'I must see her.'

'I have to report you the minute you show up. There are police in the hotel – get out – it'll be too late in a minute.'

'I've got to see her.'

'If you go now I can pretend you were never here.'

The clerk turned and began fiddling with the keys and letters behind him, his back to Walter. His hands trembled.

Walter thought for a second and made for the stairs. As he set his foot on the first step he saw the clerk look over his shoulder, catch sight of him at the stair foot and whiten, then with a grimace he reached out for the telephone.

Walter ran along the passage to the door of 288 and knocked and knocked again. The girl was a long time answering. He thought she might be asleep. When she opened the door and saw him she put her hand to her mouth.

'Oh god no, not you.'

'Yes, I promised you I'd come back.'

'How could you be such a fool.'

'Don't ask me to explain now. We must get moving. There's something wrong here – I don't know what . . . let's get going. . . .'

'You're not going anywhere.' A policeman stepped out of the bathroom, another stepped from behind the door.

'You're under arrest.'

Walter found nothing in her eyes but an unemotional pity for him, he looked into the room. The bed was rumpled and there was a book thrown down on the cover, she'd been lying on it reading. At the bed end there was a card table and two chairs, two gin rummy hands thrown down, and cigarettes, half stubbed out, smoking in an ash tray.

'I don't understand.'

'No more did the inspector. Here's this woman – lousy with dollars she oughtn't to have, here's the cupboard full of black market stuff. What's the explanation, a man I don't know gave them to me. I'd never seen him before – give her credit she's not cracked a thing about you – you couldn't have picked a loyaler little woman – well we thought you'ld be back for the money if not for the woman. And we thought it would be worth hearing you explain how you got it all.'

'A small breach of the currency regulations, a small breach of the food regulations – nothing I can't clear up . . .' Walter tried to smile at the girl.

'Well come along to the station and see how clever you can be.' The policemen started putting on their coats and gathering up their things. 'It'll be quite a wrench leaving the old place. Another day and we'd have given you up.'

'You're the biggest fool,' the girl said.

Charley Snow came along the passage. The two bogies and the doll were a surprise, what the hell now?

'What's all this?' he said.

He looked at Walter and let his eyelid flicker, a friend and fellow conspirator. He let his gun drop to the bottom of his pocket.

Walter's heart leapt, everything was going to be all right.

'What's it to you, sergeant,' said one of the Bath police.

'I want that man.'

'Well you can want, he's our prisoner.'

'Have you booked him?'

'No.'

'Well, I'll have him then.'

'You? Who says?'

'This man's wanted on an important political charge. You wouldn't want me to report you for finagling Mackinder men out of trouble by holding them on minor civil charges. I want this man I tell you.'

'You know what the situation is. Ask for him through channels if you want him.'

'I want him now. I've come for him.'

Walter went and stood by the girl.

'It's going to be all right,' he whispered it into her ear.

He took her hand. She let it lie completely passively in his. Charley seeing their two wrists close together stepped forward and snapped handcuffs on them, tying them together with steel.

'You can't do that.' The policeman stepped forward.

'On your way, Rollo, I've done it.'

'You bloody politicals are going to go too far one of these days . . .'

323

'Save it for your report. Why are you so keen to keep these two from the politicals? What's the angle? Maybe there's something here I ought to look into.'

'The hell with them, and the hell with you. Come on, Smythe, let's get back to the station and do our home work on this. I tell you, sergeant, you've gone too far this time. We'll turn in a report on this that'll break you. You see.'

'I'll be waiting. Come on you two.'

Charley sat in the back seat with Walter and the girl driving out of town. A Bath police car followed them for some miles and then dropped out of sight.

The car was on its way to headquarters in Bristol, and Charley was trying to think of a way of getting there without the prisoners. He kept looking at the backs of the heads of the other men of the car crew, crowded into the front seat, wondering what was inside them, wondering how big a risk he could take.

Twilight was falling and wreaths of mist and fog were coiling up from low-lying ground.

'Hear that?' Charley leant forward and spoke to the driver.

'What?'

'A noise in the engine, something wrong, I thought.'

They all listened.

'There!'

'I didn't hear it.'

'I heard it plain as anything.'

'Yes, I thought I heard something then,' said the man sitting by the driver.

'Better stop.'

They pulled in to the roadside. They opened the bonnet and two leant over the engine while the driver revved it up.

'Sound as a bell.'

'No, there's something in the water pump, or in the fan mounting . . . there. Plain as plain.'

Mist drifted across the roadway from a damp looking field lying between two woods.

'He can't hear it from behind the steering wheel. I'll rev her up, while he comes round here and listens.'

Charley lowered himself into the driver's seat, and pressed hard down on the accelerator pedal.

'You two can get out and stretch your legs if you want to.' He spat the words rapidly over his shoulder.

They got out onto the road and stood a few paces from the car feeling the clammy mist cold against their faces while Charley made the car engine race and idle, race and idle. Finally he set it with the hand throttle, racing, and climbed out. He passed close to Walter and spoke softly under the roar of the engine –

'When I say "Now" run. Make for that wood. It's your only chance. Best of luck.' He walked on to the group round the engine.

'Can't you hear it. There it is, there . . .' he put his hand into his pocket and found the gun. 'There it is again, now . . . NOW. . . .'

'Hey, you two, none of that . . .' The driver started round the car after them.

Walter heard the first shot as his foot touched the grass verge on the far side of the road. He felt the girl stumble and begin to fall. Then he hit the wet turf before he could get his free hand up to shield his face, someone had thrown a huge stone and hit him on the back of the head. He tried very hard to lift his head and raised it nearly a quarter of an inch, then it fell forward. His eyes were wide open in spite of the blades of grass crushed and bent against their naked pupils.

21

THE court room was in a former cinema. 'We do not wish the people's justice to be associated in any way with the formalistic instrument welded by the bourgeoisie: the dingy pseudo-gothic lairs of that disguised tyranny are not for us!'

Besides the cinema had been designed for a double bill, films and variety, and it was much easier to feed the television cameras, the microphones, the film cameras and the spotlights from the stage points than it was to wire an existing court room.

To the official eye there was nothing vulgar about the place when the conversion was finished. The jazz modern organ grilles and the allegorical nudes each side of the proscenium arch were hidden behind severe panels of scarlet hessian, the drop curtain showing Bristole Towne in Oldene Tyme had been dyed black and now formed a sober foil to the array of scarlet banners behind the chairs of the commissioners of justice. Bands of scarlet bunting with slogans printed on them hid the white and gold masks of comedy and tragedy held by dancing nudes which had formed a repeat motif along the front of the gallery and circle.

The foreign correspondents who had been brought down from London for the grand opening of the first Regional Court of Popular Justice read the slogans without emotion, cricking their necks as they stared round and up from the press table. 'The Safety of the Republic is the Only Law,' 'The People's justice is the People's need,' 'Case Law is dead law, the People's justice is born anew for every case.'

They looked round again. A renegade Anglican priest stepped into a dais over the old wurlitzer pit.

The house lights went down and a blue baby spot settled on the priest, making his christless pectoral cross shine as if it was white hot. The ushers called in sibilant whispers for everybody to stand and he read a brief interdenominational prayer. Then he vanished away, smiling all over the lower part of his face.

There was a stir and whisper as people sat down, a squad of uniformed counsel took their places. A blaze of lights focused on the prosecutor's dais, the dock, the witness stand, and the judges' bench were snapped on. The judges came in and took their places.

A correspondent from Eire turned to one of the American pressmen.

'By god, do you see that, the judges are made up for the television cameras.'

'No, it can't be.'

They were both deeply shocked for the first time.

The President of the Court hammered with a gavel, and a voice called out 'The People versus the man Fergusson, The People versus the man Fergusson.' Fergusson was brought into the summer lightning of flash bulbs, and the mill began to grind.

It was late on the third day that the case of the woman Jackson and the woman Horne was called.

The room was filled then with a thick blue fog of tobacco smoke and the tension of the early hours was gone. It only returned for an instant as each new prisoner was brought in to hear, in a process as formal as a medieval disputation. why the state was determined that he should die. A door was flung open and the prisoner's figure appeared with dramatic suddenness silhouetted against a black opening blinking at the brilliant light of the court room. Each new arrival was greeted by a sudden hush and a quick intake of breath.

The crowd knew that every prisoner must think as that door opened that the chance he had been waiting for was come at last, the trial which would bring the truth to light. The extraordinary hostile depositions which they had met fragmentarily could now be checked and the fragments put in their logical contexts, the dishonesty, and the motives of hostile witnesses could be made apparent – everything could be cleared up at last. The crowd knew that they were in fact to meet all the distortions and misunderstandings that they had been wrestling with behind the scenes in the form of absolute truth. There was an intense pathos about the prisoners at this moment of revelation – they were in the position of paranoiac lunatics on the brink of discovering that they had been sane all the time, that the conspiracies and persecutions of their dreams were true pictures of reality.

The audience knew too that the prisoners were running through the last hours and minutes of their lives. When Anne and Margery were brought in notices announcing that Fergusson and several of the second day's prisoners had already been executed were posted in the lobby. They could be seen on a board (half-way up the stairs leading to the café and bar) which had once shown what next week's films were to be. This momentary flicker of sympathy soon died away; there were too many prisoners, their cases were too much alike in broad outline, too perplexing in detail, and the warmth of the heart is quickly chilled by boredom.

'Not a bad looking girl,' said the man from Eire at the press table.

'Not bad at all,' said the American. 'I'll give you another E.'

They were playing word squares to kill time. The Irishman looked down at his scratch pad: 'I'll take it, and give you another.'

E

ALIVE

I

C

T

They listened to the indictment for a few seconds.

'All this social parasite stuff . . . that girl is definitely good looking. I'll give you another E.'

E

ALIVE

I

CE

T

'Take an "S." Did you hear that, so she was one of those. Do you believe it?'

'I've given up believing anything I hear in this place. It's all un-news anyway. Take – uh – a V.'

'A V, I don't like V. I did all I could to get out of it, but I got a pretty straight hint it would mean the end of my press facilities if I didn't come along.' He put the V in place. 'What are you doing about it?'

'Filing a precis of the nightly hand-out – the paper isn't using it – but what the hell else can I do?' He stared thoughtfully at his pad. 'There's no story in this stuff.'

ES
ALIVE
IV
CE
T

'Take an R.' He made it SEVER, and immediately regretted the IV and the TR, what words ended that way? The State's first witness appeared, a small figure, rigid with excited appreciation of the spotlights and the nozzles of the cameras aimed at her. The Republican oath came thin and shrill from her immature throat.

'One of these Socialist guides – it makes me mad to see a kid in a thing like this.'

At the witness stand an attendant finished changing the cards in the indicator above it and stepped down. 'Jeanette Jackson, daughter of the woman Jackson,' said the card.

'That's the dark woman.'

'Christ, putting up her own daughter – they have all the ideas – I wonder if the kid knows what she's doing?'

'I don't believe in any of that drug stuff.'

'What I meant was, is she old enough to realise.'

'She's got a sweet little bust. She's no innocent newcomer to a wicked world.'

They listened to the alternation of the girl's voice and the deeper rumble of the prosecutor as they built up the story. Of the avid, extravagant, woman eager for money who had badgered her husband into abandoning his constructive, socially valuable work, and then, in partnership with his mistress, forced him into a career as a black market operator. The prosecutor's voice boomed out.

'And when the heroic railwaymen were making the first stand against the encroachments of the Monarcho-Facists, what were these two women doing?'

329

'They were setting up house together.'

'Explain that further, if you please.'

'They were agreeing' it was a shrill approximation to a musical note, now that Jeanette had settled down into a chant – it carried well, 'to live together and share my father between them.'

'And was any attempt made to conceal this charming arrangement from you?'

'No.'

'And did you know what this delightful companion your mother had chosen for you had been?'

'Yes.'

'What was that?'

'No, no, no, Jeanette, no . . .'

Margery with her two eyes looking like holes in a sheet of paper was on her feet. The president hammered with his gavel, attendants hurried up towards her. Jeanette raised her voice, leaning towards the microphones, and shouted louder and louder, over and over again.

'She was a prostitute, a prostitute, a prostitute!'

'It's the first time they've lost control of one of the defendants,' said the man from Eire. 'I suppose that's worth a line.'

'If you can get it through the censorship,' said the American, raising his voice to be heard through the buzz of comment.

'I will have to adjourn this court,' shouted the president, 'if the woman Jackson does not regain her sense of decency.'

Margery slowly sank back into her seat, staring across the lawyers' tables, over the rows of curious faces, to Jeanette. She remembered her staring over the side of the boat into the luminously green water of the sea cave, like a mer-child, green and strange in the reflected light. Perhaps she was a changling, perhaps a stranger, not her flesh. Jeanette stared back, not at her, but at Anne. Anne reached out to her friend and gave her arm a gentle pat. 'Don't worry yourself, it doesn't matter what they say now.'

The prosecutor gave his witness in chief time to recover by coming over to the dock and launching into one of his explanatory denunciations.

'. . . and so it seems, comrade President, that while the national crisis was developing, while the nation was hardening its muscles and its will for the supreme test, there were those whose minds were on other things!'

He walked up to the base of the dock and stood staring up into the women's faces.

'This pillar of the respectable middle class, this model citizen Jackson, and her boon companion, the woman Horne, the toy and plaything of her man . . .'

Anne looked into his eyes and found them fixed on a point just above her eyebrows. He had a technique that enabled him to seem to be facing the defendants man to man, but he did not meet their eyes.

'Back to the old routine,' said the American. He turned back to the scratch pad and began worrying over IV and TR. They meant he was going to lose ten points on that side of the square, the time was come for bold offensive tactics. 'I'll give you U.'

'Hmn, U; I'll hand you back an R.'

'Suits me, and you can have a V back for it.'

> VES
> ALIVE
> RIV
> UCE
> TR

The man from Eire considered the thing carefully, and then suddenly saw it. 'Thanks for the V. Why do they go through all this business. Why don't they put them away quietly.' He wrote the V down in its place with a quiet satisfaction. 'It's funny too, when you work it out, what a curious jumble of morality and absolute amorality they horse about with. The prosecutor doesn't believe a word of what's going on, yet he acts just like an elder of the Free Kirk taking the hide off a detected sinner.' His square was unlike the American's.

> C VE
> RIVAL
> U L
> SIEVE
> ER

'It sometimes seems to me that this left wing stuff about expediency being the only law checks in very nicely with the puritan way of thinking. Two centuries ago the prosecutor would have claimed he'd had some sort of direct orders from god to punish these people. Take an H.' He filled in CRUSH.

'H, the hell with H. Your Catholic Irish bias comes in there. I'd say this sort of thing smacks more of the Inquisition and old Torquemada than it does of any Protestant machinery. Have an S, will you. I'll be glad when they get that kid out of here, she gives me the creeps.' He completed VIRUS. 'If there's any goddammed duller profession than ours I'd like to know it.'

'There has been a complaint that you are talking too much,' said an usher coming up behind them. 'Kindly restrict your comments to a minimum.'

'I apologise on behalf of the Irish Republic and the United States of America.'

'That's all right with me, only there's been this complaint, see?'

'We'll be good.'

When they turned back from the usher's pink face Jeanette had vanished from the witness box, and the prosecutor was examining another witness, a hotel clerk who had taken black dollars in payment for the man Jackson's hotel check. It was dull evidence and they were able to concentrate on the game. The Irishman won: his

$$CRAVE_5$$
$$RIVAL_5$$
$$USOLD_4$$
$$SIEVE_5$$
$$HDEER_4$$
$$5 \quad 55$$

beat the American's square easily.

$$HEVES_1$$
$$ALIVE_5$$
$$RORIV$$
$$DEUCE_5$$
$$LASTR_4$$
$$4 \quad 555$$

332

'Heves looks damned like a word,' said the American, 'I bet it would be if I could get at a dictionary.'

'I'm not giving it you.'

'Well, Eves then.'

'Eve hasn't got a plural.'

'It has got a plural. Here: "of all the Christmas Eves I have ever spent, that was the least cheerful." You've got to give me four for that.'

'All right. That leaves me 38, and makes you 34. I still win. It comes of having roots in an older culture.'

'You're a poor conquered tribesman from its outer margins.'

They began another square, and finished three more.

'Everybody stand please, everybody stand please,' hissed the ushers. The court stood to hear the two women found guilty as charged, and sentenced to death.

They were taken back into the old dressing-rooms and left alone in a little box of a room with a wooden bench at one side and a can in the corner. Margery felt surprisingly lightened by knowing the worst, it killed the violence of her feeling about Jeanette. She was surprised to see that Anne, dead white, collapsed onto the bench with her eyes shut as soon as they were alone.

'Be brave, Anne, I don't expect they'll hurt us, and then this nightmare will be over.'

'I'm not afraid, it's just that I felt the child move for the first time – as we were coming down those stairs.'

'Oh god . . . I'd forgotten.'

They sat in silence for a few moments while Anne recovered from her faintness.

'Why don't you tell them . . . they might give you a reprieve for the sake of the child.' But it sounded silly even as she said, 'You've never told them, have you?'

'No. I won't. I won't beg my life or its life from them.'

'I don't see that you've the right to be so proud. After all the child . . .'

'I will have it. I will have it.' She got up and walked up and down the little room. 'I can't believe I'm going to die. I won't die until I've had it. I won't just . . .'

333

The door of the room was shut and locked.

'I can't think how Jeanette could say all those things about us. . . . Suppose your child . . .?' Margery for a few seconds thought that the horror of what her daughter had done to them might reconcile Anne to dying with her own unborn. 'Your child will at least always be perfect.'

'It must live, it must . . . if only to be a monster.'

'Be brave, Anne, we've only got until tomorrow.'

There was a long silence in which Anne walked slowly round the room reading the names on the walls there were scratched here and there, already. Only three that she could find.

'I've wondered and wondered what they can be doing to Francis.'

'Perhaps they've never got him.'

'That would be almost worse – he's so young to be alone . . . oh I don't know. I suppose Jeanette is quite happy, being what these people want her to be.'

'I expect Francis is better off, if they haven't caught him.' Anne spoke absently, looking at the little window, high up on the wall. It pivoted on its central axis, neither half was wide enough for a body to go through, but the whole square . . .

'I'm going to escape.' She said it firmly. 'I'm going through that window.'

'You're sure to be caught, and if you aren't, where will you go? It isn't any use.'

The shock of the sentence was wearing off, and the horror of Jeanette's condemnation was running through Margery's head. Everything was beastly and hopeless.

'Let me stand on your shoulders, by the window.'

Margery felt her weight growing intolerable as she wrestled with the window frame.

'I can't hold you any more. I told you it wasn't any use.'

But the window frame fell out into the street with a crash, and the noise of splintering glass wasn't followed by any shout or challenge. Anne looked into a deserted back alley, dimly lit by the fading afternoon light.

'Are you going to come? I'll wait for a minute if you're going to come.'

She heard Margery speak behind her in the cell, as she hung over the ledge, say something, she couldn't make out what. She wriggled round into the right position to drop down the twelve foot of wall beneath her, and looked down into her face.

'Come on, I'll give you a handup.'

'I daren't. It's all so hopeless.'

'They're going to kill you.'

'I know. It's just that I . . . I daren't, that's all.'

'Good-bye.'

Anne hung for a second at the end of her arms, sick at the enormous distance that still seemed to be between her feet and the ground. Then she pushed out from the wall and let go, nerving herself for the shock. She walked off down the alley as soon as she recovered from it. She waited under a wall there for a minute watching the empty blank of the dressing-room window for Margery's head. She walked out into the hushed, half dead, city, alone. The light began to ebb out of the sky as night fell.

She looked through the open gates of a factory yard a few blocks away and saw a lorryman all by himself, throwing a tarpaulin over a loaded truck. He moved about slowly making the sheets fast all round the bed of the truck, working in the dimness of his parking lights. He was clearly getting ready for a run. Anne sidled in keeping close to a wall, ready to turn and run if necessary, watching for a gate keeper or supervisor who might make trouble. She was close to the driver before he saw her.

'You've no business here.'

'I wanted to ask you to give me a ride.'

'You don't know where I'm going.'

'I want to get out of town.'

'It's like that, eh? I'd be risking my neck. No, thanks.'

'Please take a chance. I've got to get away – I must.'

He gave a quick look round the deserted yard, no one in sight and all the office windows dark and blank.

'How much money have you got?'

'I haven't got any.'

They looked at each other.

'How are you going to make it worth my while?'

335

'I could.'

'I daresay you could . . .'

He looked at her with a cold grey eye, appraising her. He could pull in for an hour or so on the edge of Cound Woods, off the main road, take her, and then turn her in to the Marshfield police four miles farther on as a suspect. That would put him in the clear. The only risk would be getting to Cound Woods – she could ride under the tarpaulin, and unless there was a search on, it would probably be all right. 'All right.' She did her best to smile.

She sat between two cases and took the jolting and the swaying like a beating. She only thought one move ahead, she couldn't think any further than that. When he pulled up it would be dark, and she'd have a chance of getting away from him. If she were quick she might get out of sight before he could get round from the cab. She grew tense and ready for action every time the truck slowed down, imagining the spurt off into the darkness. Where she would go then she didn't know.

She woke with a shock, the man had lifted the tarpaulin and was shining a torch in at her. He had one hand on her knee and was shaking it to waken her, swinging it slowly with a firm grip as if she was altogether his.

'Come on out.'

'All right.' Her heart sank. She was going to have to fight for it. She was surprised to find herself trembling with exhaustion and weakness.

'Jump down, I'll catch you.'

She saw his spread arms waiting, unavoidable, and jumped down. He held her, and before she had time to say anything or even tighten her muscles, let her go.

'Not that you aren't a pretty decent armful.' She waited for his next words with a sudden certainty that she needn't bolt for it. 'I've been thinking up in front all on my own, about you having no money, and being on the run. I were a bit of a twirp asking for that. It was the look of you carried me away. It was low. To make up, here's me sandwiches, and here's ten quid. And I hope you get wherever you're going. The only thing I ask is that you don't tell on me if they get you. And the only thing I advise you to do is keep off the roads. Here you are. Give us a kiss if you can bring yourself to it.'

She found herself hugging him like a child, and giving him friendly kiss after friendly kiss on his firm cheeks. He held her like a bear and patted her back.

'There luv there, me better nature won't stand no more'n just so much of this.'

He left her suddenly and walked off round the huge looming bulk of the loaded truck. She heard the motor start, saw the lights come on, and saw the truck roll away down the tunnel of arching trees illuminated by its head lights. She waved until it was out of sight, and tears of happiness ran down her cheeks. Then she walked off alone into the dark.

During the teatime recess, the man from Eire vanished and left the American in the café talking to a woman reporter who was covering the trials for an Argentine paper. He stayed talking to her because she had the high gloss that South America produces in its wealthy and he was attracted by it. She knew that she was sexually exciting him and talked with a flashing brilliance out of pleasure at being the absolute focus of his attention. Not that she had any intention of letting him have her, with his crew cut giving him a little boy look, and his earnest slowness of bodily movement and thought he was quite impossible.

'Yeah, yeah, I see what you mean by this concept of a developing justice but I . . .'

All the time he was thinking about the look of her, and the tight skin of perfection that was stretched over her. Back home once there had been an ice storm, the air was warm and rain fell, but the ground was ice cold, and as soon as the rain – a fine drizzle – touched anything it froze. He'd picked a dead bird encased in skin of glass clear ice off a bough just outside the back door; he imagined a rose like that, any bright perfection enclosed in that dead clarity.

'Justice is the instinctive knowledge of the community about right and wrong. The decision in the case of those two women was unchallengeable – they knew, my frien', they knew what they were doing was wrong. That girl knew instinctively the situation was criminal – and that love in such circumstances

337

would be criminal – that is why she turned on her mother, and the state discovering the true instinctive law in her revulsion turned on her too. I am very impressed by this court – it is direct, natural, like a tiger. . . .'

He looked at the purple stain of lipstick on the butt of her cigarette as she waved it in a half circle and blew out a smoke cloud, she smiled at him with her eyelids half down. He had an athlete's body, perhaps . . . she moved her weight on her feet.

A little embarrassed, he lifted his cup and took a mouthful of the brown, bitter, Indian tea. God what a drink, but you had to take in so much liquid during the day.

'I like this direct, natural, way the English are rediscovering,' she said. 'It may be harsh, but it is true. It accords with the truth of the world. . . .'

I bet she bites, he thought.

'The English are rediscovering their historic founts of virtue – becoming emotional, violent, direct again – Elizabethans – I like their new muscle, their new hardness . . .' she ran on.

Back in the depths behind the scenes they were emptying the cells for the next set of prisoners who were to appear at the evening session. They came to Cell Seven and found Margery standing under the window, still nerving herself to go.

'There should be two women here, chum.'

'Let's see the list.'

'There it is, two women.'

The three men looked at each other.

'You signed for her, Ed, there's your moniker.'

'I must a put her in nex' door.'

They stood looking at Margery while Ed went to look next door.

'There's only a bloody man there on 'is own. The man Stevens it says on the list.'

They all suddenly looked at the window.

'So that's the bloody fiddle. We should have done something about those bloody windows. But who'd have thought . . .'

He went and stood on the bench on tiptoe peering out, a sandy faced man with a sharp dog's profile. 'There's the hell of a drop, you wouldn't hardly credit it.'

'What are we going to do?'

'All I know is we're in trouble.'

'We don't have to be, not if we handle it right.' Dog face jumped down off the bench. 'Stands to reason she won't say she come out of here on sentence of death if she is picked up. Stands to reason they won't be looking for her if it isn't reported.'

'I don't get it.'

'Sentence duly carried out, that's what I mean. There's all that bloody coke out in the yard. Who's to see through a bloody coffin lid.'

Dog face was sweating. His forehead was beaded, and every now and then two or three droplets joined and ran down into his eyebrows.

'It's the only thing we can do. If we're caught we won't be any worse off than if we're caught on this. If we get cracking we've an off chance of getting away with it.'

He turned to the man with the list held in place on a millboard with a spring clip.

'Get this. We go through the procedure laid down as if we had the woman, . . . the other one's down below already. Leave me do the talking.'

He snapped his fingers. The two men came to attention and suddenly looked at Margery.

'Now madam, we have a duty to perform. Will you kindly take one step forward.'

She moved like an automaton, and from some faraway place heard her own voice.

'You worked in a shop once.'

'Yes, ma'm. I was a hairdresser before the unpleasantness.'

She wondered what he was doing behind her and suddenly found that her hands were tied. She wanted to scream, but she'd forgotten how.

The man from Eire reappeared standing at right angles to the line of talk running between the American and the woman from the Argentine.

'You Anglo-Saxons are so sentimental,' she said slamming her accent onto the word to caricature it, 'so sentimental about ideas. The leetle child in the pinny who softened the strong man's heart in the Victorian novelette, you see through her now, but instead you cherish the lettle golden headed ideal. You are swaddled away from reality by your ideals, everyone can be 'appy, everyone can be well fed, everyone can be pussy and cosy and gentle . . . the world is not like that. When you wake up from your pretty dreams you will find yourself in a nightmare and you will break up, si, si, I tell you, idealism is the sickness of the soul.'

The American looked at the tiny gold cross which nestled at the spring of her breasts, where the gently swelling flesh vanished under her exquisite lawn blouse. The jungle and the inhumanity of man had eaten a Christian Empire in her home land.

'I tell you it is only your dreams that make this court seem so bad to you. Man is not good at all, not at all.' She shook her head from side to side, slowly with her rich smile.

He was a nice boy, but you couldn't have an affair with him, like all the Nord Americanos, he wasn't quite grown up.

'Sorry to butt in,' said the Irishman, 'but this is urgent. I've just been back to my hotel. I rang up the office to ask if they really wanted me to watch this farce any longer.' He dropped his voice and the three heads drew in together. 'They said I was to get out of here as quick as I could, to get to London and get an accreditation as a war correspondent.'

'What's that?'

'I thought I'd give you the tip.'

'Who's fighting who?'

'There's been some sort of Pearl Harbour, the Americans are fighting the Russians. They couldn't say much before we were cut off. That's all I know.'

'Well, thanks . . .' The American looked about at the crowded café, wondering if he was already in an enemy country. 'I'd better get to the Embassy in London. I hope to god I don't get interned — to spend a war drinking tea behind wire, that would be terrible.'

'It's tremendously exciting, a vast historical event,' said the Argentine, 'and all you think about is your little personal convenience. Oh, you idealists!'

She rocketed off into laughter.

'There's a train for London in half an hour,' said the Irishman, 'can you make it?'

'I'll pick up my things and try – I'll see you at the station.'

He waved a paw at the woman, and went off down the wide staircase at a run. He was already thinking about getting back into the A.A.F. when he got back home, it would be fine to stop this film of corruption spreading any further over the world: at any rate to do something simple that would make sense.

'They are like babies,' said the Argentine woman, 'like big babies.'

The rumour spread, and more and more of the press began drifting away to badger their offices on the telephone, for confirmation, for instructions.

Bells rang to announce the beginning of the evening session and the audience drifted back to their seats leaving the corridors and lobbies almost empty.

There was hardly anyone about when dog face came through with a single sheet of typing paper in his hand. He went to the notice board and pinned it up alongside the two other sheets already there. The palms in tubs flanking the board rattled and clicked their leaves in the draught while he did it. One man came up the steps from the lower lobby to read it when he was done, looked at the first few words, and turned away. Dog face went upstairs to the café for a cup of tea.

'No tea left, sonny. Sorry.'

'Well, make it coffee.' The grey haired, motherly, woman drew him a cup from the nickel plated urn.

'Thanks, ma.'

'They say there's going to be another war.'

'Suits me.'

'Suits you, indeed, I don't want none of it.'

'No more don't I, but I'm sick of all this bloody killing.'

He took a few steps away from the counter where he could look down at the notice board on the half landing. The red lights over the doors that came on when the court was sitting caught his eye. He thought of the coffin full of coke being

341

dumped in the long trench in the potters field, with all the other coffins. He went back to the counter.

'This coffee's as bitter as gall. It turns me up. Harn't you a crumb of sugar to spare?'

'I haven't seen any sugar since I been here. And I haven't had no complaints neither. It's your sour nature.'

'Maybe it is. Christ what wouldn't I give for . . .'

He couldn't think of anything. He put the coffee cup down and went back to his corridors and cellars out of sight, leaving a door swinging to and fro to mark his violent departure.

She watched him go with pursed lips. The coffee was perfectly all right, she didn't know what had got into people.

22

I T was two months before Anne could get back to the mill, for a week or two she drifted, begging and stealing, and then a tide of refugees from the Southern battlefields where the Americans were fighting for a beach head caught her and swept her northwards.

Someone spotted her as pregnant at a soup kitchen in Liverpool run by an Irish Roman Catholic organisation and she was nearly shipped off to Eire.

They gave her a bed in a convent hospital where she could hear the noises of the docks, the mutter of the sirens, and the engines talking softly in the dark bodies of the big ships.

During the night she dreamed of the sea widening and widening between her and home and she smelt the yellow rose from the front of the mill.

She sat in the door of the mill loft swinging her legs and plucked one of the roses from the vine which reached up towards her. She thought it was covered with dew, although it was high noon on a sunshiny day, and looking closer saw that the rose was weeping for sorrow at her going away over the dark sea.

She woke, and looked down the dormitory, along the rows of thin legged iron beds, and saw moonlit wreaths of curling river mist caressing the warehouse wall across the way. The nun sitting watching by a shaded light at the end of the room got up and came to her, rustling with starched linen, in her padded shoes.

'Is there anything the matter, can I do anything for you?' She had a pleasant singing Irish voice.

'No – it's about tomorrow. I can't go to Ireland tomorrow. . . .'

'Now, dear, don't think about that tonight. The boat's a red cross ship, and it's from a neutral country; you've nothing to dread on the water. And think of it, you'll be out of the fighting when the baby comes, taking your ease with the little man among all the eggs and butter and milk he'll need to make him strong.'

'No, it's terribly kind of you, but I must go home. I've only just remembered where I really belong. I must go back.'

'You'd best wait till morning before you make up your mind.'

'I've made up my mind. Someone else can take my place on the boat.'

'Well now, you don't have to decide until morning. I'll fetch you a glass of water, it'll help you settle to sleep.'

Anne made her way south again, through the cracks and fissures in two armies, and after two or three weeks came to Lemlade. She didn't recognise it at first, twelve feet of stone wall still bearing a faded sign 'To the Boats,' 40 acres of rubble, part of the New Inn stable yard, the chancel of the church, and a gazebo with all the windows out and half its tiles blown off. Bulldozers had cleared the roads and a military sign post spoke of new irrelevant directions, divorced from local names or purposes.

'Is this really Lemlade?' She spoke to three men who were languidly loading blocks of stone onto a cart, as if the effort were hardly worth while.

'All there's left of it.'

'Thank you.'

She walked away. The child stirred insistently, and she sat down feeling its movement with a hand pressed to her stomach.

'What have I brought you to? Suppose. . . .'

She looked eastwards towards the banks of elms and willows which hid the mill. There were about two miles to go. She walked out by the church to take the shorter field path across the water meadows to the Carp Inn. She could just see its roof through the trees, and a thin plume of smoke rising from its chimney.

She tried not to look at the burnt out tank half-way across the first field, she couldn't help seeing the posters which some propaganda unit had fixed on the outer walls of the chancel.

A sunburned G.I. with a public relations smile held out a hand

344

to all the world; 'He is for freedom, your freedom. . . .' said a line of type.

Next door a well-scrubbed family sat down to watch Mr. Everyman carve a huge turkey as lush and pneumatic as a Varga nude. Grey haired grandma smiled at dad; pretty mom, wonderful for her age, smiled at junior, so like his father. Junior grinned at dad, no sphinx would come between them with a turkey on the table; pert sis grinned across the table at grandpa in his silver rimmed specs, and he grinned right back – there comes a time in every man's career when he must hand over his carving knife to a younger man, and no hard feelings. Kindness ran off the masterpiece of commercial colour printing like molasses. All round the turkey were gay dishes heaped high with fixings and candies. Round each plate there was a zareba of matching silverware, and the tasteful glass glinted expensively. You could fill in the background of bank balances and paid up insurance policies, the well chosen common stocks, the car in the garage, the closets full of linen and good clothes, the shoes of real leather, the solid fabric of an attainable dream. . . . That one said 'America believes in the better things in life.'

She laughed, suddenly happy, 'I believed in the better things in life once. . . .'

She walked on across the field, eager now to get to the mill; thistles were scattered about, like an ugly regiment of undisciplined landsknecht, some still in purple flower, some grey headed, already letting their seed parachutes drift off.

A heavy whine grew in her ears, growing till it seemed as if a vibrating metal rod were pressing on her eardrums. She looked up and saw, far behind the sound, the smear of vapour trials across the sky, death going east. When she stared at them she seemed to see through the warm blue into the frozen violet air through which the bombers were passing. She caught a glint of silver ahead of one of the vapour trails.

There were fourteen men up there singing 'Baby, it's cold outside,' in close harmony over the inter-com making it sound like a madrigal. The big bomb for Leningrad lay quietly among them waiting for the bomb aimer's finger on the release button.

Bending her head back and being dazzled made her a little sick; she came back to earth and walked on.

The noise died away, the vapour trails widened, blended, and formed a flat white cloud. Thistle seeds drifted across the path in front of her on the quiet breeze.

'Was it because I believed the wrong things were the better things in life that I made so much misery for the people I loved?'

The grasses nodded and bowed.

'Suppose the mill is empty and deserted? Suppose Francis has disappeared? Suppose I am all alone when the time comes? Am I going to die, is the child going to die?'

The grasses nodded and bowed, moved by the mindless wind.

She stared at the front of the mill when she reached it at last, eager to see some sign of life, as a sick patient might look at the face of her doctor hoping for the beginning of a smile or a trace of confidence. Most of its windows had been blown in during the bombing of Lemlade, but sacks had been nailed over the openings to keep the worst of the rain out. Fresh wheel tracks led up to the mill door. Someone still lived there. She went to the front door of the house and tried it.

The knob turned, and the door opened.

Part of the passage roof was down, fallen plaster had smashed a chair. The house breathed a dead emptiness into her face, a damp exhalation of neglect.

'I have smashed up everything. I can bring nothing but death into the world.' She swayed forward in a dead faint.

Francis had fixed a wire to the front door so that a bell jangled in the back kitchen when anyone tried it.

He got up now and slipped two shells into the shot gun. He sat facing the door into the front part of the house holding the gun ready. He had had trouble with looters once or twice and he had found that it paid to let them take a good look at the stripped out front rooms without interference. They generally went away when they'd taken the measure of their desolate abandonment.

He waited for any least sound that might tell him the prowler was getting nearer the kitchen, but none came.

His eye wandered to his book again, spread out by his oatmeal

346

baps and his cup of hot milk, and he began to read. He had twice read all through the Comedies of Shakespeare, and the Histories and Poems. He was now on page 1122 of the Oxford volume of Tragedies.

He began dipping the oatmeal baps into crushed honeycomb that was in a bowl in front of him. He read as he licked and munched. He was careful to use one hand for turning the pages and the other for dipping the oatmeal cakes in the honey. He had got to a part that he had liked on his first reading and was glad to come round to again.

Arviragus: So, begin.

Guiderius: Fear no more the heat of the sun
Nor the furious winter's rages
Thou thy wordly task hast done
Home art gone, and taen they wages.
Golden Lads and Girls all must
As chimney sweepers come to dust.

Arviragus: Fear no more the frown o' the great
Thou art past the tyrant's stroke
Care no more to clothe and eat
To thee the reed is as the oak. . . .

He broke off, if he were sure that there were nobody about he would like to shout this bit out loud. He listened, heard nothing, and decided to go out to the front to make sure.

'Anne, Anne,' she woke to his cry, and found him kneeling by her when she forced her eyes open. 'Oh, Anne, I'd given up thinking you'ld ever get back. What have they done to you, the beasts, the beasts.'

Months of loneliness suddenly overwhelmed him and tears spurted from his eyes.

'Oh, Anne, I've been so miserable.'

'You've got to be brave, Francis,' she reached up and touched the warm tears on his cheek. 'You've got to be much braver now I've come back. I've come back to you for help.'

He helped her round into the kitchen, and fed her. When he saw her properly, his childish tears suddenly drained away. Her clothes were in rags. Her shoes had worn out long since and she had bound up her feet with strips of linen and carpet felt from a bombed house. Another wanderer had made her a sandal of old car tyre rubber that served as a sort of sole for these shapeless boots.

'How much do you know?'

'They posted a notice about you and mother outside the police station. Dusty's granddaughter came up and told me. Nobody knows what happened to Jeanette. She came once with some policemen in a car. They were trying to find me. I was hiding up in the mill roof. They used to come quite often at first, and then they stopped.'

He looked at her as if struck by a new thought.

'If you're alive, perhaps mother is.'

It didn't sound as if he believed it.

'I don't think your mother got away.'

'Nor do I.' He looked old and sad. 'I didn't know what had happened at first. I was out in Burden's sixty acre piece waiting for pigeons in a hide in the kale. I came back with eleven pigeons. And there was no one here. I couldn't make it out. And then Dusty came and told me the police had taken you all away. He hid me for the first month when the police were hot after me. Then when they eased up I came back. I searched the place for some note or something. All I found was a piece of paper behind the looking glass in mother's room. It just said "Good-bye darling." I knew when I read it I wouldn't ever see her again. But I just knew I had to wait here. I don't know why.'

She drank the sweet milk, tasting of honey, and behind the honey of the summer's flowers. She remembered Walter in his last hours of happiness in the sunlight, before he had turned his back on it and walked into the dark away from all those who loved him and the mill that he had once wanted.

'I don't mean that. I know why really.' He gulped. 'I knew if I went away my last chance was gone. I knew if I held on it would come all right. I can work the mill. After next harvest people will want grist again. They've got to come here. It's a marvellous place. There's a duck up the mill dam in the rushes where that fallen pollard is, she's got chicks – I see them every

348

day – and anyway when I grow up and things are all right again, I'll marry. We'll get new ceilings put in the rooms in front the soldiers knocked about. And I'll make the farmers give me chairs and things for grinding their corn. We'll live here. I'll never go away. Never. I'll make it just what it ought to be, a place to be happy in.'

She smiled.

'You think I'm a fool and a baby. But I know . . .'

'No, I smiled because I liked what you were saying. I know why it isn't silly about the wild duck . . . but I broke it all up once. Will you ever be able to forgive me for that? I don't know how you can. . . .'

'It wasn't you.'

'Yes.'

'No. You tried to make happiness. Mother tried too.'

He hesitated.

'Father and Jeanette wanted something else. I don't know what. I don't understand it. He was my father, and she was my sister, but they were another kind of person. They didn't want our happiness. They wanted something else.' He gestured towards the flattened place that had once been Lemlade. 'They wanted that, outside, that's their world. . . .'

'I was one of them once,' said Anne.

'And Jeanette was one of us once . . . people change.'

He fell silent and thought while she dreamed of Jeanette on the witness stand.

'You're older than I am, you know more. It's silly of me to tell you what I think, but I know. There's a real war. This war outside isn't a real war at all. There's a real war, inside, between good and evil. There's some way of knowing which side to be on. We've lost it. You and me, we're on the right side by accident. We ought to know why. The secret's somewhere here. It's something to do with the corn growing year after year, and life being better than death, and not getting anything for nothing . . . do you know what I mean?'

She nodded her head silently wondering what could be in his mind.

'I'm sure there's something quite simple that we could tell

your child when it's old enough that would give it a hold on life, and keep it going all its life. Something that would keep it from drifting over and becoming one of those others.'

He took a pan of hot water off the stove and put it on the floor beside her. He cut the rags away and began to wash her feet. She leant back in her chair. She felt he was groping after some idea about god and she wanted terribly to help him. But all she knew about religion was somehow wrong. She could remember being terribly surprised once at finding a crucifix in a cracker at a Christmas party, and she could remember a man in gaiters in an hotel making a scene because people at another table in the dining room had been served before him, she could remember seeing 'Cleanliness is next to Godliness' written up in black and red letters in a swimming bath. She wanted to say something immensely helpful and enlightening, but she couldn't think what it should be.

'We'll do all we can for each other,' she said.

He stopped drying her feet and looked up with troubled eyes. 'I've been thinking a lot, here alone, and I don't believe that's enough.'

She looked at him sleepily, listening to the mellow tick of the clock which still hung there on the wall. In a few days now her child would be born. She was back at the mill, everything would probably be all right. She couldn't think beyond that, and didn't want to. She knew the life in her was her love for Walter made real, because it was that it would be on the right side. Perhaps if she had come to hate Walter in the last few terrible months, the child would have become a demon eager to tear more lives apart. Perhaps Walter's hatred for her, and of it, had already thickened its blood with poisons, that had to be risked.

She looked at Francis again with pity. He was still a child, for all his ghastly experience, and it was only a child who could think of evil and good as two strands of cord that could be unknotted and separated.

Life was a cable woven of a thousand strands, half white, half black – they could probably never be drawn apart without destroying the cable itself.

It was a dream, a child's dream, that the inner battle could

350

ever end, that a generation could ever be born that would with one voice choose happiness and life rather than tension and death. Walter who had loved life in her and had created life in her, had also loved violence and had made death for her.

All around them whole peoples who wanted prosperity and peace made war and created poverty. It was the fate of man to love what would destroy him, that was the pattern of life.

She looked pityingly into the child's eyes which were alight with the vision of another truth and another pattern which she could not begin to see or understand.

He returned her look, sensing that her mind was set on another course than his.

'You've got to believe it, you've got to: there's something a man can know about himself, and the sky and all its stars, and night following day, and the corn growing and dying, something that can make sense of it all – if we don't find out what it is it'll always be like this, always. . . .'

The clock ticked on, measuring off the endless flow, and she smiled her gentle smile, certain only that life would go on, and that even if it were like this, always, illumined by his determination, to know, and hers, to create, it would be worth while.